Peter Lovesey's novels and short stories have won him awards all over the world, including the Gold, Silver and Cartier Diamond Daggers of the Crime Writers' Association, of which he was Chairman in 1991–2. He also won the Short Story Dagger for 2007. He lives in Chichester.

PETER LOVESEY OMNIBUS

The Circle

Do Not Exceed the Stated Dose

Peter Lovesey

SPHERE

This omnibus edition first published in Great Britain in 2009 by Sphere

Previously published separately:
The Circle first published in Great Britain in 2005 by Time Warner Books
Paperback edition published by Time Warner Books in 2006
Reprinted 2006, Reprinted by Sphere in 2006
Copyright © Peter Lovesey 2005
Do Not Exceed the Stated Dose first published in Great Britain in 1998
by Little, Brown and Company
Paperback edition published by Warner Books in 1999
Reprinted by Time Warner Paperbacks in 2002
Copyright © Peter Lovesey 1998

"Because It Was There" was first published in *Whydunit* (Severn House) 1997;
"Bertie and the Boat Race" in *Crime Through Time* (Berkley) 1996; "Bertie and the
Fire Brigade" in *Royal Crimes* (Signet) 1994; "Disposing of Mrs Cronk" in *Perfectly
Criminal* (Severn House) 1996; "The Case of the Easter Bonnet" in the *Bath
Chronicle*, 1955; "The Mighty Hunter" in *Midwinter Mysteries 5* (Little, Brown) 1955;
"Murder in Store" in *Woman's Own*, 1985; "Never a Cross Word" In *You* (*Mail on
Sunday*) 1955; "The Odstock Curse" in *Murder for Halloween* (Mysterious Press)
1994; "A Parrot Is Forever" in *Malice Domestic 5* (Pocket Books) 1996; "Passion
Killers" in *Ellery Queen's Mystery Magazine*, 1994; "The Proof of the Pudding" in *A
Classic Christmas Crime* (Pavilion) 1995; "The Pushover" in *Ellery Queen's Mystery
Magazine*, 1995; "Quiet Please—We're Rolling" in *No Alibi* (Ringpull) 1955;
"Wayzgoose" in *A Dead Giveaway* (Warner Futura) 1995

A CIP catalogue record for this book is available from the British Library.

ISBN 978-0-7515-4156-3

Printed and bound in Great Britain by Clays Ltd, St Ives plc

Sphere
An imprint of
Little, Brown Book Group
100 Victoria Embankment
London EC4Y 0DY

An Hachette UK Company
www.hachette.co.uk

www.littlebrown.co.uk

The Circle

A Note from the Writer

Shock horror! I had almost finished this book when I discovered that the Chichester Writers' Circle really exists. The shredder beckoned, but I took a deep breath and asked to attend a meeting and explain. After hearing a couple of chapters they were kind enough to say I should go ahead with publication. None of the characters in these pages resembles a member of the real circle or, thank heaven, shares any of their names. So I count my blessings, and wish the Chichester Circle continuing success and a future untarnished by anything of the sort that I imagined here.

I must also declare my links with other circles. I first heard about them from a remarkable and inspiring fellow-writer, Joan Moules. Over the years Joan has founded several circles that grew rapidly thanks to her enthusiasm. Through her I got to know the Warminster Circle, and, later, the Selsey Circle, and made lasting friendships with many of the members. I trust that they will accept this book as the total fiction it is, but also as an affectionate tribute to circle members everywhere, and, most of all, to Joan.

P. L.

Describe a circle, stroke its back and it turns vicious.

Eugene Ionesco, *The Bald Prima Donna* (1950)

1

All writing is a process of elimination.

Martha Albrand, quoted in *Twentieth Century Crime &
Mystery Authors*, ed. J. Reilly (1980)

The night of the first murder.
  In a cottage on the Selsey Road the central heating
had cooled and the floorboards were creaking. Alone and
wheezing in his bedroom, Edgar Blacker stirred, turned over,
took a few shallow breaths and settled into a dream of best-
sellers and huge profits. He was a publisher.

Downstairs, the flap on the letterbox opened and a plastic
hose was pushed through. Liquid trickled from it onto the
fitted carpet. The hose was withdrawn. The flap closed.

Seconds after, it was pushed open again. A piece of cloth
saturated with fuel was forced through. More oily rags came
after it. They made a small heap.

One cloth reeking of petrol hung from the letterbox. No
attempt was made to push it through. There was the faint
sound of a match being struck. The cloth fizzed into flame,
dropped on the other rags and they ignited at once. Two
parcels of page proofs were lying beside the door ready for
posting. The flame touched them and they caught fire.

In the next phase of his dream, Blacker was lunching with
J. K. Rowling, the creator of Harry Potter. She'd asked for
a salad. For himself he'd ordered the best item on the menu:

fillet steak *flambé*. He believed he could smell it being cooked.

The bookshelves lining two walls were perfect tinder. This cottage was stuffed with inflammable material. Even the filing cabinets were made of teak. The flames made green tongues of fire as they reacted with the cloth and the glue of the book bindings. In seconds, the shelves caught and glowed. Soon the wood was hissing.

It took a while for the fire to reach the small oak staircase at the far end of the living room but when it did the polish on the handrail burned green and yellow. The whole structure was soon ablaze. Deadly fumes were funnelled upstairs. Smoke is usually the killer in house fires. And there were no smoke alarms in this old building.

Edgar Blacker didn't get to close the deal with J. K. Rowling. He inhaled various gases, including carbon monoxide, and was called away to keep an appointment with the Chairman in the sky.

2

The compulsion to make rhymes was born in me. For those sated readers of my work who wish ardently that I would stop, the future looks dark indeed.

Noël Coward, foreword to *The Lyrics of Noël Coward* (1965)

Bob Naylor never said much about his rhymes. The world he moved in didn't go in for rhyming, and on the one night in the pub he'd confessed to being 'a bit of a poet on the quiet' he'd had the reaction you get if you say you're a cross-dresser. No one ever spoke of it after that. You don't mess with a man as powerful as Bob. But he continued to play with words, enjoying the challenge of making them rhyme in ways that amused him. Rhyming was more fun than watching television or sitting in front of a computer. He could do it in bed, in the bathroom or while driving his Parcel Force van.

One Friday night when he was making faint moaning sounds, trying to nail a word he was sure must exist, his daughter Sue looked up from her computer and said, 'Dad, have you ever thought of joining a circle?'

'Come again?'

'A writers' circle. There's one here in Chichester. I've just found the website. Says they meet at the New Park Centre on Tuesday evenings.'

'Never heard of it.'

'You have now. Come and look while it's on the screen.'

He got up and stood beside her just to show interest. It was a change from the chat rooms she spent most of her evenings visiting.

Welcome to the Chichester Writers' Circle

Whatever your interest in writing, you are guaranteed enrichment and support if you join our circle. We are creative people who enjoy words, working in poetry, fiction and non-fiction, and our interests range from fantasy to family history, from the theatre to the scene of the crime. We meet on the second Tuesday of each month at the New Park Centre and it's very friendly. Since joining the circle we have all become published writers, because what is publication if it is not making publicly known? Sample our work by clicking on all or any of the following. Then make a date in your diary. We are looking out for you.

- Extract from *Passion Fruit*, a romantic novel, by Desiree Eliot
- First chapter of *The Sussex Witchcraft Trials*, by Naomi Green
- *Unsolved*. A sample case. By Maurice McDade
- Two erotic poems by Thomasine O'Loughlin
- *Madrigor: The Coming of the Warrior*, by Zach Beale
- *The Snows of Yesteryear*, a sample chapter, by Amelia Snow
- *Tips for the Twenty-First Century*, by Jessie Warmington-Smith
- *Showing Prize Marrows*, by Basil Green
- *My Meeting with Sir Larry,* by Tudor Thomas

'Do you want me to click on one of them?' Sue asked.

Sod that for a lark. 'No thanks, love. Kind of you to mention it.'

'A writers' circle might be just the thing for you.'

'Like Alcoholics Anonymous?'

'Don't be like that.'

'They'll be serious writers. It's not for oiks like me.'

'Have it your way. But you ought to get out more.'

This from a fourteen-year-old.

In his van on the M3 next day he composed a few lines. 'Circle' is not a word that rhymes with much, but Bob liked a challenge.

> Let's see if the jerk'll
> Join a circle
> His loving daughter said
> But the jerk gave ferk all
> For the circle
> He was horribly low-bred

That summed up Bob and his writing. He was the son of a plumber and a barmaid who had parted when he was seven. With young Bob in tow, his mother had gone through at least ten cheap addresses and almost as many men. He'd failed all his exams and left school at sixteen. The only thing he'd ever passed was a driving test. He'd never read anything by Shakespeare or Dickens. Didn't look at the arts programmes on TV. Didn't drink wine or borrow books from the library. The books in the house belonged to Sue, or her mother Maggie, who'd died of leukaemia three years ago. Three years, one month and two days.

Rhymes helped him fill the times when everything went quiet.

'They'll be know-alls,' he said that evening.

Sue looked up from her homework. 'Excuse me?'

'That writers' circle. Teachers and such. I'd be way out of my depth.'

'I thought you'd put it out of your head.'

'I have. I was telling you why.'

'Oh sure.' Sue looked down again. It wasn't the home-work that made her smile.

He didn't mention the circle for two weeks, but that was par for the course. He always began with 'no way' and got more positive by stages. In his fertile imagination he was facing every hazard, the pointy-heads with university degrees who could quote Shakespeare, the old ducks in twinsets who could spell anything, the crossword solvers and the English teachers. He could picture himself reading out his rhymes, stuttering and sweating and losing his place and swearing and seeing the shocked faces around the table. Mayhem was going on in his head. When he'd faced every horror he could imagine, he would decide that, after all, it couldn't be *that* bad.

'Do you think they allow smoking?'

'Probably,' Sue said.

'I can't see it.'

'I expect they have a coffee break.'

'Maybe. What do they do at these meetings, do you reckon? Write stuff?'

She flicked her hair back. 'Why ask me?'

'And read it to each other?'

'Go along and find out.'

'You're joking.'

The following Tuesday at six forty-five he parked in front of the New Park Centre and watched who went in. New Park was also a cinema and they were showing a sexy French film, so it was difficult to tell who was part of the writers' circle, except that some of them came with bags and briefcases. Why would you need a briefcase for a sex flick? He hadn't brought a briefcase. If he went in at all he was damn sure he wouldn't be reading out his rhymes.

A youngish guy with a rucksack crossed the car park and went in. Long hair, earring, sweatshirt and jeans. Looks human, Bob thought. Not a schoolteacher or a professor. Give it a go, mate. He opened the car door and got out. If I don't like the look of the punters, he told himself, I can say I'm in the wrong room, looking for the film.

Inside, he strolled past the queue at the box office and went towards a door on the left, the only way to go if you weren't there for the film. A blonde in her forties was ahead. She glanced back to check that he wasn't anyone she knew. Deep-set blue eyes and the hint of a smile. Then she stopped, turned round and said, 'Are you a writer?'

Bob cleared his throat. 'Me?'

'It's the writers' circle in here.'

She didn't sound highbrow, and she was pretty in a way that younger women can't be, with creases that promised to be laughter lines asking to be exercised.

'Thought I might look in,' he said. 'See what you get up to.'

'Nothing we can get arrested for, more's the pity, but you're welcome to check. I'm Thomasine O'Loughlin, by the way.'

Fancy handle, he thought, but she seemed like a real person. He followed her into the meeting room where a long table and chairs were set up and nobody was seated yet. Two groups were in conversation. A man in a bow tie was holding forth in a carrying voice.

'No better, no better at all.'

Sounds like a line from Shakespeare, Bob thought. Should I look as if I've heard it before?

'He doesn't know,' the voice went on, as if reading his mind. 'I tell you, he doesn't have a clue.'

If this is how they treat visitors, Bob thought, I'm off.

'He put me on some new stuff that sends me to sleep

in the afternoons. I'll be back to see him in a day or two – if I can stay awake long enough to make another appointment.'

Smiles all round, even from Bob.

Thomasine was beckoning. 'Come and meet the chair.'

'Why? Is it special?'

'Chairman.'

'Ah.'

The chair wasn't the man with the medical problem. He was in the group at the far end. Catching Thomasine's eye, he stepped forward, a fiftyish guy in a sweater and cords who looked as if he would be more comfortable in a suit. His hair was thick and dark, too dark to be natural. The eyebrows probably were the genuine thing. They popped up. 'A new member?'

Bob tightened inside. The accent was top drawer. 'Just visiting.'

'A friend of yours, Tommy?'

Thomasine laughed. 'That's quick. We met outside the door.'

'Maurice McDade,' the chair said, gripping Bob's hand. 'Do you write?'

'Only a beginner.' Bob gave his name.

'We're all beginners in a sense,' Maurice McDade said. His speech came in bursts with overlong pauses, making him sound excited when the words came. 'The circle only came into being last year. You'd think a town this size would have had one for ages. Nobody took the first step.'

Thomasine said, 'Maurice set it up with the help of two others, Naomi and Dagmar.'

Names so posh that Bob checked where the exit was.

'We're still small,' Maurice said. 'Eleven if they all come. Like a cricket team. How did you hear about us? A recommendation?'

'The website.'

'Splendid. Miss Snow designed that. She'll be so encouraged. We'd better make a start.' He clapped his hands. 'Calling all writers. High time we put our feet under the table.'

Bob watched them find seats. Six women and five men, or six if he included himself. Average age, mid-fifties. One bow tie, five pairs of specs, a hearing aid and a wig. But also a blonde of about twenty who might have strayed in expecting to see the film.

'Before we begin, I'll introduce our visitor, Bob Naylor,' Maurice said. 'He's only taking a look at us this week. If we play our cards right, we could be up to twelve soon.'

Bob summoned a grin. He was to the left of a woman in her forties, hair streaked with silver, who had to be the secretary, already writing down the chairman's remarks. On his other side was the young guy with the earring.

Maurice spoke again. 'For Bob's benefit, I'll repeat my mantra, familiar to most of you by now. This isn't a talk-shop. We're here because we are creative people and we're not afraid to read out what we produce. This way, we are all – what are we?'

A couple of them spoke together. 'Published writers.'

'Exactly, for what is publication but making publicly known? Writing is about communication, so we're not afraid to have our efforts discussed by the others. Any writer should welcome the input of his peers.'

Sounds a pompous prat, but he's doing his best, Bob thought. Give him a chance.

The minutes of the last meeting were handed round by Miss Snow, the grey-haired secretary. Maurice asked if there were any matters arising and Bob thought of a rhyme.

> Who fancies Miss Snow?
> Anyone fantasising?
> What's that down below –
> A matter arising?

9

Cut it out, Naylor, he told himself. This may be the place for one of your rhymes, but no way is it the time.

The man with the bow tie spoke from the other end. He'd found what he called a solecism in the minutes. Miss Snow glared at him.

'And what is that?'

'The misuse of a word.' There was a hint of central Europe in his accent.

'I know what a solecism is,' Miss Snow said. 'I'm asking where it is in the minutes.'

'The foot of page one. "The circle was fulsome in its praise of Mr Blacker's talk." Fulsome is a pejorative word meaning disgusting by excess. Your meaning, in effect, is that we lavished so much praise on Mr Blacker that it made him look foolish.'

Give me strength, Bob thought. How do I get out of here?

'I thought he lavished too much praise on us,' one bold woman said. 'I had him down as a toadying sharpie, telling us we all had it in us to write a bestseller.'

Silence dropped like dead leaves in November.

Maurice said, 'Thank you, Naomi. You're never shy of giving an opinion.'

'Shouldn't the minutes say "the late Mr Blacker"?' the man next to Naomi said.

'That is a point,' Maurice the chair said. He took an even longer pause this time. 'Did everyone hear the tragic news of Edgar Blacker?' Turning to Bob, he said, 'Mr Blacker was a publisher by profession, so we invited him to speak to us. He died in a fire at his cottage the next night.'

Thinking he'd better show respect, Bob shook his head and said, 'Dreadful.'

'You don't have to go overboard,' the outspoken woman called Naomi said. 'It's not as if he was one of us. Quite the reverse. He raised the hopes of certain people around this table, making it sound an easy matter to get published. It

10

wasn't what you hear on writers' courses. It was irresponsible. They're beginners.'

'Except Maurice,' Miss Snow said. 'He's publishing Maurice's book.'

'*Was*,' Maurice said.

Miss Snow reddened. 'Oh. I hadn't thought. What a blow. I'm so sorry. You'll place it with some other publisher, I'm certain.'

'No question,' an overweight man said in a strong, deep voice. 'The cream always rises to the top.' A faint smile hovered around his lips, undermining the compliment.

'Anything else about the minutes?' the chairman said, not wanting to dwell on his personal misfortune. 'In that case, let's move on. Successes. Do we have any successes to report since the last meeting?'

A hand went up. 'A letter in *The Lady*.'

'Splendid! Well done, Jessie,' the chairman said, and there were murmurs of congratulation all round. 'Did they pay?'

'Twenty-five pounds.' Jessie, a compact, elderly woman in a purple twinset, modestly dipped her head.

'Are you going to read it out?'

'I'd rather not, if you don't mind. It's personal.'

Personal, in a magazine selling in thousands? Bob thought. These people are priceless.

'Yes,' Maurice said, with a raised finger, 'and it's the personal touch that gets the attention of an editor. Write from the heart, and you'll succeed. Any other successes?'

The man with the hairpiece said, 'My gardening column in the parish magazine, if you can call that a success.'

'Of course it's a success, Basil,' Miss Snow said. 'Everything in print is a success.'

'It's about runner beans this month.'

That was it for the successes. They went on to discuss the next item on the agenda: opportunities. Good psychology

11

on someone's part. Leaflets about poetry competitions for cash prizes were handed round. Bob doubted if his rhyming would qualify.

'The report from the chair is next. I don't have much to report,' Maurice said. 'We've been thinking about the programme for the next six months. We can afford another speaker, I think.'

'Get someone better than Blacker, then. He was a conman,' the man with the sonorous voice said on a rising note. A Welshman, Bob decided.

Basil, the gardening expert, said, 'That isn't very kind. He's only just died.'

'Doesn't mean we have to praise up his talk. I agree with Naomi. It was crap. He spent most of the time talking up his tinpot publishing business and the rest of it telling some of us we could make a fortune.'

'He offered to come back.'

'For another fat fee.'

'Not at all. I'm sure he meant to come for nothing. He saw the potential here. Publishers need writers, you know. We're the creators.'

'The talent,' Jessie the success said.

Bob looked around at the assembled talent. To their credit some of them were grinning. Thomasine winked.

'I wouldn't mind hearing from a literary agent,' said a woman who had been silent up to now.

'Wouldn't we all?' Thomasine said.

'I meant as a speaker.'

'Dagmar, my dear, that's an excellent suggestion,' Maurice said. There was skill as well as tact in his handling of the meeting. 'But it isn't easy to get an agent to come along. We tried before.'

'Can't blame them,' Thomasine said. 'They know they'd leave here with a sackful of scripts. The Bournemouth circle had an editor from Mills and Boon.'

'Waste of time,' the Welshman said. 'How many of us write romance? Two, at a pinch.'

'What's your suggestion, then?'

'Me. I'd save the money and organise an outing.'

'Where to?'

'We could visit Kipling's place, Bateman's.'

'Been there.'

'Not with a bunch of writers, you haven't. We could use it as a topic, something to write about.'

'I'd rather like to visit the Jane Austen house at Chawton,' Miss Snow said.

'Each to his own, my dear. Personally, I've had it up to here with rich young men pursued by virgins on the make. If the rest of you want to go to Chawton, fine. "Ship me somewhere east of Suez."'

'What?'

'A quote. I was quoting Kipling.'

'What about our youngest member?' Maurice the chair said. 'Do you have a preference, Sharon?'

'Wouldn't he love to know? Dirty old man,' the Welshman murmured.

The blonde shook her head. She had spent the entire time scribbling on a pad. Bob had assumed she was writing, but now she'd moved her arm he could see that all she'd produced was a page of doodles.

Maurice decided on a show of hands and the circle agreed that a visit to Bateman's would be arranged later in the year. If it was successful, he added with diplomacy, they might try the Jane Austen house the following year.

'So we come to the exciting part of the evening, our work in progress.' Maurice turned to Bob and almost brought on a seizure – but only to explain, 'We usually take it in turns to say where we are with our writing. If possible, we read something aloud and invite comments. Honest comment, no holds barred.'

'Cliché.'

'What?'

The man with the bow tie said, 'No holds barred. It's a cliché.'

With restraint, Maurice said, 'Would you care to suggest an alternative, Anton?'

'You said it already. "Honest comment."'

'Thank you for that.' It was spoken in a tone that drained it of gratitude. 'Perhaps, Anton, you would like to open the batting.'

'Cliché.'

Everyone except Anton smiled.

Anton said, 'Since the last meeting, I have not done any writing owing to pressure of work.'

Someone murmured, 'Cliché.'

'If you like I could give you ten or twenty minutes on the curse of the cliché in modern English.'

'Another time, perhaps. I happen to know there are members bursting to read out their latest work and I think they should have their opportunity. How about you, Zach?'

To Bob's right there was a movement. The young man with the earring had sunk low in his chair during the early part of the meeting and seemed to be falling asleep. He braced himself, reached into his rucksack and took out a thick, dog-eared sheaf and placed it on the table. So this was Zach. Without any preamble he began to read with extraordinary intensity. 'Gripping the great, razor-sharp, double-bladed axe forged in fire by the ironmaster of Avalon, Madrigor the fearless strode across the narrow causeway that led to the ancient castle on the mount, ignoring the savage east wind fanning his black velvet cloak and the icy sea-spray whipping his leathery calves. He had one objective and that was to vanquish the stinking hordes within and recover the mazarin stone of his ancestor, Godfric, and put its magical powers to noble employment,

14

arming him for the ordeals to come. Not even the massed ranks of the Querulinda would stand in his way now. He was transformed, invincible, super-strong. His green eyes gleamed and his teeth flashed in the glow of the setting sun. If the gods were with him he would prevail over his enemies. True, the opposition were vastly better equipped than he with their vats of boiling oil and their flaming arrows. What did it matter, the terrifying din they made by beating on their shields and chanting war-songs? The archers stared down gimlet-eyed from the battlements, crossbows at the ready, impatient for him to come within range. They were dressed in chainmail and helmets. Madrigor spurned even a shield, relying on his agility, his innate sense of timing, to avoid whatever the enemy cast in his direction. Within himself, he relished the challenge . . .'

While the tide of words poured over them, Bob glanced around the table. Not everyone was listening. Opposite him, Thomasine rolled her eyes upwards and gave a slight smile. The owner of the bow tie was looking at a competition leaflet. Two, at least, were rehearsing for their turns, scanning their scripts, their lips moving. Maurice leaned back and checked his watch.

I'm having a ball, Bob thought. This is like nothing else, this bunch of strange people united only by their desire to write. I can't wait to hear what each of them will read out. What sort of book has the chairman written and almost got into print? The doodling blonde? Thomasine, with the twinkle in her eye?

'. . . the salt of his own sweat stinging his lips, he hauled himself higher up the rock face without heeding the damage to his bare hands. Another stream of boiling oil hit the outcrop above him and splashed, sizzling behind him. He swayed to one side to avoid a flaming arrow. Having got this far, almost to the great granite wall of the citadel itself, he knew with glorious certainty that the gods had chosen to

15

favour him this day. Without their aid, he would assuredly have been struck down before getting so far. The encroaching darkness, evening's gift to the oppressed, would help him now. He still had to scale the bare wall and surmount the bastion . . .'

Maurice the chair said, 'Perhaps at this point—'

But the torrent couldn't be halted in mid-flow. '. . . above which his enemy waited to engage him.'

'Thank you, Zach.'

'Lanterns had been lit along the parapet.'

'I'm interrupting you there because we could run out of time. Speaking for myself, I wish we could go on. You've reached an enthralling part of the story.'

Zach's lips were still moving, though his voice had tailed off.

Maurice said, 'Anyone care to comment?'

'I couldn't take much more of it,' the outspoken woman said. She had deep-set, dark eyes that looked as if they could see right through you.

'I'm not sure if that counts as constructive criticism, Naomi.'

'No, I mean I'm not used to such excitement. I was there with him, climbing the castle walls. It's a tour de force.'

'Really? There's a tribute, Zach.'

The Welshman said, 'You could, perhaps, get him over the rocks and up the wall a little quicker. We all know he's going to sock it to the opposition.'

'Tudor, that's not the point,' Thomasine said. 'Zach is writing long. It's fantasy. They're big books. A fantasy writer can't get away with under six hundred pages.'

'There's more if you want,' Zach said, brandishing unread pages like banknotes.

'Unfortunately,' Maurice said, 'we'll have to deny ourselves until next time.'

'I'll be into another chapter by then.'

'Excellent. We can't wait. Thomasine, let's change the mood with something from you, shall we?'

'I can't compete with what we've just heard.'

'We're not in competition. Never were.'

'All right. I've written another erotic poem.'

There was a noticeable raising of the attention level.

'Good on you, Tommy, girl,' Tudor the Welshman said.

She took a small, black notebook from her bag. 'It's called "A Night with Rudolf".' She cleared her throat and began to read.

'Covent Garden, Nureyev alone upon the stage,
The music of *Le Corsair* rising to a great crescendo,
And I know, I know, I know, this is the one, the solo,
The thing he does so well, the reason I am here,
Two months' wages, a small fortune, my holiday in France,
For a seat in the stalls, front row. Close-up view
Of those stallion haunches in all their muscularity
    stretching the tights,
Gold tights, gold, gleaming, steaming, straining tights.
I watch him circle the stage with leaps as enormous
As the music, giving me sensations I should not have in
    a public place.
I cannot shift my eyes from his bulging masculinity.
    Wondering, wishing,
Dreaming, thrilled by the music and the man, in my
    memory I will hold
This experience for ever.'

'Oh, my word!' Miss Snow said. 'I'm all of a quiver.'

Anton was frowning. 'Was that erotic?'

Tudor said, 'If it was, it went over my head.'

'You men,' Miss Snow said. 'You have no subtlety. If it isn't in four-letter words, you don't respond at all.'

'I loved it,' Maurice said. 'Straight into our next anthology, if I have anything to do with it. Personally I never under-stood the appeal of Nureyev, but you've just opened my eyes, Tommy. Very telling, that stallion reference. What was it? "Haunches in all their masculinity"?'

'Muscularity.'

'Right. What a striking image. I would almost say rampant.'

'Whoa, boy,' Tudor said.

'I mean it. She promised us an erotic poem, and she delivered.'

'Don't. I'm getting embarrassed,' Thomasine said.

'This might be the right moment to have our break, then. Did anyone put the kettle on?'

It was good to stretch the haunches, muscular or flabby. Bob hadn't appreciated how tense he had got climbing up the castle wall and leaping around the Covent Garden stage. No one else seemed to know what to say to Thomasine after her reading, so he went over. 'That was high-tone. If the rest of this mob are up to your standard, I'm leaving right now.'

'Don't be daft. We're all beginners. You hear what someone else has done and it sounds kind of special because it's different from your own stuff. I bet you've got some-thing really brilliant tucked away in a drawer at home.'

He was about to turn this into a joke about drawers, but decided against it. He was the newcomer. 'Can we light up in here?'

'The corridor. Wouldn't say no to one myself after opening up like that. Worse than a striptease.'

After they'd both taken their first drag he said, 'Will they all read to us?'

'About half of them. Sometimes the excuses are more inventive than the stuff anyone has written. Maurice is very good at helping the timid ones pluck up the necessary. You're not timid, are you?'

'Just ask me to read and see the state of me.'

'You'll get over it.' She gave him a sudden nudge. 'Hello. Looks as if you're not the only new boy.'

Two hunks in leathers and jeans edged past and into the meeting room. They were given the welcome treatment by Maurice.

'Young and beefy,' Thomasine said. 'Nice for our Sharon. Nice for all us girls.'

To Bob's eye, they didn't look like creative writers. He watched from the doorway. Maurice had gone through his welcoming spiel and it hadn't impressed. The newcomers were doing the talking. Maurice made a sweeping movement with his hand as if to show they'd got something wrong.

'They're cops,' Bob said.

'How do you know?'

'Something about the way they're talking to him. And they work in pairs.'

'What would they want with Maurice?'

'You'll have to ask him, but I don't think you'll get the chance.' One of them had grasped Maurice's arm just above the elbow.

Maurice turned and spoke to the little woman called Dagmar.

'Our vice-chair,' Thomasine said. 'He's asking her to take over. He's leaving us.'

She was right. They steered Maurice through the door. It seemed to be voluntary, even though his face was ashen.

Thomasine went straight over to Dagmar. 'What was that about, Dag? What's going on?'

'I've no idea. Maurice asked me to take over after the break.'

Tudor said, 'I heard it all. They're CID. They want to question him about the death of Edgar Blacker.'

3

The members of the circle had clustered around Dagmar. She said, 'Maurice is no killer. He's got nothing to do with it.'

'How do you know?'

Miss Snow said, 'Oh, come on, Tudor! Edgar Blacker was publishing his book.'

This could have got nasty, but Thomasine steered them in a more positive direction. 'What are we going to do?'

'He asked me to take the chair for the rest of this evening,' Dagmar said.

'We can't go on as if nothing's happened, reading out our work. It won't be the same at all.'

'I second that,' Anton, the cliché-spotter, said. 'It would be unseemly.'

Basil said, 'Why don't we adjourn to the bar and talk things over in a more relaxed atmosphere?'

'Good thinking.'

Jessie, the writer of the letter in *The Lady*, announced that she didn't wish to be seen in a bar and was leaving, but the rest, including Bob, reconvened around two tables. An awkward situation was averted when Basil suggested it was too large a round for anyone to fund, so they bought their own.

'We've got to speak up for Maurice,' Miss Snow said when they were all around the tables again. 'We can't have our chair arrested and do nothing about it.'

'He was not arrested,' Anton said.

'Of course he was arrested if they took him away by force.'

'He went of his own volition.'

'They had him by the arm.'

'They didn't caution him. If they arrest a person, they have to issue an official caution.'

Dagmar said, 'Anton is right. Maurice agreed to go with them.'

Tudor said in an ominous tone, 'We don't know what's behind this. They must have some good reason for taking him in.'

'These days there's enormous pressure to make a quick arrest,' Thomasine said.

Anton said with a click of the tongue, 'He was not arrested.'

'It's a technicality, Anton. They can still charge him.'

Zach said to Thomasine, 'You think they're fitting him up?'

'Who knows? We know he's a good man, but do they?'

'We know sod all, my dear,' Tudor said, continuing to stir things up. 'He's a friend to us, but that doesn't make him safe in the eyes of the law. In my short life I've had a few bombshells from my friends. What do any of us know about him? Is he married?' He looked around for the answer.

'Divorced or separated, I believe,' Dagmar said after a pause. 'But he lives with someone.'

Tudor seized on this as if he was leading for the prosecution. 'Does he, indeed? How many of us knew that? He's a dark horse. Before we all march off to the nick protesting his innocence, let's get the facts straight.'

Dagmar, regretting that she'd spoken, said, 'I don't see what Maurice's private life has to do with it.'

'*Everything* in a case like this. Maybe his partner was two-timing him with Edgar Blacker.'

'Oh, how ridiculous!'

'What do the rest of you think? Naomi?' Tudor turned to the woman on his left.

She said with scorn, 'You're reading too much into this, as you always do, Tudor. Let's deal in facts, not speculation.'

'We don't have all the facts.'

'Exactly. So I say leave it for tonight.'

Tudor was reluctant to leave it. 'Let's have another opinion.' He looked across at the youngest member of the circle, still making elaborate patterns on her writing pad. 'Sharon, do you think we should all be rushing to Maurice's defence?'

Sharon looked up and turned a deeper shade of pink. 'Dunno.'

'You must have an opinion.'

'He's always been nice to me.'

'We've seen that for ourselves, my dear.'

'Nothing we can do, is there?'

Now it was Thomasine who spoke up. 'I'm ashamed of you all, if that's the way you think. We wouldn't be here if it wasn't for Maurice. He founded the circle and he runs it. The least we can do is show solidarity.'

'So right!' Dagmar said.

'But in what way?' Basil asked.

Zach said, 'If you want to take on the fuzz, count me in.'

'Please,' Anton said. 'I agree with Naomi. Let's keep this in proportion. Maurice was invited to go for questioning and he went, quite probably because he feels he has something useful to contribute. If he wants our support I'm sure we'll give it, but let's not rush our fences.' He raised his hand at once. 'All right. A cliché. But you know what I mean.'

Miss Snow said with a sharp look at Tudor, 'Just so long as we're all clear that none of us thinks he's a murderer.'

Thomasine said, 'Maurice? He couldn't murder a plate of fish and chips.'

'With the right motivation he could,' Tudor said. 'What do you think, Bob? As a newcomer, what did you make of our chair?'

Difficult. As a newcomer, Bob had hoped to be ignored. 'He made me welcome.' To focus the attention elsewhere, he said, 'This book he nearly got published – what's it about?'

There was a silence that Bob didn't understand, then several sets of eyes widened. Tudor gave a throaty laugh. 'Why didn't any of us think of that? Unsolved murders. It's all about unsolved murders.'

'Straight up?'

'I kid you not. It's a catalogue of crime. Dear old Maurice might play the part of the perfect gent, but there's a dark side to him.'

Dagmar had put her hand to her mouth.

Thomasine said almost to herself, 'I'd forgotten about his book.'

Anton said, 'If it comes to the attention of the police, he'll have some questions to answer.'

But Miss Snow was unmoved. 'It doesn't make him a criminal any more than writing erotic poetry makes Thomasine—' She stopped in mid-sentence and started again. 'Any creative person can take an interest in crime. Think of Dickens.'

'Henry James,' Anton said in a tone that invited anyone to challenge him.

No one did.

Thomasine said, 'Listen, everyone. Naomi is the only one of us who's speaking good sense. Let's stick to the facts. We'd better wait until we know the outcome of this interview. I

23

suggest we all meet here tomorrow at this time and decide on our next step.'

'So how was it, Dad?'

    'The circle? Better than I thought.'

    'Will you go again?'

    'Tomorrow.'

    'That's quick.'

    'Yeah, but we've got a murder mystery to solve. A real-life one.'

    'Get away!'

For someone credited with good sense, Naomi was behaving strangely. It was the next evening and she was cycling out from Chichester in the fading light, pedalling strongly, a strange intensity in her dark eyes.

The burnt-out cottage that had belonged to Edgar Blacker was a sad sight on the Selsey Road, south of the town. Fire investigators from the police, fire service and insurers had sifted through the charred remains and agreed that the seat of the fire had been the hallway. Arson, using some accelerant, was the only explanation. The pattern of burning had been photographed, filmed and mapped. Scene-of-crime officers had collected what evidence they could and council workmen had boarded up the window spaces and doorways. Each means of entry was sealed with police tape. Notices warned that trespassers would be prosecuted. In time, a coroner's jury would be bussed out here to inspect the scene. And if anyone was charged with the crime, teams of lawyers would want to see inside.

None of this was going to stop Naomi. She was the free spirit who had called Blacker a toadying sharpie at the writers' circle. She was wearing her gardening clothes: a light windcheater, jeans and desert boots. In the basket attached to her handlebars was a flashlight, a powerful one.

24

Her backpack contained a pair of gardening gloves, some tools she thought might be helpful and her handbag – which went everywhere with her.

She propped her bike against a tree and moved around the building, using the beam to pick out details of the fire damage. Anything of interest was noted on a small pad. The damage downstairs was extensive. Burn marks above the windows showed where the flames had leapt out after the glass shattered. She wasn't so sure what to expect upstairs. The gabled window of the bedroom where Blacker had died was scorched outside because the thatch around it had ignited, but there was no certainty that the fire had raged so fiercely inside.

After circling the cottage she shone the flashlight into the garden shed at the rear and was pleased to discover a lightweight metal ladder. Typical, she thought, as she went in. The police have been to all this trouble boarding up the place and then forgotten to remove the most obvious aid to an intruder.

She stepped outside and took a long look across the field to pick a moment when there was a gap in the traffic. Then she dragged the ladder up the garden path and propped it against the back of the building where she wouldn't be seen from the road. Although all the windows were boarded up, parts of the roof were covered only by a tarpaulin lashed to what was left of the beams. If she could get up there and loosen the ties she'd have a very good view of the bedroom.

The cottage was constructed with this single room as a kind of attic under the pitch of the roof. There was a small landing and nothing else. The bathroom was downstairs.

She put the flashlight in her backpack. She wasn't used to climbing ladders, so she mounted this one with caution. At the top she gripped the highest rung with one hand and tried loosening the tarpaulin with the other, but she wasn't strong enough. By pressing her knees and thighs against the ladder she made herself more secure, freed both hands and untied the first knot.

In a few minutes she was able to lift a section of the tarpaulin and shine her lamp into the bedroom. The worst of the damage was from water. A mattress was still on the bed and bookshelves beside it, the books now misshapen and stained. The fitted wardrobe stood open and some of the dead man's suits could be seen hanging inside, their shape gone, a green mould growing on the fabric.

She pointed the flashlight down the wall she was looking over. A chair stood against it, directly below her. She came to a quick decision, hooked the lamp over the top of the ladder, climbed up a couple of rungs and got one leg over the tie beam at the top and then the other. It was a short drop to the chair. She managed it without mishap.

Some people might have been spooked by entering a room where someone had been asphyxiated. Not Naomi. Opening drawers and cupboards, she listed what was inside and made diagrams. She felt in the pockets of all the jackets, but the only things she found were a soggy cloakroom ticket, a pack of three condoms, marked 'extra safe', and a toothpick, none of which she kept.

Still attached to the wall facing the wardrobe was a framed photo of a much younger Blacker with a blond man, grinning inanely, their arms draped over each other. They held cans in their hands, so it was probably some lads' night out, but they weren't in the T-shirts that were standard wear on such occasions. They were in suit trousers and the shirts with heavy stripes that were essential wear for young executives at one time. As she was lifting the picture off its hook the cardboard backing fell out and the frame disintegrated. No fault of hers, she decided, slipping out the photo. She popped it into her backpack. It would soon have fallen off the wall anyway.

Nothing else was worth bothering about. The thrillers and science fiction beside the bed were unusable. The socks and underclothes in the chest of drawers were heavy with damp. She opened the bedroom door and looked into a burnt-out ruin black as sin, with only stumps where the stairs had been. To take one step on what remained of the landing would have been madness. The smell of burnt wood was overpowering. She closed the door and prepared to leave.

Leave?

She had not foreseen that the only way out would be by standing on the chair and climbing up the wall to where the ladder was. It had been simple letting herself down, but the reverse was more than she could manage. Standing on top of the chair back she could only just get her fingers over the beam she'd dropped from. An Olympic gymnast would have found it a trial. She looked around for something taller to stand on. The chest of drawers, like the wardrobe, was a built-in fixture. The bed was too heavy to move. She struggled with the mattress and dragged it off the bed, but it was so wet she couldn't shift it to the wall.

'Stupid,' she said. 'Stupid, stupid, stupid woman.'

She was trapped. The window was boarded up and the door led into a black void. The cottage was isolated and surrounded with notices telling people to keep out. To shout for help would be useless. Unless she thought of something, there would be a second death in this bedroom.

4

Times have changed since a certain author was executed for murdering his publisher. They say that when the author was on the scaffold he said goodbye to the minister and to the reporters and then he saw some publishers sitting in the front row below, and to them he did not say goodbye. He said instead, 'I'll see you later.'

J. M. Barrie, speech at Aldine Club, New York, 5 November 1896

To everyone's relief, Maurice McDade was sitting in the pub, a wide smile across his face, when they arrived that evening. All the members who had been there the previous night turned up except for Naomi; a fine show of solidarity.

Tudor – the one who had practically had Maurice stitched up – was the first to clap a hand on his shoulder and say, 'Good to see you, boyo. We knew you had nothing to hide.'

'So what happened?' Anton asked, when they all had their drinks.

'A few crossed wires, that's all,' Maurice said. 'They thought they had something on me. Well, I might as well tell you, since it's bound to come out. Edgar Blacker and I had a thumping great row on the day of his death. He told me the production costs of my book had spiralled and he needed five thousand pounds. If it wasn't forthcoming he'd be forced to back down on his agreement to publish.'

Miss Snow said, 'Extraordinary.'

Basil said, 'Oh, my hat.'

Zach said, 'What a wanker.'

'Naturally I was devastated,' Maurice went on. 'He was supposed to pay *me* some money. The advance – and it wasn't much of one anyway – was due to be paid on the day of publication, which was only days away. I'd done a lot of extra work on the script at his request and he hadn't paid me anything. I told him straight that I didn't have that money to spare, and anyway it wasn't in the contract that I'd pay anything. He said if that was my attitude he had no choice but to pull the book. I was speechless. He didn't even say he was sorry.'

'This was the day someone torched his cottage?' Tudor said.

'The morning after he talked to the circle. He called me up and asked me to come and see him without a hint as to what it was about. I've toiled away at this bloody book, if you'll excuse me, ladies, for years. I really believed it was about to get into print at last. I say it myself, and it's true, that book is worthy of publication.'

'We all know that,' Tudor said. 'You've read the best bits to us.'

'Did you stick one on him?' Zach asked.

'We had an exchange of views. There wasn't a fight, if that's what you mean. I'm not a violent person.'

'Lord, no,' Miss Snow said.

'I told him what I thought of him in no uncertain terms. I don't think I've ever been so angry.'

'But you didn't torch the cottage?' Tudor said.

'Of course not!'

'How did the police get onto you?'

'They won't say.'

'Someone must have seen you. Was there anyone around when you were there?'

'At the cottage? No.'

'The cottage?' Anton said. 'He ran the business from a cottage?'

'Yes. We spoke in the living room where he has his desk.' He spread his hands. 'That's about it.'

'You convinced the police you're innocent?'

'I hope so. They gave me quite a grilling. About three hours. It was getting on for midnight when I got home last night. I felt drained.'

'Don't they have any theory as to the killer?' Anton asked.

'I was the theory. I guess the subject of my book made them suspicious.'

'Well, it would.'

Bob spoke up. 'You'll have to write another chapter now.'

Everyone laughed and it eased the tension.

'Incidentally,' Maurice said, 'some of you may be called in for questioning.'

This announcement went down like garlic bread in Transylvania. Miss Snow knocked over her lemon shandy and there was a short interval while they mopped up.

'Whatever would they want to question us for?' Anton asked.

'Surely they don't regard any of us as suspects?' Dagmar said.

'They're taking a lot of interest in us,' Maurice said.

'In what way?'

'They questioned me closely about the evening he came to speak to us, wanting to know if anyone spoke to him afterwards.'

You could almost hear the memories ratcheting through the events of that evening.

'Several of us did,' Tudor said. 'It was a heaven-sent opportunity. A friendly publisher in our midst, for Christ's sake! You don't let him get away without testing the water. I don't mind telling you I talked to him about my autobiography.'

'Don't tell me. Tell the police,' Maurice said, winding Tudor up a little. His sense of relief was making him mischievous. 'They're the ones who are looking for suspects.'

Tudor fell for it, eyes bulging. 'Telling him about my book doesn't make me a suspect.'

'What did he say?'

'Well, if you want to know, he wasn't very encouraging. He said it needed a lot of work.'

'There you are, then. That's your motive.'

'My *what*?'

'Your motive for killing him. He tells you your life story isn't worth publishing. That's a slap in the face.'

'A kick in the goolies,' Zach said.

'I wasn't pleased, I admit.'

Miss Snow said, 'But it doesn't make Tudor a murderer.'

'We know he wouldn't kill anyone, but do the police?'

Tudor, red-faced, said, 'Why focus on me? Any of you could be a suspect.'

'Except Bob,' Thomasine said. 'He wasn't here.'

'Thanks,' Bob said.

Now Basil was alarmed. 'I had no reason to kill Edgar Blacker. He led me to believe my gardening articles might be collected into a book.'

'Couldn't have read them,' Tudor said.

This could get ugly. Maurice slipped into his role as chair. 'Listen, all of you, we're getting a little over-excited and I think the fault is mine. The police didn't actually say they are thinking of any of you as suspects.'

'Witnesses, more like?' Dagmar suggested.

'We witnessed nothing,' Thomasine said. 'We weren't there when his house went up in flames.'

'Nobody was there, apparently.'

'Except the killer.'

Maurice nodded. 'Speaking from all my experience studying unsolved murders, this one is a brute. It was done at night when no one was around. The killer simply stuffed some oily rags through the front door and put a match to them. There's no DNA, no ballistics, no fingerprints. I expect the body was just a charred piece of meat.'

'Don't!' Dagmar said.

'They identify them from the teeth.'

Miss Snow took in a sharp breath.

'And all his personal papers will have gone up with the cottage,' Anton said. 'They won't have an address book to help them, or bank statements.'

'Are they certain the fire was deliberate?' Miss Snow asked.

'That's beyond doubt. They have fire experts who can tell you where it started. In this case, it was obvious.'

'So have any of you ever thought of writing a whodunnit?' Tudor asked, recovering his bounce. 'This looks like a golden opportunity.'

'Don't,' Dagmar said. 'This is serious.'

'A serious whodunnit.'

'You're trivialising something tragic and disturbing.'

'Isn't that what crime writing is all about?'

'He's winding you up, dear,' Thomasine told Dagmar.

Tudor said, 'I was making a fair point. We're always being told that writers should make use of personal experience. Write about what you know. Here we are with a murder on our doorstep – well, on Edgar Blacker's doorstep – and what are we going to do? Pretend it didn't happen? I say we should get creative.'

'You have to be a cold fish to write detective stories,' Miss Snow said. 'I couldn't possibly attempt one.'

'Do a factual piece then. The strange death of a publisher. Write it up and sell it to the *Bookseller*.'

'I wouldn't dream of doing any such thing.'

'Which is why you'll never make an investigative journalist.'

'I've no desire to be one.'

'Someone else should do it. As a circle we can't let an opportunity like this pass us by. Zach?'

Zach shook his head.

'Too busy with the big novel?' Tudor said. 'What about you, Sharon? Make a name for yourself.'

Tudor seemed to believe he had a mission to draw the pretty blonde girl into the open.

She said, 'You're joking.'

'And has this event done anything for you as a writer?'

'Give me a break,' Sharon said.

Dagmar said, 'She wants to be a fashion writer.'

'You've got me there,' Tudor said. 'Edgar Blacker in his sports coat and cords wasn't exactly the king of the catwalks. Why not stretch a point and do a piece on the two detectives who took Maurice in? They looked – what's the word? – cool.'

Sharon shook her head and went back to her doodling. Tudor's sharp blue eyes swivelled in search of someone else to wind up.

Anton said, 'Murder is too crude a topic for me.'

Tudor looked across at Basil, the gardener. 'And you're going to say it doesn't beat keeping a lawn nice. I give up.'

Dagmar said, 'It's a question of good taste, Tudor. A man we all met has died a horrible death, and we don't wish to exploit it in any way.'

'Pleonasm,' Anton said.

'I beg your pardon.'

'You can't die a death. It's a pleonasm. Either you die, or a death takes place.'

'Somebody strangle that man before I do,' Tudor said. 'Aren't we going to get so much as a pesky poem out of this murder, then?'

Bob, sensing that the spotlight was about to turn his way, acted quickly to deflect it. 'What about you, Tudor? What are you going to write?'

33

'Me? Oh, I haven't decided yet. It could be another chapter in my memoirs, especially if one of you lot is the killer.'

'That Tudor's a pain in the bum,' Thomasine said to Bob in the car park. 'He'd take over as chair if it wasn't for all the extra work.'

'Takes all sorts,' Bob said. It isn't a good idea to take sides when you're so new.

'Trust me, last night wasn't typical. You didn't see us at our best. I hope you'll come again.'

'I might.'

'You didn't give anyone your address or phone number. What if we have to cancel?'

He stalled. He was still in two minds about joining the circle. 'Because of another murder?'

'God forbid – I didn't mean *that*.'

'I'm not sure I'm up for it.'

'Up for what?' She made it sound suggestive.

He wasn't planning to get more friendly with Thomasine. She seemed fun, but he hadn't dated a woman since Maggie died. 'The circle.'

'Don't be like that. Give us another try. It's a great laugh sometimes. A riot. Really it is.'

'If I can make it, then.'

'Give me your number just in case we change the date. It's been known.'

'I'm saying I don't want to make it official.'

'And it won't be. I'm not on the committee.'

With some hesitation he told her his number. 'Sometimes my job keeps me busy at nights. I'll do my best.'

'What are you in – security?'

'A bouncer, you mean?' He smiled.

'You're big enough.'

He told her about the driving job. 'And what do you do?'

'Me? I teach . . . What's funny about that?'

* * *

It was getting on for midnight. Basil was at home making a cocoa prior to retiring and beginning to wonder when his wife Naomi would return. She'd gone out earlier on the bike without telling him her plans. She'd not shown up at the pub. However, he wasn't too concerned. They didn't live in each other's pockets. She was apt to go off 'checking some facts', as she liked to put it, and it was not unusual for her to get home late fulfilled by her researches.

After the session with the circle members, he'd busied himself in his greenhouse whilst trying to remember some of the things that had been said. Naomi was sure to want chapter and verse on every blessed thing. She'd be pleased Maurice was in the clear. They both had a high regard for Maurice.

The phone rang. This would be her, no doubt.

And it was. And she didn't sound fulfilled.

'Where have you been? I've been calling for the past two hours.'

'You know where I was. I went to the pub with the circle.'

'Till midnight?'

'No, I got back early. I've been pottering in the greenhouse pricking out seedlings.'

'While I've been trapped in a deserted building.'

'I had no idea. Where are you now?'

'Still here, you cretin.'

'Trapped inside a building? I got that. Do you need help, my dear?'

Her exasperated sigh was audible down the phone. 'Why else would I be calling? I was afraid I was in a dead spot.'

'Dead spot?'

'Stop parroting my words and listen to me. Do you know the publisher's cottage on the Selsey Road, the one that went up in flames? I'm stuck in the bedroom.'

'How on earth . . . ?'

'It doesn't matter how. Just get here as fast as you can and bring the steps. I can't climb out without them. You'll need a torch. Have you got that? The steps and a torch.'

'Yes.'

'Say it, then.'

'The steps and a torch.'

'As quickly as you can, Basil. I'm cold, uncomfortable and extremely annoyed.'

The drive home in the van added nothing to Basil's understanding. Naomi was treating the episode as if it didn't merit an explanation and Basil knew from experience that it wasn't wise to ask. For his own satisfaction he was damned if he'd tell her Maurice had been at the pub. So nothing was said.

Finally she asked, 'What seedlings?'

'I beg your pardon?'

'You said you were pricking out seedlings. What are you growing from seed this late in the year?'

'Lettuces, dear. Late lettuces. You know how we both enjoy a salad.'

Bob didn't expect a call this quick, lunchtime the next day.

'This is Thomasine. Are you working tonight?'

'Depends.'

'Could we meet? Something's happened. Well, it's Maurice. They've pulled him in for questioning again and this time it looks serious.'

She was waiting in the Feathers in South Street, and little Dagmar was with her in a state of shock, sipping an Appletiser as if it was neat whisky.

'He's been held for eight hours already,' Thomasine said.

'That's a long time considering they questioned him only the day before.'

Dagmar spoke: 'They can keep him for up to thirty-six

hours without charging him. They need a warrant to hold him any longer.'

'Dagmar works for a solicitor,' Thomasine said, seeing Bob's reaction to this legal knowhow. 'What's going on, Bob? Maurice is a pussy cat. He wouldn't commit murder.'

'How did you find out?'

'What, that he's been pulled in again? Don't ask.'

Dagmar turned a shade more pink. The best guess was that she'd overheard something at work.

Bob went to the bar and ordered a beer, wondering how this had become his problem. He hadn't even joined their circle, yet Thomasine seemed to think he could save their precious chair from being stitched up. Ah well, he told himself, it's a change from sitting at home trying not to watch *EastEnders*.

He returned to the table. As if they'd read his mind, Thomasine said, 'We need a man's help with this. If Dagmar or I go in to bat for Maurice, everyone's going to think we have a thing for him, and it's not like that. We just think he's entitled to some back-up.'

'And if you think about the other men in the circle,' Dagmar said, 'well . . .' She smiled and shook her head. 'Tudor, Basil, Zach and Anton. They all mean well, but you wouldn't choose them as ambassadors.'

'Do any of them know the police have got him there again?'

'No, it's inside information,' Thomasine said, and Dagmar blushed again.

Bob felt the weight of their confidence in him. 'I'd like to help, but I'm not sure what I can do. If the worst comes to the worst and they charge him with murder, he'll have a legal team defending him.'

Dagmar said, 'We should be doing something now. Every minute could be important.'

'Doing what?'

'We were thinking his partner may know why the police are giving him such a hard time.'

Dagmar said, 'If anyone knows, she will.'

'What's her name?'

'Fran.'

'Have you met her?'

'No. He doesn't bring her to any of our parties.'

'But they live together?'

'Yes. In Lavant,' Dagmar said. 'We had a meeting at the house once, before the club was formed, just Maurice, Naomi and me, and Fran went out for the evening. It's a nice house facing Goodwood and the racecourse.'

'The thing is, I don't really know him at all.'

'She'll know you're okay if you're from the circle,' Thomasine said. 'It's a big part of his life.'

'I need another beer.'

'Is that a good idea? We thought you might have a cup of peppermint tea to mask what you've drunk already.'

'You want me to go up there *tonight*?'

Maybe tonight was best. By the morning he might think better of it.

They were right about the house. A paved drive, coach lamps, porticoed Georgian front.

Lights were on inside. Someone had heard the chimes and came to the door and the surprise was that she was a little old lady. Not a day under seventy-five, he thought. Soft permed silver hair, pale skin, thin arms. No one had mentioned an elderly parent.

Bob had forgotten Maurice's surname. A bad start. 'I, em, come from the writers' circle. Is Fran at home?'

'You're looking at her.'

He said, 'Ah,' in a way that was meant to sound calm, and didn't. It was more the strangled 'Ah' of a patient at the dentist's.

'Who are you?' she said.

Her voice was strong. Maybe she's younger than she looks, he thought. However hard he tried, he couldn't make her under seventy. 'Em, Bob Naylor.' Honesty was needed here. 'You may not have heard of me.'

'That's true.'

'I don't look the type, I admit, but I'm the new bloke in the circle. They – we – want to help Maurice if we can. We heard they pulled him in again. Is there any more news?'

'He's still there, as far as I know.'

'We think the Old Bill have cocked up.'

'I beg your pardon?'

'The police, ma'am. They're out of order.'

'I'm sure they are but I don't know what any of us can do. You'd better come in, Mr Naylor.'

She opened the door wider.

'This way.' She showed him into a front room out of the 1950s, with three-piece suite, china cabinet, nest of tables, glass-fronted bookcase and a Swiss mountain scene over the fireplace. What was Maurice's game, moving in here with a woman so many years his senior? Maurice as a middle-aged toy boy? It was hard for Bob to get his head around that.

'Tea or coffee?'

'Thanks, but no. Just a chat. The gang – the circle – are trying to decide the best way to help Maurice, but we don't know what we're up against.'

'You're up against the police. It's good of you to offer, but what can anyone do?' She was twisting an embroidered handkerchief around her fingers.

'He told us how Edgar Blacker shafted him over the book.'

'Yes, er, that's a fair summary.'

'Said there was a thumping great row.'

'I believe there was. He felt terribly let down.'

'We feel for him as fellow writers. He also said he didn't start the fire that night, and we believe him.'

'That's reassuring.'

'Well, I guess you know for certain that he's blameless. You would know if he went out that night.'

Fran twisted the handkerchief tighter and sighed. 'That's one of the difficulties. You see, we sleep in separate rooms. About eleven that evening, I went to bed and Maurice said he was going for a walk. He often does about that time, just to look at the stars and get a little exercise before turning in. I never hear him come in. I'm asleep as soon as my head touches the pillow.'

'Shame,' Bob said, and it was an understatement.

'Yes, it is. They haven't come along to question me yet, and I'll have to be truthful if they do.'

'You said that's one of the difficulties. Is there another?'

She sighed. 'I'm afraid there is, but I couldn't possibly divulge it to you, not without Maurice's permission.'

'Something else happened?'

'A long time ago.'

'What – tied in with Edgar Blacker?'

'No. Quite separate.' She raised her hand. 'That's all I can say.'

'But you believe he's innocent?'

'I have total confidence in him, Mr Naylor. I wouldn't share my life with him if I thought he was evil.'

'I don't want to seem nosy, ma'am—'

'Fran. Call me Fran.'

'Fran. How long have you two been together?'

'Nearly ten years. He had a difficult, unhappy marriage and I only met him after it was over. You'll appreciate that there's an age difference between us and some people find it difficult to understand. If the reverse happens – an older man and a younger woman, nobody seems to think anything of it. I don't believe he regards me as a mother figure, as some people suppose, and I certainly don't treat him that way. We have a loving, relaxed relationship. Are you married?'

'A widower.'

'Perhaps you understand, then.'

'I wasn't trying to judge you, love. We've all got our lives to lead. I only asked because I wanted to know how far you two go back.'

The phone rang – and it really did ring as phones once did. It was the Bakelite model with a dial once supplied to everyone who asked to be connected. She crossed the room and picked up the receiver. 'Yes?'

She listened to the caller, and her face creased in anxiety.

Finally, she said, 'Oh,' and replaced the receiver. To Bob, she said, 'They're keeping him overnight.'

5

No, on the whole I think all writers should be in prison.

Ralph Richardson, on being asked to appear in a charity programme in support of imprisoned writers; quoted by Ned Sherrin in *Anecdotage* (1993)

The ladies were still in the bar. Three empty Appletiser bottles were lined up in front of Dagmar, and Thomasine was using a cherry on a cocktail stick to scoop up the last of her drink. Bob gave them the news about Maurice being kept overnight.

Dagmar looked devastated.

Thomasine, too, was devastated, and she had drowned her inhibitions in a series of G&Ts. 'Shit and derision – what can he tell them that he hasn't already?'

'Who knows?' Bob said. 'They think there's more.'

'And so do you, Bob. I see it in your eyes.'

'Not much I can tell you, though. Fran hinted at something and then kept the cap on the bottle. She called it a difficulty. Said it happened a long time ago.'

'Sounds like he's got form.'

'My thought exactly.'

'What do you mean – a criminal record?' Dagmar said, making it clear this was about as likely as an elephant in church.

'Right on.'

'*Maurice?*'

'What else could she mean?' Bob said.

'*Maurice?*' Dagmar said again.

'They wouldn't hold him overnight without something they can work on. Fran is in a sweat. I can tell you that.' He told them about Maurice's late night walk on the night of the murder and Fran being unable to supply an alibi.

'What's the matter with the dopey woman?' Thomasine said. 'If it was me, and my man was up shit creek, I'd speak up for him.'

'Me, too,' Dagmar said.

'No disrespect,' Bob said, 'but that lady is high-principled. She's not going to tell porkies for anyone.'

'But if she *knows* he's innocent . . .'

'She doesn't know. It's about trust, isn't it? She trusts the bloke. For her, that's enough, but it's not enough for the Old Bill.'

'Besides,' Thomasine said, spreading her hands wide, 'they'd expect his partner to lie for him. In the eyes of the law, alibis from your nearest and dearest don't amount to a fart in a whirlwind.'

'What's she like, this woman?' Dagmar said.

'Fran? Bit older than I expected. I'd say there's all of twenty years between them.'

Dagmar's eyes widened. 'That makes her over seventy.'

'That's what I thought.'

Thomasine said, 'She must be a bloody good cook, is all I can say. So what are we going to do, poppets? Tell the others Maurice is back in the nick?'

'There's nothing any of us can do for him tonight,' Bob said.

'Suppose they charge him and he's innocent?'

'Of course he's innocent,' Dagmar said, beginning to get over the shock of that age gap. 'We've got to support him.'

'There's only one way,' Thomasine said. 'We must find

out who really set fire to that sodding publisher's house. And when I say "we", I mean the entire circle, the whole kit and caboodle – all twelve of us.'

'Eleven,' Dagmar said.

'Twelve. Bob's in, aren't you, baby?'

'Yes, but what Dagmar means is that Maurice can't help us much.'

On that note of unity, they decided to leave. Thomasine got upright with difficulty, pushing at the table edge as if it was the river bank and she was in a small boat.

'You're not driving, are you?' Bob said.

'Why? You want a lift?'

'We'd better get you home,' he said, looking to Dagmar for a sign that she would help. She gave a nod.

Out in the fresh air, Thomasine swayed and grabbed Bob's arm. He helped her to his car. They eased her into the back seat and Dagmar got in beside her.

'What's this – a threesome?' Thomasine said.

'Don't be daft,' Dagmar said.

'I don't need a chaperon.'

'I do,' Bob said. 'Where do you live?'

They drove to some flats west of the city. Between them, he and Dagmar negotiated the stairs, taking most of Thomasine's weight. Dagmar found the key in the handbag and they let themselves in and opened the bedroom door. Thomasine flopped onto the bed without another word. Dagmar removed her shoes and covered her with the quilt.

On the drive back to the centre of town, Dagmar said, 'She'll be so embarrassed tomorrow. It's not a habit.'

'We've all been there.' Even as he said this to Dagmar, Bob was thinking that a lifelong Appletiser drinker probably had *not* been there.

Dagmar was still finding excuses for Thomasine. 'It's the shock about Maurice. It affects us in different ways. He's a dear man. He doesn't deserve this.'

'We'll sort it out, love. Don't let it get to you.'

He put her down beside her Mini and drove home. The speed of things, the way he'd been pitched into this, surprised him. Here he was, not even committed to joining the circle, taking on their problem as if it was his own.

When he got in, young Sue was still up and on the phone. Seeing him, she ended the call and offered to make coffee.

'Tea would do me nicely, love.'

'So have you cleared up the mystery, Dad?'

'Not yet.'

'This murder. Was it someone's house burned down with him in it?'

'Yes.'

'You could be too late, then. It was on the news. They're questioning some bloke.'

'Doesn't mean they've got the right one.'

'Hey, listen to Mr Sherlock Holmes! You want to get one of them funny hats and a magnifying glass.'

'Any more of that from you, young lady, and I'll be asking you what your homework was.'

'All done.'

'I bet. And how long have you been on the phone?'

She busied herself with the teapot.

'You weren't using your mobile, I notice.'

'I can't win, can I?' Sue said. 'If I go out, I'm in trouble for wasting my time, and if I stop in I'm stacking up the phone bill. Do you want to know about the call you had?'

'Who from?'

'Some posh bird.'

'Didn't she leave her name?'

'Big laugh, that was. "Miss Snow," she said. "Tell him Miss Snow would like to hear from him as soon as possible." Miss Snow! Is that what you call your latest pick-up, Dad?'

'She's secretary of the circle. Did she leave a number?'

'By the phone.'

He looked at his watch. Too late to return the call. He guessed Miss Snow had seen the item on TV.

He called her next morning after Sue had left for school.

'I've been sitting by the phone,' she said.

All night? he thought.

'You're the only person I can speak to with any confidence.'

'Why is that?'

'Could we meet?'

'What's it about?'

'I'd rather not say over the phone.' She was a lot more discreet than Thomasine.

'Okay. Where?'

'Do you know the women's refuge shop?'

'Charity shop? In that little lane off North Street?'

'That's the one. I'm on duty there this morning.'

'I'll come there, then.'

'We should have it to ourselves if you can get there early.'

'What time is early?'

He met her outside the shop door. She was wearing a black silk headscarf that made her look ready for the confession-box and for a moment he wondered if she was the killer and was about to tell all. But she took the scarf off when they got inside.

He helped her pick up the morning's junk mail and a few paperbacks some donor had pushed through the door. The smell of old clothes was overpowering.

'I don't know how to begin,' she said.

'We could open the door at the back, get the air flowing.' He was thinking he wouldn't work in a charity shop if they paid him. This was poky, dark and stacked high with junk.

'I'm talking about Maurice.'

But Bob hadn't yet got over the smell. 'Some air freshener would help.'

She said, 'I'm used to it. Leave the door open if you like.'

'And you do this by choice? You're a saint.'

'If you saw the state of the refuge, you'd understand. I'm on the committee, and we need new furniture badly. But I want to talk about Maurice.'

'You're going to tell me he's on the level.'

Nodding, she said, 'They're making a ghastly mistake.'

'The law?'

'Yes. They kept him overnight. It was on local radio. They don't do that unless it's serious, do they?'

He tried to look uncertain.

'He's a good man,' she said. 'Don't misunderstand me. I don't carry a torch for him, or anything.'

Carry a torch. Bob loved that. Miss Snow being racy. Looking at her now, with those worry lines and silver streaks, it was hard to imagine her carrying a torch for anyone. Twenty years ago, maybe.

Get real, Naylor. She could be your age. Probably thinks you're on the scrapheap yourself.

She said, 'I'm just so worried that he's being – what's the word?'

'Fitted up?'

'Exactly.' She switched on a strip light that flickered about ten times before coming on. 'He needs a spokesman. An advocate. You're concerned about him, aren't you? You wouldn't have joined us in the bar the next night if you hadn't wanted to help.'

To help sounded a warning bell in his head. He didn't trust himself to say anything.

'You're one of us,' she said, meaning it as a tribute. 'What is more, you took the measure of us all the other evening. I could tell by the way you conducted yourself that you had us all summed up. You didn't have a lot to say, but what you said was so perceptive.'

'Trying to fit in, that's all.'

'You see,' she said, with a narrowing of the eyes that made Bob feel like a stag being stalked, 'I happen to believe it wasn't pure chance that brought you to the circle that night. There is a destiny that shapes our ends.'

'You've lost me now.'

'You were sent, Mr Naylor. The circle needs you, and you arrived, a man with gravitas.'

'Come again?'

'People listen to you because you are who you are. It's about personality. Well, you saw what the others are like. They mean well, but heaven help us if they're all we've got as spokesmen.'

Time to back-pedal. 'Hang about – I'm no spokesman.'

'Too modest,' she said. 'Getting back to Maurice, he is in desperate need of someone to take up his case, and you're the obvious choice.'

He shook his head, but it did no good.

'So I'm about to take you into my confidence. I happen to know that Maurice was in trouble once before with the police, and once they get their claws into you . . .'

He was undermined by his own curiosity. 'What sort of trouble?'

She hesitated and took a look around the empty shop. 'You will treat this as confidential?'

'If you want.'

She started rearranging the skirts hanging on a circular rail, as if it helped to occupy her hands. 'He had a dispute with a neighbour when he was living in Brighton some years ago. I happen to know because I was living in Hove and read about it in the *Argus*. This man was extremely unpleasant. He had some kind of boatbuilding business and his garden was full of timber, front and back. I don't know all the details, but there were planks and things stacked against the fence, the fence owned by Maurice, and one day it collapsed under the weight. Maurice asked him to repair

48

it and got a mouthful of abuse. The man had two of those fierce guard dogs. Black and brown. What are they called?'

'Rottweilers?'

'Yes, and they now had the run of Maurice's garden. He was afraid to open his back door. They took over the garden, fouling it and making it their own territory. He tried reporting the man to the council and nothing was done. His life became a misery. So he took the law into his own hands. He shot the dogs with a shotgun he owned and made a bonfire of the wood that had tipped over into his garden. Unfortunately the fire got out of control and spread next door and destroyed a shed and a couple of the boats the neighbour was working on. Apparently they were worth a lot of money. The firemen were called, and the police, and Maurice was arrested. There was a lot of sympathy for him locally, but he was charged with causing criminal damage and' – she drew a sharp breath – 'found guilty and sent to prison. I can't remember how long it was – a few months, I think.'

'Bit steep.'

'I'm glad you agree.'

'Mind,' he said, 'shooting the dogs wasn't clever. That wouldn't have helped. You get the picture of a bloke with a short fuse.'

'It had gone on for months.'

'Yeah, but you can't argue it was an accident.'

'You're right,' she said.

'And it won't help him now.'

'That's why I'm so worried for him.'

'Throw in the fact that it's a fire again,' Bob said, speaking more to himself than Miss Snow.

'But the two events are quite different.'

'Unless you're a cop looking to nick someone. Then it adds up neatly. An angry man with a record of fire-raising.'

'Don't!'

'He's in deep. He had the motive, the opportunity and this. He's got no alibi.'

'But surely his partner must know where he was.'

'I spoke to her yesterday,' Bob said. 'Maurice went out about eleven on the night of the fire and she didn't hear him come in.'

She stared. 'You went to see her?'

'Thomasine and Dagmar asked me to.'

All this took her a moment to absorb, then she recovered. 'You see? We're all turning to you for help.'

'God knows why,' Bob said with feeling. 'How do you know he didn't do this?'

'*Maurice?* Oh, no.'

'You only see one side of him.'

She leaned forward and eyeballed him intently. 'Mr Naylor—'

'Bob. No one calls me that.'

'Then you must call me Amelia.'

By Miss Snow's lights this was probably as reckless as it gets. She was in earnest, no question. 'Maurice is a gentleman in every sense of the word. It wouldn't cross his mind to make an attack at night on someone asleep in his bed.'

'You mean he'd blast him with his shotgun?'

It was a flip remark and wasn't appreciated. 'Not Maurice.'

'Look at it this way, em, Amelia,' Bob said. 'If he didn't do it, we're looking for some other geezer. The police won't give up on Maurice without someone else in the frame. Are we going to do their work for them?'

'It needn't come to that.'

'Like I said, he's got no alibi. His partner Fran is bricking it, but she's no help. She knows he was out on the night of the murder and she's not going to cover up for him.'

'This is so distressing.'

'If we knew more about the murdered guy, it might help. You heard him speak to the circle. What was he like?'

'Friendly. He encouraged some of us to believe we might get into print very soon.'

'A right conman, then.' The moment he'd said this, he wished he hadn't. She had her heart set on publication, like everyone else in the circle.

Drawing herself up a little, she said, 'Well, certain of us are up to professional standards. It's in the lap of the gods whether we find a publisher. Edgar Blacker was willing to take us on, or so he was suggesting. If you don't believe me, you can look at the tape.'

There was a pause of several beats before Bob asked, 'What tape?'

'There's a video of the talk he gave us. We asked his permission to film him so that we could show it later and discuss it among ourselves.'

'I wouldn't mind seeing that tape.'

'You can borrow it if you wish. I have it at home.'

'Today?'

'If you like. I'd forgotten you didn't meet Mr Blacker. Wait a minute. I'll phone the refuge and ask someone to come in and take care of the shop.'

While Miss Snow made the call, Bob stood in front of the shelves of secondhand books, most of them dog-eared and fading paperbacks. They didn't interest him. He was basking in his own good fortune. A video of Blacker's appearance in front of the circle. He hadn't dreamed it existed.

'That's fixed.' She was back. 'Nadia will take care of the shop. She's not been here long.' She mouthed the word 'illegal'. 'Speaks good English, though.'

Whilst waiting, she made an instant coffee that smelt of footballers' socks. Bob was grateful when Nadia arrived ten minutes later, a smiling, middle-aged woman dressed, presumably, in things from the shop, because she looked as English as Miss Snow herself.

Out in North Street, the air had never smelt so fresh.

51

The wide walkways of Chichester give people the chance to move freely at the pace they like, and on the whole that is brisker than in most cities. But Amelia Snow was slower than the average pedestrian, which suited Bob, because they could talk. 'What do you write, apart from minutes of the meetings?' he asked her.

'Oh, I'm doing a book on famous Snows,' she said.

He didn't catch on. 'As in snowstorms?'

'No, no. People who share my name, like Dr John Snow, the founder of anaesthetics, and C. P. Snow, the novelist.'

'Are there enough for a book?'

'More than enough. My problem is who to leave out.'

'How far have you got?'

'I'm working on my third draft. It runs to over a hundred thousand words already.'

'Strewth.'

'They have such interesting lives. Edgar Snow, the great sinologist. Marguerite Snow, the silent film star.'

'There's that guy on TV who pops up on election night with the swingometer.'

'Peter Snow. And Jon Snow, the Channel Four News man, of course. But they're not included. I'm restricting this to dead Snows.'

'Do you read bits out at the meetings?'

'Frequently. I get the impression it goes over their heads.'

'Did you show it to Edgar Blacker?'

'I gave him a sample chapter to read. He said some flattering things, but he seems to have praised almost everybody's work.'

'Better than knocking it.'

'I don't agree with that. If you praise everything, it devalues the currency of your opinion.'

'Did he make you an offer?'

'I beg your pardon?'

'To publish the book?'

'Oh. Well, he wanted to acquire it, I'm sure of that.'

'What was his game, do you think?'

'His game?'

'What was he up to, telling everyone their work was great?'

She frowned and looked away. 'I don't know, unless he was one of those people incapable of giving bad news to anyone.'

At the Cross, they turned left into West Street. The stonework of the cathedral glowed in the morning sun.

'I live behind the Army & Navy,' she said, and a surreal picture popped into Bob's head, worthy of a rhyme.

'Is that a fact?' he said, stringing it together. He was a rapid rhymer.

'The department store.'

'Right. Got it.'

> I live behind the Army & Navy
> Knickers off for Sergeant Davy,
> Captain Billy, Corporal Jeff
> And Gordon from the RAF.

'Nice and central,' he said without a hint of his thinking. 'Convenient for everything.'

'Yes, it's small, but it suits me.' She took a key from her bag. They'd come to a terraced row of houses that opened directly onto Tower Street. 'Please come in and I'll find that videotape.'

She stepped inside and turned on a light. Just off the hallway was the room where she did her writing.

'My den,' she said with just a suggestion of intrigue.

A computer and printer on a trolley. Bookshelves. An entire set of *Who Was Who*. Plenty of Snows in there, he imagined. She also had a framed photo of a showgirl in a cat costume, but without the headgear. He took a closer look and got a whole new slant on Miss Snow.

'This you?'

'Mm.'

'Wow.'

'I did some stage work when I was younger.'

'In *Cats*? This looks like the original show.'

'Yes, but I wasn't one of the stars, or anything.'

'You must have been good.' Good figure, too, he noted. Better than good, and the cut of the costume hid very little.

'I trained as a dancer, but it's a short career unless you can act, and I'm hopeless at speaking lines.'

'So you write them instead.'

'I can't write dialogue. Biography is my forte.'

On a table in the corner was a typescript.

'Is that it?' he asked.

'Only a draft. The clean version is in the other room.'

She was such an innocent that he resisted the obvious gag.

She added, 'Fortunately I got it back from Edgar Blacker before his house burned down. It can be awfully expensive printing out five hundred pages, don't you find?'

'Me? I've never written anything that length.'

'What have you done, then?'

Oops. He stonewalled. 'The odd bit of verse. I'm not in your league at all.'

She was bending over a carton in the corner, searching for the tape. I guess we've all changed shape since our dancing days, Bob told himself.

She said, 'I'd like to write poetry, but I haven't got the talent. What sort of thing inspires you?'

'Whatever pops into my head,' he said to her rear view. 'You'd be surprised what gets me going.'

'I hope you'll read some of it out at a meeting.'

He thought of his Army & Navy lines. 'That'll be the day.'

'Got it,' she said, straightening up, holding a cassette. 'You mustn't be nervous of reading your work, Bob. I hope you keep it nicely in a notebook.'

'It's not worth it.'

'Then you can read to us at a meeting. We've all had to lose our virginity at some time – figuratively speaking – so we're a very sympathetic audience.'

'I'll take your word for it.'

'Promise you'll get a notebook and keep everything you write. They'll offer an opinion, some of them, and that can be valuable.'

'What do they do in real life?' he asked.

'The circle is real life.'

'Yes, but . . .'

'You mean, how do they earn a living? Maurice works for British Gas, at management level. Zach, the fantasy writer, who read out his work to us, serves in the record shop in South Street. Basil, the gardening man, is retired.'

'Anton?'

'Also retired. He was some kind of civil servant. Then there's Tudor, the Welshman. He sells cars, or insurance. I'm not sure which.'

'I can believe that. What about the dolly bird?'

'Sharon? She's a hairdresser. Does one day a week at college. She hasn't been with us long and to be frank I don't know how long she'll want to stay. As you saw, she doesn't contribute much.'

'Except when Tudor forces her to speak.'

'You noticed? He thinks he has a way with the ladies.'

'Then there's Thomasine. She told me she's a teacher.'

'At the girls' school, yes.'

'And Dagmar works for a solicitor.'

'You are well informed. She keeps that to herself. Who does that leave, apart from me?'

'The woman who had the letter published.'

'Jessie. She's a widow. She was married to someone quite important in the church, an archdeacon, I believe. That's only one down from a bishop. Oh, and I didn't mention Naomi.'

'X-ray eyes?'

'What makes you say that?'

'She saw right through Edgar Blacker and didn't mind saying so. She was the one who spoke up first, saying he was a bit flaky, raised too many hopes.'

'That's true, now I recall it.' She stared at him for a moment in silence. 'You don't miss a thing.'

'I bet you didn't put what she said in the minutes.'

She coloured. 'It was off the cuff. I can't put down every word.' She handed him the cassette. 'But this will tell you everything that happened the evening Mr Blacker spoke to us.'

'Thanks. And what about yourself?'

She seemed surprised by the question. 'Me?'

'Do you have a job, apart from the charity?'

'I'm a chartered accountant, semi-retired. I wouldn't call it a job. I don't even have an office. I go on site and do the books for a few local businesses I've known for years.'

'Is one of them a publisher?'

A frown. 'No.'

It was worth asking. 'Edgar Blacker wasn't a client, then?'

'Certainly not. They're all old friends like my chiropodist, my dentist and the shop where I buy most of my clothes.'

'You get some perks, then?'

'Just goodwill. You won't get an accountant to admit to "perks", as you put it.'

'I've heard of this. It's the barter economy. Like the Middle Ages. You have a skill to offer and so do your friends and neighbours. You help each other out and no money changes hands. Neat idea. If I had a useful talent, I'd be in there getting my hair cut for nothing and fruit cake at the weekend.'

'Putting accountants like me out of a job.'

Bob grinned. 'Hadn't thought of it like that.' His eyes held hers for a moment while he summed up what he'd learned so far. 'So your life is pretty busy with the charity shop and the accounting. Plus the circle. You've been the secretary from the beginning, right?'

She nodded.

'Well placed to know everyone in the circle?'

'I suppose so.'

He gave her a long look. 'All right, love. Cards on the table. Out of that lot, who could have started the fire that killed Blacker?'

She shook her head. 'No, no. I refuse to speculate. It would be abusing my position.'

'If I was another woman you'd speak out, no problem.'

'That's different.'

'I don't see why. You want me to play detective and you won't even give me the dope on the suspects.'

She put her hand primly against her chest. 'I didn't say anything about playing detective. All I said was that Maurice could do with someone to speak up on his behalf.'

Fair comment, he thought. It's Thomasine who wants me to play Sherlock Holmes.

He tried a more subtle approach. 'Speaking up is no use unless we put someone else in the frame. Look at it another way. Who gets a clean sheet from you?'

She sighed as a kind of protest, yet was persuaded to go down this route. 'Well, I can't really imagine any of the women doing such a thing. Dagmar is very proper, and so is Jessie. It wouldn't cross their minds. Naomi may be outspoken, but what you see is what you get, as they say. She'll tell you if something is wrong rather than acting on it secretly.'

'And I suppose the dumb blonde isn't committed enough?'

'Sharon? She's on the fringe really. I can't think what motive she would have. She hasn't written anything that I'm aware of, so she had no reason to be upset by the publisher.'

'That leaves Thomasine.'

She shot him a fierce look. 'No it doesn't. I can't see her harming a soul. She's a warm person, very friendly.'

'True. We're down to the blokes, then. Leaving aside Maurice, who have we got?'

'I won't be drawn,' Miss Snow said. 'I don't understand men. There's always the potential for violence in the male psyche, so far as I can tell.'

'Basil?'

She smiled, and she *was* drawn. 'Well, he's a sweetie. No, I can't see him as a fire-raiser.'

'Zach?'

'I said I won't be drawn.'

'Anton? Tudor?'

'I'm getting tired of this. Has it occurred to you, Bob, that the fire may have been started by someone from outside the circle? Edgar Blacker had his finger in other pies.'

Another zinger from Miss Snow. He'd focused so much on Blacker's visit to the circle and his death the next night that he'd failed to look elsewhere.

6

The only way for writers to meet is to share a quick pee over a common lamp-post.

Cyril Connolly, *The Unquiet Grave* (1945)

After he'd left, Bob still found it difficult to wrench his thoughts away from the circle. He asked himself if all this concern of Miss Snow's was driven by guilt. Suppose she'd started the fire that killed Edgar Blacker, planned it as a clean killing and been horrified when the police pulled in sweet old Maurice? She'd made it clear she wanted Bob in there batting for Maurice, but not doing the job of a detective. She'd be happy if Maurice was released without charge and no one took the rap.

She had a will of iron. He could imagine her getting a fixed idea that Blacker had to be stiffed. And carrying it out. But what was her motive? The way she'd told it, Blacker hadn't rejected her book on the Snow dynasty. He'd looked at the script and made encouraging noises. No, if she was the killer, there had to be some bigger reason.

He went into work and did the late shift, which meant he wasn't home until almost midnight. Sue had gone to bed and left something in a saucepan that looked murky but smelt all right. He lit the gas under it and checked the answerphone. The one message was from Thomasine:

'Thanks for looking after me last night. The less said about that, the better. The reason I'm calling is I have some news of Maurice. Bad news. I'm afraid they've charged him with murder. Can you get back to me?'

Charged him, had they?

Tomorrow, he decided.

He was tired, but reckoned he ought to run that video, so he opened a can of lager, rescued his supper before it congealed and took it into the living room.

Sue must have been watching something with the volume turned right up because the sound hit him like a plane coming in, and it was only the voices of the circle gathering in the New Park Centre. He reached for the remote.

Snatches of conversation came and went. Miss Snow was trying to persuade Tudor to give the vote of thanks. Anton had been to the doctor again. Whoever was holding the camera was making mischief with the zoom, picking out long legs in white lace tights that turned out to be Sharon's, then Thomasine at a window taking a crafty smoke, and Basil checking his hairpiece in front of a picture. Everyone except Maurice and Zach came into shot. The odds were on Zach being the cameraman.

'He's publishing Maurice,' Jessie was saying.

'Can't be too choosy, then,' Thomasine said from the window.

'What did you say?' Dagmar said.

'Joke, dear. Maurice deserves to be published. And there's a market for his kind of book, real crime.'

'Personally I wish he'd picked some more tasteful topic,' Jessie said.

'Such as?'

'I don't know. The royal family?'

'Give me strength,' Thomasine said.

'They call them three-six-fours in the library,' Tudor was heard saying out of shot.

'Who – the royals?'

'No, the people who read real crime. Three-six-four: Dewey Decimal System. Got it? Never linger round that section. Give it a wide berth.'

'What nonsense!' Dagmar said.

'I'm only passing it on, for what it's worth,' Tudor said. He was now in shot, and wearing a black velvet jacket and bow tie. 'I'm on familiar terms with the librarians. They all know me.'

'That I *can* believe.'

Miss Snow crossed in front of the camera. 'He's arrived. We ought to be seated.'

Some blurring of the images followed. A short break in the filming must have happened, because the next thing in focus was Maurice standing out front, addressing the audience. '. . . a special pleasure for me as one of his authors – shortly to be, at any rate – and I hope others in this room will be joining his list before long. As you know, he generously invited us to submit our work for consideration and a number of you took him up on the offer. Whilst we all understand the constraints on publishers, we hope very much, Edgar, that you will give us some pointers this evening on what you look for in a script. Members of the circle, please welcome Edgar Blacker.'

Polite applause, and a close shot of the murder victim. Short, with thick, mustard-coloured hair, and a tanned face suggestive of a winter holiday. Dark eyes looking over gold-rimmed specs. Corduroy jacket in dark red, striped shirt and cravat. Image was important to this man. On the table in front of him was a stack of typescripts.

'I'm going to begin,' he said in a high-pitched voice, 'by putting you out of your misery. I'm hugely impressed by everything I've read in this sample of your work. In fact, I will go so far as to say that I could see myself publishing almost all of it. I don't know why the standard of your circle is so high.

I confess that when Maurice asked me to look at some scripts I was not over keen. Is that a fair reflection, Maurice?'

Beside him, Maurice gave a little twitch of the shoulders that could mean anything.

'What I was given turned out to be a most exciting collection of scripts ranging from fantasy to family history, from verse to vegetables. No, don't smile. Publishing is a vast, all-inclusive industry and no topic is too humble to get into print. One of my bestselling books is nothing more than photos showing dogs that look exactly like their owners.'

He smiled, trying for a response, and this time didn't get one. If the audience were of the same mind as Bob, they were too busy deciding which breed the speaker was. A Dandie Dinmont?

'Well, I don't own a dog, so I'd better tell you something about myself. I've always been employed in publishing of some description, starting as tea boy at Eyre and Spottiswoode – a fine house no longer in being – and then as a packer in one of the big distributors' warehouses in Birmingham. My first editorial job was with a magazine publisher in Essex, working on several titles. After five or six years of that I got into educational books with Ward Lock. Loved it. I'd really found what I wanted to do. Stayed publishing school books until I'd saved enough to start my own business, the Blacker List, as I called it, and the rest is history.'

History that passed me by, Bob thought.

In the pause, the camera panned across the room. You can tell a lot from the backs of people's heads. The circle were taking in the spiel, but they didn't really want to know about Blacker's career. They couldn't wait to find out if he was going to offer contracts.

He started talking about the stuff he published, reading from a catalogue, and it was clear from the fidgeting in the audience that he was losing them.

Fast forward, Bob decided.

When he pressed *play* the interesting bit was under way.

'. . . an exquisite series of articles on gardening. Is the author here tonight?'

One cautious hand was raised. Basil was checking his hair-piece with the other.

'Well, sir, as you must be aware, gardening is big business. I like your approach. It's informative without being too technical for the average man.'

'Really?' Basil was almost purring.

'We'd need illustrations, of course, full colour on art paper, and you must provide a lot more text, because readers like value for money, but I'm confident we could have a success with your book. Do you have a nice garden of your own?'

'Not bad,' Basil said.

'Has it been on television?'

'Good Lord, no.'

'We can fix that for you. I have some contacts in the media.'

Basil sounded alarmed. 'It isn't up to that standard.'

'But you can make it so. Wonderful publicity. Free advertising, you see. We small publishers can't afford to advertise, so we take every opportunity we can. You'll be surprised how good your garden looks on the screen. We might also link up with the National Gardens Scheme and open it to the public.'

'It's tiny,' Basil said.

'That won't put off the visitors if we give it a good write-up.'

'They'd have to come through the house.' Basil was in danger of being steamrollered. He turned to look at someone else in the audience.

Then Naomi spoke up. 'I'm not having people through my house.'

'And you are . . . ?' Blacker said.

'His partner.'

Which was something Bob had not discovered until now. Basil and Naomi, green fingers linked with gimlet eyes, not a pairing he expected. He could imagine the look she was giving the speaker.

In a clever attempt to divert her, Blacker said, 'And did you submit a script, madam?'

'"The Sussex Witchcraft Trials."'

'Oh, I remember. Admirable. Timely, too. Right now there's a blossoming of interest in the occult.'

'Did you read it?'

'Enthralling. Meticulously researched. I was unaware such things happened in this peaceful part of England.'

'What things?'

'Well, the witchcraft.'

'The witchcraft didn't happen. That's the whole point of the book. They were innocent women.'

Blacker made a clucking sound. 'But of course.'

'Are you sure you read it?' Naomi was beginning to sound like a witchfinder herself.

'Absolutely.'

'They were the seventeenth-century counterparts of the district nurse and the pharmacist.'

'Thank you for making the point so clearly. I can see splendid opportunities here for television interviews with nurses and pharmacists asking them if they've ever thought of themselves as witches. Oh, I like it. We must speak more about this book,' Blacker said, grabbing another script and turning the pages. 'I thought these poems were highly original. Who is Thomasine?'

A hand waved just in front of him.

'Poetry, to be candid, is not a big seller. However . . . these, I thought, may well be worth developing. Wry, thought-provoking, evocative and – if I may be so bold – sometimes sensuous. It's a winning combination. Have you been published before?'

'Only in my school magazine,' Thomasine said, 'and I was up before the head when she read it.'

There was some laughter at this.

'Saucy stuff, then?'

'That wasn't how the head put it.'

'Didn't she spot your potential?'

'No. She thought some boy had.'

More laughter.

This was becoming Thomasine's show, and Blacker smiled, but without real amusement. 'I'll say this. Properly edited, pruned of a few excesses, your poems could do rather well. A tweak here, a spot of fine-tuning there. We'd need to be selective. Not all of them work so well as the best, but neither did Wordsworth's. I would envisage a series of slim volumes on various themes.'

'Suits me,' Thomasine said.

He picked up another script. '"The Snows of Yesteryear". An extraordinary project, taking a group of moderately well-known people with nothing more in common than their surname, and recounting their lives in detail. I have to say that it gripped me from the beginning. There's a touch of Lytton Strachey about this concept. Yet the author must be excessively modest, because he or she doesn't disclose his or her name.'

Maurice the chair said, 'She's our secretary, Miss Snow.'

'How fitting. I should have guessed.'

Miss Snow hadn't looked up from the minutes she was taking.

'Have you read the Strachey book, *Eminent Victorians*, Miss Snow?'

She shook her head without raising it.

'Then I can recommend it. He casts his net a little wider than you, but his refusal to be impressed by the famous folk he writes about is worth examining. It is clear that you know your subjects intimately, yet one has to be careful not to turn it into hagiography. Are you familiar with the term?'

A voice – not Miss Snow's – said, 'Lives of the saints.' It was Anton.

'Thank you. Actually I was addressing Miss Snow.'

'She's writing everything down,' Anton said. 'She can't take the minutes and talk to you at the same time.'

'I see. Well, kindly take this down, Miss Snow. With some judicious rewriting, more light and shade, a little irony here and there, I would expect to market this book as a breakthrough in biography, a whole new approach. I can see it getting reviewed in all the upmarket papers.'

She nodded her appreciation.

He reached for another script. He wasn't wasting time. 'Ah. The work of fantasy.'

'Tudor's autobiography?' Thomasine said, and there were more suppressed laughs.

'I think not,' Blacker said. 'This is a major work of the imagination by someone who calls himself Zach.'

The image on the screen jerked.

'That's me,' Zach was heard to say.

'Your real name?'

'Yep.'

'Useful for a fantasy writer. Well, Zach, are you published already?'

'No. This is my first attempt.'

'Congratulations, then. You've produced a work of epic proportions.'

'Too long?'

'No, no. I love it. What an undertaking, and how inventive. You've created your own extraordinary world, and made it real for the reader. Your warrior hero – what is he called?'

'Madrigor.'

'Yes. He's a superb creation. Larger than life, yet with enough of humanity about him to engage our sympathy. His adventures have all the excitement of Sir Walter Scott with the added element of science fiction. Have you read Tolkien?'

'Yes.'

'Like him?'

'He's the king.'

'All I can say is that you could very well become the heir to his millions of readers. I can't remember coming across a first novel of such promise. It may take time, but I have every confidence.'

Thomasine said, 'How will he reach millions of readers if you can't afford to advertise?'

'He'll sell the film rights. This story is so visual, I can picture the scenes already.'

'He'll need an agent if he's getting into film deals.'

'Not necessarily. I can handle that.'

'Don't you approve of agents?'

'Some writers find them helpful, but Zach is unknown. If he sent his script to an agent it would be dumped with hundreds of others on what is unkindly called the slush pile. It's unlikely to be read for months and then given only a cursory look. Let's not forget that some of the biggest best-sellers in history were rejected by agents and publishers.'

'*War and Peace*,' Tudor said.

'Is that a fact?'

'Probably not, coming from Tudor,' Maurice said. 'He's been known to string us along.'

'Unfair,' Tudor said.

'Come on, sweetie,' Thomasine said. 'All that stuff about being a gigolo. Do you expect us to believe that?'

'It's in my autobiography.'

'Wishful thinking.'

'My dear, you didn't know me in my prime. I was only on offer to extremely rich women. Film stars, opera singers, barristers. And they always wanted me back.'

'Bit of a stallion, were you?'

'I find this distasteful,' someone said from the front, probably Jessie, who was published in *The Lady*.

'Have you read my autobiography, sir?' Tudor asked the publisher.

'I believe I did.' He started sorting through the remaining scripts. 'Remind me of the title.'

'"Backflash". A humorous reference to the famous sketch Francis Bacon did of me in the nude. That's in Chapter Three.'

'Ah.'

'I want the sketch on the front of the book.'

'The jacket.'

'No, the birthday suit.'

'I think we're at cross purposes. Shall we discuss it afterwards?'

'The jacket?'

'The book. The contents of your book.'

'I don't see why,' Tudor said. 'Everyone else has had a public appraisal, so why not me?'

'Being autobiography, it's more personal.'

'I'm no shrinking violet. I wouldn't have written it down if I'd wanted to keep it quiet. This lot have heard the choice bits.'

'Even so, my remarks will be for your ears only.'

There was a shocked silence. Then: 'You don't like it? What's the problem? The rumpy-pumpy? I never heard of a publisher who shied away from sex.'

'That's not the point at all.'

'Easy, Tudor,' Thomasine said to calm him down.

'Very well, sir,' Tudor said with mock humility. 'I'll wait till the end if that's what you want.'

Undaunted, Blacker turned to another script. 'There's a story here entitled "Passion Fruit", a romantic novel. May I ask the author to reveal herself? I assume this is a lady, though perhaps I shouldn't.'

Dagmar's hand was raised.

'You are Desiree Eliot?'

There were stifled giggles.

'A pen name,' Dagmar said.

'May I enquire what you are really called?'

'Dagmar Bumstead.'

Two or three people seemed to be having seizures.

Blacker did his best to shame them. 'There's nothing wrong with that, you know. I prefer it to the pen name if I'm honest. Is there a reason why you didn't want to reveal your name?'

'I thought it didn't sound romantic enough.'

'There was a very fine novelist called Phyllis Bottome, and it didn't hamper her in the least. *Passion Fruit*, by Dagmar Bumstead. It sounds just right to me. Of course, if you want to be mysterious and hide behind a pseudonym, we could think of something else.'

'Dolly Brontë?' Tudor said. 'Fifi Austen.'

'Give it a rest, man,' Thomasine said.

'I have to say I'm not a reader of romantic fiction,' Blacker said, 'so I gave this to a colleague to read, and she told me she devoured it at a sitting and would have read another if you'd written one.'

'I have,' Dagmar said. 'I've got eleven more at home.'

Blacker's jaw dropped and his eyes took on a glazed, defensive look. 'Haven't you submitted any of them to publishers?'

'Repeatedly. They keep coming back with rejection letters.'

'I'm rather shocked to hear that. I believe your work is first-rate.'

'Thank you,' Dagmar said in her matter-of-fact manner. 'So will you publish it?'

He cleared his throat. 'Em, as I explained, I'm not wholly familiar with the romantic fiction market. I'll need to consult an expert before I commit myself.'

Dagmar's head dropped a little. In the audience, Thomasine turned to exchange a look with Tudor.

Blacker moved on. 'There's just one script I haven't discussed, and that's "Tips for the Twenty-First Century". As far as I can gather, it's a collection of practical information. What to do with those elastic bands the postman drops on your doorstep, and so on. As a premise for a book, it's not new, but it could be rather clever. Whose is it, may I ask?'

'Mine.' The voice was Jessie's.

'You must have spent some time collecting all the tips.'

'A lifetime,' Jessie said. 'Some were passed down through my family.'

'Such as pinching the tip of one's little finger to prevent a sneeze?'

'Indeed.'

'And the parsley leaves and vinegar to improve one's breath?'

'Absolutely.'

'You don't approve of products one can buy?'

'My tips are all based on natural substances,' she said.

'If I'm right in my instinct, and sometimes we have to follow our noses, there's a gap in the market for a book such as this,' he said, 'but I have to point out that some of the remedies sound rather old-fashioned. In view of the title, I think we should be looking for some tips involving modern technology, mobile phones and so on.'

'It's not that kind of book,' she said.

'But the title.'

'I had to change it. Until 1999 it was "Tips for the Twentieth Century".'

He said, 'I like "Tips for the Twenty-First Century". I like it very much. You've updated the title. All I'm suggesting is that you update the tips. You might have a section on text messaging.'

'I don't think so,' Jessie said. 'I don't know the first thing about it.'

'Then you're well placed to find out. By learning the basic

70

principles for yourself you can explain them for your readers.'

'No, thank you.' She wasn't going to move on this.

'What did you say your name is?'

'Warmington-Smith.'

'Let's be friendlier than that, shall we?'

'Mrs Warmington-Smith.'

'Oh, stupid me. It's here on the front of the script. Well, Jessie, any author ought to be open to suggestions. You have a fine idea for a book, but the contents do need some attention.'

'What you are saying is that the title is all right, but you want a completely different book.'

'I wouldn't go that far.'

'What else would you change?'

'It's your book, of course, but you might have a chapter about the internet. There's so much on offer. People can get free advice on planning a car journey, for example.'

'I don't have a computer.'

'Oh.' There was too much disappointment in that 'Oh'. He made an effort to brighten up. 'Well, perhaps you should invest in one and write a chapter about the difference it makes to your life.'

'It would take me years to learn. I suffer from technophobia. My book is meant for people like me who are trying to survive in a world where every other person in the street is holding something to his ear and shouting things nobody wants to hear.'

'Then perhaps this is a "How to Survive" book.'

'Possibly.'

'There are other technophobes out there,' Blacker said. 'Plenty of others. The secret of successful publishing is all about identifying a market. Let me think about this.' He set the typescript on the stack. 'Is there anyone I missed?'

Maurice said, 'I think not. Several of our members chose not to submit anything at this point in time.'

Anton said, 'Chairman, that is one of the most deplorable of all clichés.'

'Thank you, Anton.' Turning to Blacker, Maurice said, 'Anton is our vigilante, ever on the lookout for lapses of speech.'

'You'd make a useful proofreader, then,' Blacker said. 'I didn't notice a script from you, sir.'

'I wasn't ready,' Anton said.

'And the young lady . . . ?'

'Works long hours at a hairdressing salon and finds it difficult to put together anything of any length,' Maurice said with a smile in the direction of Sharon. She looked up, content to stay silent. The camera zoomed in on her notepad. Some of the doodles looked artistic.

'Length is not important,' Blacker said. 'I'd be willing to look at anything, however slight.'

'As the actress said to the bishop,' Thomasine said in an undertone that the mike on the camera picked up but Blacker did not.

'Any questions, then?' he said.

Dagmar was the first to come in. 'When can we expect to see Maurice's book in print?'

'Ah, Maurice's book,' Blacker said and for a moment he was caught off guard. Watching him now, it was obvious there was a problem. 'Yes, *Unsolved*. As soon as I saw it, I thought this is right for us. We must publish it. As to when, I don't have my schedules in front of me.'

'The first Thursday in September,' Maurice reminded him.

'There you are, then,' Blacker said. 'It's in the pipeline. Nearly through the pipeline, in fact. Another question?'

'You talked about the tips in Jessie's book,' Anton said. 'Do you have any tips of your own to pass on to the circle?'

'To assist your writing, you mean? The one thing I would recommend is to get the tools for the job. I don't mean expensive computers or reams of paper. I'm talking about a decent dictionary, for example, a modern one, not something handed down by your grandfather, and some basic reference books connected to your topic. Some sort of filing system also helps because you'll be cutting things out of newspapers and magazines. Keep everything you are ever likely to use. I'm a hoarder, and not ashamed to say it. My house is filled with cuttings and photos from years back. Letters, notebooks, videos. I wish I was better organised because I'm starting to write a memoir of my chequered career and I have to keep stopping to look for things, but it's all there somewhere. I expect you have the same problem, Maurice. You must have stacks of material on unsolved murders.'

'Quite a bit,' Maurice said. 'I've only used about a tenth of it.'

'Ah, it's the iceberg principle. What is on view isn't the whole story. There's a huge amount underpinning it.'

Anton said, 'Mixed metaphor.'

'I beg your pardon?'

'Another question,' Maurice said.

'How much do you pay?' This from Tudor, still unhappy that his script hadn't been discussed.

Maurice said at once, 'I don't think that's appropriate.'

'Why?'

'You don't ask that sort of question.'

'He's in business. We're the people offering the goods. We're entitled to know what he pays.'

Dagmar said, 'Tudor, we're not selling tins of beans.'

'That's debatable.'

'Tudor, how could you!'

'The whole thing about writers is that if they knew anything about business they wouldn't be writers anyway.'

Maurice said, 'Equally you could say that a genuine writer

doesn't do it for the money. You know very well, Tudor, that a publisher and his author come to a private agreement.'

'You mean you don't want to tell us how much you're getting?'

Blacker tried to take some heat out of the exchange. 'What a publisher pays is an advance on the royalties of the book. If it sells well, more is paid to the author. Of course a new writer is an unknown quantity, so the publisher can't be expected to risk a large amount up front, so to speak. We publishers are notoriously bad payers, and it isn't just the writers who suffer. We pay peanuts to our employees. There's a story of Billy Collins, the famous publisher, kneeling to receive his knighthood from the Queen. When she tapped him on the shoulder with the sword and said, "Rise, Sir William," he didn't get up. She tried again. Still no response. Then someone said, "Ma'am, why don't you try, 'Stand up.' *Rise* is not a word he understands."'

The audience enjoyed that. Maurice waited for the laughter to end and said, 'That seems a good note on which to stop. Thank you, Edgar. I think we'll leave it there, but before we do, I believe someone would like to say a few words?' He looked towards Miss Snow. She looked to her left.

Tudor, of all people, had been asked to give the vote of thanks.

He was on his feet. 'This has been very instructive. Let's face it, we're just a bunch of wannabes – with one exception – so the chance to meet a living, breathing publisher doesn't often come our way, and you'll have to forgive some of our dumb questions – if that isn't an oxymoron. You've given us the kid-glove treatment, sir, praised our modest efforts – for the most part – and handed down enough encouragement to keep us dreaming our dreams of rising up the bestseller lists. We wish your publishing venture every success, especially as some of us might have a stake in it. And now someone has a token of appreciation tucked away somewhere.' He glanced towards Miss Snow, who produced a glittery bag containing a bottle. 'Ah. This, then, comes with our thanks, and I invite you all to show your appreciation in the traditional way.'

Bob continued to watch until the image vanished after a few seconds. He switched off. He would run it again some time. Enough had emerged to give him new angles on several of the circle, and the murder victim, Edgar Blacker. The talk wasn't quite the buttering up he'd been led to expect. Tudor's ego had taken some knocks and so had Jessie's. Naomi had seen through the waffle about the witchcraft book. But was there enough to trigger a murder?

The expectations had been high. They'd handed in their best work wanting to hear good things. It wasn't like getting back an essay they'd written at school when they knew their place in the pecking order. These were grown-ups. No one with clout in the publishing world had judged their work in years – except Dagmar's. All those rejection letters must have been tough, but even she hadn't seen her critics face to face until now.

So what did Blacker's verdict amount to? Well, he'd wrapped it up as prettily as he could, but only Zach's science fiction got the nod. Basil's gardening stuff needed expanding, and was going to bring unwanted publicity. The reverse was true of Thomasine's poems. They needed thinning out. Miss Snow's biography had no bite to it. Jessie's tips were old-fashioned. It was obvious he hadn't read Naomi's witchcraft book or Dagmar's latest romance and whatever he thought of Tudor's life story wasn't fit to be heard by everyone else.

A few tears must have been shed that night.

7

It's not the people in prison who worry me. It's the people who aren't.

The Earl of Arran in *The New York Times*, 1962

In the morning he returned Thomasine's call.

'They've charged Maurice,' she said.

'You told me.'

'He'll be suicidal. We've got to stop it.'

'Bit late for that.' He didn't like being a downer, but when a man is done for murder, the law takes over.

'Not at all. This is the time we can make a difference.'

He soft-pedalled. 'I don't see how.'

'The police think they've got their man and the case is closed. We can have a clear run. Are you listening to me, Bob? It's down to us.'

No more gentle persuasion from Thomasine. Things had gone beyond that.

'We can try,' he said. 'But let's face it. We don't know what the police found out. And we don't have their resources – fingerprinting, DNA, all that stuff.'

Thomasine was unimpressed. 'This was a fire, remember? The house went up in flames. We're not dealing in finger-prints and DNA. This is about people's motives and where they were on the night of the fire.'

'We could find ourselves fingering someone else from the circle.'

76

'If they're guilty, what the hell?' she said. 'I don't believe Maurice is. Do you?'

He didn't answer that. 'Last night I looked at the video of Blacker's talk to the circle. I borrowed it from Miss Snow.'

'Oh?' There was a pause, and when she spoke again there was a change of tone. She sounded more guarded now. 'What did you make of it?'

'Quite a few of them came out of it with their hopes dashed. I don't know what it must feel like to beaver away for a year or more on a book and then be told it's crap.'

'He didn't tell anyone that.'

'Not exactly. But I think they got the message he didn't want to publish them.'

'Who? Tudor?'

'Tudor stands out, yes. But others were given the thumbs down as well. He didn't think much of Jessie's household hints for the twenty-first century.'

'He told her to get more up-to-date.'

'But she isn't going to, is she? She isn't capable. This is the point, Thomasine. How many of them are going to alter what they've done? Do you think Miss Snow is going to dish the dirt on the people she's writing about? I don't see it. Will the witchcraft lady – what's her name?'

'Naomi.'

'Will Naomi write stuff about spells and black magic, because that's what sells? No chance. And she won't be opening her house and garden to the public to give a puff to Basil's book.'

'In case they catch her riding her broomstick?'

He smiled. 'What I'm saying is that some of you lot were pretty pissed off by Blacker and his advice. I'm not a serious writer like the rest of you, but anyone can see it's a pain to chuck years of hard work in the bin. The question is . . .'

'Whether it's enough to justify murder. Definitely,' she said. 'If you haven't done it, you can't know how strong the feeling is. The book is part of yourself, Bob, the nearest thing I know to child-bearing. To be told it's a failure is horrible.'

'Okay. I can understand that.'

'We were all keyed up that evening, ready to pick up the slightest hint of criticism.'

'Right, so who took the biggest knock?'

They both said, 'Tudor.'

Thomasine added, 'And he's the first to take offence.'

'You want me to talk to him?'

'Would you?'

'Sure.'

'We'd better do this together. When are you free?'

'I work, remember?'

'So do I, and so does he. It'll have to be an evening, won't it?'

Tudor lived above a building society in North Street. He suggested meeting in a pub, but they persuaded him it was too public. They didn't say his voice could be heard across three continents. Just that they owed it to Maurice to be discreet.

Tudor wasn't to be deprived of his libation, as he put it. Two packs of Black Label waited on the table in his living room. The place was roomy enough for three sofas, but it wasn't the furniture that caught the eye. The walls were plastered with photos of the sort you see in celebrity magazines. The fact that Tudor was in every one didn't make the impact he intended. It seemed to Bob like desperation, this urge to be pictured with minor celebs.

Thomasine made a roundabout start. 'Tudor, baby, we're trying to prove Maurice is innocent. Thought you might have some ideas how to go about it.'

Tudor's features relaxed. He picked up a can and opened it. 'Oh, if that's what this is about, I'm your man. I don't mind admitting I had my doubts when he was first taken in for questioning, but I'm like that. I was brought up to believe the police were infallible. It's hard to shake off, that kind of conditioning.'

'You changed your mind?'

'Totally. Maurice hasn't got a ha'p'orth of malice in him.'

'The trouble is,' Bob said, 'he doesn't have an alibi either. He went for a walk on the night of the fire and his partner doesn't know when he got back.'

Thomasine said as if she were speaking only to Bob, 'If you asked most of us where we were that night we wouldn't be able to come up with cast-iron alibis. I live alone and so does Tudor.'

It was neatly done. She and Bob both looked to Tudor for a reaction.

He hesitated. 'Good point. I was at home here in bed, but I can't prove it, if anyone should ask. I wasn't entertaining Miss World.' He winked at Bob. 'Not that night, anyway.'

'And if the cops made some enquiries,' Thomasine said, 'they'd find Edgar Blacker was top of your hate list.'

'Why?'

'Because of the way he treated you at the meeting.'

He sighed, like a chess player in check. 'What – keeping me waiting for an opinion on my book? He did, the bugger. That's true. He got up my nose. Only it hardly makes a motive for murder.'

'Did he see you at the end?' Bob asked.

'A few private words. He didn't want to speak in front of the others, his point being that it was too personal. My book's a memoir, you see, an account of my life so far.'

'Were they encouraging, those few private words?' Thomasine asked.

'Helpful, more than encouraging. After all, we didn't come to be buttered up, did we? Nice to hear, no doubt, but no damned use to serious writers. Constructive criticism was the order of the day.'

'Was it really helpful, Tudor?'

'To a degree, yes. He told me it was a matter of pitching it right. I tend to treat the reader as an old chum with a shared sense of humour, giving him the occasional nudge in the ribs. Edgar Blacker didn't care for that. Wanted a more neutral style, simply telling the story without sign-posting the funny bits. I could see what he meant.'

'Anything else?'

His eyes flicked left and right. 'Well, he was a little scep-tical about some of my adventures, and I had to tell him straight that everything happened just as I describe it. He didn't seem willing to accept that an ordinary fellow like me could have been on friendly terms with so many of the great and good. As you know, Thomasine, I take folk as I find them, never mind if they've climbed Everest or won Wimbledon, and they always respond. They're only men and women like you and me. We all have to go to the bathroom, don't we? When you think of it like that, treating them as equals, you can get along with anyone.'

'Was he interested in publishing you?' Thomasine asked.

'If I was willing to make the changes he suggested I think he'd have jumped at the chance.'

'Is that what he said?'

'Not precisely.'

'What *did* he say?'

'About the book?' Tudor was stalling now. 'He said it needed beefing up, whatever that means.'

'Not enough substance.'

'Something like that. There was a danger the reader might think I was a name-dropper if I couldn't say some-thing more startling about my friends in the public eye.'

This sounded more likely. Bob tried to look mystified by the idea of Tudor as a name-dropper. 'More startling? What – badmouthing them?'

'You've got it. He was after sensation. Well, if this had been a work of fiction I wouldn't have minded, but it's my life story, for pity's sake, and these are my friends. I can't stab them in the back.'

'Out of the question,' Thomasine said.

'I'm glad you agree.'

'And is that what you told him?'

'More or less. Look, what was said between him and me doesn't matter in the least. We should be turning the spotlight on some of the others.'

Bob kept the spotlight where it was. 'Was that your first meeting with Blacker, that evening at the circle?'

Tudor's eyes gave the answer.

'You knew him already?'

'I wouldn't put it so strongly as that.'

'But . . . ?'

In desperation he started to flannel. 'There are degrees of knowing, aren't there? If you know somebody in the biblical sense, you ought to be married to them. My contact with Blacker was way down the scale. We'd met on one or two occasions, no more.'

This could be the breakthrough. Bob was pleased he'd asked the question. 'When?'

'A few years ago. I sold him some insurance. That's my job.'

'You insured him?'

'My firm did. I'm just a cog in the machinery.'

'What kind of insurance? Life?'

'I can't go into it. Confidentiality.'

'Fire?'

'Good Lord, no,' Tudor said. 'Please respect my position here. I could get into fearful trouble if head office find out I've discussed a client's business.'

'The client is dead,' Thomasine said.

'And my dealings with him have nothing to do with the case.'

'Did he ever make a claim?'

Tudor made a sweeping movement with his open hand. 'If you persist with this, I'm going to have to ask you to leave. Believe me, it has no bearing. End of discussion.'

'But we have established that you and he knew each other before the night he died,' Thomasine said.

'Slightly. Can we leave it there?'

'After the meeting – the circle meeting, I mean,' Bob said, 'did you see him again?'

'Before he died? Not me. Why all this interest in me? Have you spoken to any of the others?'

'You're not the first,' Bob said.

'You should talk to our blonde charmer, Sharon. She's not a writer. She's never read anything out. She just sits and scribbles on her notepad all the time, doodles, not words. What's she doing, coming to a writers' circle and making no contribution whatsoever?'

They left without discussing Sharon.

That same evening, the author of 'The Sussex Witchcraft Trials' called on the next Tolkien and made a bold suggestion. 'I'm looking for a partner,' Naomi told Zach in the converted railway carriage that was his home in Selsey, 'and I can't think of anyone better than you.'

'For what?' Zach said. Confident and able as he was, secure in his own home, he still felt uneasy under the hyperthyroid gaze of those brown eyes.

'For our mutual benefit.' But the tone of her voice didn't make it sound so inviting.

'Oh yeah?'

'You and I have certain things to offer each other, wouldn't you say?'

This hit Zach like a poleaxe.

'How do you mean?' He was stunned, weak at the knees and disbelieving, but to be honest with himself he'd never had an offer like this from a woman. He wasn't every girl's idea of a sexy hunk. As for Naomi, well, she scared most people rigid with her steely looks, but she was probably younger than she appeared and she had the body of a tennis player.

'A way of bringing out the best in each of us.'

His thoughts were racing now. What would Basil say if his wife had a fling? Maybe Basil wasn't giving her what she wanted. He was a pretty old guy, quite a few years her senior. He might be grateful.

Zach heard himself saying, 'You've got me interested.'

'Good. It's obvious you have a good imagination.'

True, and it was working overtime. 'Thanks.'

'Unlike me,' she said. 'I stick to facts.' She gave him a long look.

What fact does she want from me? he thought. The size of my jigger? 'So?'

'There's some risk attached to this, and I must ask you to keep it between the two of us.'

'No problem,' he said. Some risk, huh? Was it outdoor sex she wanted?

She surprised him by saying, 'I had a look inside the burnt-out cottage.'

That *would* be kinky. Thinking about it, he wasn't so sure he wanted to go along with this any more.

'You mean Edgar Blacker's place?'

'Yes.'

'You went inside? What for?'

'For the truth, of course. He was murdered and Maurice McDade has been charged with it. I don't believe for one moment that Maurice is the arsonist. Do you?'

Zach was unequal to this twist in the plot. 'I don't know. Haven't thought about it.'

'Well, it's time you did,' she said. 'This is why I'm confiding in you. I have my own ideas who the murderer might be, and I'm collecting evidence, but I can't see my way to putting it on record without risking a libel action. There's a way round it, and this is where you come in.'

'Oh?'

'We dress it up as fiction using your gift with words.'

She wanted him to collaborate in a book.

'But I'm a fantasy writer. I don't do crime.'

'You have the gift. I'll give you the plot. All you have to do is get into the mind of the killer and make it convincing. Together we can turn out a bestseller.'

'It's not my scene.'

'Rubbish. Where's your sense of adventure?'

'Can't you work with someone else?'

'Who? Basil? He's a gardener, not a writer.'

In desperation, he cast around for another suggestion. 'Dagmar? She does fiction.'

'She does daydreams for sex-starved women. And she's no damned good at it. I want a real writer.'

'But I'm working on a book already.'

'Take a break, Zach. When you come back to it your batteries will be recharged.'

Her intensity was scary, yet it played to Zach's ego. He didn't know how to wriggle out of this and he wasn't certain that he should. He still had the impression that she fancied him. 'What's in it for me?'

'That's better,' she said with the beginning of a smile. 'It's cards on the table time.'

'Was that any use?' Bob asked Thomasine in the main bar at the Feathers. They'd left Tudor in his flat looking like a frog in a dried-out pond.

Thomasine was on Martinis. 'His ego was bruised, for sure.'

'Because of what Blacker thought of his book?'

'You want to hear him reading it out. It's all "my good friend the Duke" and "my old chum Ringo". Makes you want to puke.'

'Hasn't anyone told him this before?'

'That's one of the problems in the circle. We're too damned polite to each other. It takes an outsider like Blacker to speak the truth, and even he was pussyfooting really.'

'Except he was a publisher, and you knew he wasn't bullshitting if he took one of you on.'

'Which he didn't.'

'He seemed to think Zach was all right. And he liked your stuff.'

'He wanted to get out without being lynched. Would he have published us? Would he, heck. He dropped poor old Maurice, didn't he?'

'Has anyone found out why?'

Her eyes widened. 'You were there when Maurice told us. Blacker's costs had spiralled, he said.'

'But there must have been something else. He must have had second thoughts.'

'If he did, Maurice didn't share that with us.'

'But he probably told his partner Fran.'

'Hey, smart thinking!' Thomasine said.

She made swift work of her third Martini, and they took a taxi out to Lavant.

When Fran opened the door and saw them, she said with disappointment, 'You again? I was hoping it was Maurice.'

'They charged him,' Bob said. 'They're keeping him there.'

'Yes, but I was hoping they'd realise the mistake they made.'

He didn't comment. 'This is Thomasine.'

Fran managed a faint smile for Thomasine. 'I've heard about you from Maurice.'

'Like I said, we're trying to find out what really happened,' Bob said.

'You'd better come in.'

Even on this second visit she still looked too old to be Maurice's lover. She dressed old, as well. Tonight she was wearing a white lace blouse with a cameo brooch at her neck. She offered tea and went to the kitchen to make it.

Thomasine glanced about her, at the Alpine scene above the fireplace and the willow pattern tea service in the china cabinet. 'Can't picture Maurice in this set-up.'

'Researching his unsolved crimes?'

She crossed to the bookcase. 'Even these are in a time warp. Nevil Shute. Hammond Innes.'

'They're bookclub titles. My old man had a set.'

'But what's in it for Maurice?'

'Wait till you try the fruit cake.'

In fact, it was Victoria sponge, and it came on a tray with a cloth and was placed on one of the nest of tables. Fran's hand was not too steady as she poured out the tea.

'We use this room for visitors,' she said, as if she'd overheard them. 'Maurice and I like to relax and spread ourselves out in the back room with our newspapers and magazines and my sewing. Then he has his study upstairs with his filing cabinet and all his crime books.'

'Do you help him?'

'Whenever I can. I know a fair bit about crimes that don't get cleared up. My first husband was one of the Richardson gang.'

Bob almost choked on his first sip of tea. She could not have amazed him any more if she had flapped her arms and flown around the room. This from a white-haired lady with a willow pattern tea service and a cameo brooch. Who would have thought it? The Richardson brothers ruled south London in the sixties, hard men notorious for torturing those who crossed them.

He tried to keep this as a normal conversation. 'You saw it on the inside, then?'

'He did. Women kept their distance.'

'What happened? Did you separate?'

'No. He died in prison – which is why I don't want Maurice going there.'

'It wouldn't be the first time, would it?' Seeing her reaction he added, 'It's all right, Fran. We know he's got form.'

She had gone deathly white. 'Who told you?'

'It was bound to come out.'

'He's no villain,' she said. 'Believe me. I was married to one.'

Thomasine said, 'We all know he's a lovely guy.'

'The police don't. To them he's a convicted fire-raiser.'

'It wasn't like that, was it?' Bob said. 'We're trying to find out who really should be banged up for this.'

'I wish I knew,' Fran said.

'But you know why Maurice's book deal with Blacker fell through?'

Her voice took on a different note, harder and more angry. 'Because Blacker was a low-down, conniving shyster, that's why.'

'The five-grand demand?'

Fran rolled her eyes upwards.

Thomasine said, 'The man was a tosser.'

Fran said, 'You bet he planned it all along. It wouldn't surprise me if he'd played the same trick on other writers he published. They got so close to seeing themselves in print that they paid up. It's called vanity publishing in the trade, except it's worse than that because real vanity publishers tell the writers from the start that they're expected to meet the costs. He wasn't even honest about that.'

'No wonder he was touting for business at the circle,' Thomasine said. 'I could have been caught. I was over the moon when he said my poems were good enough to publish.'

'You'd have paid the printing costs, but you wouldn't have owned the book. You'd get six free copies, and that's all.'

'I'd have murdered the bastard,' Thomasine said.

'Someone did,' Bob said.

'One of his authors?'

'We'll find out. Do you have a copy of his catalogue?' he asked Fran.

'I think so. I'll look in the office if you don't mind helping yourselves to more tea and cake.'

While Fran was out of the room, Thomasine said, 'I'll be so relieved if someone outside the circle is the killer.'

Bob had been here already. 'If they are, there's not much we can do.'

'Why? Maurice is still our chair. We've got to help him.' No one was going to duck out while Thomasine was on the case.

Bob offered her a slice of cake and she pointed out that it must have been made for Maurice. 'We can't eat his cake and walk away.'

Fran returned with the Blacker List catalogue. It was modest in size, more of a leaflet than a brochure.

'Not a lot here,' Bob said when he'd leafed through the few pages. Two of the books were by the same author, memories of Chichester in the Second World War by an old lady who lived in Pennsylvania. She'd married a GI and never returned to England. Another was the illustrated book Blacker had mentioned, showing dog owners who resembled their pets. A note on the back cover stated that the author had died shortly before publication. And the only other Blacker List title was *Shinty, Bandy and Hurling*, by a former Bishop of Chichester now living in a retirement home in Scotland.

'Strong stuff for a bishop,' Thomasine said.

'Says here they're ball games,' Bob said, '"akin to hockey". I wouldn't think any of these are bestsellers. My guess is that Blacker conned the authors into paying for publication.'

'But it doesn't look as if we have a suspect among them,'

Thomasine said. 'One deceased, one retired bishop and one old lady in Pennsylvania.'

The focus of guilt shifted back to the circle. No one said a word, but it was in their minds.

The phone was ringing when Bob got in around eleven.

'Thank goodness you're back. I've been trying on and off since nine. I didn't want to leave a message.'

He couldn't place the voice yet. 'Sorry. Who is this?'

'Amelia.'

Well, it was late, and it had been a long, taxing day. 'Come again?'

'Miss Snow.'

'Ah.'

'I – em – I need the video.'

'Why? What's up, love?' He called her love in response to the nervousness coming down the line.

'I know it's late, but can you possibly return it now?'

'Tonight?' Shouldn't have called her love, he thought. Naylor, you're getting in deep here.

She went on, 'Something has happened that I'd rather not discuss over the phone, and I'm not going to get any sleep if I don't do something about it.'

He didn't believe there were things you can't discuss over the phone. Who did she think was listening? 'Do you know what time it is, Amelia?'

'Yes, and I wouldn't be asking if it wasn't important.'

'Is it anything to do with Maurice?'

'Please come, Bob.'

What the hell? he thought. I can look after myself. 'Twenty minutes, then.'

'I can't thank you enough.'

Don't even try, he thought as he put down the phone.

He was coming out of the bathroom when Sue let herself in through the front door.

'Hi, Dad,' she called up.

'Hi, baby. Nice evening?'

'Not bad.'

He came downstairs. 'Got to slip out for an hour. Someone just phoned.'

'Yeah?'

'Yeah.' He felt as if he was the teenager.

'Girlfriend?'

'Ha ha.'

'Well, you know the saying, Dad: if you're not in bed by midnight you'd better come home.'

8

Write something, even if it's just a suicide note.

Anon, quoted in *The Writer's Chapbook*, ed. George Plimpton (1999)

'I can't tell you how grateful I am.'

Bob nodded and stepped inside. Miss Snow showed him into her writing den and closed the door behind her. She was as strung out as a line of washing.

'Did you bring it?'

He handed over the video.

Her voice shook as she said, 'The police were here this afternoon. They said they needed this as evidence. Maurice must have told them about it.'

'What did you say?'

'That it was being passed around the circle and I'd have to make some phone calls.'

'Fair enough.'

'I promised to take it in to the police station tomorrow.'

'And now you can.' He didn't understand why she needed it tonight. He could have delivered it in the morning, taken it to the nick himself if she wanted. And he couldn't see why a visit from the police had got her into such a state.

It was obvious he wasn't going to be offered a chair, so he took a step back, preparing to leave. His leg nudged a low table and a couple of magazines slipped off. He picked them up and replaced them. One was the *TV Times* and the other was *The Bodybuilder*, with a muscleman on the cover. We all get our kicks some way, he thought, amused, and warming a little to Miss Snow.

She was too wound up to get embarrassed. 'Poor Maurice must be at his wits' end,' she was saying. 'He wouldn't have told them about the video unless he was desperate.'

'Why not?'

'It's like informing on his friends. So out of character. Not the way Maurice would behave unless he was up against it.'

'If you or I were on a murder rap, we'd do the same. Anything to muddy the water.'

'But he's innocent,' she said.

'If he is, then someone else is guilty, and the odds are that it's one of the people on that video.'

Her eyes held his, and she said in a mystified voice, 'You still sound doubtful, as if you think he might have done it.'

'Open mind. I've talked to a couple of people this evening and I'm still in the dark.'

'Who?'

'Tudor and Fran. But I learned a bit more about Blacker and his dealings. He was a crooked publisher. None of his authors made any money. He took money off them.'

'Do the police know that?'

'Maurice knows. He will have told them.' He stifled a yawn. 'I'll be off, then.'

She put her hand to her throat and fingered her bead necklace. 'There's something I haven't told you.'

'What's that?'

'Later, after the police had been, I had a phone call. A man's voice. He didn't say who he was. He asked me if I was the secretary of the circle and when I said yes he said he could prove Maurice is in the clear, but I must keep it to myself. Those were his words.' She took a ragged breath, as if the memory was all too stressful. 'He said he wanted to help and he would hand me the proof tomorrow. I was to meet him at eight in the morning in the boat house near the canal basin.'

'That was all?'

'Yes. He sounded very definite. I believed him.'

'The voice. Was it disguised, muffled?'

'A bit indistinct. I didn't recognise it. Bob, I don't know what to do. Should I tell the police? If this is going to help Maurice, I don't want to jeopardise anything. I'm scared.'

'You want me to take over?'

She looked as if the sun had just come out. 'Would you?'

'Eight at the boat house. No problem.'

Bob didn't feel so confident walking to the boat house next morning. His guess was that Miss Snow's mysterious caller was some nutter who had read about the case in the papers. Every murder brings a few out of the woodwork. But it had to be checked. And nutters can be nasty.

The only boat house he knew was on the side of the canal opposite the towpath, which meant making an approach along the lane skirting the Chichester High School grounds. It took him past the police station where, presumably, Maurice was still being held – poor old soul, innocent or not.

At this time of day the choice of meeting place was clever. You had to go along a footpath past a tennis court and a couple of scout huts with acres of school field on your left. It all looked deserted. The boat house was in fact two buildings used for storing canoes. The simple wooden huts with pitched roofs stood side by side above some steps and a launching area. On previous walks along the towpath Bob had more than once stopped to watch the kids on the water attempting to roll the canoes completely over.

This Saturday morning there were no canoeists yet, but

the large metal doors had been opened, so presumably there was a session planned for later. Someone must have unlocked and couldn't be far away.

Seeing no one outside, he stepped into the first hut where the canoes were ranged on racks.

'Anyone at home?'

No response.

He came out and looked into the second hut. This one contained a trailer loaded with more canoes. Nobody was in there.

He was beginning to think the whole thing was a hoax.

He checked his watch. It wasn't quite five to eight. Give them ten minutes, then I'm off, he told himself. He perched on the edge of the trailer, took a banana from his pocket and unpeeled it. He'd left home too early for breakfast.

Saturdays were special. He liked to watch sport if possible, the real thing, not TV. He didn't mind what. If there was racing at Goodwood or Fontwell, he'd be there. Through the winter it was football: the Portsmouth home matches. He'd played a bit as an amateur when he was younger and fitter.

He looked at the time again. Eight, spot on. All over the country people were sitting down to cooked breakfasts, and Bob Naylor was stuck in a boat house without even a flask of coffee. Thanks a bunch, Miss Snow.

There was a change in the birdsong outside, the urgent repetitive warning note a blackbird makes when a cat is about. Or a person. Better take a look, he thought.

He was on his feet and heading outside when it happened. The door slammed shut – in his face.

It wasn't the wind. Someone was outside. This was a strong metal door. He heard the bar being drawn across to fasten it.

'Hey! I'm in here.'

He pushed at it and couldn't move the thing. He hammered his hand against it.

'Open up, will you? I'm inside.'

The place was in darkness. There were no windows.

'Oy!'

He gave the door a kick. Whoever was outside must have heard him. The door was solid iron and it rumbled like a beer keg when he struck it.

He shouted again.

No response.

He stopped shouting and started thinking. The doors to both boat houses had stood open. Why would anyone want to close them again? For one reason only: they knew he was inside and they meant to trap him there.

Kids, playing a prank? At this time of day he doubted it.

So what would it achieve, shutting him in here for a few hours until some member of the canoe club released him?

It was going to ruin his Saturday, that was all.

Bloody hell.

He hammered on the door and called out a few more times with an increasing sense that the effort was wasted. He'd do better to find his own means of escape. From what he could remember when the light was better, the place was well constructed. Kicking his way out through the wooden walls wasn't an option.

The floor? He stamped on it hard. It didn't feel solid. Probably it was raised on supports, as wooden buildings often are. If there was a space underneath, and he could prise up a couple of boards, he might squeeze out that way.

He guessed there were tools in here somewhere. They'd need to work on the canoes from time to time. Where would they keep them? Finding anything in virtual darkness was a challenge. He began groping his way around the trailer towards the far end, knocking over a couple of objects as he went.

Then he smelt something.

First he thought it must have come out of a pot he'd

tipped over, maybe the stuff they used to waterproof the canoes. He was intent on looking for a toolbox so he didn't really care about odours. He didn't even register for some time that he was blinking more and his eyelids were smarting. Several minutes passed before it dawned on him that the smell was getting stronger.

Even so, he continued to fumble his way along the back wall of the boat house. He found some paddles and wetsuits, but nothing so useful as a screwdriver or a crowbar.

His eyes were hurting.

Then he felt his feet getting warmer through his shoes. Crouching down, he pressed his hand against the floorboards and they were warm.

A faint sound seemed to be coming from under the boards, something between a hiss and a wheeze.

Christ, he thought, there's a fire under here. I'm trapped in a wooden building that's going up in flames any second.

He knew enough about the action of fire to understand that the smoke and noxious gases already filling the boat house would kill him before the fire incinerated him. He was spluttering and coughing.

Forget the floorboards, he thought. There's only one way out of here now and that's through the roof. He grabbed a canoe paddle and reached out for the trailer. Its super-structure was a framework designed to support three tiers of canoes. If he could get to the top he had a fair chance of attacking the roof with the paddle.

He grasped the metal side bars and started hauling himself up. The trapped smoke would be thicker up there, but this was the only option. With agility born of despera-tion, he made it to the highest level and swung the paddle blindly above his head. It made contact. Heavy contact. The roof was within reach, but it felt as solid as the floor.

He tried again. There was the sound of wood splintering and for a moment his hopes soared, then plunged. The end of the paddle was breaking up, not the boards across the roof.

Below him real flames had penetrated the floor. In a frenzy he thrust the broken paddle repeatedly against the same spot.

He guessed the boards were linked by tongue and groove, which was why they resisted the hammering they were getting. More splinters from the paddle fell on his head.

He paused to gather himself for a greater effort.

Bob Naylor, this is your life.

Go for it.

The wood rasped, as if there was movement. After several more thumps the board he was striking gave a little. Another crack and it eased upwards and tore through the felt covering. He caught a glimpse of blue sky. More furious blows detached a second board. Smoke was funnelling through the gap.

He pulled himself higher, teetering on the top rail of the trailer to get a handhold in the gap. With a huge effort he dragged himself up and through the roof and scrambled out into the daylight. For a moment he lay on the incline taking in gulps of fresh air. Then a flame ripped through the space beside him and he slithered down and dropped to the ground and sprinted across the turf to safety.

Even now, when a huge brown plume of smoke was defining the source of the fire for miles around, Bob could see nobody. Whoever had slammed and bolted that door had already quit the scene.

Bob decided to do the same. When you're in shock and filthy with smoke your first instinct is to get home. You're not ready for questions and explanations.

Then he spotted two teenage girls cycling along the path towards the boat house. He stepped out of view. Canoeists, he decided. They were in shorts and sweaters.

He walked around the other side of the blazing building

and glanced back. The girls had stopped and one of them was using a mobile. It wouldn't be long before the fire service and police got here.

He legged it back to where he'd left his car in Canal Wharf Road. Inside ten minutes he was home taking a shower.

Over a strong black coffee, while the washing machine worked on his clothes, he tried to make sense of the experience. It all stemmed from Miss Snow's caller, the mystery man who had offered the proof that Maurice was not an arsonist. It was safe to assume, wasn't it, that the call was a trap? Miss Snow herself was supposed to go to the boat house at eight.

Was what happened the result of Bob's turning up instead? A fit of anger that Miss Snow had broken a confidence and sent someone in her place? He didn't think so. The fire in the boat house must have involved some preparation. It had started from outside, under the floor, in the space between the ground and the base of the hut. To get a fire going there, you'd need more than a struck match. You'd want combustible material like paper or oil-soaked rags. The stuff would have been in place before eight, ready to ignite when the victim was inside.

If Miss Snow had gone to the boat house she wouldn't have escaped. She wouldn't have had the strength to knock a hole in the roof. She was the intended victim, and it would have worked.

Why Miss Snow? He hadn't the faintest. Was she a threat to anyone? He couldn't see why.

Was it right to tell her she'd had a lucky escape? Bob didn't think so. The poor old duck was jumpy enough already, without finding out a killer was after her. Still, in a day or two she was going to read in the local paper that the boat house had gone up in flames, and she'd wet herself then.

For the time being, he'd tell no one. Except, maybe, Thomasine. He trusted Thomasine and she was his expert on the circle.

'What a crazy thing to do,' was her reaction when he phoned.

'You can say that again.'

'I meant you, going to the boat house.'

'I was doing someone a good turn.'

'You sure you're okay?'

'A few bruises.'

'And you haven't told anyone?'

'You're the first. I'm pretty certain I wasn't seen, except by the tosser who tried to murder me.'

'Oh, Bob – what a thing to happen. You must be cursing the day you joined the circle. No one is going to blame you if you walk away.'

'No chance,' he said. 'I'm going to find out who did this, and why.'

'You don't have much to go on.'

'Miss Snow said it was a bloke who phoned. That's a start.'

'And she didn't recognise the voice?'

'He would have disguised it, wouldn't he?'

'Are you thinking it's one of the men in the circle?' She hesitated, then said with certainty, 'Tudor.'

'Why Tudor?'

'You must have said something that panicked him.'

'Last night, at his flat?'

'He was bricking it when you got onto the insurance deal he'd done with Blacker. He admitted he sold him some insurance a while back. Is that the key to all this, do you think?'

'A reason to kill me?'

'The reason is that you got too close to the truth. He thought he was getting away with murder.'

'Tudor killed Blacker?'

'And you're the fly in the ointment.'

'Thanks.'

'That's my reading of it, anyhow.'

Bob wasn't convinced. 'If Tudor wanted to set me up as a victim, why go to the trouble of calling Miss Snow? Why not make the approach to me direct? I'd still have fallen for it. I'd still have gone to the boat house.'

'Are you in the phone book?'

'No.'

'Sweetie, it's as simple as that. He calls Miss Snow, who does have your number because she's the secretary.'

'If it comes to that,' he said, 'not one of the men in the circle knows my number.'

'You think the caller wasn't Tudor?'

'I'm thinking I'll check the others out.'

'Who?'

'Apart from Tudor? There's Zach, Anton and Basil.'

'Okay,' Thomasine said, 'let's find out what they were doing at eight this morning.'

'You're going to join me?'

'You need a minder, obviously.'

Zach was going to be the easiest, so they started with him. On a Saturday morning you'd expect to find him serving in the MVC shop in South Street.

They agreed to meet outside.

'Disappointing,' Thomasine said when she saw Bob. 'You look normal.'

'What did you expect?'

'Singed eyebrows at the least.'

'I wrenched my ankle jumping off the roof if that's what you want to hear.'

'But you're not on crutches.'

'I'm toughing it out.'

They went in. Zach was easy to spot with his long hair tied

up in a ponytail. He was helping a customer in the country and western section. The discs were displayed in long racks and the place was busy, as you'd expect on a Saturday.

Zach spotted them approaching and gave a nod of recognition. He didn't have the look of a guilty man – even though the shop was less than ten minutes' walk from the boat house. They let him finish with his customer. Then he greeted them and said he was due a coffee break.

Thomasine suggested they went across the street to the Café Rouge. Zach said he would need to square it with his manager.

'Ten minutes, maximum,' he told them presently. 'All the kids come in on Saturdays. It's hell.'

'Or paradise, if you're a teacher like me,' Thomasine said.

'Here's the toughest question we have for you,' Bob said when they'd found a table. 'Filter coffee, or cappuccino?'

He didn't rise to a smile. He was nervous. 'Black, no sugar.'

Bob ordered, and wasted no more time. 'We're trying to get Maurice released and I hit a snag this morning.'

'That's the understatement of the year,' Thomasine said. 'You're lucky to be alive.'

Zach looked indifferent as to whether Bob lived or not. He was staring out at the street as if he hoped the cavalry might arrive in the nick of time.

Bob told Zach all he knew about being trapped in the boat house. 'And in confidence,' he said at the end. 'I haven't reported any of this to the Old Bill. The guy who did it must be a member of the circle, and I'm going to find out who.'

'Starting with me?' Zach's eyes were not friendly.

'You're not the first. I've already spoken to Tudor,' Bob said, without mentioning when it had been. 'No offence, Zach, but where were you at eight this morning?'

'In bed.'

'Where's that?'

'Selsey.'

South of the town, like the boat house.

'Do you live with anyone?'

'I can't prove where I was, if that's what you're asking.'

'How do you get to work?'

'Motorbike.'

'What time did you get in this morning?'

'Five to nine.'

The coffee was brought, forcing all three to lean back in their chairs and behave like other customers discussing the trivia of their lives. For Bob, the conversation up to now had felt like one-way traffic. Every answer had to be worked for. A change of tactics was wanted.

When the waitress had gone, he threw in a grenade. 'On the face of it, you've got no reason to kill me. We only met a matter of days ago.'

This drew a complete blank. Bad to worse.

'The same could be said for all the others.' Bob was forced to struggle on. 'They had no reason to kill me either. It's because I'm making a nuisance of myself that I was attacked. Thomasine calls me a fly in the ointment. The person who did it wants Maurice to take the rap for Blacker's murder.'

Zach said in a flat tone, 'You want to know if I killed Blacker?'

Now Bob went silent.

'He liked my book. Basically he said it was hot-shit, wicked.'

'I know,' Bob said. 'I saw the video you took.'

He was impassive. 'So you know I thought I was on a good thing with Blacker. That he would have given me a contract.'

'That's true,' Thomasine said. 'He said you were up there with Tolkien.'

'A bit OTT,' Zach was forced to admit.

'Raised your hopes, though,' Bob said.

Zach shot him a hostile look. 'That's it, is it? You think I found out later he was shooting a line? Got my hopes up and had them dashed? I'm not so green as I look. I could see he was stringing us along, myself and those sad old wannabes.'

Thomasine could have taken offence. To her credit, she let the comment go by. 'He was a crook, but it was wrong to murder him.'

'I agree with that. I'm a pacifist.'

'Your book is full of violence,' she said.

'So is the Bible.'

In Bob's opinion this was a blind alley. 'We don't have much time. What can you tell us about Blacker? Had you met him before he came to the circle?'

'Met him? No.'

'Knew of him?' Bob said, picking up the note of reserve in the answer.

'Not much. A couple of days before he came to the meeting he phoned me one evening. My number was on the typescript I sent in. He said he was still reading it, but he liked what he'd seen so far. Wanted to know more about me, like how old I was, if I'd been published before, what my job is. I got a buzz out of all the interest so I told him everything I could. The questions got personal. Did I own the place I lived in? Were my parents alive? Things that didn't have much connection with the script.'

'But might tell him if there was money behind you.'

'Spot on. I sucked up to the man and answered his questions. My parents are alive and my dad owns a string of antiques shops. It was only later I found myself wondering why stuff like that interested him.'

'You heard about Maurice being asked to pay for being published?' Thomasine said. 'Blacker would have done the same to you.'

'Right, but I'm telling you I only sussed later, after he was dead.'

'The night of the fire, do you remember where you were?' Bob asked.

'At home, same as everyone else.'

'Everyone else except the killer.'

'I guess.'

'You don't seem to have much respect for the other people in the circle, calling them wannabes.'

'True, isn't it? I've had to listen to some shit at those meetings. You wouldn't believe how low the standard is.'

'Why join them, then?'

'They're a captive audience. I read out my latest chapters and they listen. Where else can I go? I tried an evening class – creative writing – and it was useless. The lecturer wasn't interested in fantasy. All we did was compose haiku.'

'A Japanese form of poetry,' Thomasine said for Bob's benefit. 'Stripped to the bone.'

Zach said, 'The meetings fuel my creative engine.'

Bob tucked that away for future use, if he could only find something to rhyme with *engine*. Might not make the grade as a haiku, but he would enjoy playing with it.

'We can always depend on a reading from Zach,' Thomasine said, poker-faced. The man demanded to be taken seriously.

'You must have been disappointed when Blacker died,' Bob said to him. 'All dressed up and nowhere to go.'

'There are plenty of places to go,' he said with a glare. 'Right now I'm going back to work.'

End of interview. He downed his coffee and went.

'Funny how wrong you can be,' Bob said. 'When I first saw that young guy, I liked the look of him. He was the reason I plucked up the courage to come into the circle.'

'He's got an inflated opinion of himself. That's his problem,' Thomasine said.

'Is that all?'

'He suffers from overblown prose, and we're all too polite to tell him.'

'Hang on a minute.' He closed his eyes.

'Are you okay?'

He nodded. He was making up one of his rhymes.
'Trying to think of something?' Thomasine said.
'Getting there slowly.'
'Getting where, exactly?'
'Here.' He trotted out his latest:

'Fantasy writer, Zach by name,
Lights us up with his sacred flame,
Author in the superclass,
Arsonist, or just an arse?'

'Hey,' she said, clapping. 'That's neat! You're a poet.'

9

Show me a man or woman who cannot stand mysteries and I will show you a fool, a clever fool – perhaps – but a fool just the same.

Raymond Chandler in *Casual Notes on the Mystery Novel* (1949)

One of the maxims of murder investigation is that the first twenty-four hours are crucial. If you don't catch the killer when the body is still warm, you can resign yourself to months of doorstepping. Bob was not a professional, but he'd watched enough police drama on television to know it was important to see each of his suspects as soon as possible.

'Where can we find Anton?'

'On a Saturday morning? Probably at home doing the prize crossword in *The Times*,' Thomasine said.

It sounded possible. The champion of good English had to be busy with words. He lived in a Georgian terraced house in East Pallant, behind the council offices.

'If it was a Monday, we'd find him sitting in the public seats at a planning meeting,' Thomasine said as they walked up the narrow street. 'He likes to raise points of order.'

'I bet they love that.'

'*He* does, for sure.'

'He's the least likely, isn't he?' Bob said.

'Of our suspects?'

'Think about it. He's not really a writer like the rest of you. He didn't hand in anything for Blacker to read, and I can't think why he'd want to kill him – or me.'

'If you read Agatha Christie,' Thomasine said, 'the least likely is the one to watch out for.'

'But this sure ain't Agatha Christie.'

'I wouldn't dismiss him so easily. He's got a good brain. Had a top job in the civil service.'

'Doing what?'

'Don't know.'

'Writing ministers' speeches?'

'Winds of change and windows of opportunity? Not Anton's style,' Thomasine said.

'What else could he have worked on, then?'

'Ancient Monuments?'

'Not bad,' he said, smiling. 'Not bad at all. I could believe that.'

The brasswork on Anton's front door was polished to such a standard that they hesitated to touch it, but there was no bell, so they had to knock.

The sound of footsteps was followed by safety bolts being slid back.

'Ah, the inquisition,' Anton said when he opened up. 'I thought you would find your way to me in time.'

He was in a dark suit and striped shirt. Today's bow tie was navy with white spots. He invited them into a narrow hallway hung with engravings of castles. Bob recognised Hever, Carisbrooke and the Tower of London. Noticing him pause in front of one of them, Anton said, 'They were my responsibility once.'

'Ancient Monuments?'

'Correct. How did you know?'

Unseen by Anton, Thomasine held up a finger.

'That was before English Heritage were brought in,' Anton said. 'If you see the word "heritage" walk fast in the other direction. It means someone in a poke bonnet is trying to sell you pot pourri.'

He showed them into his front room.

Thomasine said, 'Amazing!'

Bob said, 'Toytown.'

'That's what Chichester is, basically,' Anton said.

They were standing beside a table-top model of the city, every building to scale, tiny cars lined up in the car parks. Thomasine was in raptures. 'The market cross, the cathedral, and look, here's McDonald's. Did you make this, Anton?'

'A long time ago,' he said in a dismissive tone.

'It's beautiful. The detail. These little shop signs, the boot and the wishbone. No wonder you don't have much time for writing.'

'I haven't kept up,' he said. 'Hooper's has long gone and the Shippam's sign shouldn't be there any more. I've turned my attention to this.' He went to a computer across the room and switched on. A screensaver showing the market cross lit up the screen before it switched to a map of the city. 'Are you familiar with a computer mouse?'

'If I answer yes, what's the pay-off line?' Thomasine said.

'It's a serious question.'

It had to be, coming from Anton.

'All right. Yes, I can use one.'

'Go for a virtual walk, then. See if you can find your hairdresser.'

'I don't believe this.' She used the cursor to locate Crane Street, off North Street. 'It should be here, on the left.' She left-clicked and a shop called Blinkers filled the screen. 'Yikes!'

'You can go in,' he told her.

'What?'

'Click on the door.'

The salon's interior came up, complete with altar-like counter and waiting area, basins, mirrors and chairs. 'Anton, I'm gobsmacked. That's it to the life. Perfect.'

'No, if it was perfect you'd be able to talk to your stylist and discuss what you want. That's for the next generation of software.' He said to Bob, 'Why don't you try?'

'For a hairdo?'

But Thomasine said, 'Keep off. I want to carry on playing. It's so amazing. I could do this for hours.' She found the library and looked in. Another click and she was upstairs in the reference section.

'My turn,' Bob said, and soon he was exploring the Butter Market, checking the accuracy of the places where he bought bread and fish. The controls let him turn corners and examine everything from multiple angles. 'Must be a top-class package to do this.'

'From Japan, and not cheap,' Anton said.

'So did you make the graphics yourself?'

'I had no choice. I don't think they've heard of the Chichester Butter Market in Japan.'

'How do you do it? You must have visited every shop and measured up.'

'I worked with plans all my life. Some of it has to be guess-work, but most is verifiable. Getting it right appeals to me.'

'What about private houses?' Bob asked. 'Are they in the virtual tour?'

Anton shook his head. 'One has to be discreet. I go no further than the front door.'

Hearing this, Bob found himself recalling that Edgar Blacker's killer had needed to go no further than the front door. 'How far out does this stretch?'

'The limits? It's quite modest actually. I've stopped at the ends of the four main streets, so the theatre isn't in yet and neither is the station to the south. I'd like to include them in time.'

Bob was exploring the cathedral, zooming in on the stained glass. 'Hours and hours went into this, I bet.'

'These days I get by with very little sleep.'

'How do I switch off?'

'You can leave it running. We'll go into the back room. It's more comfortable.'

He led them into a place lined with books, wall to wall. There were three armchairs and a low table.

'I'm willing to bet there's a section here on English grammar,' Bob said.

'To your right, above the dictionaries of quotations. Now, at the risk of being impolite, my time is precious. Why don't you take a seat and put me through the third degree? I assume that's what you came for?'

Thomasine said in a low voice, 'Did I spot a hanging participle?'

Anton managed a smile and said, '*Mea culpa*.'

He listened in silence to Bob's account of his escape from the boat house. 'No offence,' Bob went on, 'but I'm seeing each of the men in the circle just to clear the air, so to speak.'

'Clear the air' was a cliché, and Anton was gracious enough to let it pass with no more than the lifting of an eyebrow. 'But why confine your enquiries to the men?'

'The phone call Miss Snow took last night. She said it was a man's voice.'

'Didn't she recognise it?'

'Disguised, she thought.'

'Far be it from me to complicate matters,' Anton said, 'but it wouldn't be a huge technical problem for a woman to make her voice sound like a man's. You can buy a simple voice synthesiser in a toy shop.'

Thomasine turned to Bob. 'He's right. My girls at school played tricks on me with one. Why didn't I think of that?'

'Okay,' Bob said, 'thanks for that, Anton, but would you

mind telling me where you were this morning between eight and nine?'

'Here, doing the crossword.'

Another bullseye from Thomasine.

'How did you get on?'

Anton reached for the newspaper and held up the back page, showing the corner clipped out. 'It's in the post.'

'Finished already?'

'Come, come. I wouldn't send it incomplete.'

'So you've been out already?'

'A fair deduction, Holmes. The post office is only five minutes away. Oh, and you're going to tell me the boat houses by the canal are almost as near. I can't deny it, but the paper was delivered as usual at seven fifteen and I took just under an hour to complete the crossword – by which time you were limping home covered in soot by your account.'

'True,' Bob said, crushed.

Thomasine came to his rescue. 'We'd also like to ask about Edgar Blacker.'

'What about him?'

'Did you know him before he visited the circle?'

'No. Why should I?'

Bob said with more bounce, 'Well, if you're the killer, we have to find the reason. You didn't send in a piece of work for him to comment on.'

'True.'

'And one mixed metaphor isn't enough to justify murder,' Thomasine said.

'Possibly not.'

'So you'd need some stronger motive.'

'Such as a long-standing grudge because he bullied me at school?'

'That might qualify.'

'Or stole my girlfriend, or bumped my car?'

'Yes.'

Anton's eyes shone. He was well on top of this exchange. 'Sorry to disappoint, but I'd never set eyes on the man before that evening. If I were you, I'd try one of the others. You're wasting your time on me.'

'Why do you bother with the circle?' Bob asked. 'I was told you don't often read things out.'

He thought about that for a moment. 'I'm fascinated by people with creative minds. I don't have any imagination whatsoever. Give me a blueprint, a map, and I can work from it, but I can't start with a blank sheet. Most of them can, with varying degrees of success. That's a great gift, and I suppose I secretly hope it will rub off on me. It hasn't yet.'

'What you've done on that computer is creative,' Thomasine said.

'No. I only copy what exists already. Ask me to plan a new street of shops and I'd be stumped. The brain refuses to cooperate. So I envy anyone who produces original work.'

'Okay,' Bob said. 'How about giving us some advice? You go there to watch and listen, right? You know them all. What's your verdict? Is one of them a murderer?'

'I expect so.'

'Who is it then? Have you ever found yourself thinking this one or that one could do it?'

Anton had a pained expression. 'I don't look at other people wondering if they are murderers.'

'Yes, but if one of them is . . .'

'They're all capable. If it was a crime requiring great strength or coolness under pressure I'd say certain people could be eliminated, but this was the simplest of methods. Some inflammable material pushed through a letterbox and ignited. A little old lady could do it as well as a man.'

'*Cherchez la femme*,' Thomasine said.

'I wouldn't discount any of you ladies. That's all I'm prepared to say.'

112

'Sitting on the fence.'

'Sitting on the fence was my profession.'

Afterwards, over their second coffee break – americanos, croissants and a smoke in the Caffè Nero – Bob and Thomasine took stock.

'Creepy, that computer programme,' Thomasine said. 'I mean, it was fun to try, but when you think about it, what kind of person wants to look inside every shop in town?'

'I'd say about half the population.'

'Chauvinist.'

'If it amuses him, I don't see the harm in it.'

'He's a weirdo, Bob, you've got to admit.'

'All right. He's a weirdo, but clever with it.'

She shook her head. 'I feel uncomfortable with him, as if he'd like to put us all in his computer and control us.'

'He was honest about why he joined the circle.'

'Because he likes to be with creative people?'

'Yes, I believed that bit,' he said. 'You're a mystery to him. He'd like to get some ideas of his own and turn them into words, and he can't. The best he can do is pick holes in what you come up with, find faults in the grammar and stuff. That makes him think he's superior in some way, but deep down he knows he can't hack it as a writer.'

Thomasine brightened up. 'Bob, have you got us all summed up so neatly? This is how you're going to get to the truth of this mystery.'

'Oh, yeah? All I've managed so far is to get myself trapped in a burning shed.'

'We're picking up clues. We found out that some of these guys had links with Edgar Blacker we didn't know about. Tudor sold him some insurance and doesn't want to talk about it. Zach was in touch with Blacker before that meeting, being sounded out for a vanity publishing deal.'

'It doesn't amount to much.'

'It's more than the police have got.'

'They'll have got the video by now. Miss Snow was taking it into the nick this morning. They could follow up, find out things, same as you and me.'

'But they won't, because they've pinned it on Maurice.'

He said with a smile, 'What they need is someone like you to crack the whip.'

She gave an even broader smile. 'But because I've got such faith in you, I'm going to crack it specially for you. Are you ready for Basil?'

'Basil I can handle,' he said. 'Naomi is something else.'

Basil and Naomi lived east of the city in Whyke Lane, beyond the scope of Anton's map. Fate decreed that it was Naomi who opened the door of their Victorian semi and said an unwelcoming, 'Yes?'

She had her hair scraped back from her forehead, gleaming black, as if she was in the middle of washing it in sump oil.

'Hi, Naomi,' Thomasine greeted her. 'Perhaps this isn't a good moment? We were hoping to have a word with Baz, if possible.'

She said, 'I won't have him called that. His name is Basil. He's extremely busy just now. What's it about?'

'Circle business.' Thomasine summarised the morning's events, finishing with, 'So it's only fair that we speak to Basil now that we've seen each of the other men.'

'He wouldn't harm a fly,' Naomi said. 'He's in the back garden spraying his roses.'

'Harming the greenfly,' Bob murmured.

Naomi hadn't heard. 'You'd better come in. I'll see if he can break off for a few minutes.'

They were shown into the front room by way of the hall. To Bob's eye it seemed dark and Victorian. There was an upright piano. Old photos in gilt frames, clearly of Naomi's

114

ancestors, stood on top. The women all had eyes like hers that expected hostility and returned it fivefold. Yet someone must have got close, he found himself thinking, or they couldn't have passed on the gene that glared.

Naomi didn't leave them alone for long. 'It's not convenient,' she said, with another of those don't-even-think-about-challenging-me looks. 'He's wearing his spraying clothes.'

'Did you ask him?' Bob said.

'I don't need to ask him. I can see from the kitchen window.'

'We don't mind what he's wearing,' Thomasine said as if it was for them to decide. 'We can talk to him out there. Shall we go through?'

To Bob's surprise, Naomi stepped back to let her pass. Maybe it was all front with her. They moved into the kitchen, another dark room with dinner plates on wooden racks above an old-fashioned dresser.

Out of the window they could see Basil at work, dressed like a racing driver of the twenties in a red overall with goggles and leather helmet. His spray was just as antiquated as the clothes. It worked on the pump-action principle from a bucket. But the small garden looked to be thriving on the treatment. An arch of exquisite pink roses was formed by the weight of the blooms. A daisy on that lawn would have died of shame.

'You see?' Naomi said.

'He won't mind stopping for us.' Without asking, Thomasine opened the back door and stepped across the turf.

'Don't go too close. It's harmful to humans,' Naomi said, following her.

But Basil noticed them and lowered his spray and pushed his goggles above his eyes.

'Don't blame Naomi,' Thomasine said to him. 'She did her best to stop us, but Bob was nearly burnt alive this morning and we need to talk.'

Basil said, 'Oh my word. Are you all right?'

'I'm okay,' Bob said. 'I jumped off the roof and one leg is giving me gyp, but I'll survive.'

'Then you must come and sit in the gazebo.' He led the way up the garden towards a neat wooden structure painted white. Curved bench seats inside faced each other. Bob found himself opposite Naomi, exposed to the stare.

Thomasine gave her account of Bob's misadventure. Apart from another 'Oh my word' from Basil, she was heard in awed silence.

'So we decided to check on the movements of each guy in the circle,' she said. 'No offence, Basil. We've no reason to think you'd want to kill Edgar Blacker or Bob, but in fairness to the others, we must ask where you were about eight this morning.'

Naomi started to say, 'He was—' then stopped as Thomasine raised her hand like a traffic policeman.

'His own words, if you don't mind.'

'Eight?' Basil said, turning to face Naomi as if his memory had gone. 'I would have been taking my shower about that time.'

'So you didn't go out?'

'Yes, I was out.'

'What – taking a shower?'

'I was at the leisure centre. I go for a daily swim. I'm always in the water by seven, winter and summer.'

Unkindly, Bob found himself wondering if the hairpiece stayed on in the water. 'Breaststroke?'

'How did you guess?'

'And you never miss?'

'I can't remember a time when I did.'

'He's fitter than he looks,' Naomi said.

'Is there anyone who can vouch for you?'

'What do you mean – vouch for him?' Naomi said. 'You said a moment ago you had no reason to think he had anything to do with what happened.'

'But we're treating each of the men just the same,' Thomasine said.

'There are several other regulars like me at the pool,' Basil said, 'but we don't speak to each other. We just do lengths.'

'Don't you speak in the changing room?'

His lips formed a small circle, as if he was trying to whistle. 'It's not the thing to strike up a conversation with a fellow getting dressed. When I'm decent I might pass a few words.'

'They'd know you,' Thomasine said, 'so they ought to be able to give you an alibi.'

He still looked dubious. 'That may be so, but who's going to ask them?'

'You, initially. Then Bob and I would need to confirm it with them.'

'I don't care for that at all. I'd rather you treated me as a suspect if that's what this is about.'

'No, it's about eliminating you as a suspect.'

Basil gripped his gauntlet gloves. 'But I've no reason to harm you, Bob. I scarcely know you.'

'The way we see it,' Thomasine said, 'whoever set light to Edgar Blacker's house has reason to be worried that we're asking awkward questions. We think the arsonist set a trap for Bob.'

'I didn't kill Mr Blacker,' Basil said. 'He was perfectly civil to me.'

'I've seen the video,' Bob said. 'I think he was ready to offer you a contract.'

'Apparently.'

'But it was all a con. You know that, don't you? He'd have built up your hopes and then wanted you to put your hand in your pocket to fund the book, like he did with Maurice.'

'So I heard,' Basil said. 'It's deplorable. But I didn't know this at the time. I'm afraid I'm far too trusting.'

'You can say that again,' Naomi said.

'We didn't care for his ideas about publicising my book, opening our garden to the public,' Basil said. 'You can see the size of the plot. We're not equipped for visitors.'

And you don't even offer them a cup of tea, Bob thought. 'Had you ever met Blacker before he visited the circle?'

'He was a stranger to me.'

Naomi chose to come in again. 'It was obvious to me that he hadn't bothered to read my book on the witch trials. Even if he'd skimmed through the pages he should have realised where I stand on the question of witchcraft.'

'You were disappointed?'

'Disgusted.' She pushed a lock of black hair away from her eyes. 'He had the idea I was a believer in occult practices. How anyone could be so mistaken is beyond me.'

'Witchful thinking,' Bob said, and immediately wished he hadn't. He got the fiercest glare yet.

Thomasine nudged the talk in another direction. 'You were one of the founders of the circle, Naomi.'

'What of it?'

'You and Dagmar and Maurice.'

'So?'

'How did you meet?'

Her features relaxed a little. 'On a coach trip to Stratford-on-Avon. Basil gets travel sickness, so he didn't come. I found myself sharing a seat with Maurice. Do you really want to hear this? It's rather gruesome.'

'How?'

'It turned out he was using the trip for research into one of his unsolved murders. He'd arranged with the driver to be dropped at a village called Lower Quinton, a few miles before Stratford. An old man was murdered there towards the end of the war and it was never cleared up. Maurice was visiting the scene.'

'For some local colour?'

Naomi shrugged. 'To be honest, I wasn't all that interested

until he mentioned there were black magic associations. Warwickshire is notorious for that sort of thing. The man was found pinned to the ground by a hayfork through his throat, with the sign of the cross hacked into his chest.'

'Ugh!'

'I warned you it was gruesome.' Naomi carried on in a calm tone, 'It's a form of killing associated with the occult that goes back to Anglo-Saxon times. Any unfortunate suspected of having the evil eye was likely to be impaled in this way.'

'Ritual killing?'

'Yes. And there were local legends of a black dog. If the dog was seen, a death followed soon after. The victim himself saw it as a child on nine successive nights, on his way home from working in the fields as a ploughboy. On the tenth night his sister died suddenly – or so the story went.'

'Were there witches in the area?'

'Supposedly. The coven was said to meet at a stone circle nearby. Had done so for about three centuries.'

'And the murder was never solved?'

'Officially, no. But the policeman who investigated was certain he knew who did it. He was Bob Fabian.'

'The killer?'

Naomi's nostrils flared a little. 'The detective. Fabian of the Yard.'

'I've heard of him,' Bob said.

'Fabian believed a local farmer was responsible. Much of the talk of witchcraft originated with him. He was in trouble financially and he'd borrowed a large sum of money from the victim and couldn't repay it. He dressed the murder up to make it look ritualistic.'

'Why wasn't he arrested?'

'There wasn't enough proof. He destroyed the receipts. No witnesses. He did everything he could to inflame the superstitions. After the killing, a black dog was found on his land, hanged, close to the scene of the crime. Fabian wrote in his memoirs that the case was unsolved, but he confided later that he was sure the farmer was the killer. The whole thing played to the local fears and legends, just as the persecutors of witches have done from time immemorial.'

'It makes a good chapter in Maurice's book, I reckon,' Bob said.

'I think he used it, yes. You were asking how we formed the circle. Maurice and I got talking about the books we were writing and what a happy discovery it is to find another author. On the drive home from Stratford we picked him back up at Lower Quinton and he sat with me again and the idea emerged of setting up a group. He already knew about Dagmar writing romances, and I said I could probably rope in Basil, so we agreed to meet Dagmar and see if she was interested. She was highly enthusiastic. I expect you noticed she idolises Maurice. The circle came into being over tea and cakes in the Bishop Bell tea rooms.'

'At the cathedral?'

'Yes. We had a table outside. It's easier to talk there without being overheard.'

'Good thinking,' Bob said. 'Mills and Boon, murder and witchcraft. Some ears would prick up.'

Thomasine smiled, but Naomi was unamused. 'Nothing of the sort was discussed. We talked about the practicalities of forming the circle.'

'Was Basil there?' Bob asked, slipping into Naomi's habit of discussing her husband as if he couldn't answer for himself.

'He joined later. There were just the three of us. Basil isn't so committed as I am.'

'The garden comes first,' Basil said. 'On the long summer evenings I don't often get to the circle.'

'And I can understand why,' Thomasine said. 'It's a joy to be here.'

Walking back towards the centre of town, Bob said, 'That's it, then. All the men in the circle except Maurice. I've looked each of them in the eye trying to think, Are you a murderer, chum?'

'And what have you decided?'

'They're all a bit iffy, aren't they? Basil seems the most harmless, but he's got a scary woman pulling his strings.'

'Lady Macbeth?'

'Could be. There's Tudor, as shifty as you like, with something to hide about an insurance deal. Zach, who thinks he's a genius, and Anton, who may *be* a genius, and I don't know which is more dangerous.'

'Writers are funny people.'

'Funny peculiar?'

'That's what I meant.'

He heard himself say, 'Be careful, Thomasine.'

'What?'

'Watch your back. Someone had a go at me. It can only be because I'm asking awkward questions. And if I'm being targeted, then you're at risk too.'

10

Authors are easy to get on with – if you are fond of children.

Michael Joseph in the *Observer*, 29 May 1949

'I want you out of the way tonight,' Naomi told Basil. 'I've got someone coming to see me.'

'Who's that, dear?'

'Zach from the circle.'

'Zach? I didn't know you and Zach were seeing each other.'

He received one of her looks. 'Don't make it sound like adultery. We may be collaborating as writers, that's all.'

'And you want me to make myself scarce?'

'Yes. Why don't you prick out some more of those seedlings?'

Basil said with a touch of irritation, 'I finished that job the evening I rescued you from Blacker's house. Don't worry, I'll find something else to do.' He hesitated. 'You'll probably shoot me down in flames for saying this, but isn't Zach's writing rather far removed from yours?'

She didn't shoot him down. She said in a bored voice, as if it was so obvious he should have thought of it himself, 'We'll each bring a different perspective to the project, and that can be stimulating.'

'May I ask what it's about, this project?'

'You may ask, but you won't get an answer from me. This

is still at an early stage and we don't want other people stealing our idea.'

Basil accepted this rebuke with philosophy. 'Writing is more competitive than I appreciated before I joined the circle. In my innocence I thought it was just about self-expression.'

'You're not innocent,' she said. 'You're naive.'

Zach's motorbike roared up Whyke Lane a few minutes before eight. He braked and dismounted and marched up to the front door feeling good in his leathers. In an encounter with Naomi you needed all the confidence you could muster, not to mention protection.

She was wearing a purple trouser suit and black silk blouse. She looked him up and down.

'You'll be wanting to get out of that stuff.'

'I'm fine, thanks.'

'Don't be ridiculous. Give me the crash helmet and close the door behind you.'

'Er, yes.'

She put the helmet on the table by the door and said, 'Jacket.'

There was no future in protesting. He began the business of unfastening and unzipping under Naomi's steady gaze.

She said, 'Distinctive smell.'

'The leather?'

'Yes. Motorcycling is another world to me. I've never even ridden pillion.'

Against his better judgement he said, 'You must try some time.'

She gave a slight nod. 'I'll need to if we're going to achieve anything as a writing team. Do you have a spare helmet?'

He hadn't foreseen this as a serious possibility. 'I may have at home.' He removed the boots and stepped out of the trousers. In his T-shirt and denim shorts he felt about six years old. 'Is Basil about this evening?'

'I sent him to the greenhouse. We don't want him watching us like Big Brother.'

Basil as Big Brother was a difficult concept.

She led him into the room with the piano and her ancestors' photographs. 'A glass of wine? Good for the getting of ideas.'

'Just one, then.'

She poured him a large glass of Bulgarian red. 'Did you get a visit from the new man?'

'Bob Naylor? Yes. And Thomasine.'

'So did we. And did they tell you about the fire this morning? Naylor was lucky to get out alive.'

'It's true, then?'

'The boat house burnt down, so it must be true. But I don't think he was the intended victim. Miss Snow was the target, and she would have died. She isn't capable of knocking a hole in the roof and climbing out. We're dealing with a ruthless killer here.'

'You think it's the same person who torched the publisher's cottage?'

'I'd put money on it.'

Zach frowned. 'Why Miss Snow? She hasn't upset anyone.'

'I know,' Naomi said. 'She's Goody Two-Shoes. When she isn't working in the charity shop she's visiting the women's refuge or helping her friends with their accounts. I can't think of anyone who'd want to kill her unless it's because she's so damned saintly. There were girls at school I would cheerfully have murdered because they were like that.'

'Too good to be true?'

'No. So good and so true it made the rest of us feel like trash. At one time we tried to get up a protest about the school dinners, which were vile, unfit for pigs, and one of these little angels said that instead of complaining we ought to think of the starving millions in China. Wouldn't you have strangled someone like that?'

He grinned. 'What did you do?'

'Not much. Changed her knife and fork for a pair of chopsticks. Girls en masse are feeble when it comes to the point. A woman acting alone, or preferably with a man, is another animal altogether.' She raised her glass. 'Here's to you and me.'

'Em, sure.'

'This isn't just about writing, Zach.'

'No?' His leg gave an involuntary jerk.

'We've got to get out and about. What are they up to, those two, Thomasine and the new man?'

'Trying to prove Maurice is innocent?'

'They say.'

'You don't believe them?'

'It could be my suspicious mind, but I wonder if they're doing the same as you and me, trying to get a book out of this.'

Zach weighed this for a moment. 'I wouldn't think so. Thomasine writes poetry and I don't think Bob Naylor has written anything at all.'

'Then why has she teamed up with him?'

'Maybe she fancies him.'

'Is he single?'

'Don't know.'

'We must find out,' she said. 'We must find out everything about him. He may be the arsonist.'

'What – Bob Naylor?' Zach said, making it clear what he thought of that theory. 'Edgar Blacker was already dead before Bob joined the circle.'

'That doesn't mean he's innocent,' Naomi said. 'He could be playing a very clever game.'

'How do you mean?'

'Suppose he has some grudge against Blacker that none of us knows about, and sets his house on fire. Then he comes along to the circle and starts treating all of us as suspects.'

'But he had nothing to do with Maurice being arrested.'

'How do you know? How do you know he didn't tip off the police to raid the circle that night they came for Maurice?'

'He didn't know Maurice.'

'He may have known Blacker had just dumped Maurice and his book. We have to be alert to every angle, Zach. I'm going to get the background on our new member Bob. What's his real motive for joining the circle? He hasn't told us much about his writing.'

'That's true.'

'Can we be certain his story about the fire at the boat house is true?'

'It burned down. You just said so.'

'We've only got his word that he was shut inside.'

'You've got a suspicious mind.'

'No, I just consider every possibility. But that's not why I asked you here.' She went to the piano and started removing the photos of her family from the top, placing them face down on the stool.

Zach watched like a male spider on the edge of a black widow's web. He supposed she didn't want to make the first move while the images of her family were on display.

He crossed his legs.

But Naomi had other things in mind. She took the last of the pictures off the piano lid and opened it and dipped her arm inside. She lifted out something that was hidden in there. It was another photo, unframed. 'This shouldn't be in my possession,' she said, handing it to him. 'I took it from Edgar Blacker's bedroom wall.'

The photo still smelled faintly of smoke. It was of Blacker, much younger than when he came to the circle – in his thirties, probably – standing beside a blond man of about the same age. Zach didn't recognise him. Each had an arm over the other's shoulder. In their spare hands they held cans of lager. They were in trousers and striped shirts, as if they'd arrived in suits and discarded the jackets and ties.

'It was the only picture there, so it must have been important to him,' Naomi said.

'Is it important to us?'

Her eyes narrowed. 'If you can't tell, I must have over-estimated you.'

'The other guy? Who is he?'

'I've no idea.'

'Was Edgar Blacker gay?'

'I got that impression, didn't you? That voice. The way he dressed.'

'Haven't thought about it till now,' he said. 'I've been proved wrong making assumptions like that.'

'Look at what's written on the back.'

He turned it over. Someone had written 'Innocents, Christmas 1982'.

'Okay,' he said. 'We know when it was taken.'

'And . . . ?'

'You mean the "innocents" bit? I guess that was written later, when the relationship got more serious.'

'My thought exactly,' Naomi said. 'They meet in 1982, possibly the evening this was taken. The friendship develops into a homosexual relationship. We can only guess at how long it lasts, but the blond young man here is the love of Blacker's life, which is why he keeps the picture on his bedroom wall. Is that assuming too much?'

'Sounds feasible. But does it have anything to do with the fire?'

'That's where your imagination comes in.'

'Does it?'

'We're writing a book, remember?' Naomi said with an edge to her voice. 'You're the creative one. See if you can think of a link between this picture and the fire that killed Blacker.'

'It doesn't have to be true?'

'Of course not. Leave the truth to me. I'll try and get some background on Blacker and I may even get the facts on his friendship with this man.'

'I'm getting confused,' Zach said. 'You want me to use my imagination while you go rooting out the facts?'

'Precisely. Isn't it exciting? We'll set out the two stories side by side, incident by incident, your imaginative version and my discoveries about the actual events. To my knowledge nobody has ever attempted anything like this. It's true that writers have used real crimes as inspiration—'

'Ellroy.'

'Who?'

'James Ellroy,' Zach said. 'You wouldn't have read him. He's not your kind of writer.'

'What about him?'

'He uses real crimes like the Black Dahlia case as the structure for his imagination to work on. Truman Capote's *In Cold Blood* is another example, written almost as documentary but with the characters speaking dialogue. It's brilliant.'

'I've read Capote,' she said without enthusiasm. 'But you and I will be going one better. We're adding an extra dimension. I'll be investigating the real facts at the same time as you're doing the fictional version. There'll be tension there. Electricity.'

She leaned forward and put her hand on his arm and he felt the electricity all right. He drew away and smoothed the hairs down, but they sprang up again. 'When do we start?'

'I've already started.'

'What about me?'

'This photo is your starting point. Try to bridge the gap between nineteen eighty-two and the present.'

'Do you want me to do an outline, or what?'

'Good idea. I have high expectations of you, Zach. You have an imagination to die for.'

'Some people find it weird.'

She flapped her hand in a dismissive way. 'Pay no attention. I've been called weird myself and I take it as a compliment. We're achievers, you and I. Who knows what this will lead to? More wine?'

He decided against another glass. Just being with Naomi made him feel heady.

He plucked up the courage to ask, 'Who do you think would publish a book like this?'

'We do,' she said. 'We're in the century of the e-book.'

'The internet?'

'We publish it ourselves and release it into cyberspace. Anyone on the world-wide web can access it.'

'I've heard about e-books. Never seen one.'

'They're tucked away in obscure sites, most of them. My plan is to create a new website called www.Chichester MurderDetectives.com. Key words, you see, that search engines pick up. All kinds of people wanting to read about murder will find it, and be captivated. It's unique, this collaboration.'

'Well, yes,' he said with a tone of reserve.

'I've already purchased the authoring software. It's so simple to use. Accepts Word and WordPerfect. We don't even have to wait for the book to be finished. We can show it as work in progress.'

'Is that a good idea?'

'A brilliant idea. It's revolutionary. Visitors to our website will see the creative process at work. As it progresses and gets known, I predict that publishers will beat a path to our door. They'll be in competition to sign us up. And I don't just mean British publishers. We'll do deals with America, Japan, China.'

'Do you think so?'

'All of Europe. I know it. Never again will you and I have to submit a script and wait for some high-handed publisher to come to a decision. They'll have to make up their minds on what is out there, or risk being trampled in the stampede.'

'It sounds promising, but—'

'I'm starting straight away and I'll be looking to you to make your contribution, Zach.'

He left soon after, his thoughts in a spin.

11

I think when people die in fires it's not because of panic –
it's more likely to be the lack of panic.

Neil Townsend, divisional officer, London Fire Brigade,
quoted by Nicholas Faith in *Blaze* (1999)

Around four on the following Saturday morning most
of Chichester was asleep. The late people had given up
and gone home and the early people weren't yet ready to
go out. The occasional drone of a heavy vehicle came from
the bypass, the A27, and that was all.

In the fire station on the traffic island at Churchside,
north of the town, four of the team on night duty were
playing poker. A black and white film was running on the
TV with the sound turned down. The other firemen were
trying to get some sleep. They were dressed for action. Their
response time was excellent in an emergency, but they didn't
often get the chance to prove it.

In the shadow of a narrow alley close to the town centre
(central enough to feature on Anton's computer) waited the
solitary figure who would give the firemen a night to
remember. No one else seemed to be about, but if some early
riser had come by at this time he would almost certainly have
walked past the alley without seeing anything. The fire-raiser
was dressed in dark clothes. The plastic bag was black. It was
from Waterstone's bookshop. It didn't contain books.

The saying goes: if it works, don't fix it. The method had been used before, with success. A few quick steps to the front door. The letter-flap opened with a gloved hand and the piece of hose inserted. The trickle of fuel as it formed a pool on the floor inside. The hose withdrawn. The oily rags pushed through. The last rag ignited with a struck match and dropped through.

No one was in the street when the arsonist arrived, or left. No neighbour was watching. Even if some sleepless person had looked out of a window opposite, there was not a lot to see for some time. The pink glow inside the house could have been an electric light. If there was a smoke alarm it didn't work. The fire took hold with devastating effect, rapidly finding the stairwell. The flames leapt up, creating a backdraught. You couldn't have designed a more efficient incinerator.

It was later estimated that the fire raged for up to fifty minutes before a milkman on his way to work saw smoke and sparks ripping through the roof and raised the alarm.

The fire team responded with admirable speed once they got the shout. Three fire appliances attended. An attempt was made to gain entry through a bedroom window, but the floor had collapsed. The entire contents of the room, bed, wardrobe, dressing table and chair, had dropped to ground level and been turned to ashes.

Chichester had not seen so devastating a house fire in anyone's memory.

12

I after supper walked in the dark down to Tower-street, and there saw it all on fire at the Trinity house on that side and the Dolphin tavern on this side, which was very near us – and the fire with extraordinary vehemence.

Samuel Pepys, *Diary*, 4 September 1666

Bob stared at the TV screen. He'd just switched on, as he did most mornings while he shuffled around the kitchen making coffee and toast. The breakfast programme was supposed to get him going, encouragement that other people were already on their feet and doing a job. He didn't expect to listen to what they were saying until after his second coffee.

They were running a clip of a burnt-out house, blackened, with wisps of smoke still escaping from what was left of the roof. The style of commentary told him this was the local news slot, and he heard the name of his town. '. . . in Tower Street, Chichester, in the early hours of this morning.' Now the newsreader's head and shoulders filled the screen. 'The fire service were at the scene close to the town centre within a short time of receiving the call, but the station fire officer said it was too far advanced for them to enter the building. It is feared that a middle-aged woman lost her life. And now your local weather.'

'Jesus,' Bob said. He'd recognised the house.

He scraped his hand through his hair.

'Yesterday's weather system has passed across the country now and we can look forward to a brighter day.'

'Oh my God!'

'What's up, Dad?'

Sue had just come down in the faded Robbie Williams T-shirt she slept in, her face still puffy from sleep.

'Dad?'

'Another fire. A woman died and I know who she is.' He kicked off his flip-flops. 'I'm going out.'

'You haven't had your toast.'

He was out of the room already.

At the scene, the entire street was closed. The end was taped off and two policemen were preventing anyone from crossing the line. Bob's portable TV had given him a better view. All he could make out from here was the back of a fire tender. The only other clue as to what was happening were the acrid fumes hanging in the air, making his throat and nostrils smart.

'Which house is it?' he asked one of the cops.

'Sorry, chum. This is as far as you go.'

'Which house?'

'Why – do you live here?'

'Someone I know does.'

'The fourth along. Gutted. No one inside stood a chance.'

'Number seven?'

'It would be, yes. It's a wonder the place next door didn't go up as well.'

'Listen. Who's in charge? I need to speak to them.'

'And who might you be?'

He gave his name. 'I know the woman who lives in that house. I don't think this was an accident.'

'Okay.'

'Are you listening? I want to see the man in charge.'

'Hold on.' The officer spoke into his personal phone. After getting a response he lifted the tape enough for Bob to duck under. 'Ask for DI Cherry.'

'Dai Cherry?'

He was given a long look.

'Detective Inspector. Ask nicely.'

Ask nicely. The stupid things people say, Bob thought, as he stepped around bits of blackened debris and pools of water. Firemen were disconnecting hoses, chatting to each other, just doing their job. An ambulance and three fire tenders were still in attendance, but the main action was over. The small house was tragic to behold, every window smashed and soot stains spread across the front. A fragment of charred carpet lay on the pavement. Bob recognised the carpet pattern and felt his stomach churn.

Ahead, a fire officer with more silver on his shoulders than the others was in conversation with a tall man in a leather jacket and jeans. Bob went right up to them.

'Inspector Cherry?'

The two continued their dialogue.

'Can I have a word?'

The fire officer finished what he was saying and walked off.

The detective's gaze was on the building. He didn't even turn to look at Bob. 'You've got something to say to me?' Either he wasn't expecting much, or he was playing it cool.

'Bob Naylor, yes. The woman who lives here is called Snow, Miss Amelia Snow.'

'And?'

'Have you found her?'

No answer. This casual attitude was getting to Bob. There still wasn't eye contact. 'Because someone was out to kill her.'

'Oh yes?'

As off-hand as that. How was he going to break through this wall? 'They did their best to trap her last Saturday. You know the boat house that burned down? She was supposed to be meeting someone there. She had a phone call. Now this. It's got to be murder.'

He could have been talking about the weather for all the reaction he got. 'You're from round here, are you?'

'What?'

'Local?'

'From Chichester, yes. Did you hear what I just said? It's murder.'

'What are you then – a friend?'

'I met Miss Snow a few times in the past two weeks, that's all. Through the writers' circle. She's the secretary. Was she in there?'

'So you belong to this circle?'

'I've been to one meeting. Look, this isn't about me. I'm not important. I'm telling you Miss Snow was under threat, for God's sake.'

'I heard what you said, Mr Taylor.'

'Naylor.'

'When you've calmed down we'll take a statement. Can you call at the police station later today? Give your details to the officer over there before you leave.'

With that, DI Cherry strolled off towards a police response car.

'Bloody hell.'

Shaking his head in disbelief, Bob went over to pass on his name and address. If this was the level of interest from the police, he wasn't surprised poor old Maurice was still in custody.

'Bob!'

He turned to look at the taped-off area where the shout had come from, and his spirits had a lift. Thomasine was there waving, with Dagmar at her side. As soon as he'd passed on his name and address he went over to them.

'Was she in there?' Thomasine asked.

'Seems so. They're saying bugger all.'

'Poor little soul! It wasn't an accident, was it?'

'They're not saying. My guess is that someone torched the house, like they did Edgar Blacker's.'

Dagmar said, 'Who in the world would want to harm Miss Snow?'

He shook his head, at a loss for an explanation. 'I need a coffee. How about you two?'

The Costa shop in West Street was the nearest place open at this time. They carried their coffees upstairs, where they had the space to themselves.

'They'll have to release Maurice now,' Dagmar said. 'They will, won't they?'

Maurice wasn't high in Bob's thoughts right now. 'If it's up to the dipstick I just met, I wouldn't hold your breath.'

'Someone else will be in charge,' Thomasine said. 'If it's a murder investigation they use detectives.'

'He *was* a detective. Does anyone know what time this happened?'

'Some hours ago. I saw it on TV. If it's anything like the fire that killed Blacker, it was started at night when no one was about.'

'What a wicked thing,' Dagmar said.

'She was a sweetie,' Thomasine said. 'I can't understand this.'

'Have they got her out?' Dagmar asked.

'There can't be much left of her to get out,' Bob said. 'From what I could see, the fire got a grip before anyone arrived. It burned like a furnace inside. The place is just a shell now.'

'It's appalling,' Dagmar said. 'And you're right, Tommy. She was a lovely person, always helping people in trouble. All the work she did for the women's refuge, working in the charity shop. They're going to miss her.'

'So are we,' Thomasine said. 'She did great as the circle

secretary. Don't know why she took it on. It's not a job I'd want, with people like Anton ready to jump on any mistake you make.'

'She was glad of the chance to work with Maurice,' Dagmar said, and added at once, 'I don't mean that unkindly. She was very high-minded, and so is Maurice, but there is some satisfaction to be got by a single lady linking up with a nice man in a worthwhile enterprise.'

There speaks the romantic novelist, Bob thought. He'd always thought of Dagmar as the one who fancied Maurice the most.

Thomasine's mind was elsewhere. 'Is it safe to assume the killer is the person who phoned Miss Snow and tried to lure her to the boat house?'

'That's my reading of it,' Bob said. 'Same m.o., basically.'

'M.o.?'

'Latin, isn't it? Same method. Killing by fire. Dead simple and not much risk. They must have stuffed some inflammable material in the space under the boat house for it to go up like it did. A fire doesn't take that quickly without paraffin or something.'

'Do you think they realised it was you inside and not Miss Snow?'

'I shouted plenty. They heard me.'

'What you're saying is that it was a trap meant for Miss Snow and when you walked into it they decided you'd better go instead?'

'Abso-bloody-lutely. I knew too much already.'

'And for a time they must have thought they'd succeeded, unless they watched you climb out on the roof.'

'I sensed they'd gone by then. Light the blue touch paper and run.'

There was a silence between them for a short while, as if no one wanted to make the dread conclusion that united them. At length it was Thomasine who spoke it.

'Let's face it. These fires all have a connection with the circle. None of us is safe any more.'

'But why pick on us?' Dagmar said. 'We're no threat to anyone, a harmless group of writers. We're not the mafia.'

'Dag, one of us can't be harmless,' Thomasine said. 'Someone in the circle is a killer.'

'It could be an outsider.'

'I don't see it. Three fires, all linked to the circle. They know who we are and where we live.'

'But why? Where's the sense in it?'

'I think we've got to consider pyromania.'

'Come again?' Bob said.

'Pyromania. People with a thing about starting fires. A mental illness. They have this need to see places go up in flames.'

'I've heard of that,' he said, 'but you're wrong. Our fire-raiser is picking on people, not buildings.'

'Maybe.'

'No maybe about it. This was murder, Thomasine, murder the easy way. You don't even have to look your victim in the eye. You sneak up to the house, shove a firebomb through the letterbox and run.'

'Horrible,' Dagmar said.

'Is that how it was started?' Thomasine said.

'No one is saying yet, but the fire at Blacker's house started in the front hall. That's the method.'

'So what can we do – leave it to the police?'

He rolled his eyes. 'Right now, I have zero confidence in that lot. You and I know more about the members of the circle than the police do. Who have they interviewed? Only Maurice.'

Dagmar spread her hands in appeal. 'And he's innocent. No one can dispute that any more.'

'You think we can take this on?' Thomasine said to Bob.

Before he answered, Dagmar took a deep breath. 'It's a

huge risk, isn't it? You're the two who have been asking questions and we know what happened to you, Bob.'

He said, 'Bugger that. I'm angry.'

'Me, too,' Thomasine said. 'I want to nail this bastard, whoever it is.'

Dagmar looked from one to the other. No question: they were in earnest.

'So why was Miss Snow killed?' Thomasine said.

'She got things going in the first place,' Bob said. 'She got onto me and asked me to do whatever I could to get Maurice released. She was dead worried that the police were going to stitch him up.' He stared into his coffee. 'Well, she told me something in confidence, but I think this is the time to share it with you. Maurice did a short spell inside.'

The colour drained from Dagmar's cheeks. 'What?'

'There was trouble with a neighbour and Maurice overreacted.'

'This doesn't sound like Maurice,' Thomasine said.

'I'm not kidding. The neighbour was an arsehole. He made Maurice's life a misery. Two of his rottweilers took over the garden and Maurice flipped his lid and shot them. But the worst of it was that Maurice made a bonfire of some wood the neighbour had heaped against his fence. The fire got out of control and burnt some property including a boat that was under repair.'

'Now I understand,' Thomasine said. 'Maurice has form as a fire-raiser.'

'You said the fire was accidental,' Dagmar stressed, as if it was Bob's fault.

'That's what I was told, love, but there are two things you don't ever do in this country. You don't sit down during *God Save the Queen,* and you don't shoot somebody's pet animal. He shot two. A jury won't ignore that. He was sent down for a few months.'

'Dreadful,' Dagmar said.

'Let's keep our eye on the ball,' Thomasine said. 'Who do we think is on the shortlist for this?'

'The four fellows we've already spoken to,' Bob said.

'Basil?' Thomasine said, dubious.

'On his own I wouldn't rate him, but with Naomi breathing down his neck . . .'

She gave a nod. 'True.'

'Then there are the women, present company excepted.'

'Why?' Thomasine said with a half smile. 'Why exclude us? We could have done it, Dagmar and I, the same as anyone else. And, come to think of it, we haven't ever considered *you* as a suspect, Mr Bob Naylor.'

'I only joined the circle after Edgar Blacker was dead.'

'Ha!' she said, pointing an accusing finger, but still smiling, 'and how convenient, coming among us and putting us through the wringer, one by one. What if you were Blacker's killer for some reason none of us has yet discovered and all this is a smokescreen to throw off suspicion?'

He weighed Thomasine's theory, allowing that it was meant in fun, yet forced to admit that it had something going for it. She was so bright. 'Let's have a truce,' he said finally. 'For the time being we'll focus on the others. If we eliminate them all we'll go head to head, right?'

'Righty.'

'Righty,' Dagmar said. Bob had almost dismissed her from his mind, such was the force of Thomasine's personality.

'And here's a suggestion,' he said. 'Why don't we call a meeting of the circle and bring them up to speed on what's going on? See them as a group and find out their reactions to what happened this morning.'

'Isn't that dangerous?' Dagmar said.

'More dangerous for the killer.'

'But we don't have the authority to call a meeting. It's up to the chair and the secretary to decide about that.'

'The chair's in the slammer and the secretary's dead. If

someone doesn't make a move we'll never get them together. Who else is on the committee?'

'Dagmar and me,' Thomasine said. 'Oh, what the hell, let's go for it. What do you say, Dag?'

He did a day's work before calling at the police station to make the statement. From the cool reaction he'd got in the morning he guessed the rozzers wouldn't be too worried if he forgot the whole thing, but he had his own agenda. He was going to find out if they knew anything he didn't.

He was seen by a friendly plain-clothes man the shape and size of a shot-putter.

'Mr Naylor, I'm glad you came. We already spoke to your daughter.'

'What's she been up to?'

'We were looking for you, to make this statement.'

'Funny. No one gave a monkey's this morning.'

'It's a full-scale murder inquiry now. There was a body in the house.'

'The lady who lived there. I told your inspector.'

'It's got to be identified. We're not even certain yet if it was male or female.'

'Amelia Snow.'

'We don't take anything for granted. The fire really took off, as you would have seen. Do you want to tape this statement or write it down?'

'Tape sounds like less work.'

'I'll see which room is free.'

When they were inside an interview room and seated, the officer said, 'This is Chichester police station.'

'I know,' Bob said. 'I live here.'

'That was for the tape.'

He smiled and gave a shrug. 'Sorry, squire.'

'Twentieth of July, two thousand and five. I'm DC Shilling, the interviewing officer—'

'And I'm Bob Naylor.'

'Right. Would you read out what's on this card?'

'"I make this statement of my own free will. I understand that I need not say anything unless I wish to do so and that what I say may be given in evidence." Right?' He went over the salient details of the last few days, starting with the call from Miss Snow asking for the return of the video. 'She said someone from the police had asked for it and she was going to bring it here.'

'She did. It was handed in,' DC Shilling said.

'So it wasn't lost in the fire. Thank God for that.'

'You can thank DI Cherry, my boss. He got in touch with Miss Snow and asked her to bring it in.'

'Is he in charge of the case?'

'Was. Someone else is taking over now. A DCI from Bognor. Two suspicious deaths is a bit much for one DI to handle.'

'Plus the fire in the boat house,' Bob said.

'If it was related.'

'You bet it was related,' Bob said, and launched into his account of the mysterious phone call to Miss Snow offering information that would get Maurice out of jail. Then he explained how he took Miss Snow's place and turned up at the boat house and was nearly barbecued.

'You saw no one?' Shilling said.

'He kept out of sight, whoever he was. Or she.'

'Pity you didn't report this at the time.'

'You found out soon enough, didn't you?' Bob said. 'You could see the blaze from here.'

'But we didn't know about you.'

'If you had, you might have thought I was the arsonist.'

'Fair comment. We've only got your word that you aren't.'

Bob held up a finger. 'Hold on. Get this straight. I volunteered to tell you all this.'

'Noted. Have you got any enemies, Mr Naylor? Anyone who might want to harm you?'

He glared back. 'I told you this was meant for Miss Snow, not me. I took her place.'

'I follow that, but answer the question, please.'

'Well, I shoot off at the mouth more often than I should, but I can't think of anyone who feels that sore about me.'

'What about these people in the writers' circle?'

'What about them?'

'Anyone taken a dislike to you?'

'That'd be quick. I've only been to one meeting. They're friendly so far. When are you going to release Maurice, the chairman? There's no way he could have started this fire.'

'He's being held on a separate charge.'

'The fire at Edgar Blacker's place. Don't you think it's got to be the same guy?'

'When the forensic report is in, I'm sure the SIO will compare the two incidents and form a conclusion.'

'They're both arson, aren't they?'

'The first was a deliberate act. The fire investigator found that it started in the front hall, from something pushed through the letterbox. This one may appear similar but it's got to be confirmed.'

'Everyone says you're wasting your time on Maurice.'

'It's not up to me,' Shilling said. 'We'll see, we'll see.'

An hour later, two beers and a mushroom pizza to the good, Bob thought about what he'd learned. The fuzz were in no hurry to release Maurice. The new chief honcho needed to get up to speed with the case. They were waiting for the forensic results from the fire investigation. With so little action, the killer would be thinking this was easy-peasy.

He recalled Miss Snow's jitters about the call the killer had made. At the time he'd thought he'd solved her problem. He'd felt quite pleased with himself, doing his knight-in-shining-armour bit. Even when things went wrong at the boat house, he'd told himself he'd saved the lady from a bad experience. The thought hadn't crossed his mind that the killer would try something else.

Miss Snow was on Bob's conscience now. He was fully committed to finding the killer.

He just wished his hands wouldn't shake so much.

13

Wish I'd worn something else, Bob was thinking when he turned up at the New Park Centre in his Guinness T-shirt. This was more like a memorial service than a circle meeting. The members nodded solemnly to each other and everyone was talking in hushed voices. The sense of shock and bereavement was real. Basil and Anton were wearing black ties. Nobody was in the bright colours you'd expect on a fine summer's evening.

Even the room seemed cold.

'Are we all here yet? Is anyone missing?' Thomasine asked, and then put her hand to her mouth as if she wished she'd said something else. One absentee was on everyone's mind.

She tried again. 'Shall we get the chairs around the table?'

While this was going on, Bob made a count. Everyone except Miss Snow and Maurice.

Anton called across the room to Thomasine. 'Who's going to chair this?'

'I thought I would, if no one objects,' she said. 'Dagmar and I are on the committee. She's offered to take the minutes.'

'Is it a regular meeting, then?'

'No, darling, I think it's best described as an extraordinary meeting, don't you?'

Satisfied, it seemed, he went to a chair and sat down.

Dagmar, on Thomasine's left, said in confidence, 'Should we start with a prayer?'

'I thought we'd have a minute's silence. We're not all church-goers.'

For once there was no need to call them all to order. They'd taken their places around the table and gone silent. Thomasine explained that she'd called the meeting in Maurice's absence, but she was confident he would give it his approval as soon as he was released, as he surely would be. She said, 'We're here out of respect to the memory of Miss Snow, our secretary, and I propose that we start with a minute's silence.'

Anton said, 'Do we know for certain that she died?'

'For pity's sake,' Tudor said. 'This isn't the time for nitpicking, old boy. You don't see her here, do you?'

Dagmar said, 'I expect she's here in spirit.'

Jessie, the archdeacon's widow, said, 'Amen.'

'So if you have a problem with showing respect, why don't you take care of the timekeeping?' Tudor said to Anton. 'Tell us when the minute is up.'

'If you wish.'

'Shouldn't we stand?' Basil said.

Thomasine said this was a good suggestion.

So they stood, some with heads bowed, thinking of Miss Snow until Anton said, 'Time.'

Tudor turned on him again. 'This isn't a bloody booze-up. We're trying to show respect for a dead colleague.'

'What else was I supposed to do – whistle "The Last Post"?' Anton said.

Thomasine said, 'Cool it, guys. Let's all sit down and have a civilised discussion about where we go from here.'

'I propose Dagmar for our new secretary,' Jessie said as soon as they were settled.

'Seconded,' Basil said so fast that it had the signs of a fix.

Tudor held up both hands as if to stop an advancing train. 'Before we rush into this, let's ask Dagmar if she's willing to take the risk.'

Dagmar looked up from her notepad. 'What risk?'

'The risk of stepping into a dead woman's shoes.'

Dagmar took in a sharp breath. 'Are you saying she was killed because she was secretary?'

'I haven't the faintest why she was killed, my dear, but it has to be a possibility.'

'Surely not,' Jessie said, looking to right and left. 'We're a harmless organisation, aren't we?'

Nobody spoke, but the way Naomi rolled her eyes was eloquent enough.

Jessie's question hung in the air until Dagmar, white-faced, said, 'I think I'll stand down after this meeting.'

Thomasine glared at Tudor. 'Well, we don't have to rush this. Next time someone else may like to volunteer.'

'What are we going to do about dear old Maurice?' Basil said. 'He's still being held by the police when it's patently obvious he's an innocent man. We've had three attacks of arson and he couldn't possibly have carried out the last two.'

'I'm afraid the woodentops don't think that way,' Tudor said. 'They'll let him go when they're ready, and not before. They can pretty well do as they like.'

Zach nodded and said, 'Fascist pigs.'

'They'll be carrying out forensic tests,' Anton said. 'If the results are in his favour, they'll let him go.'

'You have a touching faith in the Old Bill,' Tudor said.

Thomasine in her stand-in role as chair said, 'One of the reasons I wanted to call this meeting is that after what's happened we're sure to get some attention from the press.'

'*Some* attention?' Anton said.

Tudor said, 'They'll hang us out to dry.'

Jessie said, 'What on earth does that mean?'

'They'll have our guts for garters, then.'

Jessie said, 'Please!' Whether it was the guts or the garters that upset her was impossible to tell.

Anton came to her rescue. 'Tudor, we *are* a literary organisation. I suggest we leave vulgarisms in the street where they belong.' For Jessie's benefit, he said, 'The gist is that the press will take advantage of us.'

'Why?' Jessie said. 'We've nothing to be ashamed of.' She hesitated and her expression altered. 'Have we?'

'It's how it looks to an outsider that matters,' Thomasine said. 'We invited a speaker to our meeting and he was killed shortly after. Our new recruit Bob was caught in another fire and almost killed. And now our secretary is murdered. People are going to point out that the circle is the common factor. We're sure to come under the microscope.'

'So what are you saying, that we'd better agree on how to deal with the jackals?' Tudor said.

'In a word, yes.'

'A spokesman?' Basil said.

'A press officer.'

'Cool,' Zach said. 'Like it.'

'Someone we can refer them to,' Thomasine said, encouraged by the support. 'If we're not careful they'll be picking us off, paying us bribes for titbits of gossip about each other.'

'How ghastly!' Jessie said. You could see in her face the prospect of her reputation disintegrating.

Naomi spoke up for the first time. She had been a brooding, unsettling presence until now. 'So who do you suggest for press officer?'

'I can handle it,' Tudor offered.

'We don't want him,' Naomi said to Thomasine. 'He can't keep anything to himself. We want someone who can stonewall.'

Basil shook his head. 'Not me, my dear.'

She said with contempt, 'I'm not talking about garden maintenance. You'd be useless. I propose Bob.'

'Me?' Caught off guard, Bob trotted out his usual excuse. 'I'm not even a full member yet.'

'That's neither here nor there,' Naomi said. 'If we appoint you, it's because you're well qualified.'

'Me? I've never done anything like it.'

'Personality-wise, you're the best we've got.'

'That's a laugh.'

'Don't you want to do this?'

'I'd rather not, if we can find someone else.'

'You see?' Thomasine said with the sweep of a hand, looking around the table. 'He's a born stonewaller.'

This produced the first smiles of the evening.

She rode her advantage like a surfer. 'Can we have a show of hands for Bob as our press rep?'

Bob was the only one who didn't raise a hand.

Zach said, 'Sorted.'

'Outgunned,' Thomasine said with a smile at Bob. 'If any of us is approached by the media, refer them to Bob Naylor. Right, Bob?'

'I guess.'

Thomasine moved on. 'We can also be certain that the police will want to question some of us, if not all.'

Jessie said in a strangled tone, 'Oh no!'

Tudor said, 'What's your problem with that?'

'I don't want a police car parked outside my house.'

'Worried about curtain-twitchers, is it? Let's face it, we're all potential suspects now. They're going to put us through the mincer.'

Jessie looked as if she'd been put through the mincer already.

'The point I'm making,' Thomasine said, 'is that Bob can cope with the press, and I'm sure he'll do it brilliantly, but we can't ask him to fend off the police as well. Each of us is going to have to deal with them individually.'

'Dangerous,' Anton said.

'Which is why I raised the matter.'

'Neat,' Zach said. 'A game plan.'

'Something like that. We're awfully vulnerable. We give out a lot about ourselves at circle meetings, and that's to be encouraged. It's part of the writing process, using our life experiences. So we all know some pretty intimate details about each other from the things we read out. I, for one, wouldn't want my innermost thoughts passed on to the police.'

'Nureyev's tights?' Tudor said.

'Tudor . . . please.'

Anton said, 'Our acting chair is speaking good sense. Let's agree not to pass on personal information.'

'Fair enough.' Tudor eyed the youngest member, Sharon, at the end of the table. 'No tittle and no tattle, right?'

'Certain people have a gift for it,' Anton said with a hard look at Tudor.

Zach said, 'All okay on that? Fingers up to the fuzz.'

Thomasine was quick to say, 'No, I'm not saying we shouldn't cooperate. Answer the questions they're entitled to ask, about your own movements, where you were on the night of the fire and so on. Just don't be tempted to comment on other members of the circle.'

'Whatever your private suspicions may be,' Naomi said, leaving no doubt she had plenty.

Dagmar said, 'I'm not bothered about talking to the police. What worries me is something far more sinister.'

'What's that?' Jessie asked.

'We're all potential victims now.'

There was a moment while everyone took that in.

'What – do you think he's going to pick us off one by one?' Tudor said. 'Why would he do that? We're just a bunch of amateur writers. No one is threatened by us.'

'Miss Snow wasn't threatening anybody. I can't think of anyone less threatening than she was.'

'We don't know why Miss Snow was picked.'

'Well, I'm going to take precautions,' Dagmar said.

'What can you do?'

'Get a letterbox fitted outside my house. Then I can seal up the front door and sleep easy at night.'

'While he lobs a firebomb through your front room window,' Tudor said. 'If someone really wants to get you, my love, they will.'

'Oh my God!'

'You're not helping,' Thomasine said to Tudor. 'Some of our members are extremely frightened.'

Tudor raised a hand to acknowledge another gaffe. 'Sorry, people.'

At this critical moment in the meeting another hand was raised. No one would have predicted that the usually silent Sharon had something to say.

Thomasine said in a surprised tone, 'Yes, my dear?'

'Are you going to ask if anyone's got a success to report?'

If anything could relieve the tension, this was it. There were smiles and some gentle laughter.

'I hadn't planned on it,' Thomasine said, 'but why not? We could do with some good news.'

'Well, you know I've always got a pencil in my hand?' She held it up for all to see.

'Right. We've seen the doodles you do.'

'A little while ago I started doing pictures of the salon where I work, the people, I mean, and just for a laugh I put balloons out of their mouths with stuff they're saying, the funny things you hear when you're in the chair with your hair in curlers. Know what I mean?'

'Captions,' Tudor said.

Anton said, 'Wrong.'

'What do you mean, "wrong"?' Tudor said.

'Speech bubbles. She's referring to speech bubbles.'

'Yeah, man,' Sharon said, looking up from the doodle

she was working on and pointing a finger at Anton. 'Any road, some of my friends thought they was wicked and why didn't I take the best stuff round to that free newspaper that started up last year. So I did, and they liked them so much they want to print them.'

'Marvellous!' Thomasine said, genuinely pleased. 'Congratulations!'

'It's not real writing, so I didn't know if it counts, but I'll be getting twenty-five pound for each strip they use.'

'Hey, that's brilliant, and don't play it down. Of course it's real writing. You'll have a regular income from your work, which is more than any of us can boast.'

'That's what I wanted to say, then.'

'Is it just the hairdresser's in this strip,' Tudor asked, 'or are you featuring other locations? From here some of the drawings seem to bear a close resemblance to members of the circle.'

She slid her hand over the paper. 'No, I wouldn't do that. It's only about the salon.'

'Pity,' he said, 'I wouldn't mind being in a strip cartoon.'

Anton chose this moment to fire another broadside at Tudor. 'You're full of suggestions. If I remember correctly, it was you who urged us all to use the fire at Edgar Blacker's cottage as the inspiration for our writing. I'm so pleased I ignored you. Now that Miss Snow has died it would be in the worst possible taste.'

Jessie said, 'Oh my word, yes!'

There was a rueful smile from Tudor.

The biggest reaction came from Naomi. She jerked forward, frowning, and looked across at Zach. 'Inspiration for our writing?'

Clearly uneasy, Zach said, 'I don't think you were there, Naomi. This was the evening we met in the pub and Maurice had just been released by the police.'

Basil started to say, 'It was the evening you were trapped—'

But Naomi cut in. 'I know which evening it was, Basil.'

Anton wouldn't let it rest. 'I propose that we agree here and now that it would be deplorable for any member of the circle to use these tragedies as subject matter for our writing.'

Jessie said, 'Hear, hear. I second that.'

Naomi turned to see if Zach would say anything.

After some hesitation he cleared his throat. 'Hold on. That sounds like censorship to me. There's a principle at stake here. Freedom of expression.'

'I agree,' Naomi said.

Dagmar said, 'Noted.'

With all the experience of a thousand meetings in the Department of Ancient Monuments, Anton said, 'Madam Chair, I have made a proposal and it was seconded. I insist that it is put to the vote.'

Thomasine was having a torrid time as the stand-in chair. For help she looked towards Bob.

Caught again. Bob wasn't used to all this procedural stuff. He'd always avoided union meetings if he could. He dredged deep and said, 'There's one thing no one has mentioned.'

'What's that?'

'Tea break.'

'Lovely suggestion,' Thomasine said. 'We can talk things over informally and come back to Anton's proposal later – if we really need to.'

Bob was outside having a smoke when Thomasine found him.

'Sorry about all that, springing it on you,' she said. 'You were great in there.'

'I know sweet f.a. about the press,' he said, offering her a cigarette. 'I once saw a cartoon I liked. This woman has just come home and is saying triumphantly to her husband, "Only my second week at the writers' circle and they've made me treasurer!"'

'Yes, and it's bloody unfair, but you'll do it in style, I know you will. What can I do in return – be your slave for a day?'

'I'll think it over.'

'A day and a night, then?'

He looked. She was smiling, and the remark was joky, but there was something there he hadn't seen in a woman's eyes since Maggie died.

In the Lewes Arms, opposite the law court and built into the ramparts of the castle, Detective Superintendent Peter Diamond spilled some beer as he threaded a route through the tiny front bar. This was where lunch was being taken. Lawyers, witnesses and relatives needed an escape.

DCI Hen Mallin was saving seats by the window, and that was where Diamond was heading. The pair of them had given evidence in what was known to the press as the Wightview Sands case, and it was over apart from the sentencing. The jury hadn't taken long over the guilty verdict.

'Hope you wanted lemon in this,' Diamond said as he handed Hen her gin and tonic.

'Always. It stops me getting scurvy. Are you staying another night?'

He shook his head.

'Duty calls?'

'The Wasps.'

'Sounds dangerous.'

'Rugby. I'm a Bath supporter.'

'All right for some,' she said. 'I'll be checking in at Chichester.'

'Why – do they have a team?'

'Chichester nick. I took a call this morning. Series of arson attacks.'

'I thought you were based at Bognor.'

'I am, but Chi is up a gum tree. What are you smiling for?'

'I was picturing it. Sounds like a panda.'

She took a long sip of the G&T. 'Whatever. They're getting a new keeper.'

When they returned to the meeting room and Thomasine called for order, Anton said, 'We're not all here.'

'Who's missing, then?'

'Zach.'

'And Naomi,' Jessie said.

'We can wait a few minutes,' Thomasine said.

'I don't think Zach is coming back,' Jessie said. 'I saw him putting on his motorcycle clothes.'

'He didn't say he was leaving.'

'I saw Naomi get on her bike and ride away,' Dagmar said.

Tudor said, 'It's a bit off, leaving like that without letting us know why.'

'It's about what we were discussing before the break,' Dagmar said with her way of seeing to the heart of things. 'Zach was talking about freedom of expression. I think they expected to be outvoted.'

'Did she say anything to you about leaving?' Thomasine asked Basil.

'I'd be the last to know,' he said. 'Naomi is her own woman. But the two of them met the other day to talk about a project, so this may have something to do with it.'

There was a pause while the others took this in.

'Hoho. Sounds to me as if we've got a couple of dark horses in our midst,' Tudor said. 'It wouldn't surprise me at all if they're planning something. This wasn't about freedom of expression. They've done a deal with the papers – dishing the dirt on the rest of us.'

Jessie gave a strangled cry and put her hand to her throat.

Thomasine said, 'Tudor, you're at it again, letting your imagination run riot. We discussed talking to the press and they said nothing.'

'Too guilty to own up.'

'You're talking about two of our colleagues. Let's have some loyalty here. They probably each had other appointments they had to hurry away for.'

'If you believe that, you'll believe anything.'

'I'll speak to them later and find out.'

Through his clenched teeth Anton drew in a long, audible breath. 'Madam Chair, before the break I put a proposal to the meeting. I now move that we put it to the vote.'

'There are only nine of us here,' Dagmar said.

'Eight if you exclude me,' Bob said. 'I haven't joined yet.'

Thomasine said, 'I was hoping you wouldn't insist, Anton. Perhaps as temporary chair I shouldn't express a view, but I think Zach had a point about censorship. There is a larger principle at stake. It would be a pity if we painted ourselves into a corner.'

'I agree,' Dagmar said.

Without looking up from her sketching, Sharon said, 'Me, too.'

'And me,' Basil said.

'Looks as if we're far from unanimous,' Thomasine said.

Dagmar said, 'And I think we need a two-thirds majority to change the constitution. There's something in it about freedom to write on any subject and in any style we choose.'

'Sorry, Anton,' Thomasine said, 'you're out of order.'

14

Reading isn't an occupation we encourage among police officers. We try to keep the paper work down to a minimum.

Joe Orton, *Loot* (1966)

'All right, boys and girls, settle down and be grateful it isn't my holiday pictures.'

Detective Chief Inspector Henrietta Mallin – better known as Hen – from Bognor, had taken over as Chief Investigating Officer on what was being called the Chichester arson case. It was a pity the city's own CID couldn't handle this one, but Hen had a good clear-up rate, and it was agreed that the local man, DI Johnny Cherry, wasn't the brightest fruit in the basket. He looked blighted before meeting Hen, and bruised after.

'This is the cottage on the Selsey Road where the publisher died,' Hen said, as the image of a burnt-out ruin appeared on the video screen. The entire CID team was watching, together with Stella Gregson, a DS from Bognor who had arrived with Hen. 'Victim was asleep upstairs and died in bed.'

She took them quickly through a sequence showing the space where Edgar Blacker's front door had been. Nothing was left of it. The floor, walls and ceiling were black and disintegrating. 'The seat of the fire,' Hen said. 'Our perpetrator stuffs some oily rags through the letterbox and puts a flame to them. From here it spreads through the main room, which was lined with books wall to wall, and into the kitchen and bathroom.'

It was difficult to make out one room from another in the blackened debris. She paused the videotape.

'We go upstairs now. People of a nervous tendency, look through your fingers.'

They were shown the head and shoulders of the dead man, the face stained by smoke, yet untouched by flames. The skin was undamaged, the eyeballs still white. 'If you were expecting roast publisher, this will come as a surprise,' Hen said. 'The bedroom escaped the worst of the fire damage. He died of a cocktail of toxic fumes. Never even got out of bed.'

The camera panned slowly around the bedroom. The used shirt draped over a chair was a touching reminder that its owner had gone to bed expecting a peaceful night's sleep. 'The thatch above this room caught fire and took out the roof, but fire burns upwards and outwards, and the door you see was closed. The fire service got here before the flames from downstairs could burn through, but the fumes seeped in through the cracks.'

'Who raised the alarm, guv?' Stella Gregson asked.

'A passing motorist with a mobile.'

'No connection, I suppose?'

'None, but you're right to mention it. The person who reports the fire is often the perpetrator. In this case, he wasn't. He was a local radio guy on his way in to present the breakfast programme.'

Some close shots in the bedroom showed how little damage there was. A framed photo of two men still hung on the wall. 'Is one of those the victim, ma'am?' a keen DC asked.

Hen referred the question to DI Cherry. 'Johnny?'

'Er, apparently . . . in his younger days.'

Hen said, 'I didn't notice this when I visited the site this morning. Was it removed and bagged up?'

'Must have been,' Cherry said.

'I'd like to see it. I should have mentioned that Mr Blacker was fifty-two, and a bachelor.'

'Say no more, guv,' the keen DC said with a grin.

Hen's eyes flashed. 'Have a care, my beauty. I don't do homophobia, and in case you're wondering, I'm unmarried and I'm straight. What's your name?'

'Humphreys, ma'am.'

'No need to blush, Humphreys. Anyone can tell you're straight as well, straight back into uniform if you make another crack like that. But let's return to someone of more importance: Edgar Blacker. His publishing company is called the Blacker List, ha bloody ha. He spent his entire career in the industry, starting as tea boy. Worked up to packer in a Birmingham warehouse. Moved down to Essex and got some editorial experience producing magazines. Do we know any titles, Johnny?'

Cherry smirked. 'Not *Woman's Own.*'

'I get you. Top-of-the-shelf stuff?'

'Mostly.'

'Then he goes upmarket into educational publishing and only recently branched out on his own.'

'Was the Blacker List a public company?' someone else asked.

'No. He owned the whole thing, put some money of his own into it and took out a loan. How long he would have survived like this we don't know, because a publisher employs loads of specialists: designers, editors, proofreaders, printers, salespeople.'

'And the writers.'

'Well, his idea was to get the writers to cover the cost. It's known as vanity publishing. Believe it or not, there are millions of people whose greatest ambition is to see themselves in print. Personally, I'd rather spend my money on a really good cause like shopping in Knightsbridge, but we're all different. Vanity publishing is okay by me so long as the writer knows what he's getting into. Blacker's writers didn't. We're holding a first-time author called McDade who was asked for five grand shortly before his book was due for publication. He didn't pay up and he was dumped. You nicked him, Johnny. Maybe you'd like to say some more.'

DI Cherry looked as if he'd prefer to say nothing, but there was no get-out. 'When we charged him he was looking bang to rights. He'd been to the house and had a run-in with Blacker on the day of the fire, and he's got form as a fire-raiser. There wasn't anyone else in the frame.' Cherry hesitated and cocked his head, as if listening to his own voice played back to him. 'However, these other fires have raised a few doubts.'

'Cue another fire,' Hen said. 'This one may appear to be unrelated. There's a link that I'll explain.'

The remains of the boat house appeared on screen with wisps of smoke still rising from the damaged roof.

'Not a private dwelling, but one of the two boat houses used by the local canoe club. It's beside the canal, a stone's throw from here. A week ago last Friday a middle-aged woman called Amelia Snow takes a call from a voice she doesn't recognise. Male. The caller says he can prove Maurice McDade is in the clear if she'll meet him at the boat house at eight next morning. I should explain that McDade is the chairman of the Chichester Writers' Circle and Miss Snow is the secretary. An extremely loyal secretary. But she's also a canny lady and she asks someone else to go in her place. He's Bob Naylor, a Parcel Force driver who recently joined the circle. Naylor gets there as arranged. The door's open, so he goes in. Through this end.'

She shone a point of light at the screen.

'Soon as he's inside, the door slams behind him. It's a

161

strong metal door and there's no way he can force it open. In minutes, the building is on fire. Some kind of accelerant was placed in the space under the floor and it spreads quickly. Luckily Naylor is pretty fit and climbs up a boat rack and batters his way out through the roof with a canoe paddle. According to his statement he saw no one.'

A long shot of the exterior, showing the hole in the roof and the blackened source of the fire in the space below the building.

'It's safe to assume Miss Snow wouldn't have got out of the boat house if she'd acted on the phone call herself. She was wise, or lucky, to ask Naylor to go in her place. Her luck ran out a week later when her dinky little town house went up in flames with her inside.'

The shell of Miss Snow's house appeared on screen.

'The fire service categorised this as a fire out of control. They were called too late to make any difference, except to limit the damage to the neighbours. A clock in the kitchen stopped at four twenty a.m., so it's a fair estimate that the fire-raiser struck up to thirty minutes before that. I went to see the building this morning. You often hear the word "gutted" used about a fire. In this case, it's accurate. There's nothing left inside except ash and some objects that resist fire. The conditions were special. A mixture of convection and radiation produced an effect known in the service as a firestorm. All that's left of Miss Snow is a few powdery bones, including parts of the skull.'

'And the teeth,' Stella Gregson prompted her.

'And the teeth. We're checking them against dental records.'

'Do we know where the fire started?' a sergeant asked.

'Front door, same as the fire at the cottage. Forensics are checking to see if the same accelerant was used.'

'Witnesses?'

'None so far, which is surprising in a built-up area like

this, but Chichester isn't exactly a hub of night life. We'll be making the usual appeals for information. It was on local telly and radio and that may help.' Hen switched off the video. 'To sum up, we have two victims, one near-victim, and a suspect, and all four have a connection to this writers' circle.' She turned to a DC in the front row. 'What do they do in a writers' circle?'

'Write, ma'am?'

'They can't spend all the time writing.'

'Do they drink?'

'*Do they drink?* All the writers I've ever heard of are winos, and most of them are weirdos as well. However, we're dealing with part-timers here, so they may not all have got the habit. Johnny, how often does this circle meet?'

'Once a month,' Cherry said. 'In the New Park Centre. Blacker gave them a talk at the July meeting. We've got it on video. They did it themselves.'

'Useful. I'll watch it after this. And was that the last meeting they had?'

'Last but one. August was the last proper meeting.'

'The last proper meeting. Do they have improper meetings?'

Laughter.

'There's a serious point here,' Hen said. 'The meetings certain individuals have outside the regular meetings could be the key to this. For example, Amelia Snow must have met the Parcel Force driver to persuade him to go to the boat house in her place. What was going on between those two? Was someone else made jealous?'

Cherry said, 'Unlikely.'

'Why do you say that, Johnny?'

'Miss Snow was an old maid.'

He regretted it.

'As opposed to a nice bit of skirt?' Hen said. 'Or a dolly bird? Or crumpet? I thought you people might have got the message that I don't do labelling. How many are in this circle?'

163

'Eleven now.'

'That's eleven potential suspects, right, and each one is an individual. So we're not calling them old maids or fat gits or, em . . .'

'Winos and weirdos, guv?' Stella Gregson said.

After a moment's extreme tension, Hen's lips softened into a slow smile. 'Thank you for that, Stell.' She made the shape of a gun with two fingers and pointed it at the side of her head. 'Let's all agree to treat them as human beings, shall we? We're going to get to know them, who their friends are, what they do for a living, where they live and what sort of writing they do. From now on, this is the incident room. I want the usual display board on this wall with all the names on it. Pictures, too, if poss.' She paused, and looked around the room. 'As for you lot, you're just a faceless murder squad, so you're going to get labels. Johnny, you're my office manager. Get us up and running today. Stella is my admin officer. I'll also be appointing a receiver, an action allocator, statement readers and indexers. Cheer up, kiddos. This could be a positive experience. At this point, I'm going out for a smoke. Ten minutes – and then I want your theories.'

Hen's smoke was a small cigar. The bliss on her face as she took the first deep drag left no doubt that this was serious dependence. 'How did they take it, Stell?'

Stella Gregson was a non-smoker used to standing among the fag ends with her boss. 'Mr Cherry's pissing his pants that you've taken over, but no one else seems to mind.'

'He thought the case was done and dusted.'

'Are you going to talk to the guy he nicked?'

'Have to. I'll read the paperwork first. It should be a feature of this case, the paperwork. Instead of "I am John Smith, unemployed, and I was proceeding up the street" we're going to get stuff like "Last night I dreamt I went to Manderley again". Some of the statements could be worth a fortune in years to come.'

Stella smiled. '"It was a bright cold day in April, and the clocks were striking thirteen."'

'Who wrote that? We don't want crazy stuff.'

'George Orwell. *Nineteen Eighty-Four.*'

'As long ago as that?' She spoke without a smile. Stella would never know if she was serious.

'Right,' she said to her murder investigation team, 'you've heard from me. I want some input from you now. Why does a decent, clean-living little lady like Miss Snow get incinerated?'

No one was rash enough to speak.

'Come on. You've had longer to think about it than me,' Hen said. 'A semi-retired accountant who also does a bit of charity work. Secretary of the writers' circle.'

The keeno, DC Humphreys, decided this was the moment to redeem himself. 'An accountant gets to know a lot about a person's finances. Could someone have panicked that she knew too much?'

'Someone with money problems? Good thought. Do we know whose accounts she managed?'

DI Cherry said in a dismissive way, 'Only a few clients she'd known for years.'

'Like?'

'Like Miss Peabody's, the private dress shop in Crane Street. I'm certain Miss Peabody doesn't have a money problem. Neither does the dentist, Michael Wheatley-Smith, nor the podiatrist, Anita Jacques.'

'Podiatrist?'

Stella said, 'Feet, guv.'

'Have you looked at any of these people's balance sheets?' Hen said to Cherry.

'No need. In Chichester, we know who's doing okay.'

'So what other accounts was she auditing?'

'Probably looked after the women's refuge she supported. She'll have done that without a fee.'

DC Humphreys said, 'Maybe she'd taken on someone else we don't know about. I was thinking how convenient it would be if the accounts were dodgy and they went up in the fire at the same time as she did.'

'Good thought, too,' Hen said, 'only let's not forget the killer had two tries. The first time, Miss Snow was invited to the boat house. There weren't any account books stored there, far as I know.'

A sergeant at the back said, 'Here's another theory, ma'am. You said she worked in the refuge. You get some hard cases ending up in those places. Junkies, alcos, illegals, you name it. What if one of them decided Miss Snow was a soft touch, and it turned out she wasn't?'

'You mean they tapped her for cash and she refused?'

'She could have threatened to report them.'

'Now that isn't bad,' Hen said, 'not at all bad. We know she visited the refuge and helped there, as well as working in the shop. It would explain the trap at the boat house, and the fire at her place. My problem with this theory is the lure, the call she took asking her to go to the boat house. The reason she was hooked is that the caller talked about proving Maurice McDade was innocent. How would anyone from the refuge know about her link to McDade? He wasn't in the papers at this point.'

'It was on local radio.'

'Was it, indeed? I didn't know that.'

Stella said, 'For starters, guv, why don't we focus on the people who knew McDade was being held?'

DC Humphreys said, 'The circle.'

'And a few others. McDade has a partner, I understand. Some of the circle may have talked to friends and families.'

'Okay,' Hen said, 'but there's another factor, isn't there? The killing of Amelia Snow is a carbon copy of Edgar Blacker's murder. I'm hoping forensics will tell us the same accelerant was used. Certainly both fires were started at the front door.'

'And by night,' Stella said. 'Are you saying Miss Snow was killed for the same reason as Blacker?'

'I'm saying the evidence points to one killer carrying out both murders. The reason may be less straightforward. You sometimes find a second murder being done when the killer gets panicky and thinks someone is on to him.'

'Was Miss Snow a bit of an amateur sleuth, then?'

'Like Miss Marple? Let's find out. Tomorrow evening I want to try something rather novel. I'm calling a special meeting of the writers' circle. When they've assembled at their usual place I'm going to tell them what the evening is all about. Then we'll bus them round here and interview every one of them, all in one evening.'

'What if they refuse, guv?'

'They won't. It's their chance to prove they had nothing to do with it. And the killer won't want to draw attention to himself – or herself – by opting out.'

'Some of them may be able to prove they're in the clear,' Humphreys said.

'I hope so. I've never had so many suspects. Any with alibis that check out will get a free lollipop from me.'

'We don't have enough interview rooms,' DI Cherry pointed out straight-faced, in case anyone should think he was getting pleasure from gumming up the works.

'Then we'll do it in relays. You'll each be assigned to one or more of these geniuses and armed with a list of questions. But don't let that inhibit you, or them. Encourage them to talk about themselves. They're storytellers. The results should be – what's the word I'm looking for? – unputdownable.'

Maurice McDade was watering the vegetable garden at Ford Prison when Hen arrived with a silver-haired DC at her side.

'Put down the hose, Mr McDade. It makes me nervous.'

He handed it to someone else. The three made themselves as comfortable as a low stone wall allowed. Hen offered

McDade one of her small cigars, but he was a non-smoker. She lit one herself. There were advantages to doing an interview outside.

'I don't know how much you've heard,' she said after introducing herself and the DC.

'About Miss Snow? I saw it on the news.' McDade had an earnest, confidential manner. On remand he was allowed his own clothes, a striped shirt and well-pressed fawn trousers. Hen reckoned he was not much over fifty, a tall, decent-looking man with an accent that would get him into the stewards' enclosure at Henley. But she wasn't going to forget his record.

'Devastating, I should think,' she said, wondering how the death of his friend played against the prospect of an early release.

He nodded. 'She was a gentle soul. I don't understand it.'

'It's the gentle souls who cop it, Mr McDade.'

'Is it certain she was murdered?'

'Well, it wasn't an accident for sure. How long had she been secretary of the circle?'

'Since the start, two years ago. She was very good at it. Kept me up to the mark. I relied on her a lot.'

'Whose suggestion was it to invite Edgar Blacker to give a talk?'

'That was down to me, one letter I didn't ask Miss Snow to write. To be honest, I was basking in my success a bit. Wanted the others to see that I actually had succeeded in netting a real, live publisher.'

'Instead of which, he'd netted you.'

He rolled his eyes upwards. 'As it turned out, yes.'

'Let's get back to Amelia Snow. You must have met her before the circle was founded.'

'Why do you say that?'

'Well, if she was your secretary from the start . . .'

'She wasn't one of the founders. Dagmar and Naomi were

168

my co-founders. I met Miss Snow at the first meeting, after we'd put a letter in the *Chichester Observer*.'

'I'm interested that you keep referring to her as Miss Snow. You must have known her well enough to use her first name.'

'Yes, it's difficult to explain. She had a ladylike manner, and it would have seemed crass to address her any other way.'

'Maybe she secretly wanted to be called Amelia.'

'I don't think so. She was immensely proud of her surname. She was writing a book about famous people called Snow.'

'Did she show it to Edgar Blacker?'

'He spoke well of it. Compared her to Lytton Strachey.'

'Lit on what?'

He looked pained, like a schoolmaster disappointed with an answer. 'One of the most famous of all biographers. Blacker said Miss Snow's book reminded him of Strachey, except that she wasn't so critical of her subjects. But that was the whole point with Strachey. He really wielded the hatchet on some Victorian demigods like Florence Nightingale. I couldn't see Miss Snow doing that.'

'So was he being sarcastic? Blacker, I mean.'

'I'm afraid so. He wasn't a nice man, as I discovered.'

'He let you down badly.'

'I'm sure it was calculated.' His voice took on a harder note. 'He'd buttered me up for months and he waited until almost the eve of publication before demanding extra money. A "cash-flow crisis". I was sure to recoup it all in royalties, he said blithely. I'm not a complete mug. I refused. Well, you must have read my statement. We had the mother and father of all rows and I walked out. I can't begin to tell you what an effort that took when I was so near to having the book in my hand. My book.'

'*Great Unsolved Murders?*'

'The title is *Unsolved*.' A faint smile. 'A single word gets larger letters on the cover.'

'Good thinking.'

'And now you're going to say what all the other policemen said, that I must be the world's leading expert on getting away with murder.'

She took her time over answering. This was a man skilled in using words. 'No, but I'm going to ask for your opinion. You've had plenty of time to think about it. Who's the arsonist?'

Maurice McDade shook his head. 'No use asking me. As a matter of fact I asked for the printer to insert a large question mark above the heading of each chapter. I don't go in for theories. That's up to my readers.'

If and when you ever get any, Hen almost said, tempted to prick his complacency. 'Put it another way, then. Some of the people in the circle took a dislike to Edgar Blacker. Should any of them be on my list of suspects?'

'You need more than just dislike to carry out a murder.'

'Which is why you're on remand, Mr McDade. You're the one he shafted.'

'You won't get me to point the finger at my fellow writers.'

'And that's why you're here,' Hen said. 'We don't have another serious suspect.'

He took a step forward and his voice rose sharply. 'But it's about my innocence, not their guilt. Look, I couldn't have started the fire at Miss Snow's. I was locked up here.'

'You haven't been charged with the fire at Miss Snow's. Can you help me with that?'

Now he was making a huge effort to sound more calm. 'I'll say this much. She rubbed shoulders with some desperate people.'

'At the refuge, you mean?'

'Yes, she took it upon herself to help them in whatever way she could. It wasn't just a matter of raising funds in the charity shop. She was often at the refuge itself, trying to counsel the clients, or whatever they're called. It did cross my mind that if one of those people confided in her, told her about a crime, for instance, and later panicked, they could have decided killing her was the only remedy.'

'We're looking into that, Mr McDade, but thanks for mentioning it. Did you hear anything from Miss Snow after your arrest?'

'Only at one remove. My partner mentioned on the phone that Miss Snow was doing all she could to secure my release. She and Dagmar and Thomasine.'

Hen played ignorant. 'Let me get these names clear in my head. Dagmar was one of the founders?'

'Yes, with Naomi.'

'Which one is Thomasine?'

'Thomasine O'Loughlin. A splendid woman, salt of the earth. She contributes so much, and in a positive way. Writes some rather good erotic poetry as well. I'd expect her to take the initiative.'

'Is that typical of erotic poets, then?'

'The initiative in proving my innocence.'

'It's all right, Mr McDade. I was being flippant. You also mentioned Naomi. Is she one of your supporters?'

'Naomi? She's more of a lone wolf. No, that's unkind. Her intentions are good, I'm sure, but she has an off-putting manner. I can't see her teaming up with anyone else, not the women, anyway.'

'Off-putting in what way?'

'Hard to explain. I always feel there's a mountain of resentment behind Naomi. She knew straight away that Blacker was bluffing when he said he'd read her book on the Sussex witchcraft trials and it was timed just right for the current fascination with the occult. She asked him straight out if he'd actually read it. Believe me, if you're eye to eye with Naomi you back down. He moved on rapidly to someone else.'

'Tell me about Dagmar, then.'

'Little Dagmar. A delightful person. Very serious, very earnest. Of Austrian or German stock, I would think. But she has this other side you'd never dream of until she mentions she's written twelve steamy romances as Desiree Eliot.'

'Written and published?'

'Not published yet, but I'm sure her chance will come. They could be a goldmine for an enterprising publisher, all those novels written already.'

'Are they good?'

'Who can tell, except the kind of person she's writing for? Romantic writers, more than any others, have to hit the spot, if you understand me.'

Hen thought she did, and managed to keep a straight face.

'It's a huge market,' he said, 'and to my admittedly inexpert ear, Dagmar's writing is equal to the challenge.'

'Did Blacker agree?'

'He said he'd shown her script to a friend who devoured it at a sitting. He was sounding very bullish about it until she mentioned she had eleven more that she'd been hawking around the publishers.'

'Without so much as a nibble?'

'Not up to now.'

'When Blacker heard this he went into reverse?'

'Well, yes.'

'Disappointing for Dagmar.'

'Shattering – but I must tell you she's a gentle soul. It wouldn't enter her mind to turn to violence.'

'You're being very helpful.' And Hen was being very arch – considering she'd looked at the video of Blacker's talk only a couple of hours before. 'There's an even more delicate flower in your little bunch, and I'm trying to think of her name.'

'Jessie Warmington-Smith.'

'That's her.'

'The widow of the archdeacon. Writes letters to *The Lady*. She's spent many years compiling a book of useful hints for everyday living. It had the working title "Tips for the Twentieth Century", and of course she had to update it after the millennium, but unfortunately some of the tips are more suitable for the nineteenth century than the twenty-first.'

'How to water your aspidistra?'

He grinned. 'I must give Blacker some credit here. He dealt with her gently. He suggested including tips on text messaging and suchlike. She wasn't impressed.'

'Struck him off her visitors' list?'

'Very likely.'

'And she'd be capable of lighting a fire. It's got to be in the chapter on household hints.'

No smile this time. 'I can't see Jessie on the streets at night with a can of petrol.'

'Why not? What was it Shakespeare said about a woman scorned?'

'I understand you, but I think it was Congreve, not Shakespeare.'

'All right, darling, have it your way. If being relaxed on the streets at night is a factor, I guess we have to look at the blonde bimbo.'

'Young Sharon?'

'What did Blacker say to her?'

'Nothing. She didn't submit any work.'

'The least likely, then?'

He frowned. He'd missed the point.

She said, 'In my job, they're the ones you're supposed to suspect the most. What brought Sharon to the circle in the first place?'

'She just turned up one week. She does day release at the local tech, I think. Maybe the tutor sent her to us. She wants to be a fashion writer, she says. She's quite a good artist, going by what she does in her notepad.'

'Does she join in the discussions?'

'Hardly at all. I do my best as chair to draw her in. It's early days. It's good to see young people joining, so we don't want to put her off.'

'I wonder what she gets out of it,' Hen said. 'When she first came, had you already programmed Edgar Blacker to give you a talk?'

He thought for a moment. 'We must have. We publish our programme in January. Sharon joined in the spring.'

'So she could have heard about it?'

He shrugged. 'It's no secret. The programme is on the notice board at the New Park Centre and in the library. That's how a lot of our members find out about us.' He looked across the vegetable patch towards the man with the hose, who was built like a gorilla. 'I ought to get back to the watering. It's not a good idea to impose on the other inmates.'

'I won't keep you much longer. There's a lady you haven't told me about.'

'I thought we'd been through them all.'

'Your partner.'

'Fran?' He looked away again and passed a hand through his hair. 'She isn't in the circle.'

'I know, but she's in *my* circle.'

He frowned as her meaning got home to him. 'You don't have to worry about Fran. She's incorruptible. Please leave her alone.'

'She has as much reason as you to have been angry with Blacker.'

'She didn't know him at all.'

Not knowing him could have made killing him easier, but Hen chose not to point this out. 'You don't mind me saying, I hope: there's quite an age gap between you.'

'So?'

'I wondered how it came about.'

'I was unhappily married for years. We separated and things

174

went from bad to worse. That business with my neighbour, and the spell inside. The divorce was . . . horrible. When I met Fran her gentle personality, her honesty, was like a revelation. She understood what I'd been through. She helped me put my life together again.'

'We know about Fran's first marriage, Mr McDade.'

'Oh God, spare us that! She made a mistake and got hitched to a criminal when she was just eighteen. He was put away with the rest of the gang almost forty years ago. You've got nothing on Fran.'

'True,' Hen said. 'Nothing at all.'

'She could have said I was at home on the evening of the fire, but she didn't. You get the truth from her. If she'd gone out that night and started the fire herself she'd tell you. You wouldn't even have to ask. She'd be round at the police station and telling you all about it the same night.'

'Remarkable,' Hen said. 'I wish there were more like her.'

'She's unique.'

She dropped the butt of her cigar and flattened it with her shoe. 'Better get back to your hosing.'

His face creased in disappointment. 'Aren't you going to let me go?'

'Not so simple,' Hen said. 'There are formalities. You were sent here by a magistrate. I'll have to explain what the hell the police were up to, and I'm not sure I know. I only started in the job this morning.'

15

I never came across a situation so dismal that a policeman couldn't make it worse.

Brendan Behan on New York's *Open End TV Show* (1959) and quoted in *The Sayings of Brendan Behan*, ed. Audrey Dillon-Malone (1997)

Pressganged into being spokesman for the circle, Bob had no chance to prepare. He spent the rest of that day and next morning fielding questions from national and local papers, as well as radio and TV people. It was jaw-dropping what some of these journos asked. Did Miss Snow have children? Affairs with clients? Was she gay?

Miss Snow?

The hardest part was giving the impression that he knew all about the poor woman. By the third or fourth interview he'd worked up a routine that seemed to satisfy them. Yes, she was a quiet, conscientious lady who doubled up as secretary and treasurer of the circle, and would be hugely missed. She was a chartered accountant. Even after retirement she'd continued to audit the books of several Chichester businesses. She was very committed to helping the women's refuge, serving in the charity shop and helping out at the house the refuge used. Any spare time was devoted to the book she was writing about famous Snows.

He didn't mention that call inviting her to the boat house. Up to now the press hadn't fully grasped the link between all three fires, and he was damned if he wanted to be put through the grinder about his own adventure.

Just when he was thinking of taking no more calls, Thomasine phoned.

'You're a star,' she said. 'No one else could have done it. I heard you on the car radio when I was driving out to Zach's. Writers' circle ten, nosy interviewer nil.'

'More like one all and playing extra time,' he said. 'What's the dope on Zach?'

'He was uncomfortable about leaving the meeting halfway through. I've got my suspicions. Anton was probably right. Those two are up to something.'

'Zach and Naomi? It's an odd pairing.'

'I know, but if she wants to use Zach, he's putty in her hands. She terrifies most men. Terrifies me sometimes.'

'Use him for what?'

'What Anton was on about. Recycling all this drama as the raw material for storylines.'

'I didn't think Naomi wrote stories. She does facts, doesn't she, the truth about witchcraft and such?'

'Yes, but Zach is the storyteller. He can wrap anything up in words and make it sound exciting.'

'Do you think so? When he read out bits of his novel I was turned right off.'

'He's the best we've got.'

'Do Zach and Naomi know anything we don't?'

'I get the feeling they do. There's something going on, Bob.'

'So what next? Do we tackle Naomi?'

'She's next, yes.'

He gave an insincere sigh. 'What a pity I'm so busy with all these press interviews.'

* * *

DI Cherry was a foot taller than Hen and showing resentment that she'd taken over this investigation, but in her philosophy the bigger they came, the easier they were to shoot down. 'What do you mean, "it's missing", Johnny? It was on the video.'

He shrugged. 'I checked all the evidence bags, and it isn't among them.'

'Was it ever?'

'Pardon?'

'Was the picture of Blacker and the other man ever removed from the bedroom and bagged up?'

Now he looked over her head, as if the strip lighting had a fascination for him. 'I thought it was. Can't be a hundred per cent certain.'

'Didn't it interest you as the senior investigator?'

'I was focusing on the seat of the fire downstairs.'

'The front door?'

'Yes.'

'And when you finished focusing downstairs did you look in the bedroom?'

'Sure, and we collected a lot of stuff, like his sleeping tablets and the clothes he'd been wearing.'

'They were hanging over the chair?'

'Right. You can see them on the video. It was taken before we disturbed anything. You can see the clothes if you want. His wallet. His credit cards.'

'Are we on the same wavelength, Johnny? Just now, all I want to see is that photo.'

'I get you. I'm not being stroppy. I was at my desk at eight this morning.'

Hen had shown up closer to nine thirty. 'Early riser?'

'No. I need the alarm to wake me at six thirty. I fit in my swim before I get here. I've always believed in leading by example.'

She ignored the taunt. 'Is it possible it's still hanging on the wall in what's left of the cottage?'

'I suppose it could be.'

'Then I suggest you retrieve it pretty fast and bring it here.'
After he'd gone she turned to Stella. 'What a bullshitter. I
asked him earlier if we had it and he told me we did.'

'In fairness, guv, he wasn't quite so categorical as that.
You asked him if it was bagged up and he said it must have
been.'

'Shifting the blame. He'll come down like a ton of bricks
on some hapless scene-of-crime officer. *Leading by example.*
So far, I'm not impressed with our Mr Cherry.' She called
across the incident room, over the heads of the civilian staff
entering data into computers, 'DC Humphreys.'

A startled face surfaced. 'Ma'am?'

'"Guv" will do, thank you. How many of the writers' circle
have you contacted about the meeting?'

'All but three . . . guv.'

'And who are they – the ones you haven't reached?'

'Zach Beale. He hasn't turned up at work yet. And Naomi
and Basil Green. I left a message on their answerphone.'

'Everyone else is signed up?'

'Yes, guv.'

'Chase up the Greens, then. And Zach.'

Another officer called. 'For you, guv.' He held up a phone.
'Forensics.'

Hen put it to her ear. 'You've got results for me?'

'Is this DCI Mallin?'

'It is.'

'Pauline Cooper, forensic odontologist, concerning the
remains found in the fire in number seven, Tower Street.'

'Yes?'

'I was asked to compare the teeth of the deceased with
the dental records of Miss Amelia Snow.'

'And?'

'As I'm sure you're aware, the skull recovered from the
fire was severely burned and disintegrating in places but

the jawbones were intact. Teeth withstand intense heat better than any other parts of the body. These were in good enough condition for me to make a comparison. I'm satisfied that we have a match with the records of Miss Snow. The number and positioning of the fillings – and there are eight – and two extractions, are more than sufficient statistically to establish identity beyond reasonable doubt.'

'I can't tell you how grateful I am,' Hen said. 'There wasn't much else to go on.'

Ms Cooper wasn't the chatty sort. It seemed to be a point of pride in the Forensic Science Service that they never revealed satisfaction in work well done, but this was a human being on the end of the line, not a cipher, and she deserved her pat on the back.

But whatever she privately thought, Ms Cooper was unemotional to the end. 'I'll send you the written report shortly and a copy will go to the coroner. Someone else wishes to speak to you now. Hold on and I'll transfer you.'

Hen put her hand over the mouthpiece and said to Stella, 'What did I do to deserve this? Two forensic reports in one call.'

This one announced himself as the gas chromatographist, but for Hen's purposes he was the ash man, the fellow who'd sifted through the remains at the seats of all three fires. He started to explain how he went about separating components of hydrocarbons, but Hen asked him to cut to the chase.

'You want to know if the fires appear to have been started using the same materials?'

'In a nutshell, yes.'

'Fire number one, at the cottage on the Selsey Road, employed a liquid accelerant and saturated rags, and this appears to have been the case with the second and third fires, at the boat house and Tower Street. The agent was gasoline in all three cases, leaded gasoline. So the answer – in a nutshell – is yes.'

'Petrol?'

'Of course it vaporises quickly, but the fact that it was leaded was useful. You have a chance of measuring the lead content. We recovered enough through seepage to make comparisons and there's no doubt all three fires employed a similar grade with a good correspondence of the lead.'

'So we have a serial arsonist?'

'I just report our findings, chief inspector.'

'Okay, and it's up to me to interpret them. We have a serial arsonist.' After she'd thanked him, Hen turned back to Stella. 'You heard my side of it? Let's start getting this mess unscrambled, Stell. The guy on remand, Maurice McDade, has to be released a.s.a.p. and we'll need a magistrate's order. He's the only one of the circle who *can't* be the arsonist.'

Naomi had arranged to meet Zach in St Martin's tea rooms, a low-beamed seventeenth-century building reached from North Street by way of a passage called the Crooked S. Most patrons came for the tea, coffee and pastries, pricy but prizewinning, and unequalled in the city. Some may have been drawn by the beautiful waitresses, also unequalled. Naomi, however, had picked the place for its dimly lit interior and honeycomb layout, ideal for people not wanting to be observed. She'd chosen a table screened by tall settles and she and Zach sat close to the wall and facing each other. The secrecy suited Zach. He'd told his boss in the record shop that he was down with flu.

'What we've got now,' Naomi said, 'is a classic murder plot.'

'I guess,' Zach said.

'There's no guessing about it. Two deaths and a near death all connected with the circle. You and I are wonderfully placed.'

'I'm not so sure of that.'

'You're not so sure of anything this morning.'

'Wonderfully placed to get murdered.'

He could have been Basil, talking like that. Naomi didn't care for it. 'Get a grip, man. I'm talking about our e-book. Imagination and investigation striding side by side. You've started work, I hope?'

'I put down a few ideas.'

'Not on the website, you haven't.'

'I'm not ready for that yet.'

'Work in progress, man. It doesn't have to be perfect. I'll hear these ideas, anyway.'

He fingered his earring. 'Like you suggested, I'm trying to draft a story that begins in the past, with Blacker and the guy in the photo, his gay lover – as we assumed.'

'You can assume anything,' she said. 'You don't have to bother with the truth. It's up to me to unearth the facts and write them down – as I'm doing, on the website – and you'd better start soon. The killing of Miss Snow gives this a dimension I hadn't dared to expect, definitely a serial arsonist at work.'

'Seems so.'

'Come on, Zach. Don't tantalise. How does your story go?'

'I had a good look at that photo,' he said. 'The writing on the back says it was taken in 1982, over twenty years ago. It would have been neat if the other guy turned out to be a member of the circle, but I can't see any resemblance.'

'There's such a thing as artistic licence.'

He shook his head. 'I've already headed in another direction. In this version, he's the second son of a duke. I've called him Jason. The family are rich, but rich, filthy rich.'

She gave an approving nod. 'That's always good in a book.'

'A castle, a house in Belgravia and a place in the South of France. Edgar Blacker – may I call him by his real name?'

Now she gazed down at her coffee. 'Maybe not. We'll think about that.'

'For the time being?'

A pause, then, 'All right.'

'He asks to use one of the family homes as the background to a photo shoot for a magazine feature, and that's how he gets to meet Jason.'

Naomi nodded again, liking it. 'They are attracted to each other and . . .'

'Jason invites Blacker to share his penthouse in London. They're very close, those two. The next thing is, Jason's older brother – the heir to the dukedom – is killed in a boating accident.'

'Lovely. Drops overboard?'

'On a sea trip off the coast of France.'

'Is it murder?'

'Of course. Blacker is responsible. While the yacht was anchored in a big marina and everyone was sleeping, he came aboard and chloroformed the brother and dragged him out of the cabin and heaved him overboard. The body isn't recovered for several days. No one suspects Blacker. No one knows he was anywhere near the boat.'

'This is more like it,' Naomi said, reaching out to put a hand over Zach's. 'You have such a fertile imagination.'

'It never sounds so clever just describing the plot,' Zach said. 'It will grab you when I get it on paper.'

'On the web,' she corrected him. 'It grabs me now. Does he tell Jason what he's done?'

'Not yet. But of course Jason is now the heir. Blacker does all he can to cultivate the relationship. For a time everything is cool. Then there are problems. Blacker is taking too much for granted, bringing clients back to the flat to impress them. There's a suspicion he's pocketing money that Jason leaves around. They fall out, big time. Jason shows him the door. Blacker goes apeshit and tells Jason what he did to ensure he inherited. He says if the murder ever gets known he'll swear he was acting under orders from Jason. He demands a big pay-off, and gets it. Do you see now? That's the back story. It's all set up for the murder of Blacker some years later.'

'By Jason?'

'Yes. Maybe Blacker has surfaced again and wants a big handout to finance his publishing venture. Jason can see this blackmail going on indefinitely.'

Naomi's eyes glittered. 'So he goes out to the cottage one night and sets it on fire? This is where our two stories touch base at a point of reality. Mine will be a faithful account of all the known facts about the fire while yours has soared away into fantasy.'

Zach nodded. 'But I'm still not clear how this will look on a computer screen. What's the reader going to make of it?'

'We'll use different fonts to avoid confusion. Mine will be in bold.'

'Why not mine?' he said, challenging.

'Because reality has to be paramount. The reader needs a structure and I'm providing it. You can be in italics if you want.'

'No, I'll stay upright. It's easier on the eye.'

With that settled, Naomi got him back on track. 'Where does the story go next? Have you thought of a reason why the other fires are started?'

'It's got to be Jason covering his tracks. He's heard about Maurice being arrested and the whole thing about the circle. He panics a bit over Maurice. You see, he has a conscience and doesn't want someone else to go down for the crime he committed.'

'That's all right – except you can't use Maurice's real name. Don't want to run the risk of libel.'

'You just said it was all right to mention Blacker.'

'That's because he's dead. You can't libel the dead. Never

mind for now. We'll think of another name later. Go on. I'm hooked on this.'

'Jason finds out who the secretary of the circle is and makes the call to Miss Snow asking her to meet him at the boat house.'

'Why?'

'To make it obvious someone other than Maurice is the arsonist. But instead of Miss Snow, Bob Naylor shows up. Jason panics, thinking they must be on to him. He slams the door on Naylor and sets fire to the place. Naylor escapes through the roof, so no one is hurt.'

'You've really thought about this,' Naomi said with admiration. 'Now, what about the fire at Miss Snow's house?'

'That's Jason again,' Zach said. 'He's under tremendous pressure by this time because he made that call and he knows all the recent callers can be traced.'

'Why didn't he think of that before he made the call?'

Zach gave a shrug. 'Carelessness? This isn't a foolproof plot yet. So he decides to set her place on fire. He's in the clear and the spotlight shifts to the circle.'

'Not bad,' Naomi said. 'A few loose ends want tightening up, but you'll get there.'

'I'm not used to writing crime stories.'

'I said you'll get there,' she said with a touch of petulance.

'Okay. Are you going to tell me how you've been getting on?'

'You can read it on ChichesterMurderDetectives.com.'

'You're not putting everything on there, are you?'

She had a special smile for that question. 'Most of it.' She paused and looked to make sure they were not overheard. 'One thing I may not make public.'

'What's that?'

'I've got a mole.'

'A what?'

'A mole.'

Zach didn't know how to respond. Alarm bells sounded in his head. She'd taken her hand away from his, but her hormones had to be churning wildly. If she offered to show him the mole, he wasn't sure what he'd say.

'I said I've got a mole.'

'I heard you.'

'Don't you want to know where?'

'Tell me, then.'

'In the MIT.'

'Ah.' He nodded as if a mole in the MIT was a common complaint.

'You don't understand, do you? MIT is Murder Investigation Team. I've got a contact in the police station.'

Relieved, he heard himself say, 'Brilliant.' Then he added, 'Who?'

'You don't need to know. But I'll tell you this, Zach. There's a woman heading the investigation now and she's an ace detective specially brought in. Her name is Hen Mallin. She's already arranged for Maurice to be released.'

'That's good.'

She shook her head. 'Not good.'

'Why?'

'It means the rest of us are under the spotlight.'

Zach moistened his lips.

Naomi said, 'We're all going to be interrogated in the next twenty-four hours.'

'Christ.'

'Yes, DCI Mallin is a tough lady. She knows about the photo of Blacker and the other man.'

'How can she?' His eyes bulged. 'I've got it at home.'

'They always take a video of the crime scene. It was still hanging on the wall at the time.'

'We'd better hand it in.'

'No. That would make you and me the prime suspects.'

'It's withholding evidence. They can do us for that.'

186

'We'll take that risk,' Naomi said with calm determination. 'Just make sure it's well hidden in case they search your place.'

He was stunned. 'Would they?'

'Is there somewhere at work you could keep it?'

'Maybe – but I don't like the sound of this one bit. Can I give it back to you?'

'No,' she said. 'They could find my fingerprints at the scene. You've got no connection with the picture. It's better if it stays with you. Keep your nerve, Zach. This isn't the biggest crime in the world. I was starting to tell you about my discoveries. Remember I was going to check up on Bob Naylor?'

He gave a faint nod. He was trying to think of places in the MVC shop to hide the photo. Behind an Elton John poster?

'He's a Parcel Force driver. Lives with his fourteen-year-old daughter. His wife died four or five years ago. I haven't discovered why he came to the circle, except he may be looking for companionship. He doesn't seem to have written anything. Can't even use a computer.'

He heard himself say, 'Neither could Dickens.'

'What?'

'Charles Dickens.' He'd spoken off the top of his head, but it felt good to get one over Naomi. 'You can write a novel with a pencil and paper if you want.'

'Naylor doesn't look anything like a writer to me.'

'We don't all have beards and bow ties. I'd give him the benefit of the doubt.'

'He seems to have struck up a pretty strong friendship with Thomasine.'

'She's a friendly sort.'

'No question of that,' Naomi said with a toss of the head. 'We've all heard her erotic poems.'

'Are you saying Bob has some other motive?'

'In the absence of any literary aspirations, quite possibly.

187

Why does the man join a writers' circle if he talks like a bricklayer?'

'That's bitchy,' Zach said.

'*What* did you say?'

'Snobbish, then.'

'Not at all. He's behaving suspiciously. He sits there taking it all in and volunteers nothing. If my first thought is correct, and he just wants to pair off with a woman, a circle like ours is a good place to find one. But if he's getting privileged information about us, then we'd better watch out, all of us.'

'But you proposed him for press rep.'

'And for a reason, to get him into the open, see what he's really like. He can't go on acting the ingenue if we thrust him in front of the media. They'll get behind the mask.'

'You don't think he's the arsonist?'

'One of us is, and he's the one we know least about.'

Zach thought about that and took a sip of coffee. 'We don't know much about some of the others. Sharon, the hairdresser.'

Naomi said, 'Her?' in a tone of contempt.

'She says even less than Bob Naylor. The typical dumb blonde. What does she get out of the circle?'

'Perfecting her communication skills?' Naomi said.

Another bitchy remark, Zach thought, but this time he only said, 'That's a laugh.'

'There's scope for improvement.'

'She did tell us about this comic strip she's going to be working on. That was a surprise.'

'Diversionary tactics? I forget what we were discussing at the time, but it stopped us all in our tracks. Now why would a pretty little airhead like that take up arson?'

Zach looked across the room to see if anyone had overheard. He said in little more than a whisper, 'Is this going onto our website? It's a bit strong for publication, isn't it?'

'I'm not accusing anyone. I'm keeping an open mind,

simply recording everything people do and say, including the police.'

He held up both thumbs in approval.

She said, 'I was telling you we're all going to be questioned. You'll find a message on your answerphone summoning you to a special meeting tomorrow night.'

'What if I'm busy?'

She shook her head. 'We should both be there, Zach. We don't want to draw any more attention to ourselves. And you may be sure the killer will be there for the same reason.'

www.ChichesterMurderDetectives.com

Welcome to our website, created by Naomi Green and Zach Beale. Share in this unique project, the writing of a real crime e-book by two authors currently under investigation for murder. Read that again if you like. It is true. We are suspects in the Chichester arson attacks and also members of the writers' circle that is the focus of these crimes. We will give the inside account. You can read our work in progress, case notes, character studies and plot ideas essential to the creation of a book.

To learn more, left-click on any of the following:

- About ourselves
- Fires 1, 2 and 3
- Victims
- Suspects
- Latest developments

You chose **Suspects**. For legal reasons, their identities are encrypted. Not one of us has a decent alibi. You don't, when the murders take place at night. As if it's a beauty contest, I'll announce them in reverse order.

11. Yours truly
Well, it's not me.

10. Zed

He's my collaborator in this e-book and I've seen enough of him to satisfy myself he's not the arsonist. He was the only person to get unqualified encouragement from Blacker – *'a major work of the imagination . . . the new Tolkien'.*

9. The Chair

He was in custody when Fires 2 and 3 happened, so it's not him.

8. Greenfingers

My husband doesn't have the guts, and aside from that he had no quarrel with Blacker. He's not a serious writer.

7. Blondie

Though present at Blacker's talk, she submitted no work, and so received no criticism. Reveals almost nothing about herself except that she was commissioned to do a strip cartoon for the local rag. She doesn't hack it as a writer, or a possible killer.

6. Parcel Force

As a newcomer, he has to be regarded with suspicion, but wasn't present at Blacker's talk and apparently never met the man. Unlikely to have caused the fire at the boat house unless his version of events is a lie and a distraction. Brash, opportunistic and doesn't have the makings of a writer or an arsonist.

5. Archdeacon's Lady

A dark horse, obsessed by status, ready to faint from shock if anyone uses a four-letter word, but secretly lusting for the Chair. Nose put out of joint by Blacker rejecting her book of tips as old-fashioned. Capable of starting fires.

4. Nitpicker

Weird – and thinks he's wonderful. Treats the circle as a shooting party, picking off cliches like game birds. I've heard he does strange things on his computer. He'd be top of this list if he had a more obvious motive. But he offered no manuscript, so didn't get the rebuff from Blacker.

3. Passionella

Another of the Chair's groupies, and a tireless writer of steamy romances. No stranger to rejections, she had her hopes raised this time, then dashed when she revealed how many of her scripts have landed back on her doorstep. Was Blacker's 'I'll have to consult a colleague' the last straw? All those years of disappointment have to find an outlet.

2. Schoolmistress

Does her damnedest to be loved by one and all, so was the first to reel in Parcel Force the evening he turned up, and that's always been the pattern. Wears her faults on her sleeve, drinks too much and smokes too many, and delights in parading her libido in her poems. Men fall for it every time. And now she visits us in our homes, trying to solve the mystery. Methinks she doth protest too much.

1. Welshman

An attention-seeker with a vindictive streak. Had the biggest putdown of all by Blacker, not even getting his self-serving trash discussed in front of us. For a man of Welshman's self-importance, that was below the belt. We don't know what was said when he finally got his script back, but it wasn't complimentary for sure. When the Chair was pulled in by the police, Welshman was all too eager to cast him as the arsonist. Then there's this insurance connection. It may amount to nothing, but I intend to find out.

YOU ARE VISITOR [347] TO THIS SITE

17

What is Charity? A monk's cloak. Why? Because it covers a multitude of sins.

Erasmus, *Responsio ad Albertum Pium* (1529)

Hen took DC Shilling with her to the women's refuge instead of Stella. 'Poor souls don't get the chance to look at a man from one week to another,' she told Stella. 'One this size should do them a power of good. Let them know we're not a shrinking police force.'

The place was on the east side of the city on the Oving Road. They could have walked it in fifteen minutes, but Hen never walked anywhere when a car was available. On the drive out, she chatted to Shilling about nothing in particular and realised he was more than just a hunk. She liked his quirky humour. When she rang the doorbell and there was no immediate answer, he said, 'Do you want me to hoof the door in, guv?'

'It's a refuge.'

'Make 'em feel at home, won't it?'

A window opened above them and a woman leaned out and said, 'Who are you?'

Hen called up, 'Police,' and flashed her ID, even though it would be hard to see from upstairs. 'Show them yours,' she told her towering assistant. 'It's not me they're scared of.'

'Oh, dear,' the woman said, 'are we in trouble again? Just a minute.'

The door was opened by the public spirit of Chichester personified, dressed in a pink suit and white blouse with a ruff. She was Mrs Courtney-Andrews, she said, and they had to be careful about visitors. She gave Shilling a wary look.

When she'd shown them into the office she explained that it was policy to open their doors to anyone in trouble – anyone female and grown-up – and this was always leading to difficulties with the authorities. 'We used to get more visits from you – the police, I mean – when our intake was only battered wives. These days it's the immigration people asking about asylum seekers.'

'Illegals,' DC Shilling said.

'Not in every case.'

'They're the ones who interest immigration.'

'Plenty about,' Hen said.

'Well, yes, and most of them are desperate, poor souls. It's a double bind, isn't it? They can't ask for asylum unless they're in the country and the only way most of them can get in is illegally. They arrive in lorries and containers – well, I don't have to tell you, inspector. We don't turn them away.'

'And you don't turn them in,' Shilling said.

'Not when they've got this far, but we make it clear that they can't stay for long. We feed them up and give them any urgent medical treatment they need and send them on their way.'

'And do they leave willingly?'

'I wouldn't say willingly in every case but we try and persuade them that they must make room for the next ones knocking on the door.'

'Who does the persuading?'

'Basically, whoever is here. We're all volunteers.'

'The reason I'm asking is that Miss Snow was a volunteer.'

194

'Oh, it's about her, is it, poor darling? We were all so shocked at what happened to her.' Actually Mrs Courtney-Andrews looked as if the sun had come out again.

'I'm wondering if she had the job of moving someone on, and maybe they felt it was unjust and bore a grudge against her.'

The logic of this got home to Mrs Courtney-Andrews at once. Her eyes widened in horror. 'What a ghastly thought! But you can't be right. Miss Snow hasn't done any counselling lately. She's generous with her time, but most of it is spent in our shop in town. She wouldn't make enemies there.'

'But she does come in here?'

'Yes, she was an accountant, you know, so once a week she comes into the office here – silly, I'm speaking in the present tense, but I still can't believe this – comes into the office and deals with the bills and puts everything in order. I don't know who'll take over. We're going to need someone with business experience.'

'She looked after the chequebook?'

'Yes, it's kept locked in one of the filing cabinets with all our papers.'

'Do you have a key? I'd like to see.'

'I don't actually carry one, but . . .' Flushing a deep pink, she bent over and unrolled a corner of the carpet and picked a ring of keys out of a large knot hole in the floorboards. 'Not the best security, I have to admit, but what can you do when about twenty of us come and go and all need to get into the cabinets at some stage?' She unlocked the first cabinet. 'It's this one, I think. The others contain all the guest files. We call our ladies guests so that they don't get the idea they are residents.'

'Everyone is given a file?'

'Yes, but I can't allow you to look at them. We ask for everything, personal papers, passports, the lot. The information here is highly confidential.'

'And compromising,' Hen said.

'In certain cases, maybe. We've looked after hundreds of women since we opened ten years ago.'

'You're not on computer?'

'No, and I think it's sensible. This is more secure.'

DC Shilling's eyes popped wider. 'What, with the keys under the carpet and twenty helpers using the system?'

'Anyone can break into a computer,' Mrs Courtney-Andrews said as if to a child. 'Besides, this is easier for volunteers to manage. Imagine trying to read a doctor's handwriting. It's all stuffed into the files.'

'You have medical records here?' Hen said in surprise.

'Dr Borzukowski holds a special surgery one afternoon a week and Mr Wheatley-Smith the dentist comes fortnightly and we keep their records here because – between ourselves – it's done from the goodness of their hearts.'

'On the q.t.?'

'You could put it that way, I suppose. A number of our guests are scared of using the National Health Service.'

'What if they need hospital treatment?'

'Then they go to a private clinic, and we negotiate a fee. Listen, what I'm telling you mustn't go beyond these four walls. It's all done from the very best motives.'

'We'll take your word for that. Have you found the chequebook?'

Mrs Courtney-Andrews pulled open the bottom drawer. 'Here we are. Account books, bills, chequebook.' She lifted them out.

Hen took them to a desk and opened the main account book. It had been kept in a neat, small hand, each decimal point precisely positioned, the last entry eleven days ago. Tidy bookkeeping didn't automatically mean everything was in order, but Hen didn't have the training or the time to look for anything irregular in these figures. Still, she was glad she'd asked to examine them. Just seeing the neatness of the entries brought her closer to Amelia Snow. She reached for the chequebook and examined the stubs. Each one was fully completed, right down to the current balance, and that told her that the account was over two thousand pounds in credit.

She returned the books to the filing cabinet. 'Did Miss Snow ever speak about the writers' circle?'

'Was she a writer?' Mrs Courtney-Andrews said with interest. 'Well, you learn something every day. No, I had no idea. She never spoke of it. What kind of writer?'

'She was doing a book about the Snows, famous people who shared the same surname.'

'Fancy that,' she said in a tone that said she didn't fancy it one bit as a good read.

'I want to ask you about the charity shop, and how it works. You must have a schedule of helpers to run it. Is that organised from here?'

'No, it's all done at the shop. They do shifts of half a day each, usually two volunteers together. When there's a problem through illness or something we can send someone from here. Some of our guests have enough English to help out, and they enjoy it.'

'So Miss Snow didn't mind working with asylum seekers?'

'Why should she?'

'I didn't meet her,' Hen said, 'but you were suggesting she was rather a private person.'

'True, but she had a heart of gold. I know for a fact that she'd often invite them back to her house for supper before they returned here.'

Hen couldn't hold back any longer. That 'heart of gold' remark got to her. 'You people mean well, I'm sure, but do you have any idea of what you're encouraging? You talk about asylum seekers arriving in containers. Who put them there? Human traffickers, some of the nastiest criminals anywhere. Word gets around that there's a place like this where illegal immigrants can be quietly absorbed into the system. Organised crime gets to know about it and before you know where you are, you're being used by vicious, callous crooks who'd snuff you out as coolly as they kill anyone who threatens their operation. I'm sorry, I didn't come here with the object of closing you down, but I'm going to have to report what I've seen this morning.'

On the drive back, she was silent most of the way apart from a sigh or a shake of her head. Alert to her mood, Shilling said nothing until they drove into the police station car park. Hen already had an unlit cigar between her lips.

'Are you thinking Miss Snow was killed by a trafficker, guv?'

'No,' she said. 'I'm not.' The cigar jiggled as she spoke.

'An illegal?'

'No.'

'One of the volunteers?'

'Good Lord, no.' She had the lighter in her hand.

'Are we back to the circle, then?'

She lit the cigar and smiled. 'We're back to the circle.'

Bob Naylor was waiting in the East Street office of Steadfast Assurance. He'd just delivered six boxes of stationery sent down from their London head office, and he was supposed to pick up a parcel that wasn't ready.

'I'm sorry, Bob,' the receptionist said. She'd been in the job for years, and she knew him well. 'It's been one of those days.'

'How long will you be, love?' he asked. 'I'm up on the pavement in Little London. If a warden comes by, I'm shafted.'

She said, 'I thought you were sitting on the edge of my desk.'

'Ooh, we're sharp this afternoon.'

'It's Mr Hackenschmidt, my branch manager,' she said.

'He promised he'd have a package ready for collection. It's important, he says.'

'Hackenschmidt – is he new? I thought it was Mr Burnley who ran this place.'

'Not since last July. He retired.'

'Lucky man. And before that' – Bob started fishing – 'the Welsh guy, Tudor.'

'*Tudor*? He was never manager. He's just one of the agents.'

'I thought he was the chief honcho.'

She laughed. 'He acts like he is.'

'Doesn't he bring in most of the business, then?'

'You're joking.'

'He was telling me about some policy he sold to Edgar Blacker, the man who was killed in that fire at the cottage along the Selsey Road. Seemed to think it was a big deal.'

'That was four or five years ago,' she said. 'Anyway, it led to a hefty claim. Mr Blacker did very nicely out of it.'

'A fire?'

'No, a manuscript that was stolen from him. We'd insured it for a five-figure sum, over twenty grand, I think.'

'Must have been special.'

'It was a public school story by the writer of those Jeeves stories, about the butler. Do you remember his name?'

'It's on the tip of my tongue,' Bob said. 'How did Blacker come by a script like that?'

'He worked in publishing, didn't he? I suppose he found it in a file and took it home. If I remember right, it was unpublished.'

'And Tudor insured it?'

'Yes, after we'd had it authenticated by two experts. Inside a year it was stolen from Blacker's house.'

'Did your lot pay in full?'

'We had to.'

'Sounds like a scam to me.'

'Hard to prove. The manuscript hasn't been heard of since. Probably in New York or Tokyo by now. Blacker banked the cheque and started his publishing business.'

'Do you think Tudor was in on this?' Bob asked.

'Hard to say. If the bosses thought so, he'd have been sacked, so I guess he's innocent.'

The buzzer on her intercom went. She opened the door of her boss's office and presently returned with the package Bob was to take.

'Be seeing you, then,' he said when the paperwork was done.

'What made you ask about Blacker?' she said.

'Just interest.'

'Funny.'

'What's funny?'

'Just that I had someone else in here this morning. Said she was from the solicitors dealing with Mr Blacker's estate. She'd heard about the claim and wanted some more details, for probate reasons, she said. I told her what I've told you. That's why it's so fresh in my mind.'

'What was she like, this solicitor?'

'Scary, actually. Right in your face. Jet black hair and piercing eyes.'

Maurice McDade was released at four that afternoon and met by Thomasine and Dagmar, who drove him back to Lavant. His wife Fran was waiting at the open door and invited them in for a celebration drink.

'You two want to be alone,' Dagmar said. 'I think we'll leave you to it.'

'Just the one, then,' Thomasine said, and got a look from Dagmar.

Fran had baked a banana cake that Maurice said was his favourite, and they drank champagne in front of the Swiss mountains in the time-locked living room.

'This has all been so unfair,' Dagmar said.

'Yes, but I don't want to dwell on it,' Maurice said. 'I appreciate Fran and my home even more now.'

'We missed you,' Dagmar said. 'We tried to have a circle meeting and it wasn't the same. No disrespect, Thomasine. You did your best.'

'We'll soon get back to normal,' he said. 'It's important that we do.'

'We've been invited to a meeting tomorrow evening,' Thomasine said, 'but that's not a proper meeting, just a chance for that new Inspector Mallin to quiz us all.'

'It's thanks to her that I'm out,' Maurice said. 'I hope she clears up this mystery soon. I had plenty of time to think when I was inside. Until this experience I never fully appreciated what pain an unsolved crime can bring. I've written about all those cases as if there was some kind of glamour to them, the ongoing mystery of who did it. Now I know how important it is to get closure.'

'Closure with the right person arrested,' Thomasine said. 'There's another book to be written about all the poor sods who've been locked away for crimes they didn't commit.'

'True, but I've got faith in Chief Inspector Mallin.'

'You're very trusting. *Saintly* is the word that springs to mind.'

'And I don't think you should have another glass,' Dagmar said to Thomasine.

18

People who write fiction, if they had not taken it up, might have become very successful liars.

Ernest Hemingway, interviewed in *This Week* (1959)

In the dark-blue minibus carrying members of the circle from the New Park Centre to the police station, Anton was saying, 'I'm so grateful my old colleagues in the civil service can't see me now.'

'You want to try riding in a prison van,' Zach said.

'No thank you.' After a moment's further thought Anton spoke again. 'When were you in prison?'

'I wasn't. I was conditionally discharged.'

'What was the offence?'

'Disorderly behaviour.'

'Where?'

'In Storrington.'

'Storrington? That's no place to misbehave.'

'I didn't. I was protesting. The hunt came through there.'

'Ha – a saboteur. I should have guessed.'

Jessie Warmington-Smith said, 'Well, I'm dying of shame. I've never broken the law.'

Zach said, 'It's only a people-carrier, for fuck's sake.'

Jessie made a sharp sound, sucking in air through her teeth.

Anton said in a low voice to Dagmar, who was sitting beside him, 'You might think Zach is the only calm one among us, but take a look at his hands. He's got the shakes, poor fellow. I wonder what causes that.'

Tudor said, 'Keep your head down, Jessie. Isn't that the bishop looking over that wall?'

'Tudor. Enough!' Thomasine said in the voice she used to subdue the third years.

They were driven around Basin Road and into the forecourt of the police station where the CID officers were waiting, among them Hen Mallin, who had gone ahead in her own car. She'd met everyone at the New Park Centre and explained how the interviews would be organised. She'd made a powerful impact, courteous, but firm. No one had complained until she'd gone and they were all in the minibus.

Good shepherd that he was to his fellow writers, Maurice McDade had turned up and was there to help the older ones step down from the minibus. This thoughtfulness was typical of the man. The police hadn't asked him to come. There was no intention to interview him again.

In Interview Room One, Anton seemed to have decided to treat this as a civil service interview, presenting a confident posture, back straight, chin up and legs crossed at the ankles, hands (after checking his bow tie) clasped lightly one over the other, resting on his left thigh.

He needed to be alert. He was facing Hen Mallin, the senior investigating officer.

'Mr Gulliver, you joined the writers' circle soon after its formation, I understand,' she said with the gentle opener he expected.

'That's correct.'

'Yet by all accounts you don't contribute much in the way of writing. What do you get out of it?'

'The cut and thrust of the meetings. I'm well to the fore in the discussions.'

'Wouldn't a debating society be a better club for you?'

'Excellent suggestion,' he said, flattering his interviewer, a classic technique. 'Unfortunately I don't know of one this side of Portsmouth.'

'So you're content to be an observer rather than an active member.'

'In which sense?'

'If you don't write anything . . .'

'Oh, that doesn't matter a jot. Most of what is written isn't fit to be read out. I contribute by offering suggestions and praise where it's due, which it seldom is.' He gave a knowing smile to the silent constable seated next to Hen.

'But you had nothing to submit to Mr Blacker when he visited the circle.'

'That is correct.' Anton smiled. 'I can see where you're coming from now. Unlike most of the others, I wasn't held up to the light and judged. I had no reason to set Mr Blacker's house on fire.'

'Let's not race ahead here,' Hen said. 'It doesn't follow that you had no reason, just that you didn't have the same reason as some of the others. You could have set light to his place because you owed him money or he once insulted your mother.'

'Neither of which is true.'

'Or you have a pathological hatred of thatched cottages.'

'What makes you say that?'

'It's just an example. You care about architecture. You worked in the Department of Ancient Monuments, I gather.'

'That is about the first true thing you've said.'

'We're on course, then. I can look forward to some straight answers. Do cutesy old cottages upset you?'

'Not in the least, as it happens.'

'Did you know Mr Blacker prior to his visit?'

'Certainly not.'

'Your paths had never crossed?'

'To save you time, chief inspector, I am absolutely neutral about the late Mr Blacker. I neither liked the man, nor disliked him.'

'Where were you on the night he was killed?'

'That's some time back.'

'But you must have thought about where you were in case someone like me asked you to account for your movements.'

'True. I was at home.'

'All night?'

'Yes, and I can prove it. My sleeping pattern is somewhat erratic, so I was working on my computer until daylight. Then I went to bed for a couple of hours. I have a dedicated phone line and I can show you my statement.'

'I'm afraid all it shows is when your computer was online,' Hen said. 'It can't tell us if you were sitting in front of it. What do you do on the computer?'

'Sometimes I'm surfing the internet. Sometimes I'm making virtual models.'

'Models of what?'

'Buildings mainly.'

'Ancient monuments?'

'And modern.'

'Real buildings?'

'Yes.' He leaned towards her and took a less defensive pose with his elbows on the table and hands linked, the two forefingers touching his chin. 'It's a project with huge potential. I should think you would find it a godsend. I'm building up a street by street reference to central Chichester. If, for example, you had a report of a shoplifting incident in Woolworths, you could pinpoint North Street and get a picture of the shop on the screen and then actually go inside.'

'We'd want a picture of the shoplifter.'

'You're asking the impossible.'

'No. CCTV does it nicely,' Hen said. 'But I'm sure you

get hours of pleasure. Let's turn to the matter of Miss Snow's death. You knew her quite well.'

'She was our secretary and treasurer.'

'Were you on good terms with her? I got the impression there was some tension between you.'

'Nothing serious,' he said. 'She didn't like her mistakes in the minutes being discussed.'

'It's a thankless task, writing up minutes,' Hen said. 'I've done it in my time. The chairman asks if there are any corrections and it's open house for everyone who wants to hear the sound of his own voice. No disrespect, Mr Gulliver, but that's how it seems from the secretary's end.'

'And it's the secretary's end that you're investigating.'

Hen gave him the smile he seemed to expect for this piece of wit.

He said, 'But we were talking about the minutes and I say mistakes shouldn't be ignored.'

'Certain mistakes can. I'd say a lot can, and meetings would be shorter as a result. I can understand why Miss Snow would feel the criticism was directed at her.'

'We were always on civil terms.'

'I believe you. I'd have heard if you weren't. People are quick to point the finger, and they haven't. From all I hear, she was an inoffensive lady.'

'I agree with that.'

'Did you ever visit her house in Tower Street?'

'No.'

'I expect it's on your computer.'

'The exterior is. I don't put the interiors of private houses into my system.'

'That would be taking a liberty,' Hen said.

'That's why.'

'And did you have any professional dealings with her in her work as an accountant?'

'No. I told you, I was a civil servant.'

'Now retired?'

'Yes.'

'Presumably you still do a tax return. I was wondering if you got help with that.'

'I do my own. There's a simple computer programme.' He altered his posture again, sitting back with his arms folded, but he was well defended. He was enjoying the exchanges.

'Do you have any view who might have killed this inoffensive lady?' Hen asked.

He smiled and shook his head. 'You said people are quick to point the finger. Not in my case.'

Andy Humphreys, the detective constable who'd got off to such a bad start with Hen Mallin, was in Interview Room Two, stuck with an old bird called Warmington-Smith who had once been married to an archdeacon. She seemed convinced she was about to get the third degree, even though a female officer was present and doing her best to calm things down. It had taken a cup of hot, sweet tea and a biscuit and all of the Humphreys charm to induce the old dear to talk at all.

'Ever since it was formed,' she was saying in a stiff voice. 'I was one of the first members to join, at the personal invitation of the chair.'

'The chairman. Maurice McDade, right – the guy we had in custody?'

'The chair. We refer to him as the chair.'

'No problem. So you joined this writers' club in Chichester. That's a bit whacky, isn't it, a club for writers?'

She shifted her head to one side like a cockatoo. 'Whacky?'

'Weird, then.'

'Not at all. Writing is a solitary occupation.'

'You took the words out of my mouth,' DC Humphreys said.

'So it's all the more helpful to get together and compare

experiences. There are circles all over the country. One learns so much about the way others work. Quite practical things, like how to set out the manuscript. A publisher won't accept anything handwritten these days. It all has to be typed, double-spaced and on one side of the paper only. Then one hears important things about literary agents.'

DC Humphreys didn't want to hear about literary agents. 'You live in the middle of town, then?'

She blinked behind her bifocals. 'Is that significant?'

'You tell me, ma'am. It's a line of enquiry.'

'I can't think why.'

'You're in Vicars Close, right?'

'This is getting personal.'

'It's only your address I'm trying to confirm. Vicars Close, right behind the cathedral. All the tenants are church pensioners, right?'

She shifted in her seat. 'I can't think why my domestic situation should interest the police. My late husband spent a lifetime in the service of the church and he wouldn't have done it without my support.'

Humphreys held up a calming hand. 'All right, all right. Lighten up, dear. I'm not questioning your right to be there.'

'I should hope not, and I don't care for strangers calling me "dear".'

'No problem.'

'But it *is* a problem. Either it's patronising or it assumes an intimacy that doesn't exist.' Jessie put in a question of her own. 'Are you a church-goer?'

'Can't say I am, ma'am.'

'But I see you have a wedding ring. I expect you were married in church.'

'Well, yes,' he said, aware that this was getting away from him.

'Baptised, too, I dare say. People use the church when it suits them and then ignore it the rest of the time.'

'It's got nothing to do with this.'

'It's got everything to do with it, young man. We're all God's children, you know. He's here in this police station, in this interview room. Never neglect your spiritual side. I'm a very practical person. I've written a book on practical tips for everyday life. But I still allow the spiritual side to play a part in my life, and so should you.'

'If you say so,' Humphreys said, wanting to reclaim the initiative. 'Now can we move on?'

'Are you listening?' Jessie said. 'You have to open your heart. Then you'll be given signs. I get them quite often because I'm receptive, like Joan of Arc, except that she heard them as voices.'

Humphreys groaned inwardly. All of this was going on tape to be listened to later by Hen Mallin and the whole of the murder investigation team.

She wouldn't stop now. 'Only last night I had a sign. Some people would find it disturbing and I suppose it might be to a disbeliever, but I took it as affirmation of all I believe in, the afterlife, the journey of the soul.'

Humphreys had been accused already of being homophobic. He didn't want to come across as a persecutor of Christians as well. 'Ma'am,' he said with all the respect he could put into the word, 'I follow what you're saying, but this is supposed to be a witness interview. Where were you on the night of the fire in Edgar Blacker's cottage?'

'At home, I imagine.'

'That won't do, ma'am. It's no good imagining.'

'I don't. Too much imagination can addle the brain. I was using an expression of speech. I meant to say that I was certainly at home most of that evening.'

'Not all of it?'

'I'm trying to be helpful. I like to go for a walk before retiring, so I wouldn't have been at home the whole time.'

'A walk – just for exercise?'

'I don't visit public houses, if that's what you're implying. Exercise isn't the main purpose. I'm taking stock of the day. The streets are pleasantly quiet.'

'How late is this?'

'Oh, it can vary. At my age you don't always feel ready for sleep before midnight.'

'Don't you feel unsafe on the streets at night?'

'In *Chichester*? No. I don't go far. I'm always within sight of the cathedral spire.'

Humphreys thought of Miss Snow's house in Tower Street, only a stone's throw from the cathedral. But what about Blacker's place, out in the country?

'I was wondering if you went for a drive some evenings. You have a car, do you?'

'Yes, but I don't use it much, and certainly not at nights. If you're thinking I drove out to Mr Blacker's cottage and set it alight, you're mistaken. Why should I wish to kill him? He called my book of tips rather clever. He said he liked it very much. A fine idea.' She had the quotes right, but was silent about Blacker's other comments.

'But you do have a car? An old car?'

'Why do you want to know?'

'You said you don't use it much. I got the impression it was old.'

'It's perfectly legal to have an old car if it has a certificate.'

This was like handling a hedgehog. 'I'm not bothered what state it's in.'

'It's about twenty years old, a Mini Metro.'

'So it still uses leaded fuel, I expect.'

'Yes, and I'm aware that it causes pollution, but I do very little driving these days, so I'm not adding much to that hole in the ozone layer.'

'Where do you keep it?'

'In my garage. We all have garages out of sight of visitors to the cathedral. Why are you so interested in my old car?

I told you I wasn't using it that night. I just went for my usual walk about half past ten.'

In another interview room, Stella Gregson was trying to get straight answers from Tudor Thomas. She'd been warned that he would keep wanting to tell her about his friends in high places. Already he'd spoken of 'my old chum Paul', meaning Sir Paul Condon, the former commissioner of the Met, a not too subtle way of reminding Stella how low she was in the chain of command. But the follow-up was clever. He'd done enough homework to know that Sir Paul had served as Chief Constable of Kent and set up the arrangements for policing the Channel Tunnel. Details like that left open the possibility that he was speaking the truth.

'You work in insurance,' Stella said, 'and I believe Edgar Blacker was a client of yours.'

'Briefly,' Tudor said, for once downplaying a contact. 'And unmemorably. I barely recognised him when he came to speak to the circle.'

'I heard you insured him for quite a large amount.'

'Not him. An item of his property. And I wouldn't say large. I could tell you about policies far bigger than that one.'

'But there was a claim.'

'The item was stolen and we paid. That's what insurance is all about, officer.'

'Twenty grand, for an unpublished Wodehouse book, is that right?'

His eyebrows shot up. 'You know, then?'

'It's our job to make enquiries. This claim came under a lot of scrutiny at the time. Some of your superiors weren't happy.'

He made a dismissive gesture. 'It's always the way when we have to pay out.'

'Is it fair to say it blighted your career? There you are, the up-and-coming agent bringing in any amount of new business. A promotion to branch manager looked certain, but it didn't happen.'

'I'm still in the job. If there was any evidence of wrong-doing I'd be out.'

'No evidence. Suspicion.'

His face had turned a shade more pink. 'Who have you been talking to?'

'Blacker seems to have launched his own publishing business with the money he got from that claim. It all happened within a year.'

'We had two expert valuations for the manuscript. There's no question that it was genuine.'

'But was the theft genuine? I've seen the case notes. There were questions about the timing of the break-in and the absence of any traces of the thief.'

'A professional. He knew when to strike and how to get clean away.'

'Our people weren't so sure.'

'They'd say that, wouldn't they, if they found nothing?'

Stella smiled. 'They found something all right, a large chunk of rock from the garden, used to smash a panel of the window. A professional wouldn't rely on picking up a handy rock. He'd have his tools with him.'

'A clever opportunist, then.'

'You've been over this before, haven't you?'

'Yes, and I don't see what it has to do with the killing of Blacker or Miss Snow.'

'If you and Blacker had some arrangement and he reneged on it, or even if you felt he owed you something, you'd be pretty incensed when he showed no interest in your book.'

He turned a shade more pink. 'You know about that as well?'

'There was a video of his visit to the circle. I've looked at it. He refused even to discuss your script in front of the others. This – from a man who'd netted a small fortune thanks to you.'

'I expected no favours.'

'You got none. There was just a "see me afterwards" as if he was dealing with a schoolkid who hadn't done the homework. Humiliating for a man like you who's rubbed shoulders with the great and the good.'

'That's true, anyway. But it doesn't make me a murderer.'

'Big blow to your self-esteem.'

'It wouldn't be the first time. As my old friend Roger Moore once remarked to me, I have more bounce than any Bond girl he ever met.'

'Anything of note?' Hen said, finding Stella and Humphreys making tea.

'Warmington-Smith runs a Mini Metro on leaded,' Humphreys said.

'Does she, indeed?'

'And likes a walk late at night.'

'She wouldn't need to walk far to Miss Snow's.'

'And she's doolally as well. Sees things.'

'What things?'

'Like Joan of Arc, she says.'

'We'll take a look at that car, and the fuel. How's it going with Tudor, Stella?'

'Slow progress, guv. I'm pressing him on the insurance angle. He's as good as admitted his career went pear-shaped when Blacker made his claim on the missing Wodehouse script. I've yet to tackle him about Miss Snow.'

'Keep with it, then. Anton's going to be a long haul, too, as I expected. Teflon-coated, that man.'

'Try the blowtorch, guv.'

'I intend to.' First, she went to look at the circle members still waiting to be interviewed. No one was complaining at the delay. Maurice McDade's calming presence was a definite help. Even the volcanic Naomi was in a dormant phase, deep in some magazine article about the internet.

DI Johnny Cherry had drawn Sharon, the blonde, in this game and she wasn't the picture card she seemed. He'd already run through his limited knowledge of hairdressing and failed to spark a response. Writing seemed to interest her even less. She chewed steadily and watched him with her big, dark-lined eyes.

'Why did you join the circle, then?'

'Dunno.'

'You must have thought it would help your career.'

'Yeah?'

'Is it helpful, what they do at the meetings?'

A shrug.

'But I expect you get something out of it.'

'Dunno.'

'I mean, through talks and things. You went to the talk Edgar Blacker gave.'

'Did I?'

'The man who was murdered.'

'Oh, got you.'

'You didn't know him already, then?'

The eyes slid upwards in denial. How could she, young, blonde and gorgeous, possibly have entered the same orbit as an old fart like Blacker?

But Johnny didn't give up. 'I've seen the video, and you're on it. You seemed to be drawing – doodling really – while he was discussing the stuff that people had handed in. You didn't hand anything in yourself, I noticed.'

She gave another shrug and said nothing.

'Do you do any writing, Sharon?'

'Not really.'

'Apart from the speech bubbles in your strip?'

'Them, yes.'

'Based on things you hear in the salon?'

'Mm.'

'Well, it's all writing, isn't it? You have to know how to spell. It's going to be a nice little earner, this, from all I hear.' Pleased with himself for the smooth link to come, he said, 'You'll be able to buy a new car. What do you drive at the moment?'

'Nothing.'

'You don't have a car? How do you get around?'

'Friends.'

'You get lifts?'

'Sometimes.'

'Perhaps you borrow their cars. Can you drive?'

She nodded. 'If I need to.'

Johnny didn't have a link for his next question. It had to come out of nowhere. 'How well did you know Miss Snow, the woman who died in the fire?'

A slight frown. 'What do you mean?'

'Did you have any dealings with her outside the writers' circle?'

'Like work and stuff?'

'Anything. Any reason to meet her.'

'Well . . .'

He jerked forward. 'Is that a yes?'

'Mm.'

'Where? Where did you see her?'

'The salon.'

Progress at last. 'She came to you to have her hair done?'

'Sometimes.'

'And did she like to talk to you when she was in the chair?'

'A bit.'

A bit. And a bit one-sided, going by this experience. It was dawning on Johnny why he'd been paired with that rare being, a silent hairdresser – Hen's way of paying him back for his earlier gaffes. 'Did she have anything to say about the other members of the circle?'

'Might have.'

'What does that mean – might have? Either she talked about them or she didn't.'

'So?'

'So what did you learn?'

'Don't bother with their names, most of them.'

This was a pain. 'Okay, let's go at it another way. Did you do her hair before the Blacker meeting?'

'Mm.'

'That was a yes, was it?'

'She wanted it nice.'

'For the meeting?'

A nod.

'And did she pass any comment?'

'Asked if I was going.'

'Any comment on the speaker?'

'Said he was some publisher.'

'That's all? Had she met him before?'

'Didn't say so.'

Johnny sighed. He was near the limit of his patience. 'Talking to you, Sharon, I find it difficult to understand how you landed this job of writing the strip. Surely you need a good ear for dialogue.'

'What's that?' she said.

'Conversation. The things people say to you. You haven't told me anything Miss Snow said to you. How on earth are you going to fill in all the speech bubbles if you don't remember what people say?'

'Simple.'

'Yes?'

'It's a knack, innit?' Sharon said.

'Explain.'

216

'Keeping it short.'

And on thinking about strip cartoon dialogue, he was forced to admit that Sharon had the knack. She was second to none at keeping it short.

Zach Beale was in such a state of trembling and twitching that DC Shilling thought he would get nowhere if he plunged straight in, so he tried to calm him down by talking music. Working in the MVC shop, Zach needed knowledge of everything from hip-hop to the classics. Shilling volunteered he was a Dido fan, trying to get some reaction, but the only response came from the officer at his side, who rolled his eyes. After more prompting Zach said he was into something he called NAM that Shilling had to have explained. It was an acronym for New Acoustic Movement. NAM was cool, pure and non-electric. Zach listed some performers. He'd loosened up enough for Shilling to throw in the first question.

'So was it a surprise to you when Edgar Blacker compared you to Tolkien?'

'What – when he gave that talk?'

'Yes. I've watched the video you made. It was you behind the camera, wasn't it?'

'If you saw it, you know what he said. He wasn't comparing me to Tolkien. He said I might pick up some of Tolkien's readers.'

'"Millions of readers" was what he said. He went overboard for your work. He was ready to sign you up straight away.'

'It's academic now, isn't it?' Zach said. 'The guy's dead.'

'Did he follow it up in any way?'

'What, after the talk was over? Said he'd be getting in touch. Not much use to me now, is it?'

'A lucky escape, then. You can show the book to another publisher. By all accounts, Blacker didn't treat his writers too well.'

'I didn't know that at the time.'

'So you must have been gutted when you heard what happened to him.'

'That about sums it up.'

'Of all the people in the circle, you're the one with least motive.' That went down well. Shilling watched the face relax a little. 'Do you have any theories who'd want to kill him?'

Zach ran both hands over his head and clutched the ponytail. 'Not my thing, naming and shaming.'

'That isn't what I heard.' Shilling said in a sharp accusing tone, 'My information is that you and Naomi Green have been doing some detective work.'

Now he flexed his legs so hard that his chair slid back. 'Who told you that?'

'You're not going to deny it, are you?'

He was silent for some time, deciding what to say. 'It's not what it seems. It's a writing project.'

'Oh, yeah?'

'Yeah. Research for writing. Writers do research all the time. It's not just imagination. You have to find stuff out.'

'I thought your thing was fantasy.'

'It is mostly.' He looked away, wanting to be anywhere but here. 'I got talked into this. She wants us to do a book together.'

'About the circle?'

'The murders.'

'And have you found out anything of interest?'

No response.

Shilling repeated the question.

'I haven't. She did. Well, she may have.'

'What's that, Zach?'

A pause. 'You'd better ask her.'

Shilling leaned forward, and being so tall he could lean a long way, his forehead almost touching Zach's. 'We're not playing hunt the slipper here. There's a killer at large. If you know something, sunshine, spill it out, or I can do you for obstructing us.'

He exhaled sharply and cried out, 'She scares me rigid.'

Shilling waited.

With an effort at control Zach said, 'She got into Blacker's cottage – after it was burned, I mean – and found a picture, a photo.'

'Of Blacker?'

'Right, and another guy.'

'It was Naomi who nicked the photo?' Any pleasure in the discovery was undermined. Shilling was furious with himself for failing to make the connection.

'Yes, but she hasn't got it now. She unloaded it on me. I've got it at home.'

Shilling stood up. 'You and I are going to your place right now to collect this picture. It's evidence.'

'She'll go ballistic.'

'You won't say a word to her or anyone else. Understood? Sit here while I tell my boss where we're going.'

Johnny Cherry was almost through the list of questions Hen had supplied.

'Something else, Sharon. We're trying to track everyone's movements on the night Miss Snow died in the fire. What were you up to?'

'The Friday?'

'Right.'

'I was out of it.'

'Meaning what?'

'Took the weekend off, didn't I?'

'Right out of it, you mean? Some other place?'

'You can ask my boss.'

'Where were you?'

'Harrogate.'

Getting on for three hundred miles away.

'What were you doing in Harrogate?'

'Conference.'

Now it was Johnny who went silent, dumbfounded at the idea that Sharon would enrol for a conference, let alone travel there. 'Can you prove it?'

'S'pose.'

'What sort of conference?'

'Books and stuff.'

Johnny rubbed his eyes and said, 'Let me get this straight. You went to a literary conference?'

'Fantasy.'

There was an awkward interval as Johnny grappled with the answer. 'What are you saying now, Sharon? You made it up?'

'British Fantasy Convention.'

Another pause.

'You're not having me on? Fantasy isn't your thing at all.'

'Who says?'

He was forced to accept that she was speaking the truth. 'All on your own?'

'Got a lift, didn't I?'

'Who from?'

'Who d'you think?'

Johnny was all attention now. What he'd just learned would throw Hen Mallin's theories into confusion. If this was true about the trip to Harrogate, Sharon was out of it, and so was Zach.

19

Anyway, [poetry] is not the most important thing in life, is it? Frankly, I'd much rather lie in a hot bath sucking boiled sweets and reading Agatha Christie, which is just exactly what I intend to do as soon as I get home.

Dylan Thomas, quoted by Joan Wyndham in *Love is Blue* (1986)

Hen said she was going to hang Naomi out to dry. 'I should have realised she's the interfering witch who's given us the runaround. Who does she think she is, breaking into a sealed building and pilfering evidence? Yes, Duncan, go now, and tell Zach Beale from me that he's just as culpable as she is in the eyes of the law. He's up to his neck, right? Make him suffer.'

'He's bricking it already, guv.'

'Only because Naomi scares him. I want him scared of me.'

After Shilling had left the room, Hen said to Stella, 'Between you and me, none of this would have happened if Johnny Cherry had done his job right. I should put him and Naomi together in a tank like two Siamese fighting fish. Let 'em tear each other to bits.'

'Looking on the bright side, we've found the picture, guv,' Stella said.

'Yes, this exercise is bringing dividends. It's the onion-skin principle. You peel off a layer and find a different one underneath.'

Stella had heard from Hen before about the onion-skin principle, but valued her job too much to say so.

'First we had all these would-be writers with their hopes dashed by the obnoxious Edgar Blacker. We were looking at anger and frustration as a motive. But now we find other stuff underneath. Tudor sold this insurance policy to Blacker and lost his company a heap of money and put his career on the skids. Naomi climbs into a dangerous, burnt-out building to nick that photo. Sharon goes off for the weekend with Zach and, bingo, they both have a lovely alibi.'

This was the first Stella had heard of Sharon and Zach. 'Get away.'

Hen explained about the British Fantasy Convention. 'She's going to show us a photo. It was taken up there on the Saturday morning with someone dressed up as Gandalf and it has a time and date.'

'Why didn't Zach tell us this?'

'He didn't get the chance yet. He's been off home with DC Shilling to pick up the picture of Blacker and the other guy.'

Stella couldn't get over that pairing. 'I wouldn't have put those two together in a million years.'

'Why not?' Hen said. 'His head is full of dumb princesses.'

After a moment's thought she returned Hen's smile. 'Now you put it like that . . .'

'They went up north on his motorbike. He paid for the room, so presumably he can show us the receipt.'

'I hope she was worth it. She strikes me as rather dull.'

'Darling, he wasn't after conversation.' Hen shifted back to the business in hand. 'So we seem to be narrowing the field. What else have we learned about our suspects?'

'Jessie goes for late night walks.'

'Yes, and runs an old car on leaded petrol. There's more

to come, I'm certain. I haven't finished with Anton yet. He thought his telephone statements gave him an alibi. Looked sick when I pointed out that they proved nothing.'

This seemed to be as far as the onion-skin principle went for the time being, so Stella said, 'Some of us are ready to start more interviews, guv.'

'Hint, hint. I'm taking too long over Anton, am I?'

'I didn't say that.'

'Well, there's no reason why you shouldn't start with someone else. Have you finished with Tudor?'

'Definitely. I'm due for Bob Naylor next.'

'The man who stood in for Miss Snow and nearly lost his life.'

'Or so he claims.'

'Right. Take nothing for granted, Stell. Go for it.'

One thing you could say in Thomasine's favour: she was willing to talk. After being stuck with Sharon for over an hour, DI Johnny Cherry felt he deserved a talker. This lady appeared relaxed and ready to treat the interview as a chat instead of the inquisition.

'You're a poet, then,' he said when the preliminaries had been got through. 'Saw you on the video.'

'Funny word, "poet",' Thomasine said. 'Visions of pasty-faced women in round glasses and sandals talking to themselves. I don't want to be one, thanks. "Writer" has a better ring to it.'

'But that's not the day job?'

'No. I teach.'

'English, I suppose.'

'Mainly. Bit of everything in my time, filling in for colleagues.'

'Hard work, teaching.'

'Satisfying, though.'

'Your poems are hot stuff – right?'

She grinned. '*You* wouldn't think so. Some of the circle lead sheltered lives.'

'Mr Blacker seemed to find them saucy.'

'That bullshitter. I wouldn't believe a thing he said.'

'Some of them did.'

'Taken in by his flattery.'

'He talked about publishing you.'

'Didn't offer me a contract, did he? Said he "envisaged" some slim volumes. That could mean anything.'

Johnny was secretly amused. None of these writers claimed to have taken Blacker's comments to heart, yet each of them could quote him verbatim. 'You weren't disappointed, then?'

'No, I didn't pin my hopes on him. Mind if I smoke? An interview room is one of the few places it's allowed, if *The Bill* is anything to go by. Keep the witness sweet.'

'Be my guest.' He was glad of the chance to check his notes. Hen had given everyone a sheet with the key questions. 'Did you know Edgar Blacker before he came to the circle?'

'I know *of* him, from Maurice, our chair.' She paused to light the cigarette.

Johnny didn't need telling about McDade. He'd arrested the rat. He still believed he was heavily implicated.

Thomasine said, 'Blacker was supposed to be publishing Maurice.'

'But you hadn't met him outside the circle? He was local, so you could have done.'

'If I did, it made no impression.'

'Let's talk about McDade, then. You're very loyal to him.'

'No more than anyone else.'

'Don't be so modest. When he was pulled in for questioning, you led the protest.'

'I wasn't alone. It was obvious he was innocent.'

'He's a popular chairman. Popular with the ladies, for sure.'

She stared at him for a moment. 'What exactly are you getting at?'

'Put it this way. If one of the other men had been under suspicion – Anton, say, or Tudor – I can't imagine you ladies would have made such a big deal of it.'

'Which ladies?'

'Miss Snow and Miss Bumstead and you.'

'Bob Naylor was with us.'

'Only after you asked him for help.'

Thomasine frowned. 'You *have* made a study of this. What does it matter now whether we lobbied for Maurice's release?'

'It matters because Maurice McDade was let down badly by Blacker, told he wouldn't be published unless he stumped up most of the money. If he didn't set light to Blacker's house that night, then it's just possible one of his female admirers did, outraged by what happened.'

She gave him a look he could have lit a fire with. 'That's twisted thinking.'

'It's a twisted crime. Do you mind telling me where you were the night Blacker's house was torched?'

'At home, like most people.'

'Any way of proving it?'

'None that I can think of. I was asleep.'

'Did you have any contact with McDade on the day Blacker made his demand?'

She drew a line along the table with her fingertip. Her relaxed manner was just a memory now.

'Did you?' he said again.

Now she took a long drag on her cigarette and blew the smoke upwards. 'I happened to meet him in town that same afternoon. I was with my first form doing a survey in East Street. I saw Maurice and he looked drained, dreadful. It was obvious something was wrong. I asked and he told me about his meeting with Blacker. Poor man. Anyone would have sympathised. If I hadn't been on school duty I'd have suggested a drink.'

Johnny Cherry glanced at the female officer sitting beside him. She wouldn't appreciate the stunning significance of what had just been said, but she'd have to give him credit for his interviewing style. He'd just made a breakthrough in the investigation.

'This was hot news,' he said.

'Unpleasant.'

'You're a sociable person.' He wished Hen were sitting in on this. He couldn't have been more tactful. He didn't say the word 'gossip', or even hint at it. 'Did you pass on the news to anyone else in the circle?'

She cleared her throat. 'I did speak to one friend – Dagmar.'

'Miss Bumstead? What time was this?'

'After I got home from school. About five.'

'What was said?'

'I told her what Maurice had told me and we agreed that Blacker was a total scumbag and a few other things I'd rather not repeat.'

'Did you agree to do anything about it?'

'No. There was nothing we could do except feel sympathy for Maurice.'

So a matter of hours before Blacker was killed, two more people had found out what a conman he was. Johnny decided to suspend the interview at this point and pass this crucial information on to Hen. She'd better be impressed. And someone would be interviewing Dagmar, and it was essential they followed it up.

After the hard time he'd had with Jessie Warmington-Smith, DC Andy Humphreys was finding his next witness easier.

'I'm just in the circle to make up the numbers,' Basil said. 'You see, my wife Naomi was one of the founders and she didn't know if they'd get enough members to make a go of it, so I was roped in. I've often thought of sliding out now that they're up to numbers. I'm not really a writer.'

'I thought you did gardening articles.'

'Not from choice. The vicar needed a volunteer to take over a page of the parish magazine. If I could find someone else to do the job, I would.'

'It sounds as if you're the kind of bloke everyone turns to for assistance.'

'A dogsbody,' Basil said and added with uncharacteristic force, 'A bloody yes-man, that's me.'

'So is it fair to say you weren't bothered by Blacker's comments at that talk he gave?'

'No,' the yes-man said. 'I was bothered all right. He had a ridiculous suggestion about opening our garden to the public. I didn't want that and neither did my wife.'

'I expect it's a lovely garden.'

Basil cocked his head and looked defiant. 'But it's private.'

It seemed easiest to move on. 'Did you know Blacker at all before he came to the circle?'

'No.'

'Did your wife?'

'Naomi had better speak for herself. I'll be in the doghouse if I say things behind her back.'

'All right. Let's concentrate on you. You're retired, I take it. What was your line of work?'

'Fire officer.'

'No – really?'

'I wouldn't mention it if I didn't mean it. Thirty-three years' service, most of it in Chichester. From a boy it was what I wanted to do. The glamour thing of riding the engine with the bell going and wearing a shiny helmet and shinning up ladders to rescue people . . . well, pretty girls in their nighties if I'm honest. I didn't include confused old men in my plans, or car crashes, or floods, or kittens up chimneys, but once I'd joined I found the comradeship to my liking, so I stayed on. The team thing, only it wasn't a game, so it meant more.'

'You'll have seen cases of arson before.'

'Plenty. But not so often with loss of life. Fire-raisers attack property usually, not people.'

Andy remembered Hen's instruction to get these people talking about themselves. 'You could write some good stories with all your experience of fire-fighting.'

'I told you, I'm not a writer. Some of the things that happen are best forgotten. You'll know that, with the job you do.'

'Did you ever rescue a pretty girl in a nightie?'

Basil managed a wistful smile. 'Not a single one in thirty-three years. The nearest I came to romance was when I met my wife. And that was a head-jam job.'

'A what?'

'She was a line supervisor at Shippam's and she had a suspicion that two of her team were not only skiving off, but up to naughties in the yard. She went to the little room and stood on the seat and tried to look out of the window. There were iron bars and that's why her head got stuck. They had to call us out to prise them open and set her free. Some of her fellow workers found it funny, but I didn't make anything of it. She must have suffered mentally because I've never known her so grateful as she was that afternoon. It was most unlike her. She invited me round for tea on Sunday and we were married inside six months.'

'Nice.'

Basil weighed the comment for a long interval. 'I suppose. What I just told you is confidential, right?'

'Right.' Only the entire CID team would hear the tape replayed. Andy returned to his list of questions. 'Happen to remember where you were on the night of the fire at Blacker's cottage?'

'At home, same as usual. I don't get out much in the evenings.'

'Do you drive, Mr Green?'

'Not if I can avoid it.'

'Spreading pollution?'

'No, just driving. I'm not much good at it. I use the bike for short runs.'

'But you do own a car?'

'Van.'

Another key question. 'What kind of fuel do you use? Unleaded?'

'Diesel. How does that come into it?'

'It doesn't,' Andy said with a barely concealed sigh. 'Diesel doesn't come into it. Does your wife drive?'

'She can at a pinch. Like me she prefers cycling. There I go again, talking about her. You'd better not quote me.'

'The van? Does she drive the van?'

'On occasions.'

'Did either of you go out on the night Edgar Blacker's cottage burned down?'

'I didn't.'

Andy waited.

After a pause Basil said, 'I can't speak for Naomi.'

'You'd know if she went out at night.'

'I wouldn't. We sleep in separate bedrooms and I take tranquillisers for my nerves. Get into bed and I'm out like a light. I have to set the alarm.'

'What for?'

'My morning swim at the Westgate Centre. I like to be in the water by seven. I need to keep fit. I'm quite a bit older than Naomi.' The logic wasn't clear. Basil may have needed to keep fit to pleasure Naomi, but escape seemed a more likely explanation.

'I see. It seems your wife has been taking an unusual amount of interest in Mr Blacker's cottage.'

'You'll have to ask her about that. Look, I may be her husband, but I'm not her shadow. I have my own life to get on with.'

This might be clever stonewalling. It came across like evasion. Whoever was interviewing Naomi was likely to turn up some fascinating secrets.

'Let's talk about Miss Snow,' Andy said. 'A friend, would you say?'

'No more than any of the others,' Basil said. 'She was a quiet lady, unlike some I could name. Always courteous. There wasn't anything you could dislike about her, if that's what you're hinting at.'

'Did she visit your house?'

'I don't think so.'

'And you didn't visit hers, in Tower Street?'

'Why should I? No.'

'I've got to ask this. Did you go out on the night Miss Snow's house was burned down?'

'Certainly not.'

Andy had run through the list. He was about to end the interview when he had an inspiration. 'How is your garden laid out?'

A frown from Basil. 'Do you really want to know?'

'I wouldn't ask if I didn't.'

'It's the narrow strip that most suburban gardens are. I've tried to introduce curved shapes in the flower beds and the path for interest, and there's a small pond and some fruit trees. I like roses, so I have a pergola with trellis work. Oh, and a gazebo.'

'A lawn?'

'Certainly.'

'Do you mow it yourself?'

He said with pride, 'I do *all* the gardening myself.'

'What kind of mower? Hover?'

'No, I prefer the cylindrical sort that gives me those beautiful stripes. Mine is a Ransom.'

'Petrol-driven?'

'I'm not out of the ark.'

'So you have a supply of petrol, leaded petrol?'

'Of course. A couple of cans in my shed.' He hesitated. 'Oh, I see what you're getting at, but you'd be wrong, quite wrong.'

Hen felt as if she was still on the dry outer layer of onion skin with Anton. While others were getting dramatic results, she might as well have gone to the canteen for a coffee and a doughnut.

'I've given this some thought,' he said when she returned.

'Good.'

'What time of the night does this arsonist choose?'

'The small hours.'

'You can't be more precise?'

'Around four a.m., in the case of the latest fire.' She added, 'I'm supposed to ask the questions.'

'So if I can prove I was at home between three thirty and five, am I in the clear?'

'I reckon you would be.'

'Excellent.' He felt in his pocket and dangled a house key in front of her. 'You have my permission to send one of your officers to check my computer.'

'We've been over this,' Hen said with a sigh. 'The fact that your computer was switched on is no proof you were there.'

He nodded. 'But if you look in my e-mail facility you'll find a record of the messages I sent and received that night, and each one has a time beside it. I'm very busy at that hour because I have friends across the world who share my interest in virtual architecture and it's a good time for an insomniac like me to communicate. When you look at the messages you won't need much convincing that they were mine. And you can do the same for the night of the first fire.'

She took the key. 'If you're right about this, I'll take back what I said. I'll get someone to drive you round there.'

She came out with mixed feelings. It would be good to get a result, yet secretly she'd rather fancied Anton as the arsonist. His calculating manner and his contempt for the rest of the circle had made him a prime suspect in her eyes.

When she came out of the interview room young Shilling was waiting in the corridor with a photo in a plastic folder. 'Guv, I've got it.'

Her mood lightened up. 'Good lad.'

They went into her office and examined the black and white shot of two grinning men, one recognisable as the young Edgar Blacker, the other, with yellowish hair, unknown to her and unlike any of the men in the circle. The pair looked similar in age. Both wore striped shirts, but no ties. They were holding beer cans. Their free hands were over each other's shoulders.

'What do you think?' she asked Shilling. 'Family or friend?'

'They don't look like family to me.'

'Nor me.'

She turned it over and found the writing. '"Innocents, Christmas 1982". Over twenty years ago. What do you make of it?'

'The "Innocents" bit? Could be, like, a joke, guv.'

She turned it over to look at the front again. 'You mean they look well plastered?'

'A couple of lads on the beer isn't most people's idea of innocence.'

'Can you see what's in the background? It's been taken with a flash and there's some heavy shadowing, but that looks like a coffee machine behind them.'

Shilling studied it. 'And maybe the corner of a notice board.'

'Suggesting it's an office. The office Christmas party? Let's do a computer scan on this. Take care of it, will you? See if we can get the background enhanced. If there are clues here, I want to see them. It may have no bearing on the case, but I can't take the chance.'

She went back to where the remaining members of the circle were waiting. That stalwart character Maurice McDade was still there with the three who hadn't yet been seen: Bob Naylor, Dagmar Bumstead and Naomi Green. They all looked up.

'Almost ready for you,' she said to them as a group. 'You've been extremely patient.'

Bob looked at his watch in a pointed manner.

'You're the Parcel Force driver? Are you working nights?'

'Early mornings.'

'It won't take that long. Stella Gregson will see you shortly. Miss Bumstead, you're with DC Shilling. That means you're with me, Mrs Green.'

Naomi followed her like a lamb.

'Is this a voluntary statement?' Dagmar asked DC Shilling.

'You took the words out of my mouth.'

'I work in a solicitor's office, you see.'

Shilling gave a nod. 'We're doing this by the book.'

'If you suspected me of an offence, you'd have to caution me and give me certain advice about my rights. But like the others I'm only here because the chief inspector asked for our help as witnesses.'

No flies on this one. 'That's my understanding, ma'am. You're the romantic novelist, I believe?'

Dagmar flushed deeply. 'I don't know about *the* – as if I was Danielle Steel.'

'What I mean is that you're the only one in the circle.'

'So far as I'm aware, yes.'

'You've written a lot of these – what do they call them? – bodice-rippers.'

'You were right the first time. Romantic novels. Twelve altogether. And now you're about to ask me with a snigger where I get my ideas from.'

'Actually, no.'

She carried on as if he hadn't spoken. 'And I can't and won't answer.'

'I wasn't going to ask,' Shilling said. 'I don't mind betting you get your best ideas at work.'

'Why?'

'Correct me if I'm wrong, but the books you write are all about women who go through a series of misunderstandings with the hell-raiser who in the end turns out to be Mr Right. You must get more than enough inspiration for stories working in a solicitor's office.'

She gave him a stare fit to impale him. 'The solicitors I work with are gentlemen through and through.'

Shilling smiled. 'I meant the clients. All the problems that are brought in, divorce and separation and disputes between neighbours.'

'That's all conjecture on your part.'

Shilling nodded and smiled. 'Let's move quickly on, then. We'll talk about the publisher, Edgar Blacker. Whose idea was it to bring him to the circle?'

'Maurice's.'

'And did everyone agree?'

'Most of them sent in their work for appraisal, so they must have.'

'Nice word, "appraisal". Better than criticism.'

'You mean we wanted to hear nice things? I'm sure we did.'

'Coming back to the question: did everyone agree it was a good plan to invite Blacker?'

'I didn't, for one. Maurice is a lovely man, but he doesn't know much about human nature. I could see it would raise unrealistic hopes.'

'Did you tell him?'

'Privately, yes. I was one of the original members, so I felt I had a right to protest.'

'Protest? It was as strong as that?'

'No, it was a civilised discussion. Maurice listened to me and then gave his point of view. He thought it would do us all good to get a professional opinion on our work. He really felt it was for the best. In the end he talked me into sending in my latest, saying it would show Mr Blacker that one of us at least was capable of finishing a novel.'

Listening to this little lady speaking in her earnest tone, with never a hint of a smile, Shilling wondered how she had reacted to being rejected – for what, the twelfth time? – but in the presence of people she regarded as inferior writers. 'And did Blacker appreciate your work?'

'He seemed to think it was all right, but when I pressed him about possible publication, he backtracked fast and said he'd have to show it to someone else.'

'So did you let him keep it?'

'No, and I'm glad I didn't. It would have been lost in the fire.'

'You picked it up at the end?'

'Yes, it was stacked on the table with the others.'

'Did he say any more?'

'He was busy with Tudor. I collected mine and Miss Snow's. She asked me to. She was busy handing out competition leaflets.'

'You must have felt a bit down at the end.'

'I'm used to it. There's no sense in building up your hopes.'

'So with the benefit of hindsight you were right. It was a mistake inviting Blacker to the circle.'

She nodded. 'But he'd still have pulled the rug from under Maurice.'

'Ah, yes.' Shilling gave the smile that said he had a good card to play. 'You were one of the first to know about that, weren't you?'

'What – the fact that he reneged on his agreement to publish?'

'Is that why he was killed, Miss Bumstead?'

Her voice shook a little. 'How would I know? I can't answer that question.'

'Certain people heard how badly he'd treated Maurice the same day it happened, before the fire, and you were one of them. Thomasine O'Loughlin spoke to you about five that afternoon.'

'You're well informed.'

'How did you spend the evening?'

'Doing some ironing and taking a bath. I was too troubled to write. You need to be in the right frame of mind.'

'You did nothing about Blacker?'

'What could I have done?'

'You didn't go out later that night?'

'Of course not.'

'Do you have a theory as to who the arsonist was?'

'If I did I wouldn't divulge it to you. My thoughts on the matter have no relevance whatsoever.'

'I can't agree with that. I'd say you're a shrewd lady.'

'Perhaps that's why I won't be drawn.'

Shilling felt he was losing this one. Two nil down at half-time. 'I want to ask you about Miss Snow. I dare say you feel worse about her death than Blacker's.'

'She was one of us, so I would.'

'One of the founder members?'

'Not quite, but she joined soon after.'

'A valued member?'

'She brought some organisation to our circle. She was

a conscientious secretary and a treasurer we could all trust.'

'Functions you could have performed, with your experience.'

'Possibly, but rather selfishly I wanted to participate fully in the meetings, not take notes and collect subscriptions. Miss Snow played only a muted part in the discussions.'

'No one disliked her?'

'How would I know that? I'm not a mind-reader. From my point of view there was nothing you could dislike about her.'

'As secretary, did she have any secrets, anything on the members?'

'I doubt it. She knew if anyone owed money, but the dues aren't excessive. We pay two pounds for each meeting we attend. When anyone is short, they can give an IOU.'

'After the fire at Blacker's cottage, and Maurice McDade's arrest, you linked up with Thomasine O'Loughlin and Bob Naylor to try and prove Mr McDade was innocent.'

'Certainly.'

'Why those two?'

'Because Thomasine shared my sense of outrage, and she's a good ally, very astute.'

'And Naylor? He'd only just met McDade for the first time.'

'Thomasine thought he would be a help. We needed a man, really, and none of the others were suitable. Tudor can't disguise his jealousy of Maurice, Anton has no tact, Basil is under Naomi's thumb and Zach is, well, a bit immature.'

If she can sum up men as pithily as that, Shilling thought, she's probably got me pigeon-holed as well.

'You'd had long enough to give Naylor the once-over.'

'Thomasine said he was kosher.'

'Is she Jewish?'

'I don't think so. It's the way she talks. I knew what she

meant and I respect her judgement. She and Bob did all the questioning.'

'They didn't invite you?'

'Three people on one's doorstep would have been too many.'

'One is too many if you've got a guilty conscience.'

At the end of the interview Shilling found himself thinking it was a smart move on the parts of Thomasine and Bob, taking it on themselves to question other people in the circle as if they themselves had no case to answer.

Stella had already run through the set questions with Bob Naylor. He hadn't been present at the crucial meeting of the circle when Blacker addressed them, hadn't joined the circle at that stage, hadn't even heard of Blacker.

He said.

But hell's bells, had he made up for lost time! Borrowed the video from Miss Snow. Joined forces with Thomasine O'Loughlin and Dagmar Bumstead to try and establish McDade's innocence. Questioned Mrs McDade and just about everyone else. Gained the confidence of Miss Snow. Gone in her place to the boat house. Made a voluntary statement to DC Shilling. Got himself elected as press spokesman.

A right busybody.

'And on top of everything else you're a writer?' Stella said.

'Trying to be,' he said.

'Books, is it?'

'Christ, no. I fool around with bits of rhyming stuff, that's all.'

'Are you going to give me a sample?'

'No way. It's pathetic.'

So he wanted coaxing. Stella only ever played the wheedling woman in the cause of duty. 'Go on, I'd really like to hear a sample.'

He sighed. 'Don't know if you'll get this. I was playing about with some lines while I was waiting.' He fished in his back pocket and took out what looked like a cheap diary.

'Eleven local writers
Lead the cops a dance.
Who's for an excuse-me?
No chance.'

'Not bad,' Stella said, 'but it dates you. Anyone under forty wouldn't know what an excuse-me is.'

'Tell me about it. I have a daughter of fourteen. They should come with phrase books.'

'What does your wife think of your writing?'

'She died.'

Whoops. A pause for respect. 'Sorry. Let's talk about what's been happening since you made your statement to DC Shilling. There was a meeting, right?'

'Yeah, and I was dropped in it and made press officer. I'm not even a paid-up member and they want me as their spokesman.'

'Which you do very well. What else was decided?'

'Not much. Two of the party left early.'

'Zach and Naomi.'

'If you know it all, why ask me?'

'So why did they leave?'

'I do remember one thing we agreed,' Bob said, 'and that was not to slag off fellow members of the circle.'

He could bat for England, this one. 'But you just told me you're not a member.'

'Nice try, but I like these people – all of them. I've got to know them quite well, their hopes and fears.'

'One of them is almost certainly a murderer.'

'Okay – and ten of them aren't. Until I know which one, I'm going to respect them all.'

'You still see yourself as an amateur sleuth, do you?'

He took in a sharp breath and it was no more than a stage effect. 'Bit sarky, that. I was only helping out, like. This was before you and your boss took over. No disrespect, but the police work wasn't up to much.'

'They weren't getting cooperation from everyone. You didn't report the fire at the boat house.'

'Did.'

'Eventually – only after Miss Snow was dead. If you'd come forward earlier they might have saved her life.'

'How?'

'They could have warned her to be careful.'

'That Inspector Cherry? He didn't give a toss when I tried to talk to him. He couldn't find his arse with both hands, that one.'

She should have said something in Johnny's defence. Just couldn't find the words. All she managed was, 'Leave the sleuthing to us, Mr Naylor. We don't want any more people going up in flames.'

Hen was glad she'd left Naomi to last. Thanks to young Shilling's good work, she had a trump to play and she used it straight away. 'What have you got to say about the photo of Blacker and the other man?'

Naomi blinked and gave nothing away.

'You've got yourself in deep shit, crossing a police line and going into that gutted building.'

She was given one of Naomi's smouldering glares.

'You won't have been told we recovered it from Zach's house.'

The eyes narrowed. 'Who told you? Basil?'

'Your accessory, Zach Beale.'

Now it was raw disgust that registered. 'Wimp.'

'He's not very happy with you, either. He could be facing a prison term.'

240

'What for?'

'Concealing evidence. Conspiracy to obstruct the course of justice.'

'Oh, come on,' Naomi said. 'It's only a photo. Your people would have picked it up if it was any use to them.'

'They didn't want to disturb the scene,' Hen said with the licence her position gave her. 'But you did. I haven't yet decided what we'll throw at you, unlawful entry, theft. Why did you do it?'

After some thought, Naomi said, 'It was there.'

'Like Everest, you mean? The difference is that you crossed a police line to get to it. The place was taped and sealed.'

'It was something that belonged to him. A point of contact.'

Hen found herself frowning. This was a strange woman. 'What are we dealing with here – messages from the dead?'

'No.'

'"A point of contact", you said.'

'I'm a writer. I'm treating what happened as a project.'

'Writing about it?'

'A murder inquiry from the inside. I went to the house to get a sense of the place, and the man.'

'Don't give me that horseshit, Naomi. I think you went there to clean up.'

'What?'

This thought had just come warm and unintended to Hen. 'You returned to the scene to remove evidence that might incriminate you.'

An impact at last. A look of panic. 'You think I'm the arsonist?'

'The more I listen to you, the more likely it becomes.'

'You're wrong. Listen, you couldn't be more wrong. I went out of curiosity. The picture was hanging there, so I took it.'

This chimed in with what Zach had said. 'Okay,' Hen said, with a deliberate shift from blame to consultation. 'Let's have your views. What did you learn from the photo?'

'It's guesswork,' Naomi said, but she was deeply serious. The threats had shaken her. She knew her best chance was to make herself useful.

'Carry on.'

'If he kept it on his bedroom wall, the other man in the picture must have been important to him. They had their arms around each other.'

'Buddies?'

'Possibly. I don't recognise the man. He isn't one of the circle.'

'Agreed.'

'And something was written on the back.'

'"Innocents, Christmas 1982".'

'Yes, I didn't know what to make of that. My first thought was that Blacker and the other man had got into something shady at a later date, and the comment was written later.'

'Something shady?'

'A relationship, maybe. Twenty years ago we were less open about gays. It can't have been too much of a disaster or he wouldn't have kept the picture on his wall.'

'You said that was your first thought. Was there a second?'

'That they later got involved in some criminal act.'

'Do you have any evidence of this?'

Naomi shook her head. 'It's only a guess, but it would account for the "innocents" comment. A scam they both got into.'

Hen said, 'If they did, we have no record of it. Blacker was clean.'

'I've got another theory, then. Suppose they both fell for some confidence trick. A third person duped them. That would give another meaning to "innocents", wouldn't it?'

'Sure would. Any idea who this third person might be?'

'The killer,' Naomi said. 'The arsonist.'

'Covering up old crimes? You've obviously given this a lot of thought. Who do you suspect?'

'Is this in confidence?'

'Of course.'

'That pain in the arse, Tudor.'

20

All these courts must be lit, and our detectives improved. They are not what they should be.

Queen Victoria, letter to Lord Salisbury, 10 November 1888

'After that, I need a bevvy. How about you?' Bob said.

Thomasine smiled. 'Mind-reader.'

It was just after ten. Neither of them said so, but one good reason for choosing the Ship, the hotel at the top of North Street, was that no one else from the circle was likely to be in there. They had enough in common not to need other company now.

Thomasine asked for a gin and tonic. 'Don't worry,' she added. 'You won't have to put me to bed. The other evening wasn't typical. Dagmar and I had almost two hours to fill while you were visiting Fran . . .'

'I'd forgotten,' he said with tact.

'. . . and there was all the stress of Maurice being arrested.' Then, catching up, she said on a sharper note, 'What do you mean – forgotten? You visit a lady's bedroom and forget about it? That's not very gentlemanly.'

'I'm such a perfect gent I wiped it from my memory.'

'Oh yeah?'

When he returned with the drinks, she said, 'I don't know if you heard the buzz back there in the nick about Zach

244

and Sharon. He took her to Harrogate last weekend. Some fantasy convention.'

'Zach and Sharon? Strewth.'

'So they're off the list of suspects now.'

'Nice work if you can get it. Another one in the clear is Anton,' he said. 'He proved he was at home and online at the time Miss Snow was killed. The sad bastard sits up every night at the computer.'

There was a moment while each absorbed what the other had said.

'So who's left?' Thomasine asked. 'You, me and who else?'

'Tudor.'

'Basil and Naomi.'

'Jessie.'

'And Dagmar. That's it.'

'How many's that? Seven?'

'Five really,' Thomasine said. 'I'm in the clear and so are you, or I wouldn't be sitting here with you. You weren't around when Blacker was killed.'

'That doesn't wash with the police,' Bob said. 'They reckon I had a run-in with Blacker at some time in the past.'

'In that case, why are you supposed to have joined the circle?'

'To muddy the waters. You lot are the obvious suspects. I can stir up more trouble as an insider.'

'That's stretching it a bit. If it was a game of chess I might believe a theory like that, but you're not going to draw attention to yourself when you don't need to.'

'That's not what they think.'

'High risk if you're the arsonist.'

'Which I'm not.'

'And as you're not, it's no picnic to be one of the circle. Two people have died. Someone else could cop it.'

'Scared?'

She hesitated and took a deep sip. 'Who wouldn't be?'

'Have you worked out why Miss Snow was killed?'

'Because of something she knew?'

Bob said, 'I think it was because of what she had in her possession. That video of Blacker's visit.'

She frowned. 'But we all know what's on the video. We were there, all except you, and you've watched it.'

He nodded.

She added, 'There's nothing except some cringe-making footage of people hoping to be told they are geniuses and finding out they are not.'

'Something on it pinpoints the killer.'

'I can't think what.'

'Either something Blacker said, that sealed his fate, or something one of the circle said that reveals them as the killer.'

'And they didn't want it known? But Miss Snow handed the video to the police.'

'The killer didn't know that,' Bob said. 'If you think back, most of the circle thought she was in charge of it.'

'She was. She was the secretary, she needed it to help write the minutes and she kept it as a record of the meeting.'

'But she lent it to me – well, I asked for it – and then she called me late at night saying she needed it back because the fuzz had called it in. Only you and her knew I'd borrowed the thing. As far as anyone else was concerned, it never left her place.'

'And you think that's why she was killed?'

'Got to be, hasn't it, if it fingers the killer?'

'But she handed it to the police.'

'Like I said, the killer didn't know about that. The fire at Miss Snow's was mainly to destroy the evidence.'

Thomasine shivered. 'That's horrible.'

'Makes sense, doesn't it?'

'She was killed for that pesky video? And in reality she'd

given it to the police, so she needn't have been killed at all?' She gave a nervous, angry sigh. 'Bob, that's too cruel.'

He stared down at his drink. 'What it means is Blacker's death is still the key to all this. His pep talk to the circle gave something away that triggered the second murder. Be nice if we could run that video again.'

Thomasine's eyes widened. 'If we told this to the police, maybe they'd let us look at it.'

He shook his head. 'Policemen like amateur detectives about as much as they like losing their helmets.'

The circle members had been allowed to leave, but their interrogators were in for a longer night. Hen had summoned them to the incident room for the debriefing. 'A worthwhile exercise,' she summed up. 'Not much in the way of deathless prose, but three interesting alibis to check. Stella has already contacted the hotel at Harrogate and it seems Zach Beale and Sharon paid for a double room and made full use of it.'

'What does that mean? They were at it day and night?' Andy Humphreys said.

'There was a conference going on,' Shilling said.

'Is that what it's called?'

'Envious?' Stella said.

Hen said, 'And Anton's computer appears to show he was sending e-mails at the time Miss Snow's house was being torched. It looks as if we're down to seven. What is more' – she pointed to the enlargement Shilling had made on the computer, now displayed on the board behind her – 'we may have a real breakthrough with this photo Blacker had on his bedroom wall.'

'Or a bloody great red herring,' Johnny Cherry murmured.

'You said something, Johnny?'

'No.'

'Because I want everyone's take on this. Two guys in striped shirts with their arms around each other's shoulders, one of them Blacker. It looks like a celebration. They're holding drinks. On the back someone – presumably Blacker – has written "Innocents, Christmas 1982". We don't know the identity of the blond man. He doesn't resemble anyone in the circle. There's a coffee machine in the background and part of a notice board and over to the right could be the corner of a desk.'

'Office party?' Humphreys said.

'That's my assumption.'

Stella said, 'He was in publishing all his life, so it's a good bet this is a publisher's office.'

'We can find which firm he was with in nineteen eighty-two,' Shilling said. 'Maybe that way we can identify the blond guy.'

'Your job, then,' Hen said.

Johnny said as if the relevance of this had escaped him, 'Why are we taking so much interest in one picture from over twenty years ago?'

'Because we haven't established a definite motive for Blacker's murder.'

'I thought we had. I thought we'd agreed he made a fatal error by trashing the writers' work. One of them took it to heart and put a match to his house.'

'That's only a theory. I'm not a writer looking for a publisher and I don't know how desperate they get.'

'They'd murder just to get into print.'

'You say, Johnny, but I can't help feeling it isn't enough. I'm not ruling out some grievance from way back.'

'A blast from the past?'

'Why did he have this picture on his bedroom wall and what does that word "innocents" mean? We don't know. It may be a factor in the case. I want it checked, in any event. Meanwhile let's look at the writers we have left on our list. Which of them really shape up as killers? Some of them seem more serious contenders than others.'

'Basil isn't serious,' Andy said. 'Not about writing. He's a serious gardener. The writing is secondary.'

'How did the interview go?'

'Fine. He's very open. Told me things I didn't need to know, like how he met Naomi.'

'Now you've started, you've got to tell us, Andy.'

He gave them the story of Naomi with her head stuck in the toilet window at Shippam's. Even Johnny Cherry laughed.

'So Basil was in the fire service,' Hen said. 'That's hard to picture.'

'But useful to know if you ever get your head stuck,' Duncan Shilling said, and got an easy laugh from the team and a pointed look from Hen. The young man had a knack of running off at the mouth.

Andy Humphreys said, 'He also goes for an early swim.'

'How early?'

'Not *that* early. Around seven. He's older than Naomi, he says, so he needs to stay fit. But he's relaxed about it.'

'True. He's pretty laid back. Unlike his wife.'

'Naomi. She's capable of anything,' Stella said. 'Those eyes!'

'Capable of nicking a picture from a burnt-out house, anyway,' Hen said. 'Yes, I interviewed Naomi myself, and she's – how shall I put it?'

'Spooky?'

'I was going to say committed. She claims she's writing the inside story of the investigation from the point of view of a suspect. A good excuse for some very odd behaviour.'

'Confirmed by Zach,' Shilling said.

'Which means Zach believed it, no more than that.'

'But if Naomi is the killer, would she have taken the risk of using Zach as a collaborator?'

'Why did she use him?'

'For his writing skills. He's the one Blacker said was the new Tolkien.'

'So it was to be a writing partnership?'

'That's his explanation, guv, and he seemed to feel he was forced into it.'

'Okay,' Hen said. 'We have Naomi as a contender. Who else? What about Tudor Thomas?'

'I interviewed him,' Stella said, 'and he came over as confident when I tackled him on the insurance he'd sold to Blacker.'

'The stolen Wodehouse manuscript?'

'Yes. It was obvious he's been questioned before and he thinks he's watertight on this one. It stinks to high heaven, and it probably scuppered his career prospects, but he smiles and answers the questions like a man who knows he can't lose.'

'Do you think they did a deal and split the payout?'

'You can see it in his eyes as he says the opposite, guv. I suggested to him that Blacker did the dirty on him over his own manuscript and there was a glimmer of agreement about that, but not enough to pin the murder on him.'

'He can feel safe about any deal they did now Blacker is dead.'

'Yes, but Blacker wouldn't ever have admitted to the fraud. I don't think that's enough for a motive.'

Hen turned back to Andy Humphreys. 'Who did you see first – Mrs Warmington-Smith?'

He reddened at the memory. 'We got off to a bad start. She seemed to think I was attacking her for living in a house owned by the church. When we got round to her movements on the two nights in question she admitted she goes for late-night walks.'

'How late?'

'After midnight sometimes. She's a poor sleeper. The walks are just in the cathedral area. She also owns an old car that runs on leaded. I asked if she ever uses it at night and she says she doesn't.'

'She would, wouldn't she?'

'Maybe, but she didn't have to tell me about the walks.'

'Agreed. What do you make of her personality? How does she shape up as a potential arsonist?'

Humphreys drew in a long breath. 'She came out with some weird stuff. Gets signs and that, like Joan of Arc, she said.'

'What, heavenly voices?'

He nodded. 'She told me God was in the interview room with us.'

'Only place he can get a smoke,' said Shilling, and got another laugh.

'She said some stuff about the journey of the soul.'

'Are you saying she's strange enough to go to the top of our list?'

'Don't know about that. She wasn't bitter about Blacker or Miss Snow. I don't think she hated either of them.'

'Okay, there's a question mark over Warmington-Smith. That leaves us with Thomasine O'Loughlin, Bob Naylor and one other.'

'Dagmar Bumstead,' Shilling said. 'The one you can easily forget. I interviewed her. She keeps a low profile, even though she was one of the founders of the circle. Very discreet about everybody. Works for a solicitor.'

'She doesn't leap to mind as a suspect, I agree,' Hen said. 'Remind me what she writes.'

'Romances. That's the surprise. She's got them stacked up at home, all unpublished.'

'That's how she gets her rocks off,' Humphreys said. 'Writing about it.'

'And some people get theirs off talking about it,' Stella said with a glare.

Shilling said, 'It's easy to overlook Dagmar, but she's close to the centre of things. A friend of McDade, the chairman, and of Thomasine O'Loughlin. She and Thomasine were the most active trying to get McDade released from custody.'

'But what had she got against our two murder victims?'

'Blacker showed some interest in her script and then dropped her like a hot brick when he heard she'd had so many rejections. That must have hurt.'

'But why would she have wanted to kill Miss Snow?'

Shilling was silent for a moment, then came out with a profound remark. 'Why would anyone want to kill Miss Snow? On the face of it she was a harmless little lady, but she had a few secrets, didn't she? She was an accountant, so she probably knew if anyone in the circle had money problems. She was secretary and treasurer of the circle.'

'Worked in a charity shop,' Johnny chimed in. 'Knew who bought their clothes secondhand.'

'Are you saying Dagmar was strapped for cash and didn't want anyone to know it?'

Shilling shook his head. 'I can't be certain of that, guv.'

'But worth a thought. All right. That leaves Tommy and Tuppence.'

This got some blank looks.

Hen was shaking her head, disappointed in her squad. 'You're not with it, are you? Agatha Christie's amateur detectives. I've got all the tapes.'

Nobody said a word.

She went on, 'I'm referring to Bob Naylor and Thomasine O'Loughlin. Stella, you spoke to Naylor. What do you make of him?'

'Bright guy. Popular. They all seem to trust him.'

'Too good to be true?'

'If he is, it's a good act, guv. He makes you smile, too. Mind, he's pushy. Give him another week and he'd take over that circle completely. He makes all the other guys look like extra baggage.'

'Capable of murder?'

'Well capable. But I can't see why.'

'Unless there's something in his background we don't know about.' Hen sighed and said in a voice already thinking of other things, 'There's still plenty to be discovered about all of them. So what's new on Thomasine O'Loughlin?'

You could almost see Johnny Cherry pump himself up for this. 'I interviewed her and it was pretty sensational. She admitted that she met Maurice McDade in Chichester on the afternoon before Blacker was killed.'

'What for?'

'It wasn't prearranged. It was chance. She was out with her schoolkids doing a survey. But the point is that McDade told her how Blacker had ripped him off. Thomasine knew about it, guv. And she told Dagmar.' He folded his arms. In Johnny's view, no more needed to be said.

Thomasine finished her second G&T. 'It's been a long day.'

'One for the road?'

She shook her head. 'Tired.'

'I'll call a taxi.'

She placed her hand over Bob's. 'I was wrong earlier. I take it all back.'

'Take what back?'

'About you being ungentlemanly. You're a perfect gent.'

'Not all the time.'

'No?'

Their eyes met and hers had an invitation.

He said, 'But tonight I have to get back.'

'Something on TV?'

'Ouch,' he said. 'That's below the belt.'

In the taxi, halfway there, he said, 'It wouldn't be a bad idea to put a block on your letterbox at nights.'

'And how would I do that?'

'Have you got a screwdriver and some screws? I'll do it for you.'

'Now?'

'But I do have to get back after.'

She leaned her head on his shoulder. 'Just like Cinderella.'

21

EOD

Text message abbreviation for END OF DAY.

Just after midnight, Jessie Warmington-Smith changed into her walking shoes, put on a jacket and stepped outside. For her, this was routine, a time to breathe the cooler air and put the day's frustrations to rest. Minor frets – and there were always minor frets – had a way of getting out of proportion and interfering with sleep if she didn't take this late stroll through the streets. Some people thought she was nervous, the widow living alone, but they were mistaken. Jessie had an iron will. What unsettled her was loss of dignity, threats to her status as a person of good family and a respected member of the church.

The evening walk worked so well every time that she had put it into 'Tips for the Twenty-First Century'. Anyone would benefit. So many people relied on sleeping tablets and herbal remedies without realising that one needn't take anything at all before going to bed except fresh air and gentle exercise.

She started along Vicars Close, noting the darkened houses and the lights at certain windows. She knew which of her neighbours retired early and which liked to read in bed. The canon in the next house but one always watched television until late with the main lights turned down. She couldn't imagine what he found to look at because a lot of late-night television was unsuitable for a man of the church to view. His was the only house apart from hers where the lights were on downstairs.

Some might have been wary of venturing into the streets so late. Not Jessie. She'd once had her handbag snatched in broad daylight outside Woolworths, but never a problem at night. After midnight you could walk up South Street to the Cross and past the cathedral along West Street without seeing a soul. This was her shortest circuit. If she felt more energetic she would try other routes. The one walk she'd given up was Tower Street, and that was because it depressed her to go past the blackened ruin that had been Miss Snow's.

Tonight she passed the limping man with the little white Jack Russell and as usual he raised his hat and said, 'Good evening.' That was another thing about the streets at night. People were more civil.

She took a deep breath and looked up at the stars. Her troubles always seemed less when she studied the night sky. That offensive young policeman who'd got under her skin was just one more example of the brashness that passed for confidence these days. When he'd called the circle 'whacky' – implying that she was whacky too – it was a stupid insult. She was glad she hadn't let it pass. He had no right to make a slur like that. And he hadn't the right to call her 'dear' either. What was he – all of twenty-five years old? He should be forced to attend the circle and learn the power of words. She doubted if he realised how offensive he'd sounded. That poor beginning had set the tone of the interview. If he'd been more civil at the start she might not have taken it as provocation when he questioned her about her address, her late-night walks and her car.

Out here in the vastness of the night, the whole episode could be dismissed more easily. DC Humphreys was just a silly young pup. A more respectful approach would have got him better results. As it was, she'd gone a bit overboard and no doubt confirmed his opinion that she was a batty old woman. It had been a mistake on her part to talk about her visions. Young people of his sort watch any number of films about scary goings-on, yet wouldn't recognise the supernatural if it tapped them on the shoulder and passed the time of day. To be open to such experiences you needed to have lived a bit, not filled your imagination with were-wolves and vampires.

Opposite the Tower Street turn she hesitated, conscious that she was depriving herself by no longer including it in her walks. Perhaps tonight she ought to reclaim the route. Or tomorrow. On balance she thought tomorrow was a better idea. Or the next night. The whole point of the evening stroll was to shut out unpleasant thoughts.

The moonlight gave her the opportunity to stand below the fourteenth-century bell tower and watch the clouds passing above the crenellated top, giving the illusion that the tower itself was on the move. Some nights, when the wind was strong, she could almost believe that the whole structure was tipping over and about to crush her. She found that quite exciting.

She moved on, passing the comforting statue of St Richard giving his blessing, and the west door of the cathedral with the dear, carved faces of the Queen and the Duke set into the arched stonework. She was sorry that Giles, her late husband, the archdeacon, had departed this world before seeing the results of the stone-cleaning. It had transformed the cathedral.

Back through the cloisters she went, stepping a little faster. The lighting wasn't so good here and this was the only part of the walk that she didn't enjoy. Footsteps echoed on the stone flags and you could imagine someone was behind you. It was built around a former burial ground. She had to come this way to get to the passage leading to Vicars Close, so she was sensible about it. She didn't let her imagination dwell on the gravestones she was walking over and the memorials set into the wall. Instead she thought about the letters she had to write and the shopping she had to do in the morning.

As she approached her house she saw the light go out in the house next door but one. The canon had decided to turn off the television and go to bed.

She let herself in and closed her door and bolted it. She wouldn't be turning her lights out. It put burglars off if you left them on. Another Tip for the Twenty-First Century.

Zach was in bed in his railway carriage home, but not asleep. He had promised to stay awake until midnight, so he was correcting the latest chapter of his epic novel, *Madrigor*. This was the only writing project that mattered. He couldn't raise any enthusiasm for Naomi's e-book. Was it wishful thinking that she would give up on him if he contributed nothing else? Almost certainly. Each day she left messages with red priority tags on his e-mail. At some stage he would be forced to confront her and say he wanted to pull out.

He looked at the digital clock by his bed. Two minutes to go. Put the script in its folder and shoved it under the bed. Took a sip of water. Reached for his mobile and switched on. Texting was a new experience and he wasn't too familiar with the language. He had a suspicion Sharon enjoyed sending cryptic messages he struggled with. She insisted on this midnight ritual.

Here it was: the first message.

PMFI

No use. He couldn't work it out, so he tapped in one of the few abbreviations he did know: PXT (please explain that).

Back came: PARDON ME FOR INTERRUPTING

NO PROBLEM, he wrote. IM IN BED

THINKING OF ME?

258

OF COURSE
NICE THOUGHTS?
NAUGHTY
GMTA
Oh Christ, he thought. There she goes again. What's that?
But he didn't need to ask. She texted it in full:
GREAT MINDS THINK ALIKE
THANKS SWEET DREAMS
WITH U IN THEM
PLEASE
ILU
He could work that out. Now it was a matter of signing off.
ILU2
HAGN
PXT
HAVE A GOOD NIGHT OO
OO was OVER AND OUT. Zach switched off and turned
out the light.

In his flat above the building society, Tudor was at work on
the latest chapter of his autobiography. It was after midnight,
but when the mood took him and the ideas were flowing,
he lost all track of time. He tended to write like this, in
bursts of inspiration. He'd seen inspiration described by the
American writer Stanley Ellin as 'a sort of spontaneous
combustion – the oily rags of the head and heart'. A great
way of putting it. He would have written to Mr Ellin and
told him so, but unfortunately Mr Ellin was dead. Famous
people enjoyed being reminded of quotable things they'd
once said, and Tudor made a point of collecting their wise
and witty sayings to trot out when the chance came, either
in a letter or face to face. It was a pity so many memorable
things had been said by people who were dead.

His own wise and witty words were flowing tonight. He
was writing up his latest experience, the interview with the

police. The chapter already had a title: In the Frame for Murder. He was now putting into vivid prose – with a little dramatic licence – the account of his grilling at the hands of DI Stella Gregson. He portrayed her as a formidable adversary, picked for her forensic skill, beady-eyed, probing, springing a series of surprise questions that he countered brilliantly. 'But even as I parried her cut and thrust,' he wrote, 'I was aware that her patience could snap at any time and I might presently find myself in a cell being kicked to kingdom come by a bunch of booted bobbies, so I took some of the edge off my responses with shafts of wit. And you may be sure I reminded her that I was on a social footing with the Chief Constable and the Lord Lieutenant of the county.'

Splendid alliteration there, *a bunch of booted bobbies*. Almost worthy of his old chum Dylan.

Going over the interrogation in his mind, he couldn't help thinking he was still the prime suspect, and while it was good to be the centre of attention, it was worrying as well.

Damn! He'd hit the wrong key because his hand was shaking.

The police had this theory that Edgar Blacker had treated him badly. And of course it was true. Blacker had behaved outrageously, considering how the bastard had done so handsomely out of the insurance claim.

Yes, he thought, I'm definitely in the frame for the killing of Blacker. But they'd have a job to pin the killing of Miss Snow on me. There was no history of bad feeling with Miss Snow. So they'd had to content themselves with questions about my movements on the night of the Tower Street fire. Living alone, as I do, I couldn't produce an alibi. I wasn't at work on my computer in the small hours of the morning, like that anorak Anton. Nor was I having a dirty weekend in Harrogate with Sharon. Now that was a turn-up. Who would have thought a little cracker like her would have fancied Zach the nerd?

However Tudor looked at it, the list of suspects was worryingly short.

Blast! He'd hit another wrong key and *turning* had come on the screen as *burning*.

In her bungalow in Belgrave Crescent, Dagmar Bumstead lay awake wondering if she'd done the right thing. Earlier in the day she'd had a man round to seal her front door with two metal plates, inside and out. He'd fitted a new, self-contained letterbox attached to a post near the front gate. On the face of it, this was proof of her innocence, the reaction of a frightened woman.

Yet a cynical detective might view it differently, as a desperate bid to deflect attention, the killer trying to portray herself as the very opposite of what she was. Dagmar couldn't be sure how the police mind worked. She'd been impressed by DC Shilling. His attempts to ambush her had been pretty effective. He'd reminded her that she knew about Blacker's betrayal of Maurice ahead of the first murder. He must have got that from Thomasine; no one else knew. He'd also laid a trail inviting her to show disapproval of Miss Snow, suggesting that she could have done a better job as secretary of the circle. If Shilling was typical of the police investigation, they weren't going to take a fortified front door as proof of innocence.

Too wound up to sleep, she put on the light and looked for a book to take her mind off her present worries. She picked up *Pride and Prejudice* and was soon immersed in the intrigues of Elizabeth Bennet and Mr Darcy.

Basil was locking up when Naomi called from upstairs, 'What are you doing?'

'The usual, dear.'

'What did you say?'

'Checking the doors and windows.'

'Well, don't. I may need to go out.'

Basil went upstairs to the room where Naomi was at work on her computer. She'd been there all evening.

'Do you know what time it is?' he asked.

'I don't particularly care.'

'Ten past one. Isn't it a bit late to be thinking of going out, my dear?'

She didn't look away from the screen. 'Don't fuss, Basil. Go to bed.'

'What – and have you call me out at some ungodly hour? Remember what happened last time?'

'You're not going to let me forget, are you?'

'Are you meeting someone?'

'For pity's sake. If I wanted to visit a lover I wouldn't be telling you about it, would I? It's research, man. I'm trying to get into the mind of a killer who works by night.'

Basil sighed. 'You were a lot easier to live with when you were doing the witchcraft book.'

Thomasine was asleep.

Bob was having his last cigarette of the day. It was a good thing he'd come home because young Sue had been waiting up for him, sitting alone with a torch, scared to go upstairs. She'd been trying to add a new DVD player to her hi-fi system and the electricity had gone. The poor kid hated the dark. It was only a matter of the trip switch going, but she didn't know how to fix it. Bob mended the faulty fuse and gave her a cuddle and she was now asleep.

He didn't need reminding that he was a parent still and she was just fourteen, for all her eyeshadow and street talk. Had he been tempted to stay the night at Thomasine's? Yes, for about five seconds. They both knew that fixing the

262

letterbox was just an excuse to get him there. But he'd taken the job seriously and fitted a piece of plywood, accepted a can of beer and left. Thomasine would be thinking he was a dead loss, a man in need of a large dose of Viagra.

> Watch out lady, here comes Bob.
> Invite him in and he's on the job.
> But when he says he needs a screw
> It's for your letterbox, not you.

Actually he liked Thomasine a lot. He cared about what she thought of him. He cared so much that he was nervous of telling her he had a fourteen-year-old daughter who had to come first.

22

Fire is emphatic business. It doesn't fool around.

Shelly Reuben, *Origin and Cause* (1994)

That night another fire was started in Chichester. For the arsonist, the stakes were higher. Just getting to the scene was high risk. The city was nervous. The papers and television were already talking of a serial fire-raiser. The police were under orders to look out for suspicious behaviour. Everyone on the streets at night was a potential suspect.

So every parked car might contain someone on watch. Behind every curtain could be a detective, or one of those amateur snoopers who make a call to *Crimestoppers*.

But the planning took account of the risks. The arsonist picked a route that gave plenty of cover and made sure each stretch of the way was safe to use, once waiting in a shop doorway for ten minutes for some lone walker to pass right out of sight.

At the chosen house, it was the same *modus operandi*. The rags, the fuel, the flame. Then a quick exit from the scene, quick, but not obvious, leaving behind a fire that would take and spread, devouring everything combustible. We fill our homes with wooden furniture. Usually the floors, doors and staircase are of wood. Most curtains and blinds catch fire readily. Paper in the form of newspapers, magazines and junk mail is shoved through the door every day and often left in the hallway. No wonder so many domestic fires cause maximum destruction and death before the firefighters arrive.

This one was quick and deadly. It happened in Vicars Close.

23

It was a maxim with Foxey – our revered father, gentlemen –
'Always suspect everybody.'

Charles Dickens, *The Old Curiosity Shop* (1841)

The first Hen Mallin knew of it was at six thirty, when she stepped out of the shower. She could never hear the phone when the water was going. Didn't want to. She grabbed a towel and her mobile. I don't need this, she thought.

'Another? . . . Vicars Close? That's . . . Oh God. And is she . . . ? I'll be there shortly.'

Grim-faced as she drove from Bognor, she tried to get a grip on what had happened and what it meant. A third death by fire in Chichester. Another of the writers' circle murdered, and by night, the victim at home, in bed, at her most vulnerable. This would panic the rest of them. And give the press a field day. Proof positive that a serial killer was at work. She could hear the questions already. Why hadn't the police given twenty-four-hour protection to the members of the circle? How many more fatal fires would have to take place before the arsonist was caught?

Pick a number, she thought from the depths of her despair.

Fire engines, two of them, were drawn up in Canon Lane, on the south side of the cathedral, the closest they could get to the fire. A mass of pipes snaked up the narrow lane that fronted the terrace. There was barely room to put her feet down. But at least Vicars Close was cordoned off at each end, barring the gawpers.

Wisps of smoke still rose from the smashed windows of the burnt-out, saturated house. The fire had been contained in the one dwelling. The rest of the nicely maintained row appeared to have escaped, even the adjacent houses. White fronts and cared-for gardens made the contrast more poignant.

Hen lit a cigar and took a fortifying drag.

Stella Gregson was standing in a bed of purple irises in the trampled remains of the garden. 'Seems to have happened around four thirty this morning, guv, just like the others.'

'Witnesses – or is that too much to hope?'

'None so far. Uniform are knocking on doors.'

'Who reported it?'

'A shop window-cleaner, name of Meredith. He saw the smoke from South Street and came to investigate. That was just before six. The fire had ripped through the place by that time.'

Hen stepped over some of the hoses to speak to the senior fire officer. 'Any conclusions yet?'

'It was started at the front, I can tell you that.'

'Like the others. Petrol through the letterbox?'

He hedged a little. 'The investigation team hasn't been through yet.'

'But you have.'

'All I can give you is a personal observation.'

'Like I said, petrol through the letterbox?'

He smiled in a way that confirmed it.

'You took the decision to remove the dead woman?'

'We had to. The floor was starting to go. It's a wonder we contained it to the one house. These old buildings had solid walls. Fifteenth century.'

'Is there much left of her?'

'It's not pretty, but she isn't ash, like the last one.'

'Just the one victim?'

'Please God, yes. That's all we found. She lived alone, according to the neighbours.'

'That's our information, too.'

He scratched his unshaven face. 'Do you think the point of this was to kill? Who'd want to—'

'Thanks,' Hen cut him off. Speculation had its purpose, but not now. 'Appreciate your help.'

She returned to Stella. 'Not much we can do here until it cools off, Stell. We've got to move fast on this. I want to know where each member of the circle spent the last twelve hours. See if anyone spoke to Jessie late yesterday, in person or by phone. Look for signs of guilt, examine their hands, ask to see their shoes, clothes, vehicles, garages, outbuildings. Check for fuel, evidence of it, the smell of it.'

'We'll need warrants for all that, guv.'

'Sod that. They owe us their cooperation. If they refuse, we know who to focus on, and they'll be aware of that. Get the team working on it pronto, will you, before the press start badgering them.'

'The entire circle?'

'The whole boiling lot of them. Even the ones we think are in the clear. This is an inside job, Stell. We've met the killer, so we're ahead of the game. We don't know why the bugger is doing this, but we've got to nick him before he does another.'

'Him, guv? You said "him".'

'I take it back. Him or her. While you attend to that, I'm calling a press conference. They'll be screaming for a statement and they can have one, so at least I'll know they're sitting in front of me while you guys are doing the business.'

She was right about the media interest. She called the conference for ten thirty and it was standing room only. Some of the nationals – papers, TV and radio – were represented. From this point on, the pressure would be intense.

She was good at this and she handled their probing without once losing her grip. The questions were predictable, fishing for the quote that she refused to give, the admission that she was at a loss. On the contrary, she told them, a number of promising leads were being followed up.

Then she did four television interviews. As if that wasn't enough, she was summoned immediately after by the assistant chief constable and asked – in a roundabout way – if she was up to it. This time she did snap back. She told him she knew what was being hinted at and, no, she didn't need the Regional Crime Squad muscling in, and what was more she took it as insulting that it was even being considered. Her clear-up rate was second to none in West Sussex and she looked to her superiors for support in the shape of a generous overtime budget.

He huffed and muttered things about headquarters, and Hen came out knowing she was on limited time, but she knew that already.

She drove to the mortuary for a look at the body, a necessary duty, however distasteful. Fire is a great concealer. The possibility always had to be kept open that injuries had been inflicted first.

Just before the sheet was drawn back she reminded herself that the likely cause of Jessie Warmington-Smith's death was smoke inhalation. She would not have felt the flames. Horrific as the flesh injuries were, they were postmortem burns.

Standing beside the body she reflected on the irony that the killer is never forced to view his victim on a mortuary slab, as the investigator must. You would need to be callous indeed not to be affected by the spectacle of the fire-damaged corpse in those clinical surroundings. The nearest a murdering arsonist comes to the consequence of his crime is a glance at the photographs in court.

She saw enough to confirm Jessie's identity, then went in search of fresh air and a smoke.

In theory it was lunchtime, but she wouldn't be able to face food for a long while. She called the team to the incident room for a briefing and began by sharing the sparse information she had. The fire fitted the pattern of the others. It had started in the front hallway, by the door. There were no signs of a break-in, so concealing a theft wasn't the reason for the fire, as is sometimes the case. The victim had died in bed, probably from smoke inhalation. The fire chief was suggesting a likely time of origin between four and five in the morning. No witnesses had yet been traced, for all the door-to-door enquiries.

'So run it past me,' she told her team. 'What did you discover?'

Silence. No one wanted to go first.

Then Stella said, 'Do you want a summary from me, guv? There are ten surviving members of the circle and we've talked to nine of them this morning. The odd one out is Bob Naylor, and he left home early for work. He's a Parcel Force driver and he's on a long-haul job to Bristol. We've made contact and I'm seeing him tonight. Of the others, we had good cooperation from everyone.'

'But nothing helpful?'

'I didn't say that.'

'Get to it, then,' Hen said. 'Who are you talking about?'

'Naomi Green admits she went out during the night, she thinks at about three a.m.'

An avalanche of new possibilities crashed into Hen's brain. 'What on earth for?'

Stella turned to Andy Humphreys. 'You'd better explain.'

He pulled out his notes. 'I interviewed them both – the Greens, I mean. They'd heard about the fire on local radio, so it didn't come as a surprise to them. I spoke to Naomi first and she was very straightforward in her answers.'

'Was Basil present?'

'No, guv. He went out to do something in the garden.'

Johnny Cherry said, 'Like disposing of an empty petrol can?'

Typical bloody Johnny.

Hen said without even a glance in his direction, 'Andy, tell us what Naomi had to say to you.'

'The first time round she didn't admit to anything. She claimed she was working at her computer, entering stuff on her website until well after midnight. She keeps late hours apparently.'

'Website?'

'It's some kind of diary she and Zach are writing.'

'An insider's view. We know.'

'Only Zach isn't pulling his weight, so it's all down to her, she says.'

Johnny said, 'He's shagging Sharon instead.'

'Shut up, Johnny. Naomi was working till late, you said?'

'Basil went off to bed about one a.m. and she went – I'm quoting her – "some time after". They don't sleep together.'

'Yes, we established that before. She didn't say precisely when she got to bed? You asked, I take it?'

'She wasn't sure. Didn't check the time.'

'Unlikely, but go on. Did you look at her hands, shoes and so on?'

'She showed me them without any fuss. I thought I was doing well, getting so much cooperation out of her. I didn't pick up any petrol smell. At that stage she had the all clear as far as I was concerned. Then I interviewed Basil.'

'Alone?'

He nodded. 'Naomi went off to do some more writing. Basil confirmed he got to bed around one, like Naomi said, while she was still using the computer.'

'And?'

'I asked him if he would have heard Naomi going to bed and he said no.' Humphreys put in a personal observation.

'They're a funny couple. If they were in this together they could give each other alibis easily.'

'But they don't,' Hen said, 'so we assume they aren't.'

'Then he added something that really dropped her in it. He said he heard the front door go when she went out. He said this in a matter-of-fact way as if we both knew all about it. I said, "She went out?" And he said, "Yes, doing research." I asked what time it was and he said it must have been between two and three. He said he knew she was going because she'd told him not to lock up.'

'Did he hear her come in?'

'No, he fell asleep. This morning they both got up late.'

'I'm not surprised. So you spoke to Naomi again?'

'I did, and she didn't turn a hair when I said she'd not told me the whole truth. She said she hadn't lied. She just didn't think it was important.'

'Oh, that old applesauce. Did you ask what she was up to?'

'She said she was' – Humphreys quoted from his notes – '"getting a sense of what it must be like on the streets at night". She's trying to get into the mind of the arsonist, she says. I said she'd better come up with something better than that and she turned quite stroppy. She said I was incapable of understanding how a serious writer worked and a lot of stuff like that.'

'So how did you handle it?'

'I asked where she went and what sort of research she did.'

'Good.'

'She took the van and drove into town and parked in North Street in one of those spaces at the top end.'

Hen pictured North Street: the paved walkway ended halfway up, north of the red-brick Council House, and traffic could approach through St Peter's and park at the side. 'Did she say why?'

'Research.'

'I know. Researching what?'

'She didn't explain, guv.'

'And you didn't press her?'

Stella came to his aid. 'You know who lives in North Street, above the building society? Tudor.'

'So he does,' Hen said. 'Did she mention Tudor?'

Humphreys said, 'No, guv.'

'What happened, then?'

'Nothing, according to her. It was all about atmosphere – the city at night.'

'Atmosphere, huh? The action was in Vicars Close. Are you sure she didn't go there?'

'She was very clear about that, guv. She stayed where she was.'

'Imbibing the atmosphere?'

'I suppose.'

'How long for?'

'About an hour. Then she reckoned she'd got what she wanted and drove back home and went to bed.'

'She says.' Hen was silent for a while, brooding on what she'd heard. 'I wonder what else wasn't important enough to mention. It's all right, Andy. I'm not taking a swipe at you. You did good, lad.' She turned back to Stella. 'And what else did we glean? Were the rest of our beauties all tucked up in their little beds by three a.m.?'

'Pretty much, guv. Some went later than others. Anton was online on his computer, and can prove it. Tudor was writing a new chapter of his life story until late, but reckons he was in bed by two.'

'Anyone away from home?'

'Not this time.'

'And that's the sum of this morning's interviews?'

'The bits worth mentioning.'

'Statements on my desk before you leave tonight. Wait.'

Hen put up a restraining hand. 'I haven't finished. I want to pick your brains. Here we are with a third death by arson. One rather unpopular man and two inoffensive women. We had a few theories as to why Edgar Blacker was murdered. Fewer for Miss Snow. And I can't think of any reason at all why Jessie had to go. Can you?'

'She was an easy target,' DC Shilling suggested. 'Like Miss Snow.'

'Lived alone, you mean?'

'And in the centre of town.'

'That's risky, surely?'

'Plenty of escape routes, plenty of cover.'

'Fair enough, but you seem to be assuming they were killed for no other reason than convenience.'

Shilling gave a shrug. 'If the idea is to pick off members of the circle one by one, it makes sense to start with the easy ones.'

Johnny Cherry said as if to a child, 'Blacker was the first to go, and he wasn't in the circle.'

'All I'm saying,' Shilling said, 'is that the two women were sitting ducks.'

'No, you said the idea was to pick off members of the circle and I'm challenging that assumption.'

Hen sensed that there was more behind Cherry's remark. The man was still a peevish, grudging presence at meetings, unable to get over his displeasure that the investigation had been taken from him. But if he had something to contribute she wanted to hear it. 'What's your take on this, Johnny?'

'I reckon more than one person is involved.' He paused to watch them all sit up, and it certainly created interest.

'Go on. We're listening.'

'As you know, I nicked Maurice McDade, the chairman, for the murder of Blacker, and I still think the case would stand up in court. Okay, someone else must have started the fire at Miss Snow's, but McDade could have been behind that, too.'

Frowning, Hen said, 'That's unlikely, isn't it? Miss Snow was a friend of his.'

Johnny was enjoying this, spacing his words for maximum effect. 'She was the one who knew about his past, his jail term. And she betrayed him. She told someone else. Who did she tell? Naylor, the new man. And who nearly died in a fire at the boat house? Naylor.' He looked around for approval, and there were certainly some eyebrows raised. 'Then Miss Snow herself was killed.'

'Who are you suggesting did this?'

'McDade's partner, Fran.'

Shilling gave a long, low whistle. Everyone else was dumbstruck.

Hen's stomach gave a lurch and her self-confidence plummeted. She'd forgotten Fran. All this concentration on the circle members had clouded her judgement. It was a whopping oversight, and she'd been shown up in front of the team. She grappled with the concept for some seconds. Johnny, sod him, was right. Fran was well placed to know what was going on and had a motive. Digging deep for a scrap of credibility, she said, 'She's rather elderly to be a fire-raiser, isn't she?'

Johnny dismissed that with a sneer. 'Is there an upper age limit for arsonists? As far as I know, Fran isn't disabled. She's devoted to McDade. Maybe she acted with his encouragement, maybe not. Let's not forget she was married to one of the Richardson gang.' He leaned back in his chair, savouring the impact he'd made. 'If it was up to me . . . But of course it isn't.'

'If it was up to you, what?'

'I'd find out where she was on the nights of each of the fires.'

Hen said, 'We can do that, but before we get too excited how does the latest fire fit into this hypothesis?'

'We don't know until we question Fran. Jessie Warmington-Smith was one of the founders of the circle,

275

wasn't she? It could be that she, too, knew about McDade's past form.'

He'd obviously thought this through. Hen hadn't looked outside the circle because it seemed that the crimes required inside knowledge. His theory had to be tested. Hen said she would follow it up.

'You can send me,' he offered.

'I'll do it,' she said. There were limits.

No one pointed out that if Johnny's theory was right, Hen had made a fatal mistake in releasing Maurice McDade. No one needed to point it out. They all knew Jessie Warmington-Smith might still be alive.

She made another effort to claw back some respect. 'I'm still giving high priority to Naomi Green. I want a printout of everything on this website of hers. Duncan, will you see to it?'

'No problem,' Shilling said.

'And we'll demand the same from anyone else who has been writing about the case. Tudor, for example. Who interviewed Tudor?'

Stella raised her hand.

'Why the long face, Stell?'

'He's not going to like this.'

'He'll be flattered,' Hen said. 'They're writers, these people. They want to be read.'

She wound up the meeting. Johnny Cherry had a grin as wide as a grand piano. His intervention had rocked the team's confidence in her. Divided loyalties threatened.

DC Shilling was the last to leave, and for one humbling moment Hen feared he was going to offer sympathy. But it was something else. 'I've got a scrap of information for you, guv. Don't know if it helps. It's about that photo of Blacker and his unknown friend. You asked me to find out where he was working at Christmas, nineteen eighty-two, the year it was taken.'

'And?'

'He was with a magazine group called Lanarkshire Press.'

'Up in Scotland?'

'The name's misleading. It operated from a trading estate in Tilbury. You know Tilbury? Thames estuary.'

'I know Tilbury. Go on.'

'They specialised in men's magazines, soft porn.'

'I remember someone saying Blacker had done a bit of that.'

'None of them were big sellers. They kept trying different titles, producing a couple of issues and then thinking of something else. Like *Headlights* made a big thing of boobs and *Hot Buns* was mainly bottoms.'

'Okay, I get the drift,' Hen said.

'Well, towards the end of eighty-two, they had this idea of a mag with pictures of girls who were supposed to be amateurs and first-timers. Some men prefer them to professional models.'

'Like "Readers' Wives".'

'Same idea, except that the title they came up with was "Innocents".'

'Was it indeed?' she said, her spirits lifting a little. 'So the writing on the back of the photo wasn't what we thought at all. It wasn't a comment on the two blokes, it was a porno mag and they were at the Christmas party. Nice work, Duncan. That's a mystery solved. A small one, but who knows how useful it may be?'

'No problem, guv.'

'Good. Now you can impress me even more by finding out who the other guy was.'

Inside the hour she was doing penance, sitting on the chintz sofa opposite the Swiss mountain scene in Fran's front room in Lavant, a tray of tea and fruitcake in front of her. She hadn't dismissed the idea of Fran as the arsonist, but she had to stretch her brain to picture this silver-haired old lady patrolling the streets in the small hours with a can of petrol and a bundle of oily rags. The thing that made her hesitate was the voice. Tough, hard, resolute.

'I'm surprised you have the gall to come back,' Fran said as she poured the tea, making it clear from the start that she was no pushover.

'I'm the one who released Maurice,' Hen said. 'When I took over he was already in custody.'

'What's this about, then?'

'Like I said on the doorstep, it's more about you than Maurice.'

'You bastards never let go, do you?' Fran said with all the bitterness of long experience. 'Just because I made an unfortunate marriage a long time ago, I'm listed as a lowlife for ever. How do I get through to you people that I was never involved in crime?'

'It's not about the past. It's about last night. I expect you heard another woman died in a fire in Chichester.'

'That. It was on the radio.' Not much sympathy there.

'She was one of the circle. You probably knew Mrs Warmington-Smith.'

A shake of the silver curls. 'They're just names to me. The circle is Maurice's baby. I'm not interested in writing.'

'You haven't met the members?'

'One came on his own when Maurice was in custody. Bob, he said his name was. I'd never even heard of him. He was back later with a woman, something like Tamsin.'

'Thomasine O'Loughlin.'

'They said they were trying to get Maurice released so I took them at their word. I'm very trusting.'

In trying to assess her character, Hen hadn't thought of 'trusting'. Words like 'canny' and 'hard-nosed' sprang more readily to mind, try as Fran might to cultivate the little old lady look.

'Can we turn to last night, or, rather, early this morning between three and five? We're asking everyone where they were.'

'Here, as usual.'

'Is there any way of proving it?'

'Maurice will tell you.'

'Thanks, but it would count for more if there was some independent proof.'

'That's ridiculous. What do you expect, some neighbour knocking on the door at four in the morning?'

'Point taken,' Hen said. 'Do you drive?'

'Can do, at a pinch. I rely on Maurice mostly.'

'But you keep your hand in? Sensible. What make of car is it?'

'Ford Escort.'

'An old model?'

'Depends what you mean. The mileage has gone round the clock.'

'I'd like to see it before I go. Have you used it today?'

'We took a shopping trip into town.' She gave a sharp, impatient sigh. 'Listen, you're wasting your time with me. I've got nothing against the writers. Maurice gets a lot of pleasure from the meetings, and I'm happy for him. There's no earthly reason why I would want to set fire to people's homes.'

'Oh, if we're dealing in earthly reasons, I think there's one you have to face,' Hen said. 'The second victim, Miss Snow, knew about Maurice's past, the prison sentence, and she blabbed about it to Bob Naylor, the man you met. Each of them was attacked by the arsonist – fatally, in the case of Miss Snow, though Naylor escaped. Both incidents happened while Maurice was in custody, which let him off the hook, but not you.'

Her hands formed bony little fists and she leaned forward, glaring. 'Maurice's past is public knowledge. It was in the papers at the time.'

279

'The Brighton papers, yes, but hardly anyone in this town knew of it. Most of the circle hadn't the faintest idea. They respect him. Miss Snow had the potential to blow away his reputation.'

Fran switched to a more defensive tone. 'Nobody told me Miss Snow was putting this about. I agree it would have angered me. I don't know what my reaction would have been except I wouldn't have torched her house. That's sneaky and detestable. I'd have had it out with her, face to face. Besides, I didn't even know where the Snow woman lived until I read about the fire in the paper.'

'Presumably Maurice has an address list for the circle.'

'If he has, it's in his office upstairs and I don't go in there.'

'But you know where to look.'

'That's unfair.'

'Where is he right now?'

'In Chichester library, I should think. That's where I left him. He'd arranged to meet one or two of the circle there, to talk over this latest fire.'

'So you drove home alone? You do use the car?'

'Just as I said, at a pinch. I may be older than Maurice, but I'm not decrepit, you know.'

Anything but, Hen thought. This was a foxy lady with a sharp mind. 'Do you keep a can of petrol here? People sometimes do, as a back-up.'

'You'd have to ask Maurice. He deals with things like that. You haven't had a slice of my cake.'

'I've got no appetite, thanks. Mind if I look at the shoes you were wearing?'

'Wearing when?'

'This morning, when you drove the car.'

'What for?'

'Just to check. It's my job.'

Shaking her head, Fran got up and left the room and

presently returned with a pair of flat-heeled brogues. Hen examined them and found no trace of petrol or of burning, but then she wouldn't have expected this with-it old woman to leave anything so obvious.

She asked to see the car and took the opportunity to poke around the garage in search of the spare can of petrol. She didn't find one.

'Are you sure you don't want a specimen of my DNA as well?' Fran said.

The sense of failure still nagged at Hen as she drove back into town. Johnny Cherry, blast him, had touched a raw nerve. No question: Fran was a suspect now and should have been from day one.

www.ChichesterMurderDetectives.com

Latest Developments on the Chichester Arson Case from Naomi Green

It's all over the papers and television, so you'll know. The arson attacks in Chichester continue. Yesterday another of the circle, Jessie Warmington-Smith, died in a house fire deliberately started in the same way as the others. It was a shock to us all. Jessie was not an easy person to get on with, but who am I to talk? Whatever one thinks about her, she didn't deserve this.

For me, it was a hugely frustrating night. Having decided the conditions were ideal for another arson attack (dry, warm, new moon), I put on dark clothes and trainers and left the house about twenty to two and drove to North Street to keep watch on the Welshman. Took up position in a shop doorway opposite and was encouraged to see the light still on in his flat over the building society. He was still my number one suspect. So I was ultra-cautious. I waited nearly an hour and then the light went out. Expecting him to come out immediately, I watched the door to the street. Nothing. There's no back door. He had to come out that way. I kept watch for another hour and twenty minutes. Finally, around four thirty, with the sky already getting lighter,

I decided this wasn't to be the night. Stiff-legged from standing for so long, I returned to the car and drove away.

I discovered later what had happened. The fire was in Vicars Close, up by the cathedral, while I was keeping watch in North Street – so I'm forced to conclude that the Welshman was not responsible. He was at home in his flat while I was watching.

Everyone is asking why the arsonist should have chosen Jessie this time. Is it because she was a soft target? She lived alone in a quiet terrace and unlike some of the others she hadn't taken any precautions against someone pouring petrol through her letterbox.

Later, we were all questioned about our movements. Guessing how the police would react, I was going to say nothing about my night's adventure, but Greenfingers, stupid oaf, blurted it out. I should have realised he'd throw me to the wolves. In the end I managed to convince them what I was doing was research for this book, but it took some while.

And so the focus has to shift again. If Welshman is off the list, and so are The Chair, Nitpicker, Zach and Blondie, who is left? I can forget Greenfingers. Only the Schoolmistress, Passionella and the new man, Parcel Force. Two strong-minded women and one man who reveals very little about himself. But what motive could any of them have?

The police have a new theory: two perpetrators working together. Interesting. There are several partnerships within the circle of suspects.. By this I don't mean man and wife. You might think of Basil and me as a team – unless you know our situation. Mostly these are twinnings of another sort. I thought I'd found an ally in Zach, but he has disappointed me. Ever since he went to the Fantasy Convention with the dumb Blondie he seems to have lost interest in the e-book. If you visit this website regularly you'll know he promised to collaborate with me, and he had some promising ideas, but he has produced nothing. It's his loss. I've registered over a thousand hits since I installed the hit counter.

Partnerships? Well, we have The Chair and his lady.

Parcel Force, the new man, and his friend Schoolmistress (wanting to see him after lessons, I suspect).

Romantic novelist Passionella and Schoolmistress (yes, her again, they're old chums).

And Zach and Blondie.

The point about two killers working together is that they can cover for each other. Some of the alibis the police have checked out would be worthless. It would throw everything back into the melting pot.

I am going back to my list to see who ought to be suspect number one. I'll keep you informed of everything that happens.

YOU ARE VISITOR [1021] TO THIS SITE

25

You shan't evade
These rhymes I've made.

Catullus (87–54BC) *Fragments*, trans. Sir William
Marris

'Just to recap, you were at home all night?'

'All night,' Bob said.

'But you were up early?'

'My job. I was on the Bristol run.'

'Which meant leaving home at . . . ?'

'Five thirty.'

'So you got out of bed at what time?'

'Quarter to five. "Early to rise and early to bed makes a
man healthy, wealthy and dead."'

Stella Gregson smiled. 'One of yours?'

'Wish it was.'

'You're sure about the time?'

'I leave it to the last possible second to pull back the
duvet. Quick shower and shave, sling on some clothes, slice
of toast and a cup of coffee, in that order if my head is
working. Then off.'

'A quarter to five this morning? No earlier?'

'I told you. I like my bed.'

'And of course there's no way to prove you were there
all night?'

'How could I? Ah – you mean like someone sharing my bed? You reckon?'

'Fair enough,' Stella said. She'd enjoyed interviewing him. 'You said that wasn't one of your verses just now?'

'James Thurber.'

'But you do write poetry. You read me a sample when we last met.'

'Doggerel is a better word.'

'I thought it was all right.'

'It's meant to raise a laugh here and there. Things that happen to me, people I meet. Nothing deep.'

'Is any of it published?'

'God, no. I'm a beginner.'

'I noticed you write it down in a pocket book.'

'An old diary. When I first came to the circle one of them told me to keep everything. Most of it's crap.'

Stella leaned forward like a conspirator. 'Anything on the other members? I'd love to read some more.'

He hesitated. 'Well, some of it's a bit . . . you know, below the belt. I wouldn't want them to read it.'

'But I'm not in the circle,' Stella said. 'And there aren't many laughs in this job.'

'All right.' He put his hand into his hip pocket and took out the small black diary. 'Don't expect Tennyson, will you?'

'I wouldn't want him, thanks. He's dead, isn't he? May I keep it overnight? I'll take care of it.' She slipped it into a drawer, and for a moment Bob Naylor looked as if he'd been duped and didn't understand how.

'We're done.' Stella parted the slats of the blinds. 'She's waiting for you downstairs.'

'Who is?'

'Your friend from the circle. That's Dagmar's little car, isn't it?'

He looked out. 'Doesn't mean a thing.'

But when he emerged from the police station it was

Thomasine who stood outside the car waving. Dagmar was at the wheel. 'We thought you might be hungry if you came here straight from work,' Thomasine said. 'I got you a bite to eat from the pasty shop. It's still warm, I think.'

'Kind of you.'

'Some of the circle are in the bar at the New Park. We would have had a meeting, but it doesn't seem right somehow. We thought we'd join them.'

'Okay with me.'

It was good to see Maurice there, restored as the father figure of the circle, his big hand clasped round a pint glass. Less good to see Tudor, flushed with the drama of another death and ready to badmouth anyone who couldn't be there. Of the ladies, only Thomasine and Dagmar had come.

'Why on earth should this happen to Jessie?' Dagmar said.

'Obvious,' Tudor said. 'She got up someone's nose.'

'You don't murder people just because they upset you.'

'Oh, but you do. Well, plenty of murderers do. Let's face it, she put herself on a pedestal. Holier than thou, forever reminding us she was once married to an archbishop.'

'Archdeacon.'

'What's the difference? You wouldn't think there was any, the way she went on. You'd never find her drinking in this bar, for instance.'

Thomasine said, 'She obviously got up *your* nose, Tudor.'

'You know yourself, there were times when she would have made a nun feel guilty. As for us, we were the children of darkness.'

Maurice said, 'Let's try and be more charitable, shall we? There was nothing in Jessie's attitude that remotely justified anyone killing her.'

Dagmar said, 'Thank you, Maurice. I can't abide people who speak ill of the dead.'

Tudor said, 'So you're carrying the torch now, are you?'

'What torch?'

'Our moral conscience. Someone has to do it, I suppose. Well, you want me to be more charitable. Here's a more charitable theory for you. She was killed because of that book she was writing.'

'"Tips for the Twenty-First Century"?' Thomasine said in disbelief. 'What's the problem with that?'

A knowing smile spread across Tudor's face. 'No problem any more. It's all gone up in flames, hasn't it, like "The Snows of Yesteryear", another apparently inoffensive book. Has anyone yet considered the theory that it wasn't the people the killer wanted to destroy, it was the books?'

'That's bullshit,' she said.

'So were the books. This is literary criticism taken to the ultimate. Kill off bad books before they get published.'

'Tudor.'

'Yes?'

'Does your mother know you're out?'

Bob saw this descending into a slanging match. 'Hold on, hold on. We're all on edge,' he said. 'Let's keep it friendly, huh?'

Maurice backed him. 'The circle has always been about support for each other. Together, we ought to be able to make some sense of what's happening. In some ways we're better placed than the police to get to the truth of it. We have a fair idea what we're all about.'

'We're creative people, or we wouldn't have joined the circle,' Dagmar said, extending the idea. 'How can any of us be a murderer? Killing is destruction, the very opposite of what we are.'

'Unless one of us joined for the wrong reason,' Thomasine said with her peculiar talent for speaking up at the wrong time.

'What do you mean?'

'That they had an agenda of their own and are using the circle as a cover for their killing.'

Tudor rose to this at once. 'A cover? You've got something there. We know who the *bona fide* members are. They're the people who write stuff and read it out week after week.' The direction of his thoughts was clear as he eyed the others seated around the table. 'Maurice finished his book and delivered it. Dagmar has done about twenty.'

'Twelve,' Dagmar said.

'That's enough to prove you're genuine. Thomasine has a great folio of erotic verse.'

'Poetry,' Dagmar said.

'And far from great,' Thomasine added.

'Sorry. Poetry. Great in number, by any standard. We all admire your body – of work.' He paused to have his wit appreciated. 'And I've completed over a hundred thousand words of autobiography.'

While this was going on, Bob felt the spotlight moving inexorably his way. 'That makes me the killer,' he said, to cut short the process. 'Nothing to read out. No form at all as a writer.'

Thomasine was quick to defend him. 'You're not the only one, Bob. Anton never reads his work in our manuscript sessions.'

'Neither does Sharon,' Dagmar said.

'Right,' Thomasine said. 'She just doodles through the meetings.'

'Yeah, but they're the ones with the alibis,' Bob said. 'On the night Miss Snow was killed, Anton was using his computer and can prove it and Sharon was up in Harrogate.'

'And Zach was up in Sharon,' Tudor added.

'Tudor, why do you have to lower the tone at every opportunity?' Thomasine said.

'Like I said, it comes back to me,' Bob said. 'No alibi. Bugger all to show as a writer.'

Concern was etched deeply in Thomasine's face. 'What about your rhymes? It's no good being coy about them.' She hesitated, but not for long. 'He's a wiz at making up funny rhymes.'

There was a silence. Then Maurice said, 'Could we hear one?'

Bob's leg jerked under the table. 'This isn't the moment, is it? I'd rather be the number one suspect.'

'Go on,' Thomasine said.

Dagmar said, 'Do it, Bob.'

He took a deep breath. 'I guess there's the "Writers' Prayer".'

'What's that?' Maurice said. 'Let's hear it.'

'A bit of nonsense really. Don't know if I can do it from memory:

Lead me not into temptation,
Overusing punctuation.
Kindly show me where to drop
Comma, colon and full stop.
But if I falter, grab me, please,
And cut out my apostrophes.'

There was a silence that threatened to go on for ever. Tudor's eyes had opened wider and Dagmar's had closed, it seemed, in embarrassment.

Maurice was the first to speak. 'You wrote that?'

'Like I said, this isn't the time.'

'It's good.'

Maurice's approval always carried weight in the circle. There were murmurs of agreement.

'When did you compose it?' he asked.

'I wouldn't say "composed". "Made it up" is more like it. Today, while I was out on the road.'

'You see?' Thomasine said to them all with undisguised pride. 'He's one of us.'

Tudor gave a hollow laugh. 'I bet that pleases him no end.'

Hen Mallin worked until after midnight, repeatedly reviewing the videotapes of Blacker's visit to the circle and the witness interviews the team had carried out. Somewhere in that lot was the arsonist, unless it was Fran, the one person she hadn't got on tape. She wasn't excluding Fran. But it was hard to visualise any of them with the level of cruelty required. Even Naomi, the most obsessive one, seemed focused on writing a book, not taking a life.

She was late getting in next morning and there wasn't much to encourage her in the latest report from the forensic lab. Samples had been taken of the lead content of petrol owned by certain suspects. The residues of the leaded petrol used by the arsonist gave at least a reasonable chance of making a comparison. Basil had a couple of cans in store for his motor mower. Checks on the old cars owned by Dagmar and Fran had confirmed that they ran on leaded. Zach ran his motorbike on leaded. None of the samples matched.

She showed the report to Stella. Trying to be helpful, Stella said it was one more factor in the case, something to add to their database.

Hen was not so upbeat. 'It doesn't help us at all, Stell. All this proves is that we haven't found the killer's supply. Any of those people could have used a can we didn't trace.'

Stell nodded. 'Are we checking the local petrol stations?'

'Done. They have no idea. A can can be bought in the shop or filled at the pump.'

'And you can bet this killer isn't going to use a local garage.'

'I did have one thought,' Hen said. 'Bob Naylor.'

'What about him?'

'He's a Parcel Force driver. Presumably they have their own depot where they fill up.'

'They'd be using diesel, guv.'

'Yes, but it's a garage set-up. The odd can stored there for private use. Have someone check it, Stell.'

Stella's eyebrows rose. 'You rate Bob Naylor as the arsonist?'

'He's the newcomer, isn't he? You interviewed him. What's your opinion?'

'I rather liked him, tell you the truth.'

'But did he tell *you* the truth?'

Later, towards midday, DC Shilling found Hen in the incident room.

'Guv.'

'Mm?'

'I've got something for you. Remember you asked me to track down the second man in the Blacker photo?'

'*Innocents* magazine.'

'Right. It turns out he was the owner of Lanarkshire Press, the publisher of all those men's magazines. Mark Kiddlewick.'

'Have you found him?'

'Sort of.'

'He's not dead?'

'No.'

'Banged up?'

Shilling shook his head.

'So what do you mean by "sort of"?'

'He changed his name by deed poll in nineteen eighty-seven. He was Marcus Chalybeate after that.'

'Bit posh.'

'It was meant to be. He sold his publishing interests and wanted to forget them. He went into the health club business just when it was really taking off, got in with a couple of hotel chains and started equipping hotels up and down the country with all the latest treadmills, rowing machines, weightlifting gear and the rest of it. The turnover was huge. He started buffing up his image, making donations to charity and the Labour Party, rubbing shoulders with the great and the good. Five years ago he was given a life peerage. He's Lord Chalybeate of Boxgrove now.'

'I think I've heard of him,' Hen said. 'Not that I've ever stepped inside a health club. Where can we see him?'

'Problem there,' Shilling said. 'He's unavailable.'

'What do you mean – "unavailable"?'

'I made enquiries. He has a secretary and she says his diary is full for the next week. The government are trying to get some bill through the House of Lords and every vote is crucial.'

'I'll see him in London, then.'

'You won't get past that secretary, guv.'

'Watch me.' She handed him the phone. 'Get me the number.'

Without another word, Shilling pressed the buttons and handed it across.

'Is that Lord Chalybeate's secretary?' Hen said. 'Good. May I speak to him? . . . Detective Chief Inspector Mallin of West Sussex Police . . . Isn't he? Oh, but I think he'll make an exception for me. Tell him it's about an old colleague of his at Lanarkshire Publishing, Edgar Blacker. Yes, Blacker . . .' In a short while she winked at Shilling. 'Lord Chalybeate? Good of you to come to the phone. DCI Mallin here. Bit of a blast from the past, this. I need to see you urgently about your connections with the late Edgar Blacker. You probably heard he was murdered . . . This afternoon, please . . . That will do nicely. Three thirty? . . .' She put down the phone and said to Shilling, 'Do you own a suit and tie? Get home and togged up. We're meeting him at the Garrick Club.'

They didn't step far into the Garrick. Just enough to announce themselves to the porter. Lord Chalybeate was waiting at the top of the steps and came down when he heard his name. He was silver-haired now and wore designer glasses and a pinstripe suit. He was just recognisable as the man in the photo.

'I thought I'd take you to my hotel,' he said with one hand steering Hen out to the street again.

'Here will do,' she said. 'Your time is precious and so is mine.'

'We can talk more freely there.'

He was well organised; he had a taxi waiting. They were driven along the Mall and past the palace to the Goring Hotel in Beeston Place, around the corner from the Royal Mews.

'Would tea and sandwiches in the garden suit you?' he asked.

They stepped right through the small hotel to the rear, where a large square lawn was intersected by a paved path. No one else was there. They chose a spot in the shade and the tea and sandwiches arrived while Lord Chalybeate was still talking about the advantages of living close to Victoria Station.

'Do you remember Edgar Blacker?' Hen asked as soon as the waitress had stepped away.

'Not particularly well,' he said. 'It was a brief association.'

'Is that a joke?' she asked.

'What?'

'Brief, briefs. Girlie magazines.'

His face was a mask of displeasure. 'What about them?'

'You published them, didn't you?'

After a long pause he said, 'The odd title. It was a tiny part of our output. Glamour mags, we called them in those days.'

'Blacker edited some of them.'

'Probably.'

'I'm telling you,' Hen said. 'He did. One of the titles was

294

Innocents. We found a picture on his bedroom wall of the two of you with your arms around each other's shoulders at what looks like an office party. On the back is written "Innocents, Christmas 1982".'

'I wouldn't recall it.'

'Wouldn't recall, or would rather forget?'

'Both,' Chalybeate said. 'It's not a time I wish to revisit.'

'But you remember the magazine?'

'Just about.' He looked away. 'We were publishing scores of titles on any number of topics: music, motoring, wildlife, sport. The top-shelf stuff was a tiny part of the output.'

'That you'd rather forget.'

He shrugged and tried to seem unconcerned. 'In fact it was all very tame. More nudge-nudge, wink-wink than porn.'

'Blacker was your editor, right?'

'Yes.'

'He seems to have looked back on his time at the magazine with some affection. He kept that photo for over twenty years. Have you any idea why?'

'No.'

'Arms around each other. You must have been close.'

Chalybeate held up a warning finger. 'You won't tar me with that particular brush, inspector. I'm straight and always have been.'

'Was Blacker?'

'I'd be surprised if he wasn't.'

'Perhaps he was simply proud to be linked with a peer of the realm, then. Found the photo in a drawer and thought, "Lord Chalybeate and I were mates once." Helped his self-esteem.'

Chalybeate gave a shrug, and it seemed like acquiescence.

'Did he try to make contact again?'

'He may have done.'

'He set himself up as an independent publisher. He'd have been looking for financial backers.'

'I dare say.' His tone suggested he was thinking of other things. Or trying to.

'Did he put the bite on you, Lord Chalybeate?'

A sigh. 'All right. You know, don't you? I chipped in a couple of grand, mainly to keep him quiet. I'm a politician. I could be in line for a government post. We have to be squeaky clean these days.'

'Hush money.'

'I don't care for the term, but that's what it amounted to.'

Hen exchanged a glance with Shilling. 'And there was no guarantee that he wouldn't come back for another handout.'

'If you're thinking I caused the man's death, forget it,' Chalybeate said. 'I was in Los Angeles until last weekend attending the World Fitness Fair.'

'Actually we're investigating three separate deaths by fire,' Hen said. She let him stew before adding, 'You're not a suspect.'

He relaxed as if he'd just completed a lift on one of his machines.

Hen said, 'But I'd like to know more about the men's magazines.'

He tried laughing it off. 'That was over twenty years ago.'

'Blacker was editor, and you owned the titles, right? What was his role exactly? My impression of soft porn is that it's more pictures than words.'

'There's a certain amount of text. But, yes, the pictures sell the magazine.'

'Would he have taken the pictures?'

'No, no. We had a couple of professional photographers.'

'Blacker hired the models and set up the photo sessions?'

'Yes, and chose the shots for publication.'

'The girls were professional models?'

'In the main.'

'Not all of them, then? The idea of a magazine like *Innocents* was that the girls hadn't posed nude before. Am I right?'

'Supposedly they hadn't. You can make it look like an amateur shoot in a number of ways, varying the lighting and the location, and so forth.' He was more willing to talk now he'd been told he wasn't a crime suspect.

'So they weren't amateurs?'

He rolled his eyes.

Shilling said, 'Blue, but not true blue,' and got a glare from his boss.

'Some did it for love, if you know what I mean,' Chalybeate said.

'I'm not sure if I do,' Hen said.

'When we could persuade a girl to pose, we did. These were low-budget mags. Any savings we could make were a bonus.'

'How did you find such girls?'

'Don't look at me personally. This was more Blacker's department than mine. My understanding was that some of them were pickups. He'd buy them a few drinks and chat them up, flatter them into stripping off.'

'Drinks or drugs?'

His mouth gave a twitch that answered the question.

'Same old trickery men have used on gullible girls from time immemorial,' Hen said. 'I'm not surprised you want to distance yourself from all that.'

'Blacker, too,' he said. 'Let's be fair. He was trying to cut it as a serious publisher.'

'But not without some gentle blackmail to fund it.'

'I wouldn't call it that.'

'I do,' Hen said. 'And if he'd lived you can bet your life he'd have been back to you for more.'

26

*One can survive everything nowadays, except death, and live
down anything except a good reputation.*

Oscar Wilde, *A Woman of No Importance* (1893)

The printout of Naomi's website material on what she called
'The Chichester Arson Killings' amounted to thirty-three
pages. Each now bore Hen's imprint, the whiff of cigar.

She'd asked Stella to look through it.

'Done?'

Stella nodded.

'Close the door.'

Stella knew what was coming. The anger had brought a
kind of paralysis to Hen's normally mobile face.

'It's obvious, isn't it, that someone's been talking out of
school? This stuff about two people working together. It
comes straight from our last meeting.'

'I thought so, guv.'

'Scumbags. I knew as soon as you and I walked into this
nick we were in for a hard time, but I didn't reckon on this.'

'They're not all bad.'

'One is, at the very least. One of the team is bending
Naomi's ear. Who is it? Who did the interview with her?'

'The first one? You did, guv.'

'No – the latest. After Jessie was killed.'

'Andy Humphreys.'

'*Him?*'

'Don't rush in, guv. I know he got off to a bad start with you, that crack about gays, but he's keen.'

'Too damn keen if he's playing his own game, feeding titbits to one of the suspects.'

'Want me to talk to him?'

'No, I will.'

Stella feared for Andy. She'd seen Hen in warlike moods, but this was Armageddon. 'It could be one of the others.'

'I don't think so. Who else in the team has spent time with Naomi? Duncan Shilling hasn't been near her. I made a point of clobbering Johnny Cherry with the dumb blonde. It's Humphreys, bang to rights.'

Stella decided to let her simmer for a while. Finally, she said, 'What about this website? Shall we close it down?'

'No need, if I plug the leak. Most of it's self-serving rubbish. Let the woman rant on as much as she likes.' Realising that she was ranting herself, she gave a half-smile and made an effort to lighten up. 'I must say I enjoyed some of these names. Nitpicker.'

'Passionella.'

'I wonder what she calls you and me.'

'Better not ask,' Stella said. 'Anyway, I've read it, like you asked. Seems to me she wants to be a part of the action even at the cost of drawing suspicion on herself. Basically the diary shows she's in the clear, if it's true. And this latest entry supports Tudor's statement that he was at home all night.' She reached for another stack of printed sheets.

'Tudor.' Hen pulled a face. 'His stuff is even more of a pain to read. Remind me what he says about yesterday. Don't give me earache by reading the whole thing.'

Stella picked up the printout of Tudor's book and turned to the last sheet. '"And so to bed about three in the morning, dog-tired, pooped and tuckered, but with another two thousand words of purple prose in my trusty computer."'

'Can you beat it? These bloody writers think they're God's gift. But you're right, Stell. Three a.m. was when his light went out according to Naomi.'

'So they're both in the clear.'

'Apparently.'

'Which means Naomi is right. We're down to the last three. Or four, if we include Fran.'

'Five,' Hen said. 'Naomi doesn't know if Basil went out that night, and neither do we.'

'*Basil?*' Stella had some difficulty grasping Basil as a serious suspect. 'He's easy to overlook, I'll grant you. Inoffensive, modest, devoted to his garden. Is he the worm that turned? But if he is, wouldn't he turn against Naomi? He had nothing against Blacker, or Miss Snow or Mrs Warmington-Smith.'

'Nothing we know about,' Hen said, and then added, 'He stays on my list.'

'He's on the fringe,' Stella said, giving serious consideration to Basil for the first time. 'Doesn't regard himself as a serious writer. Only joined to make up the numbers. I wonder if he hates the lot of them.'

'Might do.'

'But he's an ex-fireman. They don't start fires, do they?'

'Coppers can go wrong, so why not firemen?'

'He'd have to be a nutcase.'

'Whoever is doing it has to be a nutcase,' Hen said. 'But if you think about it, we're left with the level-headed ones. Dagmar never says anything outrageous. Thomasine is more animated, but has her feet on the ground. Fran has a kind of worldly wisdom learned from those years as the wife of a gangster. And Bob is the guy on the Clapham omnibus.'

'The Parcel Force van.'

'Right. Your all-round good egg. Not a nutter among them that I can see.'

The mention of Bob reminded Stella of something. She

opened the drawer of her desk and took out the diary he had loaned her. 'While we're looking at their literary efforts – I didn't tell you about this, guv.'

'What is it?'

'Bob's poems. His doggerel, he calls it.'

'He lent them to you? He's very trusting. I wouldn't lend you an umbrella on a wet day.'

'Thanks!'

'Anything of interest?'

'I haven't had time to read them.'

'Let's hear one, then. They can't be worse than these other literary efforts.'

Stella thumbed through the pages and smiled. 'Here's a sample:

> Is Basil green
> When his wife is seen
> With the new Tolkien?'

'Likes his puns, doesn't he?' Hen said, not much impressed.

'Okay,' Stella said, turning to another page. 'Here's one about a cat:

> Amelia was a dancing cat, I'm able to disclose
> Before she started writing the lives of all the Snows.'

'We're into T. S. Eliot territory now,' Hen said. 'One of the few things I remember from school, his poems on cats. Is there any more?'

> 'At the local writers' circle she sits beside the Chair
> Keeping minutes of the meeting with single-minded care.
> If the members criticise her she might give a little shrug
> And privately remember how she used to cut the rug.

301

At home, she does her writing and if it doesn't flow
She'll choose another chapter, start another Snow.
But as the night approaches and the work gets really
    tough
She allows herself a memory of how she'd strut her stuff.
For Amelia was a dancing cat, I'm able to disclose
Before she started writing the lives of all the Snows.'

'What's he on about here?' Hen said, frowning. 'This is
Miss Snow, right?'

'Must be.'

'Does he know something we don't? You're the one who
interviewed him. Did you ever hear about Miss Snow being
a dancer?'

'Sounds unlikely, guv.'

'Is it his quirky sense of humour?'

'He's got that for sure.'

'How would he know what she got up to? He was new to
the circle.'

'He did visit her house on two occasions, once to borrow
the video of Blacker at the circle and once to return it.'

Hen raised both thumbs. 'You're right, Stell. I was forget-
ting. I'm sure you questioned him about the visits?'

'Of course. I thought we covered everything. He doesn't
hold back.'

'But the dancing didn't come up?'

Stella shook her head. 'Does it matter?'

'Don't know yet.'

'What time are you expecting your dad?'

'Depends,' Sue Naylor said on the phone.

'On what, love?'

'On the job. Like sometimes he's here when I get in from
school and sometimes he gets in really late.'

'It's not regular hours, you mean?'

'Yeah.'

'Does he have a mobile?'

'For emergencies only, he says. He don't like me calling when he's on the road.'

'What's the number?'

Hen got through to Bob directly. The signal wasn't good, but she heard him say, 'Thanks a bunch. Is this how you nick people, then, calling them up on the motorway?'

She said, 'I want to ask about one of your poems.'

'Come again?'

'The things you write.'

'For crying out loud – I'm doing seventy on the M27 and you want to talk about writing?'

'The one about the dancing cat. "Amelia was a dancing cat".'

'I don't believe this.'

'Amelia was Miss Snow, right? Is there any truth in it – in the dancing, I mean?'

'Yeah.'

'She told you this herself?'

'Yeah.'

'Right. Where are you now?'

'Just passing Rownham services.'

'You'll be home shortly, then?'

'If I don't hit the bloody barrier, I will.'

'I'll be waiting at your house.'

These intervals of inactivity were a trial for Hen. She found herself thinking about the traitor in her team. Betrayal may not cause physical injury, but it hurts. By God, it hurts. The question of who had leaked Naomi the inside information troubled her almost as much as the identity of the arsonist. She'd been over it in her mind many times, recalling things that were said, meetings, interviews with suspects. She felt it ought to be possible to work it out. She could have asked

Naomi – who would be evasive, but might cough it up eventually – but she preferred not to. Pride in her leadership demanded that she cleared this up herself. After all, the possibilities were limited. Stella wasn't the source. If she couldn't trust Stella she might as well jack in the job now. That left three names: Humphreys, Shilling and Cherry.

All logic said it was Humphreys. He knew Naomi. He was the one who'd interviewed her. But his denials had been solid and convincing.

Shilling was a more likeable lad than Andy. Brighter, too. He'd solved the mystery of the writing on the back of Blacker's picture. To Hen's certain knowledge he hadn't interviewed Naomi. Yet he did have this unfortunate knack of speaking up at inappropriate times. Immaturity, probably. She couldn't have absolute confidence in him.

And that left Johnny Cherry. If anyone had a vested interest in undermining her, it was Johnny. He couldn't handle the fact that the case had been taken out of his lap and handed to her. He was jealous, cynical and probably knew in his heart that he couldn't hack it as head of a murder investigation team. But there was a problem. Johnny, like Shilling, had had little to do with Naomi. Johnny had interviewed Sharon and Thomasine, but he'd scarely even spoken to Naomi. Satisfying as it might be to pin the blame on him, logic suggested otherwise.

Bob and his daughter lived in a council semi in Parklands, a large estate to the west of the city. Inside, it had the clutter you would expect of a place occupied by a shift-worker and his teenage daughter. Sue Naylor kicked aside some Tesco bags to clear a path to the living room. She was pretty without make-up, dressed in baggy jeans and a sleeveless top that displayed her tattoos. She went back to watching a soap on TV while Hen and Stella cleared some space on the sofa and sat down.

Bob arrived soon after, shaking his head at the idea of two detectives interested in his rhymes. But his temper had improved now he was off the road. He filled a kettle.

'Sure,' he said when Hen asked about Miss Snow, 'I didn't make it up. She was a dancer and a cat.'

'How do you mean?'

'She was in the musical, *Cats* – the original West End version. The chorus, I think. She had a photo on her wall of herself in tights and a cat costume. Nice figure, too. Surprising, isn't it, what some quiet little ladies have got up to in the past? She didn't seem the chorus girl type. I asked if it was really her and she said it was.'

'She must have been proud of it.'

'To have the picture on the wall? She didn't make much of it. I'm trying to remember what she said. Some stuff about dancing being a short career. Is it important, then?'

'Is that all?'

'There was some more, but not about the dancing. She was a bookkeeper, wasn't she? Retired, but still did a few audits for old times' sake, her dentist and what are those people who cut the corns off your feet?'

'Chiropodists.'

'No.'

'Excuse me,' Hen said. 'I know about chiropodists. I get my feet done by one in Bognor.'

He snapped his fingers. 'Podiatrists.'

'Same thing, buster.'

'Okay, don't get heavy with me. As I pointed out to her, she was working the old barter system. She did their books and they did her feet and her teeth.'

'It sounds as if she opened up with you.'

'A load of stuff about Maurice, the chairman. She was all steamed up on account of him being nicked for the fire at Blacker's house.'

'What sort of stuff – his past?'

He hesitated, and it was clear that he was stalling. 'A bit of this and that.'

'His time in prison?'

A look of relief. 'Right, so you know all about that. And how he was sure to be stitched up unless we did something about it. She meant well.'

'I'm sure. And she wanted your help?'

'Anyone's. She wasn't the only one trying to help Maurice. Thomasine and Dagmar were worried, too. He's popular with the ladies.'

'Getting back to Miss Snow, how did she first approach you?'

'Phone. She asked me to come to the shop.'

'The charity shop where she helped out?'

'I met her there before we went round to Tower Street. She was running it single-handed. The place stank of old clothes. I wouldn't have stuck that job for ten minutes.'

'If she was alone in the shop, what happened when she took you home? Did she have to close?'

He said with a flash of annoyance, 'Don't you believe me? I'm telling it straight. She phoned the women's refuge and asked for someone to take over. We waited for her, a foreigner called Nadia or some such. Refugee, I reckon.' He winked without letting his face soften. 'That's what a refuge is for, refugees, isn't it?'

Provocation. Remembering her visit to the refuge with DC Shilling, Hen let the question remain unanswered. She was investigating serial arson, not illegal immigrants. 'Moving on, you made a second visit to Tower Street. Is that right?'

He nodded. 'The night before I was caught in the boat house fire.'

'What happened?'

'She said she needed the video back. It was late in the evening. After eleven.'

'What did you think?'

He looked straight into her eyes. 'I could have thought I'd got lucky.'

'Be serious.'

'She was in a state.'

'DI Cherry had asked her for the video, guv,' Stella said.

'So you went to the house,' Hen prompted Bob.

'And I could tell it wasn't just the video she was worried about. She told me about this call she'd had setting up the meeting in the boat house.'

'What was the pretext?'

'He was claiming – this was a man's voice, she said – to have the proof that Maurice McDade was innocent and he was willing to hand it over the next morning at eight.'

'She didn't know the voice?'

'It was indistinct, she told me.'

'But definitely male?'

'That was what she said.'

'You understand the importance of this?' Hen said. 'We believe this was the arsonist. He tried to set up the meeting in the boat house with Miss Snow and he meant to kill her there.'

'He nearly did for me instead.'

'Yes, and we don't know whether he knew it was you in there when he torched the place. You were lucky to escape.'

'Tell me about it!'

'But Miss Snow was still the real target, and he set light to her house at the next opportunity. The key to all this is the reason why these women – Miss Snow and Mrs Warmington-Smith – were targeted. Their homes went up in flames, so any personal documents, pictures, other evidence that could be of interest, were destroyed. That's why your memory of the interior of the Tower Street house is important to us. We didn't know about her theatrical experience.'

'Does that link up, then?'

'Now you're asking. It may tie in with the other victims in some way.'

Bob smiled. He was more relaxed now. 'I can't picture Jessie Warmington-Smith as a show girl.'

'Like you say, you find out surprising things when you dig a bit. Have you any theatrical experience, Bob?'

He pulled a face. 'Christ, no. I couldn't go on a stage to save my life.'

'Amateur theatricals?'

It was obvious he didn't like being pressed. The petulance returned. 'I said no.'

'Why not?' Stella said. 'You're an outgoing guy. You seem to get on with people. Women obviously feel comfortable with you.'

'Where's this leading?' he asked, tight-lipped.

'Let's get back to Miss Snow,' Hen said quickly. 'Did you notice anything else that might tell us more about her?'

'No.'

'More pictures?'

'Some family photos.'

'Books?'

He sighed, making it clear that all this was an imposition. 'A dictionary. Some books of quotations. Set of *Who Was Who*.'

'Nothing out of the ordinary?'

'I did see a fitness mag with some muscleman on the cover.' He couldn't resist a gag. 'I guess his name was Snow.'

'What was it called?'

'Now you're asking.'

'Try.'

'*The Bodybuilder*, I think.'

'I can't picture Miss Snow pumping iron,' Hen said. 'Why did she have a magazine like that?'

'For the pictures?'

She gave a chesty laugh. 'Maybe. Maybe.' She turned to Stella. 'There could be a link with Lord Chalybeate here. Does he still publish magazines? We'd better get hold of one.'

'Lord who?' Bob asked.

'Doesn't matter,' Hen said, sensing as she spoke that she'd closed him down too quickly. She didn't want him digging any more than he had. 'Anyway, thanks to you we've learned a thing or two about Miss Snow. What about Mrs Warmington-Smith?'

'What about her?'

'Did you visit her at home?'

'Do you mind? She was old enough to be my gran.'

She repeated the question.

He said, 'I don't think anyone was invited there. She put up the shutters if you tried to get near. A very private person.'

'She can't have been all that private if she came to the circle and read out her work.'

'None of it was personal. It was how to make pickled onions.'

'Didn't any of them know her well?'

'I doubt it.'

'She wasn't timid,' Hen said, trying to get a better response. 'She didn't mind going for late-night walks.'

'I wouldn't know about that.'

'She seems to have fancied herself as a psychic as well.'

'Sidekick?'

'Psychic. Like Joan of Arc.'

He shook his head. 'That's news to me.'

'She didn't hear voices. She saw things, apparently.'

'And ended up as toast, just like Joan of Arc.'

In the car, Hen said to Stella, 'What was that line of his about Miss Snow doing her secretary bit? ". . . she sits beside the Chair . . ."'

'". . . taking minutes of the meeting with single-minded care."'

Hen pondered this for a while. 'He's a bloody good observer. Remember the video of Blacker's visit? She had her head down right through the meeting. Even when he discussed her book she didn't speak. As I recall it, other people spoke on her behalf as if she wasn't there. Maurice McDade. Anton Gulliver. And when Blacker delivered his verdict on the script she still didn't say anything.'

'Is that important, guv?'

'Might be.' She went silent, alone with her thoughts again. The car travelled to the next traffic lights before she started up again. 'There could be something in this, Stell. Why was she so quiet? A secretary taking minutes isn't like a short-hand typist. They're not trying to catch every word. They're summarising. They have a chance to chip in with a comment here and there. You'd think she'd want to speak when her book was being discussed. Not a word.'

'I expect she saw him after the meeting.'

'No. She avoided him. Dagmar picked up the script for her. Miss Snow was supposedly too busy handing round competition forms. She asked Dagmar to collect her script.'

'Why?'

Hen's thoughts were slotting into place. She sensed she was on the brink of something significant. 'The moment Blacker walked into that room, Amelia Snow wanted the floor to swallow her up. She recognised him from way back.'

'An ex-boyfriend?'

'Worse than that.'

'Someone she'd dumped?'

'Much worse.'

'A rapist? He raped her when she was a young girl?'

'If he did, he got away with it. He's got a clean record. No, Stell, I'm wondering if it has to do with his time as editor of those men's magazines. Amelia Snow was a chorus girl. What year did *Cats* open?'

'Must have been in the early eighties.'

'You sure of that?'

'I was taken to see the original show as a birthday treat, round about my seventh birthday. That would have been January, eighty-two. It had been running some months already.'

'Let's say eighty-one, then. The timing is spot on. Eighty-two was the date of the "Innocents" photo. We're dealing in coincidences here, but when you get enough of them it adds up to something bigger. Do you see what I'm getting at?'

'Not really.'

'She had a nice figure. Did you hear that?'

Stella's mouth shaped as if to whistle as she grasped what Hen was saying. 'Blacker got her to pose for one of his porn magazines?'

'Chatted her up, got her drunk, talked her into stripping off for the camera. That's the way they got their dirty pictures according to Lord Chalybeate. After it, she'd feel used, abused, mortified. She'd do her best to forget it. Then, twenty years later, the guy who seduced her walks into the New Park Centre to lecture the circle on publishing. No wonder she kept her head down. Does that sound possible?'

Stella weighed it before answering. 'Up to a point.'

'What's wrong with it?'

Hen waited for Stell's answer. They'd worked together long enough to be frank.

'They're both dead, Blacker and Miss Snow. Who would have wanted to kill them both, and why? The theory is all right, guv, but it doesn't seem to fit what happened.'

'It does,' Hen said, feeling and sounding more confident than she had at any stage. 'Someone else had a reputation to protect, a big reputation.'

27

But where are the snows of yesteryear?

François Villon, *Le Grand Testament* (1461), trans. D. G. Rossetti

Andy Humphreys shook his head and said, 'No way, guv.'
'I ask myself what's in it for you,' Hen said. 'Did I cut you up so badly when we first met? Is that why you did this – to get revenge?'

'I've done nothing wrong.'

'Come on. You're the one Naomi talked to. To her you're the face of the Chichester police.'

'But I wouldn't disclose information.'

'She told you about this website. You must have known it would all go on the internet if you blabbed.'

'Exactly. So I didn't.'

'She's clever enough to tease out the information indirectly.'

He shook his head. 'I swear, guv. I gave her nothing. Our meetings weren't mentioned once.'

'Have you had any contact with her apart from the interview?'

'Not a word.'

'Someone has.' She brandished the sheaf of paper that was Naomi's e-book. 'Someone talked at regular intervals. These are peppered with inside information. Yesterday's meeting – when we discussed the theory of two suspects working together – is already on the bloody website.'

'Not because of me.'

'All right, then. If it isn't you, who·else has been mouthing off?'

'I wish I knew.'

In the face of his steady denials, she was beginning to lose confidence. He *had* to be the snitch, didn't he? 'I'd think more of you if you put your hand up to this.'

'It's untrue.'

'I'm going to find out, you know. If the truth doesn't come from you, I'll get it from Naomi herself. And if she gives me your name, it's the end of your career.'

Bob met Thomasine at Woody's, in St Pancras, at the end of East Street. As there was a noisy crowd in the bar, he suggested they move into the eating area, and it happened with no fuss that he took her for a meal for the first time. She'd eaten already, so she toyed with a salad starter, but he was hungry and ordered the sirloin. They shared a carafe of red wine.

He asked if she'd heard of Lord Chalybeate.

'Not the sort of company I keep,' she said, adding, after a pause, 'I'm more comfortable with van drivers.'

'Any old van drivers?'

'Only those who write funny verse.'

'But you've heard of Chalybeate?'

'Isn't he the bloke who made a fortune out of the fitness craze? He's always in the papers.'

He told her about the visit from Hen Mallin and the police interest in Miss Snow's spell as a dancer in *Cats*. Thomasine said she knew nothing of this. 'You didn't tell me.'

'I thought everyone knew.'

'I don't think any of us did. *Cats?* Amazing. She must have been a top-class dancer and she never mentioned it. Isn't that strange? Come to think of it, she said very little about herself at meetings. She'd talk about the famous Snows she was writing about, and that was it. I just took it she was so careful what she said because of her accountancy work–client confidentiality. She did the books for some people in business.'

'She was quiet by nature, wasn't she?'

'But in a different way from Jessie, who was a bit of a snob, if that isn't speaking unkindly of the dead. Amelia – Miss Snow – was guarded about what she said, but I don't think she had delusions of grandeur. Anyway, you were telling me how Lord Chalybeate's name came up.'

Bob nodded. 'The police asked me to try and remember anything at all about the inside of Miss Snow's house in Tower Street. All they'd seen of it was after the fire. One rather surprising thing I noticed at the time was a magazine called *The Bodybuilder*.'

'Get away!'

'Straight up. Some clone of Arnie Schwarzenegger flexing his pecs on the cover. Not the sort of reading you expect a single lady to have on her table, but there you are – it's all about what turns you on. As soon as I mentioned this, Inspector Mallin said there could be a link with Lord Chalybeate, and it was obvious that was a name that had come up before.'

'Not in the circle, it hasn't,' Thomasine said. 'I'm intrigued.'

'He doesn't live round here, does he?'

'We can look him up.'

'In the library tomorrow?'

'Can't wait for that. Let's check him out on the internet. Tonight.' She smiled. 'Okay, it sounds like I'm trying to get you round to my place again. It wasn't meant that way.'

'But I'll come,' Bob said.

* * *

Hen, also, was talking about Lord Chalybeate. 'Well, the motive isn't hard to find. He's got an interest in seeing off Blacker and Miss Snow.'

'To save his reputation, you mean?' Stella said.

'He's been polishing up his image for years, putting all the murky stuff behind him. He was plain Mark Kiddlewick at one time. Changed his name by deed poll to Marcus Chalybeate, and now he's a life peer in line for a government job.'

'Definitely wouldn't want it known that he published porn.'

'He was giving money to Blacker just to keep him quiet. That much we know for sure. Then I believe Miss Snow recognised Blacker and it began to look as if the whole sleazy story would come out.'

'If it's true,' Stella said.

'What?'

'About Miss Snow posing for pictures.'

'Fair enough. It's just a theory at this stage. And there are two big problems with it.'

'What are they?'

'Chalybeate claims to have an alibi,' Hen said. 'He was in America at the time of the murders.'

'Can he prove it?'

'Simple to check.'

'Want me to do it?'

'No, Stell. I've got another job for you.'

'You said there are two problems, guv. What's the other one?'

The edges of Hen's mouth twitched into a smile. 'As you know, I listen to my Agatha Christie tapes when I get the chance. There are rules to a good whodunnit. Dame Agatha would never introduce the killer this late in the story. So I'm hoping it doesn't turn out to be Chalybeate. I want it to be one of the other buggers we've been tracking all the time.'

'Is that what this is to you – a whodunnit?'

'I do enjoy a good mystery, Stell. And a whopping surprise at the end.'

'But *we* shouldn't be surprised. We've got to work it out.'

Hen gave her smoker's laugh. 'You're so right.'

'You mentioned a job you want me to do.'

'It could take some time.'

'What is it?'

'You've got a good idea what Miss Snow looked like, haven't you?'

'I've watched the video.'

'An earlier picture would help. I'll see if we can get some stills from the original production of *Cats*.'

'Aren't you going to tell me?'

Hen said with deliberate obtuseness, 'Let's go there first.'

'Eleven thousand results,' Thomasine was saying in the room she used as a study. 'This could be a long night.'

Bob watched over her shoulder in awe. Young Sue had her computer, but he'd never taken much interest in the thing. Sue had used it mainly for games until texting on the mobile phone became the big thing in her life.

Thomasine explained that she was using a search engine called Google to access every reference to Lord Chalybeate on websites across the world.

'This will be his official website,' she said as a stylised logo of two figures came up on the screen, a woman on a treadmill and a weightlifter. 'Don't suppose it will tell us what we want to know. That would be too simple. Wow, he's a major player, though. Look at this list of gyms.'

From the speed with which she moved through websites, dismissing the 'duds', as she called them, she was well used to surfing the net. Even so, the process was taking time.

Ten minutes later she gave a squeak of excitement. 'This is more like it, from some political agitator's site: "Marcus

Chalybeate's friends in the House of Lords might be surprised to learn that he was once plain Mark Kiddlewick. He changed his name officially in 1987." Kiddlewick. I think I'd change that if I was stuck with it. Now we'll make a search and see if anything comes up.'

She went back to Google and keyed in *Kiddlewick*.

'Not so impressive. A mere twenty-seven.'

Most of the twenty-seven were horseracing sites. There had once been a steeplechaser called Kiddlewick. 'No pun intended,' she said, 'but you get all kinds of horseshit you don't want. You have to be patient, and I'm not.'

She'd almost exhausted the list when a Mark Kiddlewick came up in a directory of publishers. '"Magazines, various, adult. Lanarkshire Press, Tilbury, Essex." I wonder how adult magazines come into this.'

Bob looked at his watch. This search had been going on for some time. Sue would be alone at home. She didn't like going to bed until he was in.

Thomasine was intent on her surfing. 'Tallyho. Now we see if Lanarkshire Press yields anything.'

She could keep working that search engine for hours.

'I'd better be off,' Bob said.

She turned to look at him. 'So soon?'

'It's after eleven. Early start tomorrow. Can't fall asleep at the wheel.'

She came downstairs to see him out. Thanked him for the meal.

'Just a couple of lettuce leaves?' he said.

'Next time, the twelve-ounce porterhouse steak.' At the door, she reached for his hand. 'That's not the real reason, is it, about falling asleep at the wheel? You don't have to go, Bob.'

'But I do.'

She mouthed the word *why* and didn't speak it.

This was a defining moment and he had to be honest. It was high time he told her he had a teenage daughter.

So he did. And when he'd finished, he did his best to ease the tension by adding, 'It's funny when you think about it. I'm the one who has to be in by eleven.'

'And are you divorced?'

'Maggie died three years ago. Leukaemia.'

She closed her eyes. 'Sorry – shouldn't have asked.'

'Should have told.'

'What's your daughter's name?'

'Sue.'

'And she's fourteen, you said? The kids I teach are that age.'

'Different school, though.'

'Right. I'd know her if she was in one of my classes. If she takes after you she gives her teachers a hard time.'

'She's sharper than me.'

'Sounds awesome. I'd love to meet her some time. Oh God, why am I making all the running?'

He made some of the running himself. He put his arm round her and kissed her, a real kiss, and it felt good.

After Bob had left, Thomasine made herself a coffee and then went back to the computer. A pulse was beating in her head. She wasn't ready for sleep and didn't want to spend the next few hours in an emotional state like one of her teenage students. So she gave her full attention to the computer, surfing the net for references to Lanarkshire Press, clicking on anything that came up. It took her into some sites she wouldn't normally have gone near. She was used to 'spam', the unwanted e-mail, much of it obscene, that she had to delete each time she opened her inbox, but visiting dubious websites was unavoidable if she was to find out more about Kiddlewick, Chalybeate, or whoever he was. If it had to be so-called erotica, she was going there. Good thing her classes didn't know she was accessing stuff like this, she thought.

She found the all-important link at about one fifteen in the morning. A site was offering secondhand magazines for sale and you could click for more information – obsessively copious information that listed the entire contents of every issue, together with the names of publishers, editors, writers and photographers. No pictures, mercifully. Here, in a monthly called *Innocents*, published by Lanarkshire Press, was the name Edgar Blacker, editor.

This, she was certain, was why the police had been so interested in Chalybeate, the one-time publisher of porn trying to shake off his past and pursue a political career. They'd found the link with Blacker, and when Bob had mentioned the fitness magazine at Miss Snow's, they'd seized on the possibility of a second link, to the arsonist's next victim. Was Miss Snow into physical culture? Unlikely. Thomasine thought it more likely that she'd bought the magazine because of its Chalybeate connection. Maybe she'd done some digging herself when Blacker was first invited to the circle. She was secretary, so she'd have discussed it with Maurice at an early stage.

Satisfied, she turned off the computer and went to bed.

In the morning Hen drove out with Stella Gregson to the Sussex police evidence depository. Every police force has to provide storage for the millions of items and tons of paper used in investigations. Even after a case has gone to court and a conviction is secured, all the main materials, including items not produced in the trial, are retained, kept in plastic boxes in case of an appeal or a reinvestigation.

These buildings were the size of warehouses, strictly functional, boxlike and secure. The one unlocked for them was the second largest on the site and contained thousands of magazines and books seized in raids authorised by the obscene publications legislation.

'Welcome to wankers' world,' Hen said.

'You've made my day, guv.'

'There's a lot of hardcore stuff here, but luckily we're not looking for that. When a raid takes place they don't have time to sift through everything, so they clear the shelves and bring it all back here, the mild as well as the really gross.' She turned to the custodian, a veteran with a face like a blocked sink. The porn had long ago lost all appeal for him. 'Where can we find nineteen eighty-two?'

'They'll be dusty.' He escorted them around the metal stacking system and pointed to a row of boxes reaching up to the roof beams. 'The ladder's over there, in eighty-six.'

'Fine.' To Stella, she said, 'Lanarkshire Press publications, remember. From memory, that would include *Innocents*, *Headlights* and *Hot Buns*.'

Stella groaned. 'Couldn't you have asked one of the men, guv?'

'They'd be useless at spotting a face. Think about it.'

'Yes, but—'

'You don't have to look at the squidgy bits.' From her bag she produced a photo of a young woman in a top hat, tailed jacket and tights. 'This should help. I did some phoning late yesterday. Amelia Snow, *circa* nineteen-eighty, courtesy of the Megastar Theatrical Agency.'

Stella gave it a look. 'She's very young. I'm not sure I'd have picked her out.'

'But you will now – if she's here.'

'So am I on my own?'

Hen pointed to the No Smoking sign. 'I wouldn't last ten minutes. That's the way it is, sweetie.'

'How will I get back?'

'Don't worry. I won't forget you.' She opened her bag again and took out some polythene gloves that the SOCOs used. 'You see, I'm looking after you.'

* * *

It was a pity Bob was at work. Thomasine woke up too late to call him with her news about Lord Chalybeate. Thanks to school holidays she didn't have to go in. Instead she cooked some breakfast and then strolled into town and looked along the magazine shelves in Smith's. But not for the *Times Educational Supplement.*

The Bodybuilder was a monthly so there was a good chance that the issue Miss Snow had owned was still on sale. No difficulty finding it in the sports section. The bronzed hunk on the front stood out from the cricketers and footballers. She shelled out her two pounds fifty, and went next door to Starbucks for a quiet read. She had a good look round first to make sure one of her little bubble-gummers wasn't sitting across the way.

This was the right issue. Inside was a three-page illustrated article about Marcus Chalybeate under the heading LUCKY GYMS. No reference, of course, to his less exalted career as plain Mark Kiddlewick. The piece was all about his brilliance in foreseeing the boom in fitness. 'It is fair to claim Marcus Chalybeate has done more to improve the health of the nation in the last ten years than the combined efforts of seven Secretaries of State for Health.' It continued in the same vein. Rather boring, really. Except it left no doubt in Thomasine's mind that this was a man who could be terribly damaged if his days as a purveyor of porn were revealed. What had *Hot Buns* and *Headlights* done for the health of the nation?

But she almost knocked over her coffee when she saw the picture of his Sussex home, 'a barn conversion at Bosham, near Chichester'. Just down the road. Wasn't opportunity one of the key elements in a crime, along with motive and means? This, surely, raised Chalybeate to favourite in the suspect stakes. She couldn't wait to see the place. Couldn't wait, and wouldn't.

* * *

Stella had been given some tacky jobs in her years in the police, but this was the tackiest by a long way. Even the feel of the old magazines between her polythene-covered fingers was unpleasant. They smelt musty, they were stained, the paperclips had rusted and the pages dropped out when handled. All that, she tried telling herself, would have been true of a batch of old knitting magazines. You couldn't blame the subject matter for the state they were in.

Certain copies, luckily, could be put to one side straight away. *Headlights* catered for breast fanciers, men who'd never matured past infancy. Without exception the models had enormous boobs. Did they have implants in 1982? In abundance, it seemed. She pitied the poor models. How could you get comfy in bed with all that to tuck away? Mercifully, the picture of Amelia Snow in *Cats* showed a normally proportioned woman, so the entire stack of *Headlights* could be returned to the shelves, along with *TNT* (Two Nifty Tits) and *BSH* (British Standard Handful).

'Grow up, guys,' she said aloud.

She started turning the pages of *Innocents*, which at least featured models she recognised as her own species. Innocent most of them were not, she thought. Their attempts to look inexperienced were about as convincing as chocolate pennies. Some, she guessed, must have had a few drinks before going in front of the camera because the lipstick was badly applied or the hair needed fixing. If nothing else, it supported the story that Blacker used alcohol as the persuader.

Three or four magazines in, and she knew which pages to ignore. The joke section, the letters and the car feature, and the news of the latest X-rated films. There were whole sections of adverts for phone sex. Like any job, it got easier as you persevered.

Things were making more sense at last, but Hen was still unsure why Jessie Warmington-Smith had been murdered.

She needed more on Jessie's past. Was it too much to hope that Jessie, too, had once been a chorus girl?

The widow of an archdeacon?

Heaven forbid!

She would take another look at the video of Jessie, and ask Andy Humphreys, whose interview it was, to sit with her. He looked ten years older since their last encounter.

'Do I really have to, guv?' he said. 'It makes me squirm each time I look at it.'

'Why?'

'She gave me the runaround, didn't she? I've taken no end of flak from the others. That stuff about my wedding, and my christening. "We're all God's children." I took a right pasting.'

'It wasn't a stand-up fight, Andy. It was about getting information, and you managed that.'

'At a cost, guv.'

'If you keep whingeing, I'll invite everyone to sit in.'

They ran the video, and it was hard to ignore Andy's unease, on screen and off. Some of his questions begged for a sharp response: 'That's a bit whacky, isn't it, a club for writers?'

Hen put Andy to the back of her mind. What had Jessie said about herself? She was one of the first members of the circle, 'at the personal invitation of the chair'. A staunch supporter of Maurice McDade then. This was followed by some flimflam about the benefits of being in a writers' circle. Then the outrage at having her grace and favour living arrangements discussed: 'My late husband spent a lifetime in the service of the church and he couldn't have done it without my support.' She moved on to the offensive after that, questioning Andy's church-going.

Then came that weird claim that she was in touch with the supernatural. 'You have to open your heart. Then you'll be given signs. I get them quite often because I'm receptive, like Joan of Arc, except that she heard them as voices.'

Joan of Arc, no less. Jessie didn't suffer from low self-esteem.

'Only last night I had a sign. Some people would find it disturbing and I suppose it might be to a disbeliever, but I took it as affirmation of all I believe in, the afterlife, the journey of the soul.'

Did she think she was psychic?

'Stop the tape and spin it back. I want to see that section again.'

Andy sank deeper into his chair.

Hen watched and listened a second time and then let the tape run on. Jessie insisted she'd been at home on the night of the fire at Blacker's house, 'or most of it'. Then she spoke about her habit of walking at night before going to bed, when the streets were quiet, 'but always within sight of the cathedral spire'. Andy had asked if she ever took the car out at night. She spotted straight away what was behind the question and pointed out that she had no reason to kill Blacker, who had said something favourable about her book of tips. But she'd admitted she owned an old Mini Metro that ran on leaded and she kept it in her garage somewhere out of sight of visitors to the cathedral.

The interview ended soon after.

'Are you thinking she had some kind of premonition, guv?' Andy asked.

'Of what?'

'Her own death.'

'Why do you say that?'

'The bit you wanted to hear again, about the journey of the soul.'

'I get you. The answer is no.' She got up and took out one of her cigars. 'Did we check Jessie's lock-up?'

'Lock-up?'

'The place where she kept her car. Did someone look inside?'

He said, 'I'm sure of it, guv,' in a way that said he wasn't. 'Do it now. *Now.*'

She would have gone herself, but she'd just seen something she hadn't expected. Stella, back from the evidence depository already. She was with Johnny Cherry and a couple of others, leafing through a magazine.

Hen went over. It was a copy of *Innocents*, now open at the centrefold of a naked blonde face down on a bed and turning to look at the camera, which must have been positioned between her knees. The foreshortened view left nothing to the imagination. The girl's face, of negligible importance in a shot like this, and small as a thumb-print, was just visible looking over her raised shoulder. The features weren't in the sharpest focus, but were clear enough to recognise. She had a look of genuine surprise, as if she'd just been woken up.

'Is that her?'

'I'd put money on it, guv. It says "Mandy, 19, Our Innocent of the Month", but it's Amelia Snow, looking drunk as a skunk. Your hunch was right.'

28

'Will the advancing waves obey me, Bishop, if I make the
  sign?'
Said the Bishop, bowing lowly, 'Land and sea, my Lord, are
  thine.'
Canute turned towards the ocean. 'Back!' he said, 'thou
  foaming brine.'

W. M. Thackeray, *King Canute* (1910)

Thomasine had driven out to see where Lord Chalybeate
lived. Bosham, pronounced 'Bozzum', is a sailing village
of great antiquity, built on an inlet four miles west of
Chichester. It is a much visited place, with a Saxon church
depicted in the Bayeux Tapestry, a watermill (now occupied
by the sailing club), and fine, changing views from the shore
road. Here King Canute is said to have commanded the tide
to turn, and many a visitor to Bosham has wished for the
same result. The water looks benign, but regularly washes
over parked cars below Lane End. The local sport is watching
the drivers return too late.

She soon discovered what escapes most visitors, that
however attractive are the large properties along the shore-
line, there are even more splendid residences inland and
to the east. Here, with the help of a postman, she found
the Chalybeate house. To describe it as a 'barn conversion',
as *The Bodybuilder* had, was to do it an injustice. Maybe it

had started as a barn, but it had been transformed into something on a grander scale, with a drive and outbuildings, all set back from the road in wooded grounds.

She saw this through tall wrought-iron gates incongruously set into a low wall that could easily be stepped over. Not that she planned to explore the house this afternoon. The purpose of the trip was to locate the place.

As she turned away, a small red Fiat drove up to the gate. The woman inside put down her window.

'Were you looking for someone?'

'Lord Chalybeate, actually,' Thomasine said. 'It doesn't look as if he's home.'

She was friendly enough. She looked about Thomasine's age, with black, frizzy hair. 'He isn't, and he won't be, I'm afraid. I'm Kate, the housekeeper.'

'He doesn't know me,' Thomasine said, giving her name. Then she thought up a pretext for being there. 'I'm a local teacher. Not Bosham. Chichester. I'm trying to set up new projects for the girls, interviewing local celebrities.'

'You'd better make an appointment. He's in London through the week. Only comes down weekends. But I'd better warn you he doesn't like people coming here. This is his getaway place.'

Thomasine's eyebrows pricked up. 'Ooh. Like that, is he?'

'No, not like that. He's always alone.'

'I'm with you. Just likes to chill out?'

Kate the housekeeper laughed. 'The opposite. He's straight into the sauna when he gets here. Well, he would be, wouldn't he? Got to test the products.'

Thomasine had to think a moment before guessing that saunas were supplied by Chalybeate Fitness, or whatever his company was called. 'So if I came back Saturday . . .'

'After phoning for an appointment.'

Thomasine thanked her and drove back to Chichester.

* * *

Hen Mallin had called the murder investigation team to an eight a.m. meeting, so they assumed she had something important to announce. She'd not been seen in the police station before nine up to now.

The meeting was brief.

She arrived precisely on time and started without even a 'good morning'.

'I shouldn't need to say this. These meetings are in confidence. Everything that goes on in this nick is in confidence. Anyone in breach of that confidence isn't fit to be in the police, let alone CID. So listen up and then button up.'

Looks were exchanged. Tensions were running high in the team. Hen's efforts to identify the leaker had upset almost everyone.

'I'm confident of arresting the arsonist before the end of this week. I'm ninety per cent sure who it is. The next stage is to bring them out of the woodwork.'

'*Them*?' Johnny Cherry said. 'My theory was right? Two people working together?'

'I used the word "them" to avoid saying "him" or "her".'

'Do you have to be so mysterious?'

She said with measured emphasis, 'In the circumstances, yes.'

Nobody chose to take her up on this.

'As I was about to say, the next stage is to bait a trap. You'll all be involved and it's going to mean at least one late night, so keep yourselves free.'

'Do we have a breakthrough?' DC Shilling asked.

'Were you listening, Duncan?'

'Sorry, guv.'

'That's all.'

Not much of a meeting. Insubordination was in the air.

She called across the room, 'Johnny. A word in my office.'

DI Cherry shrugged and grinned at his colleagues, quite willing to fan the flames. He was one of the lads these days.

But with the door closed behind him and only Hen for company he took a different line. 'Good idea, keeping that lot in suspense.'

'You think so?'

'Who are we talking about?'

She wasn't drawn. 'I notice, Johnny, that your hair is damp.'

'Always is, this time of day.'

'Your morning swim?'

'Right.' He attempted a mild dig. 'Normally it's dry by the time you come in.'

'Which is why I'm here this early today. I wanted to be certain. Where do you do this swimming?'

He paused before answering. 'The Westgate Centre.'

'Each morning?'

'Yes.'

'You know what's coming, don't you?'

He shook his head, but his eyes gave a different answer.

'It took me a while to work out,' Hen said. 'Time I should have been spending on the trail of the arsonist. Instead I was doing something I deeply resent, forced to question the loyalty of my own team, probing their statements, accounting for every action, looking for Naomi Green's source. Finally I listened again to one of the witness interviews and made the connection.'

Johnny assumed an air of executive solidarity, one SIO in sympathy with another.

'He mentioned it in passing,' Hen went on, 'how he sets his alarm for an early start. He's there at the Westgate Centre, doing his lengths just like you, every day before eight. Basil Green.'

A muscle flexed in Johnny's right cheek, but he made no comment.

Hen wasn't expecting him to put up his hand. She said, 'I wouldn't know how long this has been so, but I've no doubt you two exchange a few words in the changing room.

He's friendly and there's a topic you both have an interest in: this investigation.'

All the colour had drained from Johnny's face.

'All this time,' Hen said, 'I was thinking one of my team was passing information to Naomi. I forgot Basil. He's easy to forget. Even Naomi ignores him most of the time, but I bet she listens when he tells her what he learned from you at the pool.'

Now his shoulders sagged, and he made a visible effort to brace them.

Hen continued in the same measured tone, holding down her fury. 'When I realised it was you, I asked myself if it was carelessness, stupidity really, thinking your friendly chats with Basil weren't doing any harm. I wish it were so. But this is the real world and you're an experienced detective. You knew it would get back to Naomi and you knew she was writing these case notes, or whatever she calls them, on the internet. Johnny, you were acting out of spite, deliberately undermining my investigation.'

He held his hands open in appeal. He had to deny it. 'No.'

'Shut up. I haven't finished. You made it clear from the day I stepped into this nick that you were stropped off. Fair enough, being replaced as SIO was hard to take. You were entitled to feel let down, humiliated even, and the fact that I'm a woman made it harder. I knew better than to expect a hundred per cent from you. What I didn't expect was betrayal. I didn't think anyone on the team would breach security as you did.'

'It wasn't deliberate.'

'It was. There was stuff appearing on that website that you'd passed on to Basil. I was troubled about it. You knew I laid into Andy Humphreys, assuming he was the rat. One of your mates was getting it in the neck because of something you'd done, and what did you say? Sweet fuck all. To

330

call you a rat is to insult rats. I can't think of any vermin as contemptible as you.'

Such was the force of Hen's words that Johnny didn't even shake his head. He stood like a guardsman, staring ahead. Finally he moistened his lips and said, 'I suppose it's no use saying I'm truly sorry.'

'Save that for Andy and the others. It won't impress me.'

'Are you going to report me?'

'As of now, I'm not even thinking what I'll do about you. There's a killer out there and I'm trying to find the best way through this mess.'

'Do you want me to stand down?'

'What did you say to Basil this morning?'

'This morning?' He took a moment to cast back his thoughts. 'Nothing much. I knew you were closing in, so I didn't want to give too much away. I was telling him how you were looking at the videos again.'

'Did you tell him why?'

'I don't know why. I just heard from Andy that he sat in with you when you watched the Warmington-Smith interview.'

'So have you told Basil about the link with Lord Chalybeate?'

'No.'

'You swear it? Can I believe you, Johnny?'

He said with a stricken sigh, 'I don't expect you will.'

Hen studied him for what seemed a long interval. Then she said, 'I'm going to take a huge risk with you. I wish I didn't have to. I'd rather rely on anyone else, but I have no choice. Tomorrow morning, you go for your swim as usual.'

His mouth fell open like a trapdoor.

'And you talk to Basil and I'll tell you what to say.'

Long trips for Parcel Force had meant early starts and late finishes for two days. Late on Thursday evening Bob was catching up with messages left on his answerphone.

'Thomasine speaking. Expect you're working. I've had quite a day already. Got something amazing to tell you. I'll try later.'

'Hello, Bob. This is Maurice. Maurice McDade. Just to let you know that the funeral for Amelia – Miss Snow – will be next Monday, at noon, at the crematorium in Westhampnett Road, and, sadly, Jessie's follows on Tuesday at three in the cathedral. Neither of them had much family, so I'm hoping we can get a good turnout of circle members.'

'Just me, Thomasine. Time's running out. I was hoping to bring you in on this. I'll try again if there's a chance.'

'Anton Gulliver speaking. I don't know if you have internet access. If you do, you might care to look at this website Naomi Green has created. I've no idea where she gets her information from, but she's regularly broadcasting libellous statements about most of us under the cloak of pseudonyms that are themselves distasteful. Thought you should know, as press officer for the circle.'

'Bob? This is Dagmar. I just wondered if Thomasine is with you. I can't seem to get through to her.'

'Sorry to trouble you, old man. This is Tudor. Anton got through to me earlier about some website Naomi Green is publishing on the internet. Apparently she's been touting me as the fire-raiser and I'm hopping mad. Is she doing this as a private individual, or is it the circle website? Get back to me soon, won't you?'

'Hi. Sharon here. Got another success to report. Catch you later.'

29

www.ChichesterMurderDetectives.com

Latest developments from Naomi Green

An extraordinary twist in the case, thanks mainly to me. Do you remember my visit to the burnt-out ruin of Edgar Blacker's house? I removed a photo from the bedroom wall. The police had left it hanging there, thinking it was unimportant. It showed Blacker with a second man, apparently at a party. On the reverse someone had written 'Innocents, 1982'. This picture is now in the hands of the police and they have identified the second man.

I have to be careful here. The man has an interest in keeping his past a secret. He has changed his name since the 'Innocents' picture. He once owned some men's magazines – the sort that have to be kept on the top shelf – that were edited by Blacker, and *Innocents* was one of the titles. Yes, Blacker, the puffed-up publisher who came to our writers' circle and delivered judgement on our literary efforts, used to edit sex magazines.

But let's put the spotlight on the second man, although I have to say he gets plenty of attention already. Yes, he's rich and famous. These days he is a highly successful businessman who has made a fortune from the fitness craze, persuading the public to use gyms and equipment he supplies. But that isn't enough for him. He has ambitions for a career in government and is being tipped for a job in the next reshuffle. He wouldn't want his association with Blacker and those smutty magazines being leaked to the press just as he is waiting for a call from Number Ten.

Lord Gym (as I'll call him, because he has a title) was interviewed this week in a London hotel by the Sussex police investigating Blacker's murder. They are looking for a connection with the murders of Amelia Snow and Jessie Warmington-Smith. That old phrase 'helping the police with their enquiries' doesn't entirely fit what happened. He wasn't a lot of help. They want to speak to him again and they are looking for a fuller and more frank account of his association with Blacker. The opportunity will come at the weekend at his country house. Can it be just a coincidence, I ask, that he lives only four miles from Chichester? He'll be there late Friday evening. Expect the police to knock on his door on Saturday morning.

The members of the writers' circle will be relieved to know someone else is taking some of the heat. Not many of them realise who they have to thank.

YOU ARE VISITOR [3896] TO THIS SITE

30

There is no trap so deadly as the trap you set for yourself.

Raymond Chandler, *The Long Goodbye* (1953)

The stake-out was in place. Sixteen officers, uniformed as well as CID, were hidden in and around the grounds of Lord Chalybeate's house in Bosham. All were in radio contact with Hen Mallin, who was in the house directing from an upstairs room. The transport was parked away from the house in the grounds of a school.

The overcast sky was an advantage for those in hiding. Even six-foot-five Duncan Shilling was well concealed in a rhododendron plantation near the main gate. But the conditions would also provide cover for the suspect. It was difficult spotting anyone without the help of moonlight.

In the house, Hen went downstairs to have more words with the housekeeper. Keeping Kate on side was vital. She'd cooperated well considering her future employment was at stake, allowing all these officers to have the run of the house and grounds. Now that the operation was under way it was essential she didn't lose her nerve and try and contact Lord Chalybeate, who hadn't been informed. Poor dear, she was like the teenager who'd thrown a party on the night her parents were coming home.

'Does he call ahead to let you know when he's arriving?'

'Only if he's going to be late.'

'And he likes to take a sauna when he gets here around ten thirty?'

'Yes, I've switched it on as usual.'

'Then what?'

'He has a late supper. I've made a filled baguette for him.'

'Should have asked you to make seventeen.' She added, 'Joke.' Panic had spread over Kate's face.

'You do think he'll be okay with all this?'

'I'm sure of it,' Hen said with the certainty of a doorstep evangelist. 'We're here to protect him and his property, aren't we? Why don't you make some more coffee for us both?'

She returned upstairs and checked that everyone was still in radio contact. 'As soon as you see the car at the gate, let me know, Duncan. It's a red Porsche.'

'I won't be able to tell the colour, guv. I can hardly see the back of my hand, it's so dark.'

'You'll see the headlights. No other car's going to come visiting this late, apart from the suspect's, and they're not going to use the front gate.'

'Suspect could be here already, laid up somewhere in the grounds.'

'Let's hope so,' Hen said. 'We don't want a no-show after all this trouble.'

She glanced at her watch. Ten minutes – if Chalybeate hadn't been held up. After that, it was a matter of seeing if and when the arsonist chose to act. The m.o. suggested around four a.m. However, this was a markedly different location from the others. A house of this size wouldn't catch fire as quickly or as completely as the other buildings had. If the real purpose of the arsonist was the murder of Chalybeate, the ideal place to torch was the sauna, a separate building constructed mainly of wood. He wouldn't survive ten minutes in there.

The coffee arrived.

'I just want to get this clear,' she said to Kate. 'When he drives in, he leaves his car down there by the front door and then goes for his sauna. He says nothing to you?'

'Not usually. I hope not,' she said. 'I'm not much of an actor. He'd see something was wrong as soon as he looked at me.' She was cracking up.

'Correction,' Hen said. 'Something isn't wrong, sweetie. It's right. We're making sure he's safe. You've done nothing he could object to.'

Her radio buzzed. 'Excuse me.' She moved a few steps away and turned her back. 'Mallin.'

It was Andy Humphreys, from out in the road. 'Found a car up the lane, guv, a bit far from any houses. Engine still faintly warm. No sign of the driver.'

'Do an index check.'

She lit a cigar and waited. Could it really be as simple as this to nick the arsonist? If so, Andy Humphreys was Detective of the Month.

'Guv, the vehicle check gives the owner as Thomasine O'Loughlin. Twenty Blake Avenue.'

Thomasine? Not the name she expected or wanted.

'Does it, by God? Can you disable it?'

'Will do.'

'Are you alone?'

'There's assistance not far away if I need it.'

'Have someone keep it under obbo.'

She put out a general message that Thomasine's car had been found and she was presumed to be in the grounds. 'Tell me the moment you spot her, but don't approach her. Repeat, don't approach her.'

Kate, saucer-eyed, still lingered with the tray. 'So is it a woman?'

Hen told her to wait downstairs. These were dangerous moments.

'Snap it up, Chalybeate,' she said aloud.

She leaned out of the open window and willed his head-lights to penetrate the darkness. The only light was the tip of her own cigar.

Another five minutes went by. He was overdue now.

Over the radio came Johnny Cherry's voice. 'Someone passed me on foot, heading straight towards the house. Shall I follow?'

'Man? Woman?'

'Can't tell.'

'Stay put.'

She crushed out the cigar and ran downstairs. Kate came out of the kitchen and said, 'Is he here?'

'Where's the switch for the security light? Oh bugger!'

Too late. Two halogen lamps triggered by the approaching figure flooded the entire housefront and drive in brilliant light.

There was no doubt now that the figure was Thomasine O'Loughlin, dressed for action in a tracksuit and trainers, and caught in the dazzle like a rabbit. But she wasn't carrying petrol or a bundle of oily rags. This wasn't what Hen wanted. She flung open the front door.

Lacking a loudhailer, she put her hands to her mouth and shouted. 'Police. Get down, get down, get down. Face down on the ground, hands stretched in front of you.'

Total compliance. Thomasine sank down.

'Move yourself, Johnny!' Hen shouted.

Johnny Cherry stepped into the pool of light and hand-cuffed her.

'Bring her in here.'

Seconds after Thomasine was bundled inside, the security light went out.

'I'm just praying he didn't see that,' Hen said. 'If he did, we might as well all go home and watch TV.' To Thomasine, she said, 'What were you playing at? Oh, don't bother. You looked at the website and worked out what was happening.'

'I didn't know you would be here,' Thomasine said, her eyes awash with shock and humiliation.

'My job, isn't it? Johnny, take her into a back room somewhere and cuff her to a radiator. We've got a real situation to deal with – if she hasn't fouled it up.'

Before Johnny had marched Thomasine out of the room, Hen's radio crackled. Duncan's voice. 'Porsche just arrived, guv.'

She could hear it herself moving up the drive.

'Thank God for that. Talk about nip and tuck.'

She slammed the front door and returned to her observation point upstairs. If Lord Chalybeate decided to enter the house instead of using the sauna he'd find it as he would expect.

The security light was activated again. The Porsche came to a halt on the gravel area in front of the house. Hen swayed back from the window so as not to be caught in the light. She couldn't see Chalybeate, but she heard the car door slam, followed by steps across the gravel that seemed to be going away from the house. She risked leaning closer to the window.

He was definitely walking towards the detached wooden building that was the sauna.

She let out a long breath and muttered, 'Have a good sweat.'

Now the real stake-out could begin. Breathing more easily, she got back in radio contact and told her team, 'The heat's on, boys and girls.'

They were under orders to keep watch, keep in contact and do nothing until they got the order from her. According to Kate the housekeeper, Chalybeate took about forty minutes over his sauna. Patience was wanted now. The security light had gone off. All was quiet.

Her thoughts focused on the arsonist, waiting somewhere in the darkness with a can of petrol and some rags. Killers

339

may be cunning, but they seem incapable of changing their m.o. Why mess with a formula that works? But there *was* a change here, an enforced change. The timing had to be earlier than usual. Would that be a disincentive? Hen hoped not. In open country here, well back from the road, with no other neighbour within hailing distance, there was no need to delay until the small hours.

Another cigar.

The suspense was hard to endure. She would have avoided this tiger trap with its attendant risks if at all possible. She preferred a simple knock on a suspect's door. In this case it was not possible.

Chalybeate had turned on the interior light of the sauna and the windows on two sides were sharply outlined. Steam suffused with light was already wafting from the tops of the windows and the little chimney on the pitched roof.

Fifteen minutes passed, and seemed like fifty.

Then the radio silence was broken. Stella's voice. Stella's position was close to the sauna. 'Someone approaching.'

'Okay, this is it, Stell. Don't go too soon. I want them stinking of petrol, right?' She radioed everyone and ordered them to move in closer to the sauna and await the order.

Steam in large amounts was billowing from the sauna. It was easy to picture the middle-aged, bollock-naked man inside, ladling water on the hot stones, unaware of the arsonist closing in, or the police in wait. He'd never have agreed to do this.

But it put a heavy responsibility on Hen to get the timing right.

'Guv?'

'Stell?'

'Suspect at the door.'

'Okay,' Hen said in as calm a voice as she could manage. Everyone on the team was listening. 'Can you see the can?'

'Not yet, but I think the door's open.'

This had to be it. She couldn't risk waiting any longer.

'Go, go, go!'

She'd have liked to lead the charge, but she had to get down the stairs and across the drive to the sauna entrance. She was in time to see in the glare of the lights the suspect felled like a tree as three of the team grabbed at the same instant. The resistance was brief and useless, the cuffs in place and a hood over the head.

'Top result,' she said. 'Bring 'im in the house.'

Keen to see who the prisoner was, they streamed through the front door and into the hall and surrounded Hen and the prisoner. She asked Shilling to remove the hood. There were gasps from the team.

Hen said, 'I don't believe this.'

They had nicked Bob Naylor.

He was blinking a lot. 'Something in my eye,' he said. 'Do I have to wear these bracelets?'

'What was he carrying?' Hen asked Stella.

'Nothing, guv.'

'No petrol? Smell his hands.'

Shilling lifted the cuffed hands and sniffed at them, causing the prisoner to bow. 'Nothing I can tell, guv.'

'What the hell were you up to?' Hen asked Naylor when he'd been allowed to straighten up.

'Look, my eye's giving me gyp.'

Ridiculous. 'Someone give me a tissue,' Hen said.

Stella produced one and Hen wiped the corner of Naylor's eye. 'Now will you tell us what you're doing here?'

His words came in a burst. 'I was trying to find Thomasine, wasn't I? She's here somewhere. Her car's on the road outside. I get back from work today and listen to my calls and there's this message she's left and some others about a website I ought to be looking at, so my daughter got it up on the screen and I guessed straight away what Thomasine was up to. Bloody dangerous, going it alone, but she's like that – fearless. It took me some time to find out where Lord Chalybeate's place is, but I did, and came looking.' He paused. 'She's got to be somewhere around here.'

'In the back room,' Hen said with resignation. 'You two have screwed up an entire police operation. Why couldn't you leave it to us?'

'Guv.'

Hen turned to listen to Stella, who was by the door. 'What's that?'

'The sauna's on fire.'

31

You must think about people's reactions to a fire in terms of the three basic stages of making sense of what's going on, preparing to act and then acting.

Professor David Canter, quoted by Nicholas Faith in *Blaze* (1999)

And it was well alight, flames and sparks leaping high into the night sky.

It couldn't get any worse than this. Now there was a helpless man about to be incinerated.

She told Stella to call the fire service. Then she raced across the drive with the rest of them to see what they could do.

Not much. The door to the sauna stood open and the fire had ripped through the ventilated area where you were supposed to cool off. Chalybeate's only chance of survival was that the closed inner room of the sauna was insulated to hold in the heat. But it was all made of timber and would soon be ablaze.

'No way we can reach him,' Johnny said. 'Can't get through that lot to the inner room.'

'Then we'll force our way in through the walls.' Hen looked around for something to use. There wasn't much at the front of the house.

The sauna had a solid look. Chalybeate didn't go in for flimsy building. This wasn't a job for shoulders. Or boots.

She stared across the drive.

'Can someone start the car, please?'

'The Porsche?' Johnny said.

Hen didn't answer. There was only one car in view.

'Duncan?'

DC Shilling knew about cars. First he opened the door of the Porsche and checked that the key wasn't inside. Then he released the bonnet lid and started loosening the leads to make a contact. The ignition fired and the engine started. He slammed down the lid.

'Go on, then!' Hen said.

Shilling got in, revved the engine like a racing driver on the grid and drove the Porsche straight at the sauna. Some of the wood splintered and some of the car buckled and there was glass everywhere, but the meeting of metal and wood wasn't a total success. He reversed and tried again. This time there was a definite splitting of the tongue-and-groove facia of the building, not to mention a concertina effect in the Porsche. It must have been well designed because it still responded when Shilling went into reverse. At the third attempt most of the bonnet burst through the structure. With a rending and scraping, Shilling backed away. A hole the size and shape of the knee-space under a desk was left. And out of it crawled a naked man.

'Is he all right?' Hen said.

Stella and Johnny got to Chalybeate together and helped him upright. He was wide-eyed and shocked, but unhurt. They hustled him away from the burning building with little time to spare. A sheet of flame ripped through the space he'd come from.

Kate the housekeeper came running from the house with a white bathrobe. Speechless, Chalybeate drew it round his shoulders. Whether it was the near-death experience, or the destruction of his sauna, or his Porsche, it was all too much.

'Where's the boss going?' Stella said.

Hen was haring away into the darkness.

344

32

If you want to write fiction, the best thing you can do is take two aspirins, lie down in a dark room, and wait for the feeling to pass. If it persists, you probably ought to write a novel.

Lawrence Block, *Writing the Novel: from Plot to Print* (1979)

All I needed was a steady table and a typewriter.

Agatha Christie, *An Autobiography* (1977)

So what had caused Hen to run? In the last minutes the clouds had parted over a large section of the sky and areas of the garden were now moonlit. She had good night vision and near the limit of her range she'd spotted a movement. Something or someone was running at speed across the lawn towards the main gate.

On impulse she set off in pursuit. She was no sprinter, and not athletic in any way. Determination powered her. She ought to have sent someone else, but the time it would take to tell them was too long. The quarry was already swallowed by the darkness. She let her short legs carry her at the best speed she could manage across the turf. And somehow she got the figure in sight again, saw that it was human for sure, dressed mostly in dark clothes.

She felt certain this was the arsonist. She'd read somewhere, some time, that the sickos who do this stuff like to remain at the scene to watch the result of their crime, deriving satisfaction that was as good as sex. This one, though, was a killer first, an arsonist second. The psychology didn't necessarily apply.

Her legs started to ache and her throat had gone dry, but she ran on. She wasn't closing the seventy metre gap and she couldn't think how she would, but at least she had the killer in sight. She guessed there was a parked car or a bike nearby, even though the team hadn't located it. This was where the chase was heading. The first target was the main gate.

The running movement interfered with her vision in this faint light. She couldn't make out much more than the flash of white socks or trainers. At this distance there was no chance of identifying the person or what else they were wearing.

Then she had her first piece of luck all day: the fire engine moving fast along the road. She saw the pulsing blue light before she heard the siren.

The person ahead saw it, too, and veered sharp left, so as not to be sighted by the fire team. Helpful to Hen. She cut the angle and reduced the distance between them. Better still, as the fire engine reached the gate, the arsonist stopped and crouched at the foot of a tree.

Hen ran on, realising with an upsurge of adrenalin that she hadn't been spotted yet. I'm going to get there, she thought, without any conception of how she'd cope. She got to within twenty metres before she was seen.

And now it was down to whose legs moved faster. The arsonist was up, but not away yet. Hen, so near now, raised her strength for a last surge of speed. She could hear the breathing coming in gasps and thought, this bastard is feeling worse than I am.

The gap closed to a couple of metres and Hen flung herself forward. As a rugby tackle, it wouldn't have pleased a purist, but it was effective. Her right hand grabbed a shin and held on. The other person tipped forward and toppled over.

Hen scrambled to get a better hold. She needn't have troubled, because the fall had taken any fight from the fugitive.

The stink of petrol was unmistakable.

She took the handcuffs from her back pocket and slammed them on. After catching her breath she managed to say, 'You're nicked.'

Andy Humphreys was the first to get to her, followed by Duncan Shilling and two others.

'Who is it, guv?' Andy said.

Hen was still on the ground beside her capture. 'We haven't met before, and she hasn't spoken yet, but this is Miss Snow. Amelia Snow, supposedly burnt to ashes over a week ago.'

Now that she had her first proper look at the Chichester arsonist, a terrified middle-aged woman, lips quivering as she gasped for air, Hen had to admit to herself that the chase hadn't been quite the physical challenge it had seemed.

'Duncan.'

'Guv?'

'Arrest her for the murder of Edgar Blacker. And give her the caution. We're doing this by the book.'

Overnight, Miss Snow's clothes were taken for forensic examination and there was little doubt what they would confirm. When Hen Mallin and Stella Gregson faced her across the table in Interview Room One next morning, it was apparent that she was ready to tell all. There was that stunned look of capitulation Hen had learned to recognise in first offenders. Miss Snow's first night in a cell had not resulted in much sleep. The red-lidded eyes had been to the abyss and looked over. The hands would not stay still.

She hadn't even tried to tidy her hair.

After Stella had spoken the necessary words for the tape, Hen said, 'I have to give you credit, Miss Snow. You gave us the runaround for longer than I care to admit. It was only in the last twenty-four hours I seriously began to think you might be alive, only when we found the nude shots of you in that sex magazine. But let's deal with this in sequence, shall we? It's a complex case and I'm not sure my colleague believes in it even now.'

Miss Snow gave a despairing shrug that didn't augur well.

Hen hoped she wasn't going to go silent on them. 'It's a matter of record that you posed for those photos. Were you primed with drink? It looks as if you were.'

Now she nodded, but added nothing.

'So you weren't a professional model?'

A faint sigh said enough.

'You were tricked, and you regretted it for the rest of your life?'

She managed an audible, 'Yes.'

Hen had the good sense not to dwell on the humiliation. 'You did everything possible to put the episode behind you, and it seemed you'd succeeded. You got your professional qualifications in accountancy. You had a good career and earned plenty of respect in Chichester, doing charitable work as well as keeping the books for some of the pillars of local society. You joined the writers' circle and became their treasurer and secretary. You had hopes of being published soon. Am I being fair?'

She responded with a firmer, 'Yes.'

'Well, you're going to have to help me now. We want to hear in your own words about Edgar Blacker.'

Miss Snow shook her head, but in regret rather than denial. She began to speak in a clear, soft tone, articulating every word. 'I didn't know until he turned up at our meeting that he was the man who took those vile pictures.' She hesitated as if to draw on her reserves of strength. 'If you know the sort of person I am, it's incredible that I posed like that. It beggars belief. And I still don't know how it happened.' She dipped her face to avoid eye contact. 'He introduced himself at a party we had for one of the dancers in the show I was appearing in, said he was a photographer and how photogenic I was and how I ought to have a portfolio of pictures. He said he'd seen me dance and I was so much better than the others that I could easily become a solo performer – the kind of flattery you want to believe, and do if you're a stagestruck girl, as I was. Well, the next day I turned up at the house he called his studio. I'd brought a suitcase of costumes as he suggested. I knew it was risky in a way, but I was a showgirl and I'd met men before and kept them at arm's length if I needed to. He took a few pictures of me in costume and then we had lunch. He'd brought in some cold chicken and salad.'

'And drinks?'

'Yes, and he must have added some drug, because I came over very strange soon after, giggly and talkative. When we went back to the photography . . . Do I have to describe this?'

'Please.'

'I have only the haziest memory of what went on. I was changing costumes and he came behind the screen and caught me half naked. He said I was beautiful and I shouldn't be afraid to display myself. He drew me towards the lights. I was dizzy. I couldn't stand up straight, so he sat me on the sofa. Then it's just a blur. I don't know what else he did to me. I feel nauseous talking about it. I'm not denying that the pictures were taken.'

'We can move on, then,' Hen said. 'When did you find out they were in the magazine?'

'When it went on sale, six months later. He sent me a copy from their office in Tilbury suggesting I could earn big amounts of money if I posed again. I can't begin to describe how appalled I was. He hadn't used my real name, but if any of my friends or family saw the pictures, they'd know me. The pictures were in sharp focus, obviously taken in brilliant light. They destroyed my confidence totally . . . totally. I dreaded that any man I met would have seen that disgusting magazine and recognise me. I stopped the dancing. Stopped all social contact. Moved house. Applied myself to the bookkeeping course. It took me years and years to recover. Well, I say "recover". I didn't ever recover. I mean it took me all that time to get to the point where I was when he entered my life again.'

'When he came to speak to the circle?'

'Yes, after nearly twenty-five years. Normally I'd have made the arrangements for a speaker, but this time Maurice did it all, because he knew Blacker personally. So when he walked in I had the most dreadful shock. He was older and had spectacles and his hair was coloured, but the face was the one I'd seen in a thousand nightmares grinning at me from behind a camera.' She paused and bit her lip, reliving the memory. 'I can't describe my feelings. I wanted to dash out of the room, but everyone would have asked why. So I kept my head down, taking the minutes. Even when he talked about my script I didn't speak.'

Hen nodded. 'We've seen the video.'

'Then you'll know what he said towards the end, that his house was filled with photos from years back and he was starting to write his memoirs. I died when he said that. My life ended.'

'He must have photographed scores of girls,' Hen said. 'Why should he pick you out from the rest?'

'He was going to keep coming to the circle, wasn't he? Through his friendship with Maurice he was forging a link with us and he offered to come back and they accepted. They wanted to encourage him, some of them, at least. To have a publisher in their pocket was too good to be true.'

'You could have left the club.'

'Impossible. I was treasurer and secretary, remember. I had all the files at home. Maurice wouldn't have let me drop out. He'd have made it his mission to keep me aboard.'

'You couldn't see any closure?'

'Exactly. I had to do something about that beast and his house full of pictures. It wasn't enough just to get rid of him. The cottage and all its contents had to go as well. So a fire at night seemed the only remedy.'

'You didn't waste much time.'

'I was desperate. I had a spare can of petrol for my old car. I knew his address because it was my job to send him his fee for the meeting. I drove out there the next night and pushed oily rags through the door and poured in some petrol and put a match to it. The place soon caught alight.'

Hen was listening intently. She needed to know why. 'You're a quiet, respectable woman leading a useful life. Couldn't you think of any other way of dealing with it?'

'I thought I'd explained. He'd visited me in my thoughts almost daily for years. I had nightmares. He was my personal demon, leering at me when I was at my most vulnerable. Nothing short of destroying him would do.' Her intensity left no doubt.

'Let's move on,' Hen said. 'The next development is what foxed us all. How on earth did you think of faking your own murder?'

'It was a build-up of events I hadn't planned. I thought I'd got away with the burning of the cottage. Well, I think I had.'

'Just about,' Hen said.

'Then, to my horror, you arrested Maurice and charged him with it.'

Stella said, 'That wasn't DCI Mallin. That was DI Cherry.'

The finer points of the chain of command didn't interest Miss Snow. 'And it came out that Maurice had once been sent to prison for some incident involving burning his neighbour's garden fence.'

'And boat,' Stella said.

'It was looking certain that Maurice would be put on trial for my crime. He's a good man, truly good. I couldn't allow that to happen. First of all, I thought of letting it be known that you were wrong about Maurice, that the arsonist was still at liberty. I couldn't just make a phone call to the police station or I'd give myself away. And I couldn't tell anyone. So I decided to demonstrate that the fire-raiser was still at liberty by starting another fire. I made use of our new member, Bob Naylor.'

'With his agreement?'

'No, no. He didn't know what I was doing. How could I confide in anyone? He's a strong man, willing to help. I made up a story telling him someone had offered to hand me the proof that Maurice was innocent. I'd been invited to the boat house early Saturday morning to collect it. I asked Bob to go in my place.'

'And then you nearly killed him.'

'No, that was never going to happen, and it wasn't my intention.' The firmness of the answer gave an insight into Miss Snow's resolve.

Hen started to say, 'He had to break out—'

'Through the roof, yes. I'd been to the boat house before. I often walk along there. I'd looked inside. The boat racks reach right up. Any fit man could climb up and make a hole in the roof. I knew he'd find a way out. He's strong because of the work he does.'

'According to his account, he was lucky to escape.'

'But the fire had to be convincing. Basically I used the same method, except that the petrol and rags were stuffed underneath the boat house. I kept out of sight when he arrived, but as soon as I'd closed the door on him I lit the rags. Then I left, before the fire was obvious.'

'Lovely burn-up, but all to no purpose because it didn't succeed in getting Maurice McDade out of the remand centre.'

Miss Snow's eyes moistened.

Hen could imagine the desperation. 'All right,' she said, 'let me try and see it your way. Everything was going pear-shaped. You had a great affection for Maurice and he was still being blamed for your crime. Bob Naylor and Thomasine had set themselves up as amateur sleuths, going round asking questions. Naomi was doing much the same on her own account. Soon enough someone was going to find out you were the arsonist. It was then that the solution came to you: faking your own death by fire.'

After a moment's consideration she gave a nod.

'A huge step to take,' Hen said. 'It could only be justified if it achieved that closure you needed so much because not only did it mean wiping away your life as Amelia Snow, the well-respected Chichester lady, but it meant killing someone else. A second murder, the murder of someone who had done you no harm at all.'

Her lips tightened, but she didn't deny it.

'This is how things got out of proportion, isn't it?' Hen said. 'Your freedom was paramount. You needed an out. You'd found a way of killing that was well within your capacity, hard to detect and simple to carry out. You didn't see the victim choke and burn to ashes so it was all at one remove.'

Miss Snow was listening intently. She hadn't challenged any of Hen's version yet.

'I think you must have read about fire victims being identified by their teeth. Am I right? In a serious fire, that's often all we have.'

This was rewarded with a nod so slight it might have been a nervous twitch.

'Thanks to your charity work at the refuge you had access to women who would not be missed if they disappeared. Foreign immigrants, asylum seekers, some of them illegal, in that trap where they can't ask for asylum unless they're already here, and they can't get here except illegally. Non-persons.'

On Hen's right, Stella gave a little intake of breath as she anticipated what Hen was going on to say.

'You decided one of these women should die at a fire in your house in Tower Street. You sometimes had them there for meals and to stay overnight. I don't know what method you used to subdue her. Sleeping tablets crushed up and mixed with the food? Something that ensured she would be out to the world when the fire started. She died and was reduced almost to ashes, but the teeth were preserved well enough for identification purposes. When they were checked by the forensic odontologist against your dental chart, the match was perfect. How was it done?' She turned and addressed the question more to Stella than Miss Snow.

Stella shook her head.

'Crucially,' Hen said 'these people's dental records were kept at the refuge because the dentist only came there as an act of charity. The women weren't registered with the National Health Service. I've been to the refuge and seen where the records are kept. I've seen the security, or lack of it, the key kept under the carpet.' She paused. 'On the back of the brown folder is a chart recording the patient's fillings and extractions. It was simply a matter of making out a new folder with your victim's dental chart and putting your name at the top. Right?'

Miss Snow nodded.

'And how was it possible to switch your victim's dental chart for yours?' Hen put the question in a tone suggesting she knew the answer, and she supplied it. 'You still did the bookkeeping for your dentist.' With a half smile at Stella she said, 'Say "Ah".'

Stella said, 'Oh.'

The attention shifted back to Miss Snow. 'Who was she – the woman found in your house?'

Nothing could be gained from evasion any more. 'Her name was Nadia. She helped me in the shop sometimes. She was about my age.'

'How could you do this to someone you knew?'

'You may not believe this, but it's true. Nadia wanted to die. She'd suffered badly in Bosnia, although she never went into the details. The memories were torture to her. She told me more than once that if she had the courage she'd kill herself.'

'That eases your conscience, does it?'

'No. Nothing can ease my conscience.'

'Did I get it right, about the dental records?'

'Yes.'

'And did you drug Nadia on the night of the fire?'

A nod. 'She was well out. I didn't want her to suffer.'

'After the fire, you had to disappear. Where did you go?'

'Into lodgings in Petersfield. I was planning to get right away, to start a new life abroad, but I still had some things to attend to in Chichester. I needed to remove all the evidence that Nadia had existed. Her passport and other documents were still at the refuge. She'd never have left without them. Questions were sure to be asked. It worried me so much that I decided to take the risk of a night visit to the refuge.'

Hen said, 'That's how you were spotted by Jessie Warmington-Smith, on one of her late-night walks.'

She tensed. 'You *know* about that?'

'As she told it, she saw something supernatural, the proof of life after death, or some such phrase.'

355

Stella quoted from the interview with Andy Humphreys that had given so much amusement to the team, '"The afterlife, the journey of the soul." She thought you were a ghost.'

'We frightened each other,' Miss Snow said. 'I saw the look of recognition and I thought she was sure to give me away.'

'Is that why you killed her?'

'Yes.'

Stella said, 'But I don't think she would have given you away. When she was interviewed she didn't mention your name.'

'I know. I looked at the website.'

'The *police* website?' Hen said.

'Naomi's. She was reporting everything that happened.'

'Yes, you're computer-literate, being a writer.'

'I designed the circle website,' she said with a glimmer of pride.

'So you came to the opinion that Jessie hadn't told us about seeing you?'

'Yes, but there was no certainty she'd keep silent for long. I couldn't take the risk after all I'd done already.'

'Which was why she had to go? Your third murder.'

'Each one was out of necessity.' She was still playing the little woman driven by events.

'You drove in from Petersfield at night. Where did you leave the car?'

'Behind the Bishop's Palace. I wasn't seen. I set light to Jessie's house and got clean away and that should have been the end of it.'

'Until you looked at Naomi's website again and saw that we were talking to Lord Chalybeate. The whole scandal you'd tried to bury was resurfacing. Chalybeate was under suspicion of killing Blacker – and you – to wipe out his sordid past. He would insist he wasn't personally involved in taking pictures of you and all the other women. He'd make it clear that Blacker was your real enemy. The suggestion was bound to arise that you killed Blacker.'

Miss Snow took over the narrative in a flat voice. 'And then everything would unravel. As soon as it was suggested I murdered Blacker you'd be asking yourselves what I did to cover up the crime. You would have worked it out. So I decided Chalybeate had to be silenced as well. And I walked into your trap.'

'You didn't baulk at another murder?'

'I thought it would be the end of it. Each time I believed that.'

Hen let the statement stand unchallenged. No doubt Miss Snow was sincere, just as all serial killers promise themselves the next one will be the last. You had to have some sympathy for this pathetic little woman. If she had never met Blacker her life would have developed along quite different lines. Whether she would have lived happily ever after was an open question, but she wouldn't have ended up on trial for murder.

'Can I ask you something?' Miss Snow said.

'What's that?'

'When I'm in prison will they let me write my book?'

'I'm sure of it,' Hen said, thinking she'd have the time to write a shelf full.

On the second Tuesday in October the circle had its regular meeting at the New Park Centre. The attendance was well down. Maurice, as chair, announced that the membership had dropped by two. Jessie Warmington-Smith had died tragically and Amelia Snow's new situation meant she had, in effect, resigned.

'What are you talking about – "new situation"?' Tudor said.

Anton said, 'Euphemism.'

Tudor said, 'Euphemism, my arse. She's banged up, as she ought to be.'

357

Dagmar said, 'That wasn't necessary, Tudor.'

'Don't waste any sympathy on Miss Snow,' Tudor said. 'Some of us were put on the rack because of what she did. I was virtually accused of murder. Maurice went to prison. Jessie's dead. And look at what she's done to the circle. How many are we? I make it eight.'

Anton said, 'Seven.'

'What do you mean, seven? I can see eight of us.'

'One is not a member officially.'

'That's me,' Bob said.

'Only seven members, then,' Tudor said. 'Who else is missing?'

Naomi said with a strange smile, 'Basil says he has a prior engagement. He had a load of manure delivered this afternoon.'

'And Sharon has resigned,' Maurice said.

'That's no surprise,' Tudor said. 'She wouldn't have become a writer in a million years.'

'Owing to pressure of work,' Maurice said and took a letter from his folder. 'She sent this. I'd like to quote a little of it, in view of Tudor's opinion. "I heard this week that my strip has been picked up by some American guy to be syndicated (how do you spell that?) in four hundred newspapers right across the world. I won't have to do no more shampooing. I've made it, big time."'

Thomasine said, mocking Tudor's accent, 'Chew on that, boyo.'

Tudor was lost for words.

'She left a message on my answerphone about a success,' Bob said. 'I didn't think it could be this good.'

Thomasine said, 'It's nice when someone strikes it rich. Good for the circle.'

Maurice agreed. 'What do you think, Bob? Are you going to join us now?' His eyes flicked briefly towards Thomasine and then back to Bob. 'You could get lucky, too.'

Do Not Exceed the
Stated Dose

Contents

Foreword

Are you sitting comfortably?

The appeal of a short story is that it may be read at a sitting, comfortably. In bed, bath, aircraft, cruise ship or train; waiting for one's case to come up in court; under cover of a prayer book in church; propped up against the cornflakes packet over breakfast.

For the writer, also, compactness has attractions. Over the years I have plotted, if not written, short stories in many of the locations mentioned above. Occasionally an idea emerges from a few minutes in one memorable place. In this collection, "The Pushover" was inspired by the sunset celebration at Key West; "Bertie and the Boat Race" by a strange incident at the Henley Regatta; and "The Odstock Curse" by the sight of a gravestone on a dark day in a churchyard in Wiltshire.

To tell it to you straight, your comfort is not high in my priorities. If these stories are comfortable reading I am failing in my job. My hope is that you will find in them crimes that make your heart beat faster and twists that take your breath away. One or two at a sitting ought to be enough—which explains the title I chose.

Peter Lovesey

Because It Was There

They are dead now, all three. Professor Patrick Storm, the last of them, went in August, aged eighty-two, of pneumonia. The obituary writers gave him the send-off he deserved, crediting him with the inspiration and the dynamism that got the new theatre built at Cambridge. The tributes were blessedly free of the snide remarks that are almost obligatory two-thirds of the way into most of the obits you read—"not over-concerned about the state of his dress" or "borrowing from friends was an art he brought to perfection." No such smears for Patrick Storm. He was a decent man, through and through. A murderer, yes, but decent.

The press knew nothing about the murder. I don't think anyone knew of it except me. Patrick amazed me with it over supper in his rooms a couple of years ago. He wanted the facts made public at the proper time, and asked me to take on the task. I promised to wait until six months after he was gone.

This is the story. About January, 1975, when he had turned sixty, he received a phone call. A voice he had not heard in almost forty years, so it was not surprising he was slow to cotton on. The words made a lasting impression; he gave me the conversation verbatim. I have it on tape, and I'll reproduce it here.

"Professor Storm?"

"Yes."

"Patrick Storm?"

"Yes."

"Pat, late of Caius College?"

"'Late' is the operative word," said Patrick. "I was there as an undergraduate in the nineteen-thirties."

"You don't have to tell me, old boy. Remember Simon Brown?"

"To be perfectly frank, no." He didn't care much for that over-familiar "old boy."

"Well, you wouldn't," the voice at the end of the line said in the same confident manner. "I had a nickname in those days. You would have known me as 'Cape'—short for 'Capability.' Does it ring a bell now?"

Patrick Storm had not cast his thoughts so far back in many years. So much had happened since, to the world, and to himself. The thirties were another age. Faintly a bell did chime in his brain. "Cape, you say. Are you a Caius man yourself?"

"The Alpine Club."

"Oh, that." Patrick had done some climbing in his second year at Cambridge. Not much. He hadn't got to the Alps. The Welsh Mountains on various weekends. He didn't remember much else. So "Cape" Brown had been one of the Alpine Club people. "It's coming back to me. Didn't you and I walk the Snowdon Horseshoe together, with another fellow, one Easter?"

"Climbed, old boy. Climbed. We weren't a walking club. The other chap was Ben Tattersall, who is now the Bishop of Westbury, would you believe?"

"Is he, by Jove?"

"You remember Ben, then?"

"Certainly, I remember Ben," said Patrick in a tone suggesting that some people had more right to be remembered than others.

Cape Brown said, "You wouldn't have thought he'd make it to Bishop, not the Ben Tattersall I remember, telling his dirty joke about the parrot."

"I don't remember that."

"The parrot who worked for the bus conductor."

"Oh, yes," said Patrick, pretending he remembered, not wanting to prolong this. "What prompted you to call me?"

"Old time's sake. It's coming up to forty years since we asked some stranger to take that black and white snapshot with Ben's box Brownie on the summit of Snowdon. April 1st, 1936."

"As long ago as that?"

"You, me and Ben, bless him."

"If what you say is right, he can bless us," Patrick heard himself quip.

Cape Brown chuckled. "You haven't lost your sense of humour, Prof. Might have lost all your other faculties—"

"Hold on," said Patrick. "I'm not *that* decrepit."

"That's good, because I was taking a risk, calling you up after so long. You could have had a heart condition, or chronic asthma."

"I've been fortunate."

"Looked after yourself, I'm sure?"

"Tried to stay fit, yes."

"Excellent. And you're not planning a trip to the Antipodes this April? You're game for the climb?"

"The what?"

"The commemorative climb. 'Walk,' if you insist. Don't you remember? Standing on the top of Snowdon, we pledged to come back and do it again in another forty years. The first suggestion was fifty, but we modified it.

Three old blokes of seventy might find it difficult slogging up four mountain peaks."

Patrick had no memory of such a pledge, and said so. He had only the faintest recollection of standing on Snowdon in a thick mist.

"Ben didn't remember either when I phoned him just now, but he doesn't disbelieve me."

"I'm not saying I disbelieve you . . ."

"That's all right, then. Ben has all kinds of duties for the Church, but Easter is late this year, and April 1st happens to fall on a Thursday, so he thinks he can clear his diary that day. He's reasonably fit, he tells me. Does a fair bit of fell walking in the summer. You'll join us on the big day, won't you?"

It would have been churlish to refuse when the bishop was going to so much trouble. Patrick said he would consult his diary, knowing already that the first week in April was clear. "Where are you suggesting we meet—if I can get there?"

A less decent man would have made an excuse.

April 1st, 1976, in the car park at Pen-y-pass. The three sixty-year-olds faced each other, ready for the challenge. "*We* may have deteriorated in forty years, but the equipment has improved, thank God," Cape Brown remarked when the first handshakes were done.

Ben the bishop allowed the Almighty's name to pass without objection. "I think I was wearing army boots from one of those surplus stores," he said. He looked every inch the fell-walker in his bright blue padded jacket and trousers and red climbing boots. Patrick remembered him clearly now, and he hadn't altered much. More hair than any of them, and still more black than silver.

If the weather was favourable, the plan was to walk the entire Horseshoe, exactly as they had in 1936. A demanding route that each of them now felt committed to try. And a sky of Cambridge blue left them no last-minute get-out. There was snow on the heights, but most of the going would be safe enough.

"Just before we start, I'd like you to meet someone," Cape said. "She's waiting in the car."

"She?" said Patrick, surprised. He had no memory of women in the Alpine Club.

"Your wife?" said the bishop.

Patrick could not imagine why a wife should be on the trip. What was she going to do while they walked the Horseshoe? Sit in the car?

"A friend. Come and meet her."

She was introduced as Linda, and she was dressed for climbing, down to the gaiters and boots. However, she was far too young to have been at Cambridge before the war. "You don't mind if Linda films us doing bits of our epic?" Cape said. "She won't get in our way."

"She has a cine-camera with her?" said the bishop.

"You'll see."

Linda, dark-haired and with an air of competence that would have seemed brash in the young women of the nineteen-thirties, opened the boot of the car and took out a professional-looking movie-camera and folding tripod.

"I didn't know you had this in mind," Patrick said confidentially to Cape Brown.

"I thought it was just the three of us," the bishop chimed in. "Three men."

"Don't fret. She'll keep her distance, Ben. Just pretend she isn't there. How do you think they film those climbs on television? Someone is holding a camera, but you never see him. We're the stars, you see. Linda is just recording the event. And she's a bloody good climber, or she wouldn't be here."

In the circumstances it was difficult to object. Nobody wanted to start the walk with an argument. They set off on the first stage, up the Miners' Track towards Bwlch y Moch, with Cape Brown stepping out briskly between the blue-black slate rocks and over the slabs that bridged the streams. Linda, carrying her camera, followed some twenty yards behind, as if under instructions not to distract the threesome on their nostalgic trip.

They paused on Bwlch y Moch, the Pass of the Pigs. Below, Llyn Llydaw had a film of ice that the sun had yet to touch. They hadn't seen a soul until now, but there were two climbers on the coal-black cliff across the lake. "Lliwedd," said the bishop. "I remember scaling that with the Alpine club."

"Me, too," said Cape. "Wouldn't want to try it at my age. Shall we move on, gentlemen?"

The path leading off to the right was the official start of the Horseshoe. Crib Goch, the first of the four peaks, was going to be demanding as they got closer to the snowline. Towards the top it would need some work with the hands, steadying and pulling.

Once or twice Patrick Storm looked back to see how Linda was coping. She had the camera slung on her back and was making light work of the steep ascent.

After twenty minutes, weaving upwards through the first patches of snow, breathing more rapidly, Pat Storm was beginning to wonder if he would complete this adventure. His legs ached, as he would have expected, but his chest ached as well and he felt colder than he should have. He glanced at his companions and drew some comfort from their appearance. The bishop was exhaling white plumes and wheezing a little, and Cape Brown seemed to be moving as if his feet hurt. He had given up making the pace. Patrick realised that he himself had become the leader. Aware of this, he stopped at the next reasonably level point. The others needed no persuading to stop as well. They all found rocks to sit on.

"In the old days, I'd have said this was a cigarette stop," Patrick said. "Time out to admire the view. I'm afraid it's necessity now."

The bishop nodded. He looked too puffed to speak.

Cape said, "We set off too fast. My fault."

They spent a few minutes recovering. Each knew that after they reached the summit of Crib Goch, the most challenging section of the whole walk lay ahead, a razor-edged ridge with a sheer drop either side, leading out to the second peak, Crib-y-Ddysgl.

Presently a cloud passed across and blotted out the sun. The cold began to be more of a problem than the fatigue, so they went on, with Patrick leading, thinking what an idiot he had been to agree to this.

Unexpectedly Cape said, "Tell us a joke, Ben. We need one of your jokes to lift morale."

The bishop managed an indulgent smile and said nothing.

Cape moved shoulder to shoulder with him. "Come on. Don't be coy. Nobody tells a dirty joke better than you."

Patrick called across, "We're not undergraduates, Cape. Ben is a bishop now."

"So what? He's a human being. You and I aren't going to think any the worse of him if he makes us smile. He isn't leading the congregation now. He's on a sentimental walk with his old oppos. Up here, he can say what he bloody well likes."

They toiled up the slope with their private thoughts. Climbing did encourage a feeling of comradeship, a sense that they were insulated from the real world, temporarily freed from the constraints of their jobs.

Cape would not leave it. "The one that always cracked me up was the bus conductor and the parrot. Remember that one, Ben?"

The bishop didn't answer.

Cape persisted, "I can't tell it like you can. I always get the punchline wrong. This bus conductor was on a route through London that took him to Peckham via St Paul's and Turnham Green. He got fed up with calling out to people, 'This one for Peckham, St Paul's and Turnham Green.'"

"No," said Ben unexpectedly. "You're telling it wrong. He was fed up with shouting, 'This one for St Paul's, Turnham Green and Peckham.'"

"Right," said Cape. "I can't tell them like you can. So what happened next? He bought a parrot."

The bishop said in a monotone, as if chanting the liturgy, "He bought a parrot and taught it to speak the words for him. And the parrot said the thing perfectly. Until one day it got in a muddle, and said, 'Bang your balls on St Paul's, Turnham Green and Peckham.'"

Cape Brown made the mountainside echo with laughter and Patrick felt compelled to laugh too, just so that it didn't appear he disapproved. The joke was at the level of a junior school of forty years ago. Odd, really, that a bishop should have retained it all this time, but then not many risqué jokes are told to bishops.

Ben Tattersall's face was already pink from the effort of the climb. Now it had turned puce. He took a quick glance over his shoulder. Fortunately Linda and her camera were well in the rear.

The cloud passed by them, giving a stunning view of the Glyders on their right.

Scrambling up the last steep stretch, they reached the summit of Crib Goch in sunshine. Ahead, the mighty expanse of Snowdon was revealed, much of it gleaming white. Cape Brown unwrapped some chocolate and divided it into three.

"Shouldn't we offer some to your friend Linda?" Patrick asked.

"She's not my friend, old boy. She's just doing a job."

And when Linda caught up, she did her job, circling them slowly with the camera, saying nothing.

"So what's the world of academia like?" Cape asked Patrick, when the filming was done and they were resting, trying not to be intimidated by the prospect of the next half-hour. "At each other's throats most of the time, are you?"

"It is competitive at times," Patrick confirmed.

"And is it still a fact that a pretty woman can get a first if she's willing to go to bed with the prof?"

"In my case, definitely not."

"A clever woman, then."

"A clever woman gets her first by right," Patrick pointed out.

"The clever ones don't always have the confidence in their ability," said Cape. "They can be looking for another guarantee."

"I won't say it hasn't happened."

"We're all ears, aren't we, Ben?" said Cape.

The bishop gave a shrug. He was staring out at the black cliffs of Lliwedd. He'd looked increasingly unhappy since finishing the joke about the parrot.

Patrick sympathised. Out of support for the wretched man, he felt an urge to be indiscreet himself, to share in the impropriety up there on the mountain. "There *was* a student a few years ago," he said. "Quite a few years, I ought to say. She was very ambitious not merely to get a first, which was practically guaranteed because she was so brilliant, but to beat the other high flyers to a research scholarship."

"And she gave you the come-on?" said Cape.

"I knew what she was up to, naturally, but it still surprised me somewhat. This was in the nineteen-fifties, before casual sex became commonplace. One summer afternoon in my rooms in college, I yielded to temptation."

"And she got her scholarship?"

"She did. She went on to get a doctorate, and she is now a Government Minister." He named her.

"That's hot news, Pat," said Cape. "What was she like in bed— playful?"

"All this is in confidence," said Patrick. He looked across at Linda, and she was filming the view, too far away to have heard. "It was terrific. She was incredibly eager."

"You heard that, Ben?" said Cape. "The Minister bangs like the shithouse door in a gale. Don't go spreading it around the clergy."

Ben Tattersall was hunched in embarrassment.

Patrick felt a surge of anger. The whole point of his story had been to take the heat off Ben. "How about you, Cape? Ben and I have been very candid. We haven't heard much from you—about yourself, I mean."

"You want the dirt on me? That's rich."

"Why?"

"Ironic, then. Fine, I can be as frank as you fellows, if it keeps the party going. You may not have seen me in forty years, but I'll bet you've seen my work on television. Have you watched The Disher?"

"The what?"

"The Disher. The series that dishes the dirt on the rich and famous. It's mine. I'm the Disher. As you know if you watch it, my voice isn't used at all. You have to be so careful with the law. No, my subjects condemn themselves out of their own mouths, or the camera does it, or one of their so-called friends."

Patrick was too startled to comment.

The bishop said, "I don't get much time for television."

"Make some time about the end of February. You'll be on my programme telling the one about the parrot."

The bishop twitched and looked appalled.

"I mean it, Ben. That's my job."

Patrick said, "Remember what day it is. He's having us on, Ben. She didn't film us when you were telling the joke. I checked."

Cape said, "But you didn't check the sound equipment in my rucksack. It's all on tape. The parrot joke. And your sexy Minister story, Pat. We don't expect you to talk to camera when you spill the beans. We tape it and use the voice-over. A long shot of us trekking up the mountain, and your voices dishing yourselves. Very effective."

"Let's see this tape-recorder."

Cape shook his head. "At this minute, you don't know if I'm kidding or not. I'd be an idiot to confirm it, specially up here. But I warn you, gentlemen, if you try anything physical, Linda is under instructions to get it on film."

"He's bluffing," Patrick told the bishop. "He probably sells used cars for a living."

Ben Tattersall was on his feet. "There's a way of finding out. I'm going to ask the young woman. Where is she?"

Cape said, "She went ahead, to film us crossing the ridge."

It was becoming misty up there, with another cloud drifting in, and Linda was no longer in view.

"This will soon blow across," Cape said. "We can safely move on. Then you can ask Linda whatever you like." His calm manner was reassuring.

The others followed.

Curiously enough, the snow was not a handicap on this notorious ridge. It was of a soft consistency that provided good footholds and actually gave support. Had the night before been a few degrees colder, the frozen surface would have made the near vertical edges a real hazard.

The mist obscured the view ahead, which was a pity, because the rock pinnacles and buttresses are spectacular, but Patrick was secretly relieved that he was unable to see how exposed this razor edge was. He kept his eyes on the footprints Cape had made, while his thoughts dwelt on his own foolishness. What had induced him to speak out as he had, he could not think. To a degree, certainly, it was out of sympathy for Ben Tattersall after that mortifyingly juvenile joke. There was also, he had to admit, some bravado, the chance to boast that a university professor's life was not without its moments. And there was the daft illusion that this expedition somehow recaptured lost youth, with its lusts and energy and aspirations.

I must be getting senile, he thought. If it really does get out, what I told the other two, the tabloid press will be onto her like jackals.

He had never heard of this television programme Cape claimed to work for. But in truth he didn't watch much television these days. He preferred listening to music. So it might conceivably exist. Some of the things he had seen from time to time were blatant invasions of people's privacy.

No, the balance of probability was that Cape was playing some puerile All Fools' Day joke. The man had a warped sense of humour, no question.

On the other hand, a programme as unpleasant as The Disher—if it existed—must have been devised by someone with a warped sense of humour.

"It goes out late at night on ITV," Ben Tattersall, close behind him, said, as if reading Patrick's thoughts. "I've never seen it, but a Master of Foxhounds I know was on it. He resigned because of it."

"It's real?"

Cape Brown, out ahead, turned and said, "Of course it's real, suckers. You don't think I was shooting a line?"

In turning, he lost balance for a moment and was forced to grab the edge of a rock while his feet flailed across the snow.

"Hold on, man," said Patrick, moving rapidly to give

assistance. He grabbed the shoulder strap of Cape's ruck-sack. Ben Tattersall was at his side and between them they hauled him closer to the rock.

In doing so, they disturbed the flap of his rucksack. Out of the top fell a sponge-covered microphone attached to a lead. It swung against his thigh.

Patrick stared in horror and looked into Ben Tattersall's eyes. Despair was etched in them.

"Look away."

"What?" said the bishop.

"Look away."

Impulse it was not. These things always appear to happen in slow motion. Patrick had ample time to make his decision. He put a boot against Cape Brown's arm-pit and pushed with his leg. The fingers clutching the rock could not hold the grip. Cape let go and plunged down-wards, out of sight, through the mist. He made no sound.

"He lost his grip," Patrick said to Ben Tattersall. "He lost his grip and fell."

Nobody else had witnessed the incident. Linda was far ahead, her view obscured by the mist.

Cape Brown's body was recovered the same afternoon. Multiple injuries had killed him. The sound equipment in his rucksack was smashed to pieces.

Each of them appeared as a witness at the inquest. Each said that Cape lost his grip before they could reach him. After giving evidence, they didn't speak to each other. They never met again. Ben Tattersall died prematurely of cancer two years later, and was given a funeral attended by more than twenty fellow bishops and presided over by an archbishop.

Patrick lived on until this year, having, as I explained, confessed to me that he had killed Cape Brown. He need not have spoken about it. How typical of him to want the truth made public.

And there is something else I must make clear. As Patrick explained it to me, his story about the Minister offering to sleep with him to earn her scholarship was pure fabrication. Nothing of the sort happened. "I made it up," he said. "You see, I had to think of something worse than a bishop telling a dirty joke, just to spare him all that embarrassment. After I'd concocted the story, I knew if it went on television everyone would believe it was true. People *want* to believe in scandals. Her career would have been ruined, quite unjustifiably. So you can imagine how I felt when I saw that microphone fall out of the rucksack."

You must agree he was a decent man.

Bertie and the Boat Race

People close to me sometimes pluck up courage and ask how I first became an amateur detective. I generally tell them it began in 1886 through my desire to discover the truth about the suspicious death of Fred Archer, the Tinman, the greatest jockey who ever wore my colours, or anyone else's. However, it dawned on me the other day that my talent for deduction must have been with me from my youth, for I was instrumental in solving a mystery as far back as the year 1860. I had quite forgotten until some ill-advised person wrote to my secretary to ask if HRH The Prince of Wales would care to patronise the Henley Regatta this year.

Henley!

You'd think people would know by now that my preferred aquatic sport is yachting, not standing on a towpath watching boats of preposterous shape being manoeuvred along a reach of the Thames by fellows in their undergarments.

The mystery. It has a connection with Henley, but the strongest connection is with a young lady. Ah, the fragrant memory of one I shall call Echo, out of respect for her modesty, for she is a lady of irreproachable reputation now. Why Echo? Because she was the water nymph who loved the youth Narcissus. The real Echo is supposed to have pined away after her love was not returned, leaving only her voice behind, but this part of the legend you can ignore.

She was the only daughter of a tutor at Christ Church College, Oxford, and I met her during my sojourn at the University. I was eighteen, a mere stripling, and a virtual prisoner in a house off the Cornmarket known as Frewin Hall, with my Equerry and Governor as jailers. My father, Prince Albert, had rigid views on education and wanted me to benefit from the tuition at Oxford. Sad to relate, he deemed it unthinkable for the future King to live in college with boisterous young men of similar age. Six docile undergraduates of good family were accordingly enlisted to be my fellow students. They attended Frewin Hall and sat beside me listening to private lectures from selected professors. I don't know who suffered the greatest ordeal, my fellow-students, the tutors, or myself. I was not academically inclined. The only inclination I had was towards the stunningly pretty Echo.

I met her first across the dinner table, Papa having insisted that dinner parties should feature in my curriculum. I was to learn how to conduct myself at table, use the cutlery, hold a conversation and so forth. Most of my guests were stuffed-shirts, the same studious fellows who shared my lectures, together with various professors and clergymen, but, thank heavens, it was deemed desirable for members of the fair sex to be of the party. Some of the tutors brought their wives. One—I shall call him Dr Stubbs—was a widower and was accompanied by his daughter.

Echo Stubbs. My pulse races now at the memory of her stepping into the anteroom, standing timidly so close to her father that her crinoline tilted and revealed quite six inches of silk-stocking—I think the first sighting I had of a mature female ankle in the whole of my life. When I finally forced my eyes higher I was treated to a deep blush from a radiantly lovely face. Her black hair was parted at the centre in swathes that covered her ears like a scarf. She curtsied. Dr Stubbs bowed. And while his head was lowered I winked at Echo and she turned the colour of a guardsman's jacket.

I shall not dwell on the subtle process of glances and signals that sealed our attachment. She didn't say much, and neither did I. It was all in the eyes, and the barely perceptible movements of the lips. She enslaved me. I resolved to see her again, if possible in less constricting company. I lost all interest in my studies. Every waking moment was filled with thoughts of her.

My difficulty was that she and I were chaperoned with a rigour hard to imagine in these more indulgent times. If my beautiful Echo ventured out of Christ Church, you may be sure her po-faced Papa was at her side. The only opportunities we had of meeting were after Morning Service at the Cathedral on a Sunday, when every word between us was overheard by General Bruce, my Governor, and Dr Stubbs. So we spoke of the weather and the sermon while our eyes held a more intimate discourse altogether.

During lectures I would plot strategies for meeting her alone. I seriously considered ways of gaining admittance to the family's rooms in Christ Church by posing as a College servant. If I had known for certain which room my fair Echo slept in, I would have visited the College by night and flung gravel at her window. But in retrospect it was a good thing I didn't indulge in such heroics because we had lately been troubled by a series of burglaries and I might have suffered the embarrassment of being arrested. My amorous nature has more than once been the undoing of me and it would have got me into hot water even at that tender age were it not for a piece of intelligence that reached me.

The worthy Dr Stubbs, I learned, was a rowing man. He had been a "wet bob" at Eton and a Blue at the University. For the past two years he had acted as umpire at the Henley Royal Regatta.

I've already made clear my views on rowing, but I happened to be in possession of two useful facts about Henley. The first: that it was *de rigueur* that the fair sex patronised the Regatta in all their finery, congregating on the lawns of the Red Lion, near the finish. And the second: that the umpire followed all the races from the water, rowed by a crew of the finest Thames watermen. Do you see? I had the prospect of Dr Stubbs being aboard a boat giving undivided attention to the races whilst his winsome daughter was at liberty on the river bank.

I devised a plan. I would go to Henley for the Regatta and hire a small craft, preferably a punt, without revealing my identity to anyone. I would furnish it with a hamper containing champagne and find a mooring close to the Red Lion. As soon as Echo appeared, I would invite her aboard my punt for a better view of the rowing. Need I go into the rest of the plan?

Now one of the unfortunates who sat with me through those dreary lectures in Frewin Hall was a runt of a fellow called Henry Bilbo, about five feet in stature, and he happened to be the coxswain to the College First Eight. I'd noticed Bilbo being treated with undue civility by Dr Stubbs long before I learned of his connection with the Boat Club. If anyone else, myself excepted, arrived late for a lecture, he would be severely rebuked. Not Bilbo. He was an arrogant little tyke, too.

"You would appear to lead a charmed life, Henry," I remarked to him one morning after lectures.

"Oh, I have the measure of old Stubbsy, Your Royal Highness," he told me. "We rowing men stick together. He's relying on us to win the Ladies' Plate at Henley this year."

"Henley, when is that?" I affected to ask. I didn't want Bilbo to know how eager I was.

"The Monday and Tuesday after we go down. Don't you know, Bertie? It is the Royal Regatta."

"Only because my father condescended to be the Patron," I said. "Because it's Royal by name, it doesn't mean Royal persons are obliged to attend. Rowing bores me silly."

"Won't you be supporting us?"

"I have other calls upon my time," I said to throw him off the scent. "Do you have a better-than-average chance of winning?"

"Only if we can match the Black Prince," he told me.

"Who the devil is that?"

"First Trinity. The Cambridge lot. They've won it more times than anyone else. They're defending the Plate. But with me at the tiller-ropes, we should give them a damned good race. Dr Stubbs has stated as much."

"He takes an interest, then?"

"He's our trainer. It matters so much to him that he's passing up the chance to be umpire this year. It wouldn't be sporting, you see, for Stubbsy to show partiality."

This was devastating news, but I tried to remain composed. "So he won't be on the umpire's boat?"

"Didn't I make that clear? He'll be on the bank, supervising our preparation. You really should be there to see us." As a lure, he added, "The adorable Echo has promised to come."

Trying to sound uninterested, I commented, "I suppose she would."

"She'll watch us carry the boat down to the water and

launch it. She'll be all of a flutter at the sight of so many beefy fellows stripped for action." He grinned lasciviously. "Her pretty chest will be pumping nineteen to the dozen. Wouldn't you care for a sight of that?"

"Sir, you exceed yourself," I rebuked him.

He apologized for the ungentlemanly remark. I'd always thought Bilbo ill-bred, even though his father was a Canon of the Church of England.

After he left, I spent a long time considering my options. If Dr Stubbs was to be on the bank, he would expect his daughter to be beside him. My punting plan had to be abandoned.

On the same afternoon, I announced my intention of calling on Dr Stubbs at Christ Church. I sent my Equerry to inform him how I liked my afternoon tea: quite simple, with poached eggs, rolls, cakes, scones, shortcake and a plate of preserved ginger. Anything else spoils dinner, in my experience.

The beautiful Echo was not at home, more was the pity. She had left early to visit a maternal aunt, her father explained. I came to the point at once. "I understand, Dr Stubbs, that you are taking a personal interest in the College Eight."

"That is true, sir. We have entered for the Ladies' Plate at Henley."

"I should like to be of the party."

"You wish to pull an oar, sir?" he said in some surprise, for I had never evinced the slightest interest in rowing.

"Heaven forbid," said I. "My intention is merely to accompany you and any other members of your family who may be with you."

"There's only Echo, my daughter. She likes to watch the rowing. We'll be honoured to have you with us, Your Royal Highness. I think I should mention, however, that I will be occupied to some degree with the College Eight."

"You needn't feel responsible for me," I assured him. "I'm capable of amusing myself."

He said, "I'm sure the stewards would be honoured if you would present the trophies, sir."

There was only one trophy that interested me. "No," I told him firmly. "I prefer to attend *incognito*. Once in a while I like to behave like one of the human race." I helped myself to another cake.

I could see that his mind was working over the consequences of this arrangement. He said, "I wouldn't wish you to feel encumbered by my daughter. It could be embarrassing—you, sir, in the company of a young lady. I could easily arrange for her to join another party."

Encumbered? "On the contrary, Dr Stubbs," I said, "if anyone is to join another party, it is I. Your charming daughter's place is at your side, encouraging the crew. After all, they have entered for the Ladies' Plate. To have a lady in attendance is a good omen."

He said, as he was bound to say, that my presence was equally indispensable. "I just hope there's a Ladies' Plate to win on the day," he added. "At the rate the silver is disappearing from the colleges, I wouldn't bet on it. There was another burglary last night."

"Oh?"

"Yes, at Merton. A fine pair of candlesticks was taken. The fellow got in through a pantry window, apparently. He's deucedly good at squeezing into small spaces."

"Is it a youth, do you suppose?" I suggested.

I could see he was impressed by my acuity.

On my way out, by the porter's lodge, I met Bilbo. He'd seen which door I came from, so I was forced to admit the reason for my visit—the ostensible reason, at any rate.

"You want to cheer us on?" he piped in disbelief. "I thought you regarded rowing as a silly sport."

"I wouldn't even call it a sport," I confirmed, "but one

likes to support one's *Alma Mater*. Who knows? Perhaps I'll be so captivated by the sight of you fellows that I join the Boat Club myself."

He said, "It's back-breaking for the oarsmen, Bertie."

"But a sure way to impress the ladies."

"Indeed," he enthused. "Echo Stubbs treats me like one of the gods since I got into the First Eight."

"But you're only the cox," I commented with disdain.

"With respect, Bertie, that shows how little you know about it," he had the neck to tell me. "The coxswain is the brains of the boat. The rest of them rely on me to steer the best course, and that's no little achievement at Henley."

I could hardly wait for the regatta. Not for one moment did I believe Bilbo's boast that Echo held a torch for him. It was unthinkable. Apart from everything else, she was several inches taller than he.

The Ladies' Plate was decided on the Tuesday, and it started cloudy, but by lunchtime the sun condescended to appear and we had a perfect afternoon for the Aquatic Derby. Glorious Henley. That dimpled span of water with its wooded heights and enamelled banks was occupied by hundreds of floating picnic parties, whilst others promenaded along the river bank. There is no question that rowing brings out the most gaudy attire, and not only among the fair sex. If an invasion of crinoline had transformed the scene, it was matched by the effrontery of the coloured blazers and boaters on view. The scene was exhilarating, even for one without a jot of interest in the contests on the water. I will admit to having a *conquest* in mind.

Amid such gaiety I was able to move inconspicuously, scarcely recognized (for in those carefree days my likeness was not in every illustrated newspaper one opened). At leisure, I strolled the length of the course, sniffing the new-mown hay and rehearsing my overtures.

My thoughts were sharply interrupted at three o'clock, when a gun was fired in the meadows to warn those afloat to clear the course. A few minutes later the celebrated crew of London Watermen came dashing through the bridge, transporting the umpire ceremoniously to the start. What a pity it wasn't Stubbs.

The Ladies' Challenge Plate was the fourth race on the card. No preliminary heat had been necessary. It was to be a straight race between First Trinity and Christ Church, a distance of a mile and a quarter from the starting point above the Temple Island to the winning post opposite the Red Lion, below the town bridge.

The Oxford boats were sheltered under a large tent erected beside the river on the far side of the bridge. The scene here was in stark contrast to the merriment along Regatta Reach. An air of serious endeavour prevailed, the oarsmen preparing for the ordeal to come, nervously pacing the turf, saying little. The observers here seemed also to be infected with the sense of what was at stake. They stood at a respectful distance. I spotted Echo at once, looking ravishing in the Christ Church colours, standing with her father.

I doffed my boater and Echo gave a sweet curtsey.

"Please," I said. "No ceremony. Let's all be family today." Turning to Dr Stubbs, I asked, "Are the crew in fine fettle?"

"The best I've seen, sir," he told me. "They've been here for a week, staying at the Red Lion, getting in hours of practice."

"Not at the bar, I trust," said I, evincing a delightful laugh from Echo. "Shall we offer them our good wishes?"

"Oh, yes!" said Echo, with a shade more passion than seemed appropriate. She made a beeline for a diminutive figure in blazer and flannels whom I recognized as Bilbo.

"He's our cox," said Dr Stubbs, as if I didn't know. "He steers a canny course."

"Is there some skill involved?" I said.

"Good Lord, yes. The steering is paramount. He'll be steering for the church."

I didn't understand. I hadn't heard that Bilbo had religious affinities. "Do you mean Christ Church?"

"No, sir. You misunderstand me. Henley Church is the object to have in one's sights until Poplar Point is cleared. We've drawn the Berkshire station and that should be to our advantage. He'll make it tell. You'll see."

Not choosing to add to the adulation, I passed a few words with several of our oarsmen, who would, after all, be putting their bodies on the rack to win the race. But I kept an eye on what was happening and I saw Echo blush deeply more than once. I hoped nothing indiscreet had been said. Finally, Dr Stubbs himself went across to remind Bilbo that it was time to lift the boat off its trestles and take to the water.

Even I will admit that I was stirred by the sight of eight blades cutting the water in concert as they moved into the stream to row down to the start. But we couldn't linger. Stubbs had decided to watch the race from Poplar Point, a quarter of a mile from where we stood.

As we threaded a route through the crowd, with Dr Stubbs leading, I turned to Echo and enquired if she was feeling nervous.

"Terribly," she admitted.

I leaned closer and confided, "If you'd care to hold my hand and give it a squeeze, I wouldn't object in the least."

She blushed and murmured her thanks.

I said, "Speaking for myself, the main excitement will be standing close to you."

She lowered her eyes. I have that effect on the fair sex.

Stubbs was right: Poplar Point was a fine vantage place, even if we had to stand shoulder to shoulder with others. I took out my binoculars. There were signs of activity from the Umpire. The crews were poised for the off. I saw Bilbo take a hip-flask from his pocket and knock back a swig of whisky to calm his nerves. Dr Stubbs enquired if I had a good view. I put down the glasses, eyed his daughter and said I could see everything I wanted.

At length the word was given, and the oars dipped in. The Black Prince had the better of the start and for two hundred yards kept a narrow lead. The Christ Church men remained calm, pulling splendidly, their blades scarcely creating a ripple. Bilbo put his megaphone to his mouth to raise the rate.

"If they can stay in contention, the Berkshire station will be in their favour towards the finish," I told Echo, exhibiting the expertise I had picked up from her father.

Some know-it-all turned and said, "They'll need it with this wind blowing. The Bucks station will be sheltered by the bushes. Christ Church are going to struggle."

Beside me, Echo was taking quick, nervous breaths. I felt for her right hand and held it. My own pulse quickened.

Christ Church came up level as they approached the first real landmark, at Remenham. I thought I heard Echo say, "He can do it!" She was so involved in the race, poor child, that she ascribed a personality to our boat.

Steadily, with never more than a canvas between them, the crews approached Poplar Point. Echo was pressing so close to me that I could feel the steel hoops of her dress making ridges in my flesh. It was peculiarly stimulating.

Then a strange thing happened. Something fell into the water from the Christ Church boat: Bilbo's megaphone. It floated a moment before disappearing. Bilbo half-turned, and evidently decided he could do nothing about it. They had reached the critical stage of the course and they were definitely in the lead, but he was steering dangerously close to First Trinity's water.

The umpire picked up his own megaphone and his voice travelled over the water. "Move over, Christ Church."

"What's wrong?" I asked.

"He's in danger of fouling," said Dr Stubbs in a strangled tone. "Move over, man!"

As if he could hear, Bilbo tugged on the rudder, but too powerfully, for our boat lurched to port, and was now in danger of running aground.

"What's his game?" cried Dr Stubbs. "He'll lose it for us."

The Black Prince had drawn level. In fact, it was slipping by whilst our erratic steering was causing uncertainty in the boat. The crew were losing their form, bucketing their strokes, uncertain whether to reduce their effort as the boat veered off course.

"For God's sake, pull to starboard, man!" Dr Stubbs bawled. Bilbo couldn't possibly hear.

Echo let go of my hand and covered her eyes. I put a protective arm around her shoulders. Her Papa was far too occupied to notice.

The Christ Church boat was out of control. It glided inexorably towards the bank. People in punts screamed in alarm. Parasols fell into the water. The bows hit one of the punts with such force that the front of the eight rode straight over it. A man tumbled into the water. The stern dipped below water level. It started to sink. Several of the crew freed themselves and leapt clear. I looked to see what Bilbo was doing, for his inept steering had caused this catastrophe, but he remained at his post, head lowered, as the water crept up his chest.

Meanwhile, the Black Prince rounded Poplar Point in fine style and cruised towards the finish, past the band of the Oxford Rifles on their raft and the cheering thousands along the banks and in the stewards' grandstand. The drama at Poplar Point had been unseen by those at the finish and they must have waited vainly for Christ Church to come into view.

My pretty companion was in distress. "Oh, Bertie, we must see if he's all right! We must go at once!"

We made the best speed we could down to the towing path. But movement was difficult in the throng of people anxious to observe the accident. We couldn't get close. Someone was being lifted from the water. There were shouts for a doctor.

"Who is it?" I asked. "What's happened?"

"The coxswain. He went down with the boat and almost drowned."

"Henry?" cried Echo. She fainted in my arms—some consolation for the lamentable end to my romantic afternoon.

"Hold on, sir," said Dr Stubbs. "I've got some whisky here." He felt into his hip pocket. Then tried his other pockets. "Where the devil is my flask? Hell's teeth, I must have dropped it in all the excitement."

They took Henry Bilbo to the local cottage hospital. We visited him there and found him in a more serious state than any of us expected, in a coma, in fact. He would not respond to anything that was said. Some of the crew volunteered to remain at the bedside, but I deemed it wise to escort Echo and her father out of that place as soon as possible. I didn't care for the look of Bilbo, and I was right. He never recovered consciousness. He died the same night.

It was widely assumed that the wretched fellow had been too overcome with shame over his mistake to free himself from the sinking boat. In college circles, he was being spoken of as a martyr.

This was the point in the story when the detective in me first began to stir. I couldn't for the life of me understand why Bilbo had behaved so oddly. The more I thought about it, reviewing the events of that afternoon, the more suspicious I became that there was something rum about his death. I recalled watching him drink from that flask of whisky at the start, beginning the race competently in charge, but later dropping the megaphone over the side and, shortly after, losing control of the steering. Had he imbibed too much?

Without reference to anyone except my Equerry, I returned to Henley a day or so later and spoke to the doctor who had conducted the post-mortem examination. He appeared satisfied that drowning had been the cause of death. He insisted that the classical signs (whatever they may be) had been present. I asked if further tests would be carried out and he thought this unlikely.

"What caused him to drown?" I asked.

"The inability to swim, sir."

"But this was in shallow water."

"Then perhaps he was trapped in the boat. These matters are for the coroner to investigate."

"Trapped?"

"Conceivably he was exhausted."

"He was the cox," I shrilled in disbelief. "He hadn't even lifted an oar."

Far from satisfied, I asked if Bilbo's clothes had been retained. The doctor said they had been destroyed, as was usual in such cases. The only item not disposed of was a silver hip-flask. It would be returned to the family.

I asked to see it.

"Returned to the family, you say?" I queried, turning the flask over in my hand. "To Bilbo's family?"

"That is my understanding. Is there something amiss, sir?"

"Only that the initials on the outside are not Bilbo's," said I. "'A.C.S.' doesn't stand for Henry Bilbo. These are the initials of Dr Arthur Stubbs, of Christ Church College."

I was in no doubt that I had recovered the lost hip-flask.

Better still, it had been well corked and some of the liquor remained inside.

"If this does, indeed, belong to Bilbo, I shall see that his family receives it," I told the doctor. "If not, I shall return it discreetly to Dr Stubbs. We don't want poor Bilbo's reputation being muddied for any reason." With that, I took possession of the flask.

On the train back to Oxford, I was sorely tempted to take a nip of the contents of that flask. What a good thing I didn't, because when I turned matters over in my mind, it seemed wise to discover some more about the liquor Bilbo had swigged prior to the race. Without speaking to anyone else, I took it the next morning to be analysed by Sir Giles Peterson, the leading toxicologist of the day, who was resident in Oxford.

Eventually he told me, "Your Royal Highness, I examined the contents of the flask and I found a rather fine malt whisky."

"Only whisky?"

"No. There was something else. The mixture also contained chloral hydrate."

"Chloral?" said I. "Isn't that what people take to send them to sleep?"

"Yes, indeed, sir. Many a nursemaid uses it diluted to subdue a troublesome child. It's harmless enough in small quantities, but I wouldn't recommend it like this. The whisky masks the high concentration."

"Could it be fatal?"

"Quite possibly, if one took about 120 grains. Death would occur six to ten hours later." He hesitated, frowning. "I hope no one offered this to you, sir."

I laughed. "Certainly not. Whisky isn't allowed at my tender age."

The laughter vanished later, when I considered the implications. Somebody had laced Dr Stubbs's whisky with a lethal dose of chloral. By some dubious set of circumstances it had come into Henry Bilbo's possession. He had imbibed and rapidly succumbed during the boat race.

Who would have plotted such a dangerous trick, and why? One's first thought was that one of the opposing crew had sabotaged our boat, but I could think of no way it could have been done, and even Cambridge men are not so unsporting as that.

After pondering the matter profoundly, I arrived at the only possible explanation. I decided to share my thoughts with Dr Stubbs. I made an appointment and called at his rooms at six in the evening.

But I was in for a surprise. Instead of the manservant, or Stubbs himself, I was admitted by Echo—the first I had seen of her since the fatal afternoon. She looked *distrait*. Beautiful, but *distrait*. And dressed in black.

"By George, I didn't expect to be so fortunate," I told her.

She pressed a finger to my lips. "Papa is asleep. He hasn't been feeling well since the regatta. It upset him dreadfully."

"But I made an appointment."

She nodded. "And I took the liberty of confirming it. I wanted a few minutes alone with you, Bertie." She ushered me into their drawing room.

I could scarcely believe my luck.

"What did you want to discuss with Papa?" she asked.

"Oh, it can wait," I told her, seating myself at one end of a settee.

She remained standing. "Was it about the flask?"

I confirmed that it was. I told her about the lethal mixture.

"Lethal?" said she in horror. "But chloral is a sedative, not a poison."

From the look in her eyes I knew for certain that she—my innocent-seeming Echo—had spiked her father's whisky, and I knew exactly why.

"Whoever was responsible simply intended to make your father sleepy," I suggested.

"Yes!" said Echo.

"You—the person responsible, I mean—that person planned that your father should feel so tired that he would lie somewhere on the river-bank and take a very long nap. You would be free—free to dance the night away at the Regatta Ball."

She nodded, her brown eyes shining.

"Only the plan misfired," I pressed on. "Henry Bilbo picked your father's pocket."

"Henry?" she piped, shocked to the core. "You're implying that Henry was a thief? Oh, no, Bertie!"

"Oh, yes," I disabused her. "I don't like to speak ill of the dead, but he was a bad lot, a burglar, responsible for that spate of thefts we had. He was just a titch, after all. Quite easy for him to get through small windows. I've no doubt that he was the one. And when your father came over to speak to him before the race, Bilbo couldn't resist the temptation. He saw the flask in your Papa's back pocket and slipped it out."

She put her hand to her throat. "Not Henry!" She swayed ominously.

I stood up and supported her in case she swooned again. "Come and sit on the settee. Your secret is safe with me, my dear."

She stared at me, aghast that I had worked it out.

"After all, my pretty one, your motives were unimpeachable."

"Were they?" she whispered, wide-eyed.

I embraced her gently. "All that you wanted was some precious time alone with me whilst your father was out to the world. That *was* your reason for tampering with the flask, was it not?" I gently probed.

"You won't tell anyone, Bertie? Not even my Papa?"

"You can count on me."

Her response, like the Echo in the myth, was to present her adorable mouth for a kiss.

And in spite of the myth, Narcissus did not disappoint her.

Bertie and the
Fire Brigade

One of the favourite pastimes of the British while reclining in a hammock is to think up worthwhile jobs for the Prince of Wales. Everyone from the Sovereign downwards has his two-pennyworth, regardless of the fact that most of the occupations suggested are utterly unsuitable for me. I can't imagine how the idea got abroad that time hangs heavy on my hands. Between laying foundation-stones and receiving visiting Heads of State, I have precious little time for my social obligations, let alone earning "an honest crust," as one newspaper impertinently proposed.

However, since the rest of the nation indulges in this sport, why shouldn't I? I'll tell you how I could have earned a handsome living if circumstances allowed. As a detective. Given the opportunity, I would certainly have risen to high rank in the police, for my deductive skills as an amateur sleuth-hound are well attested, if not well known. And I could also have made a decent show as a fireman.

Yes, a fireman.

The great British public is largely ignorant of my pyro-exploits, as I call them, my adventures with the gallant officers of the London Fire Brigade. I don't mind confiding in these memoirs that I have attended fires all over London for the past twenty years. Frequently—when not attending to affairs of state—I can be found enjoying a game of billiards at the fire station in Chandos Street with my old chum, the Duke of Sutherland, another gentleman fire-fighter, while we wait for the alarm to be sounded. We both have the kit, you know: full uniform, with helmet, boots and axe. Oh, how I relish the ride on the engine, bell jangling, horses at the gallop!

Are you intrigued? Then I shall tell you more. I once triumphantly combined my skills as detective and fireman. It happened in the summer of 1870 when I was twenty-nine and "under fire" myself, so to speak. There had been some deplorable publicity in February of that year when I was called as a witness in a divorce case, to emerge, I may add, with my character unsullied, utterly unsullied. The husband who had been so misguided as to name me and several other gentlemen had his petition dismissed on the grounds that his wife was insane and could not be a party to the suit. The wretched newspapers, not content with the result, mischievously set out to stoke up republican sentiments. I remember shortly after being hissed in the theatre and booed at Ascot. *At the races.* Mind, when a horse of mine won the last race, the same fickle crowd cheered me to the echo. I remember raising my hat to them and calling out, "You seem to be in a better temper now than you were this morning, damn you!"

A few days later, on the Friday, I was at my club, the Marlborough, enjoying a short respite from affairs of state in a foursome of skittles, when a message came for Captain Shaw, my partner for the evening. A fire had taken hold in Villiers Street, a mere quarter of a mile away. You must have heard of Shaw, the intrepid Chief of the London Fire Brigade, immortalized by W. S. Gilbert in *Iolanthe* and stigmatized by Lord Colin Campbell in the most notorious of all divorce cases. Personally, I always had a high regard for Eyre Shaw, whatever may or may not have happened with Lady Colin on the dining-room carpet of the Campbell abode in Cadogan Place. The man is a dedicated fire-fighter, so dedicated, in fact, that he chooses to live beside the fire station in Southwark Bridge Road, a particularly unsalubrious area. His house, which I have visited, is most ingeniously fitted with speaking-tubes in every room so that Shaw can be promptly informed of fires breaking out.

Immediately news of the Villiers Street fire was conveyed, Shaw apologized for interrupting our game and called for the helmet which he keeps at the club for just such an emergency.

"Sir, would you care—"

"I should take it as a personal affront not to be included," I informed him.

Ideally, I like to ride to a fire in full kit on the running-board of the engine, but on this occasion we had no time to call at Chandos Street to dress the part, so we hailed a cab and made the best speed we could down Pall Mall to Trafalgar Square and into Villiers Street by way of the Strand.

An awesome scene confronted us. Villiers Street is a narrow, dingy thoroughfare beside Charing Cross Station, sloping quite steeply down to the Thames. It is always cluttered with coffee-stalls, whelk counters, hot potato-cans and wood-and-canvas structures festooned with gimcrack rubbish, and this evening the news of the fire had brought hundreds of sight-seers off the Strand, the station and adjacent streets. The naphtha flares mounted on the stalls showed us a daunting spectacle from our elevated view in the four-wheeler, wave upon wave of toppers, bowlers and greasy caps.

The cabman confided his doubt whether he would succeed in moving the vehicle through such a throng. The feat would not have been impossible, but it would have been deucedly slow in execution, so we elected to climb out and make our own way. Fortunately, the Chief Fire Officer is instantly recognizable when he dons his helmet and to repeated cries of "Make way for Captain Shaw!" we progressed down Villiers Street like Moses through the Dead Sea. As for me, I held on to my hat and followed close with eyes down and collar up, or we should never have got through.

Bright orange flames were leaping merrily at the windows of a large building almost at the bottom of the street and the Chandos Street lads were already at work with two engines. The proximity of the Thames meant that a floating engine had also been deployed. Shaw at once sought out the man directing operations, Superintendent Flanagan, and established what was happening. I knew Flanagan passably well as a competent officer who could handle a hose more expertly than a billiard cue. Like Shaw himself, he was Irish, more than a touch pleased with himself (a weakness of the shamrock fraternity), but conscientious and a respected leader of men. I'd once met his wife at Chandos Street, and a prettier, more beguiling creature than Dymphna Flanagan never crossed the Irish Sea. She had that combination of raven hair and lily-white skin that is unique to Irish women. You can tell the impression she made on me because I seriously thought afterwards of suggesting to some London hostess that she added the Flanagans to the guest-list on an evening I was coming for supper. Finally I abandoned this intention. I was willing to put up with Flanagan's brash manners for an evening with his winsome wife, but I felt that I couldn't inflict him on my fellow-guests.

"Is anyone inside?" was Shaw's first question.

"No, it's empty," Flanagan told him as confidently as if the house were his own.

"You're sure?"

"Sure as the Creed, Captain. The owner died last Friday. There was a manservant and he was dismissed the next day."

"Who told you this?" I asked.

"One of the stall-holders, sir. They miss nothing."

"You say the owner died. The corpse . . . ?"

". . . was moved to the mortuary the same evening, sir."

"Who was he?"

"A retired bookbinder, name of Millichip. It's a pity he was moved from the house."

"Why on earth do you say that?"

"Curious to relate, Mr Millichip was Chairman of the London Cremation League."

"The what?"

He repeated it for me. "They advocate disposal of the dead by burning."

"What a heathenish idea!" I commented. "The Church would never sanction it."

"Ashes to ashes, sir."

Damned impertinence. I wish you could have heard the uppish way he said it, for the tone would have told you volumes about his bumptiousness. Captain Shaw quite properly put a stop to this morbid exchange. "If you'll pardon me, sir, you'd better redirect your hoses, Mr Flanagan. The fire is starting to take hold on the top floor."

Shaw's assessment was correct. It never ceases to amaze me how swiftly a fire can spread. In spite of the best efforts of the crews, huge forks of flame ripped through the upper storey in minutes, sending showers of sparks into the night sky.

"What the deuce burns as fiercely as that?" I asked, but

Shaw had left my side to assist in the work of raising a fire-escape ladder, the better to direct jets of water onto the roof, where slates were already cascading off the rafters. I should have realized that a bookbinder might possess samples of his work, for it later transpired that the top floor was practically lined with books.

But I wasn't there, as most bystanders were, merely to goggle. I set to, and organized a human chain to convey buckets of water from the river as an auxiliary to the pumps. I doubt whether any of my shabby helpers recognized me, but they deferred at once to the authority represented by my silk hat and cane.

For upwards of an hour, we struggled to gain ascendancy. The falling slates became a considerable hazard, and I was obliged to borrow a helmet from a fireman who readily conceded that my skull was more precious than his own. As so often happens, just as we were getting control of the fire, reinforcements arrived from Holborn and Fleet Street. The stop, to employ a term we fire-fighters use, came twenty minutes before midnight. The house was a mere shell by that time.

Wearily, we senior fire-fighters gathered by the nearest coffee-stall and slaked our thirst while the firemen were winding up the hoses. Flanagan looked ready to drop and I told him so.

"I'm feeling better than I look, sir," he said.

Firemen work longer hours than the police or the army. Even a Superintendent takes only one day off each fortnight as a matter of right. Of course he slips away when things are quiet, but he is constantly on call.

"What exercises me about this fire," I remarked to Eyre Shaw, "is how it started. If no one was inside, what could have set it off?"

He nodded, taking my point. The wily Captain Shaw hasn't much faith in the theory of spontaneous combustion.

He said an investigation would be set in train first thing next morning. I offered to take part, if not first thing, then as soon as my other engagements allowed.

My dear wife, the Princess of Wales, had retired by the time I returned to Marlborough House, or she would certainly have passed a comment on my appearance. As it happens, we have separate bedrooms, so it was not until breakfast that she tackled me. By then, of course, I'd bathed and changed my clothes and really believed she would have no clue how I'd spent the previous evening. She doesn't altogether approve of my pyro-exploits. Such is my optimism that I'd forgotten that Alix has a keener sense of smell than your average bloodhound. More than once it has been my undoing over breakfast, and not always due to smoke fumes.

"You really ought not to spend so much time with the Fire Brigade, Bertie. I can smell it in your hair."

"Oh?"

"If your Mama had any idea, she would be deeply shocked."

"Mama is shocked if I cross the road," said I.

"Where was the fire this time?"

I gave Alix an account of my evening and told her about the advocate of cremation who had unluckily been removed to the mortuary before his house burnt down. "If his timing had been better, he'd have had his wish. I wonder if one of his supporters put a match to the place in the belief that the body was still inside."

Alix commented, "It would be rather extreme, burning down an entire house and putting Charing Cross Station at risk."

"True, but someone must have started the fire. The servant wasn't there. He was dismissed the day after Millichip died."

"Who by?"

"One of the family, I gather."

"Well, the servant must have been unhappy about losing his job so suddenly," Alix mused aloud, and then added emphatically, "He came back with a match to deprive the family of their inheritance."

It's often said and often demonstrated that women are illogical. Obviously I married a notable exception. I wouldn't have thought of the servant as an arsonist, but Alix was onto him already.

I'm in the habit of taking a constitutional at 12.15, and that morning I directed my steps to the site of the fire, where I discovered Superintendent Flanagan and his deputy, First Class Engineer Henry Locke, in earnest conversation with a tall young man dressed in mourning.

"Your Highness, may I present Mr Guy Millichip, the son of the late owner of this house?"

The young man's grip was clammy to the touch. You can tell a lot from a handshake. I should know; I've shaken more hands than you ever will, I'll warrant, gentle reader. A clammy hand goes with a doubtful character.

"My condolences," I said. "All this must be a fearful shock, coming so soon after your father's passing. Was he a sick man?"

"No, Your Royal Highness. It came out of the blue."

"A sudden death?" My detective brain was already working on possibilities.

"Yes, sir. His heart stopped."

"Isn't that always the case?" said Flanagan in his irritating Irish lilt.

Millichip glared. "I meant to say that the doctor diagnosed a sudden heart attack. The post-mortem has since confirmed it."

"I see. And was anyone with your father when he died?"

"Only Rudkin, the manservant."

"Where were you at the time?"

"Of Father's death? In Reigate, where I live. I hadn't

seen him for over a year. When I noticed the announcement in *The Times,* I came to London directly."

"And dismissed Rudkin directly?"

"He'll find other work. I gave him an excellent character, sir."

"Where is he to be found?"

"Rudkin? I have no idea. He resided here."

"Until he was dismissed?"

"Yes, sir."

"And now he has no address? You consigned him to the streets?"

"I had no use for his services and no certainty of being able to pay his wages, sir."

Here, Flanagan's deputy, Engineer Locke, observed, "You'll inherit something, surely? Aren't you the only son?"

Young Millichip shook his head. "I don't expect to get a brass farthing. Father made it abundantly clear that the entire proceeds of his estate would go to the London Cremation League." He spoke without rancour, as if remarking on the weather. Then he showed himself to be human by adding with a slight smile, "Their windfall has been somewhat reduced by the fire."

"Has the will been read?"

"Not yet, sir. The family solicitor will reveal the contents after the funeral, but I know what's in it. Father told me months ago, when he drew it up. That's why we fell out. I was incensed. It was the last conversation I had with him. Those cremation people will blue it all on beer. They're Bohemians for the most part. Writers and artists. Trollope, Millais, Tenniel. People like that. They meet once a month in some plush hotel in the West End with no prospect of achieving their aims."

"If it isn't impertinent to ask, how much was your father worth?"

"A cool three hundred pounds, sir."

"That's a lot of beer."

When the young man had left us, Flanagan pre-empted me by commenting, "I recommend that we look for signs of arson."

"I should have thought that goes without saying," said I in a bored voice. "Clearly the servant must be found and questioned at once."

"The servant?" said he, as if I'd named the Archbishop of Canterbury. "I was about to suggest that Millichip must have set the place alight."

"Millichip? But why?"

"To deprive the Cremation League of its legacy. He's a very embittered young man, sir."

I wasn't persuaded. However, we had much to do. I proceeded to examine the building with Flanagan and Locke. The ash was thick on the ground, but so are shoeblacks at Charing Cross, so I didn't hesitate. It's fascinating to look at a gutted building with a man of Flanagan's experience. He had no difficulty in finding the seat of the fire, which was in the basement, close to the street, and he rapidly concluded that arson was the most likely cause. By picking at fragments of ash and sniffing his finger and thumb he was able to inform us that a paraffin-soaked rag had been used as tinder, probably set alight and pushed through a broken window by the arsonist.

"So simple, if a person is really bent on destroying a house," he said. "We had a similar case two weeks ago, didn't we, Henry?"

"That is correct, sir," Locke confirmed without much animation, for it presently emerged that the Friday in question had been his day off duty and he had missed a spectacular blaze. As he'd also missed the Villiers Street fire for the same reason, Henry Locke had every right to feel deprived. Most of the calls the fire service deal with are chimney fires, which can be very tedious.

"An empty house in Tavistock Street went up like a beacon," Flanagan explained for my benefit. "We fought it for three and a half hours. It belonged to the eminent zoologist, Professor Carson. He left on a trip to the Amazon a couple of days before. The police are investigating."

"How could I have missed it?" I mused aloud, then remembered that a supper engagement had taken me to Gatti's restaurant on the night in question and to a private address thereafter. I was bending my efforts to *raise* a fire that night, so to speak, not to dowse one. "Well, the police have a straightforward task in this case. I shall instruct them to detain Rudkin, the servant."

I spoke confidently, showing my contempt for Flanagan's theory that Millichip was the arsonist and incidentally omitting to mention my reservations about the efficiency of the Metropolitan Police. Straightforward their task may have been, but in the event the raw lobsters required five days to find Rudkin, in cheap lodgings in the shabby district of Notting Hill. I had him brought to Chandos Street Fire Station for questioning on the following Thursday.

James Rudkin may have looked the worse for wear from his new way of life, but in deportment and speech he was still the gentleman's gentleman, with airs of refinement. I suppose he was forty-five years of age, dark-haired, with mutton-chop whiskers going grey. He claimed to know nothing whatsoever about the fire. "This is calamitous. When did you say it occurred, Your Royal Highness? Last Friday? Was there serious damage?"

"Never mind that," I told him, eager to catch him out, for Flanagan and Shaw were sitting beside me, and I wanted to prove a point or two. "Where were you last Friday evening?"

"Me?" He piped the word as if to imply that anything

connected with himself was unworthy of consideration. "You wish to know where *I* was, Your Royal Highness?"

Indifferent to the wretched fellow's play-acting, I tapped the ash from my cigar and waited.

Rudkin hesitated, apparently collecting his thoughts. "Last Friday evening. Let me see. Oh, yes. I was at South Kensington, at the Art Training School."

"The Art School?" I said in total disbelief. "You're an artist? I can't believe that. How could you afford the fees?"

"Oh, I wasn't required to pay a fee, sir. They paid me. I was, em, sitting."

"*Sitting?*"

"Well, reclining, in point of fact, sir. The School advertised for models and I applied. It was force of necessity. I needed the money to pay for a night's lodging."

"I follow you now. What time was this?"

"The class lasted from 7 to 9 p.m., sir, but I had to report early to remove my clothes."

"Good Lord! You were posing in the buff?"

"It was the life class, sir."

I turned to Eyre Shaw. "At what hour did the fire break out?"

He coughed nervously. "Approximately 8.30, sir. Certainly no later."

That evening, I told the Princess of Wales that her theory about the servant had been confounded and in a manner acutely embarrassing to me personally. "Rashly I asked the fellow if he could prove this extraordinary alibi of his and he said there must be twenty drawings of his anatomy from every possible angle. He couldn't swear that every one would be a good likeness, but I was welcome to enquire at the school. Imagine me—asking to examine drawings of a naked man."

"It wouldn't be advisable, Bertie."

"Don't worry, my dear. I may have been a trouble to you

on occasions, but I'll not be caught looking at drawings of a butler in his birthday suit. I'm just relating the facts so that you can see how mistaken you were. Rudkin cannot possibly be the arsonist. It was such a persuasive theory when you mentioned it."

"I'm not infallible, Bertie."

I sniffed. "Regrettably, it seems that Flanagan—that bombastic Irishman from Chandos Street—is the one who is infallible. Young Millichip put a match to the house to prevent it from passing to the London Cremation League. I shall suggest to the police that they arrest him in the morning. Frankly, I'm not interested in questioning him a second time."

Alix continued with her sewing.

"It's a great pity," I maundered on, more to myself than Alix. "I should have liked to have solved a case of arson. I shall have to bide my time, I suppose. My chance will come. It's becoming a common crime—every other Friday, in fact."

"Speak up, Bertie."

Alix is somewhat deaf.

"I said arson happens every other Friday. A slight exaggeration. A house in Tavistock Street three weeks ago, and the Villiers Street fire last week."

She stopped her sewing and gave me a penetrating look. "You didn't mention two cases of arson when we discussed the case."

"At that time, my dear, I hadn't heard about the Tavistock Street fire. I missed it. I was, em, otherwise engaged that evening . . . putting the world to rights with the Dean of St Paul's, if I remember correctly."

"Two houses set alight?" said Alix.

"Two."

"On Fridays?"

"Yes."

"Both started maliciously?"

"Apparently, yes."

"Was anyone hurt?"

"No, no. Both houses were uninhabited."

"Then let us suppose both fires were started by one individual. How would he—or she—have known that no one was inside?"

I said, "I'm damned if I know. One individual? What makes you say that?"

She ignored my question. "Presumably, the late Mr Millichip's death was reported in the newspapers."

"That is true," said I. "His son read it in *The Times*."

"And do you know the identity of the owner of the Tavistock Street house?"

"That was Carson, the explorer. He left for the Amazon three weeks ago."

"Was his expedition reported in *The Times*?"

"It may well have been. He's a famous man. I'll speak to the editor and find out, if you think it's important."

She gave a slight shrug and lowered her eyes to the needlework. Poor Alix. She never knows whether to encourage me in my investigations. But she'd said enough to stoke up my analytical processes again. I asked myself whether it was conceivable that some wicked arsonist was lighting fires at random. No, not at random, but by reference to *The Times*. If so, it would be devilish difficult to identify him. What facts did we have? He was a reader of *The Times*, presumably a Londoner. He selected houses that were empty and he favoured Friday evenings for his fire-raising. Would there be another fire this week, or next? If so, where?

There was a panic below stairs when I asked the head butler for the entire week's issues of *The Times*. Normally I never see a copy that has not been freshly ironed and then they tend to get creased and sprinkled with cigar-ash in the course of my perusal. Lord knows what happens after I've finished with them. One thing was certain: the prospect of retrieving six copies and getting them fit for inspection caused my head butler's eyes to resemble coach-lamps, even after I assured him that ironing would not be necessary. In the end, six immaculate newspapers were supplied from heaven knows where and I set to work compiling a list of recently vacated properties. Within a short time I realized the scale of the task I'd set myself. The deaths column alone ran to fifty or sixty names each day. I therefore confined myself to names in the vicinity of Chandos Street Fire Station, where the two previous fires had taken place. At the end of two hours, I had a list of twelve residences that I considered prime candidates for arson.

I was so pleased with my detective work that I showed Alix the list. Somewhat to my surprise, she laughed. "Oh, Bertie, what will you do now—travel the district on a bicycle keeping watch on all these houses?"

"That isn't the object," I explained. "If one of them goes up in flames tomorrow night, I shall know for certain that my theory is correct. The arsonist selects the houses from *The Times*."

"And then you can make another list next week," said Alix with a lamentable lack of sensitivity.

"What else do you propose?" said I chillingly.

"I make no claim to be a detective, but I would look for a motive, my dear."

"It's all very fine to talk in such terms," I protested, "but why would anyone put a match to a house? To see a damned good fire. Believe it or not, there are people who derive a morbid pleasure from watching a property go up in flames."

"Oh, I believe it, Bertie."

"They are known as pyromaniacs."

She regarded me steadily. "Yes."

"Then what is the use of looking for a motive?"

"There may be a more practical motive."

"I doubt it," said I.

But later, in bed—my own bed—I paid Alix's last observation the compliment of considering it at more length. Suppose there was a practical motive. Why set light to a building if it isn't for the undoubted satisfaction of seeing it ablaze? It wasn't as if some insurance swindle was involved in either incident, so far as I was aware. And there was no attempt to put anyone in personal danger; in fact, the reverse was true. The arsonist appeared to have gone to some trouble to select an empty house and so avoid an accident.

In the small hours of the morning, a theory began to form in my brain, a brilliant theory that I was perfectly capable of putting to the test. It encompassed both motive and opportunity. I could hardly wait for Friday evening to learn whether the arsonist would strike again.

He did not.

I had to wait another full week and compile another list of properties from *The Times* before this drama came to its conclusion.

Two weeks to the day since the Villiers Street fire, I took high tea instead of supper and arrived at Chandos Street Fire Station sharp at 7. Captain Shaw had not yet appeared and nor had the Duke of Sutherland, so after changing into my fireman's uniform I had a game of billiards with Superintendent Flanagan and beat him soundly. Then I put my proposition to him.

"If there's a fire this evening, I'd like to have command of one of the escapes—with your consent, of course."

He pricked up his eyebrows. Generally, I'm content to take a subordinate role in fire-fighting. "Is there a reason for this, sir?"

Damned impertinence. I ignored the remark. "You have no shortage of escapes?"

"Oh, we have more than we ever use."

"Mine can be surplus to requirements, then." I added cuttingly, "I wouldn't want to hamper the work of the London Fire Brigade through inexperience."

He had the grace to mumble, "That's unthinkable, Your Royal Highness."

"Very good, then. And Flanagan . . ."

"Sir?"

"We won't mention it to the others."

"As you wish, sir."

George Sutherland arrived soon after, and restored my *joie de vivre* in no time. He's an old friend and a marvellous eccentric who happens to own more land than any other man in the kingdom. The Shah of Persia (another notable eccentric) once advised me that Sutherland was too grand a subject and I'd be well advised to have his head off when I come to the throne. I never miss an opportunity to remind George of this.

The alarm came at twenty minutes past eight. A house at the Leicester Square end of Coventry Street was well alight. Marvellous! It was on my list. The owner had died ten days ago, according to *The Times*.

I told nobody the significance of the address at this juncture. I was playing a cautious hand, by Jove. I made sure that I was last in the rush to the fire-fighting vehicles. I watched two engines and an escape being whipped out, bells jangling. Flanagan and George Sutherland were aboard the first to leave.

My team of two firemen waited deferentially for me to step up to the driver's box, and I took my time, making certain that everyone else was out of the yard and would be clear of Chandos Street before we followed.

"All ready, Your Highness?" the driver asked.

I nodded. "Except that we shall not be going to the fire. Kindly drive to Eagle Street."

"*Eagle* Street, sir."

"Eagle Street, the other side of Holborn."

"I know it, sir, but I didn't know there was a fire there."

"Wait and see," I said cryptically.

We set off northwards up St Martin's Lane. People are pretty considerate when they see a fire appliance coming and we rattled through to High Holborn at a good trot.

"Has the engine gone ahead, sir?" the driver enquired.

"An engine won't be required," I told him. Perhaps I should explain that an escape, such as the vehicle I had commandeered, is simply a cart with extending ladders. The fire engine is the vehicle that provides the steam for the pumps. It is unusual, to say the least, for an escape to attend a fire in the absence of an engine. You can imagine the look on the face of my driver. The look became a study in disbelief when we turned into Eagle Street and there was no engine and no fire. Not even a puff of smoke.

"Shall I turn about, sir?" he asked.

"No," I told him. "Draw up outside number 39."

"That's Mr Flanagan's address," he informed me. "Our Superintendent."

"I'm aware of that. Just do as I say."

We trundled to a stop. There was no sign of a fire at 39, Eagle Street. Nobody was at the windows shrieking, or on the roof.

"Raise the main ladder," I ordered. "And make as little sound as possible."

The firemen exchanged mystified glances. Fortunately, they didn't dare defy me. They cranked the ladder upwards.

"That will do," I presently said. "Now can you swing it closer to that large window at the top?"

I made sure that the top of the ladder didn't touch the window-sill, but it was pretty close. "Is it stable?" I asked. "In that case, I'm going up."

Watched by an interested collection of bystanders, I mounted the ladder briskly, as firemen do. I have an excellent head for heights and this was only three storeys high, so I went up almost without pause. I drew level with the window and looked in. This being a September evening, there was still a good light and the curtains had not been drawn. What I saw may offend some readers; it would have offended me, had I not been prepared. Indeed, I might well have fallen off the ladder.

This was the Flanagans' bedroom. There was a large double bed, occupied by the personable Dymphna Flanagan and a man who couldn't possibly have been Flanagan, because Flanagan was fighting a fire in Coventry Street. Without wishing to be indelicate, I have to say that Dymphna and her visitor clearly weren't discussing Irish politics. They were naked as cuckoos. I should state here that I'm no prude, and I'm no Peeping Tom either. The reason I remained staring into the room for two more minutes is that I needed to be certain of the man's identity. I was waiting for him to turn his head. When he did, our eyes met. He saw me on my ladder and I saw Engineer Locke, Flanagan's deputy.

I had fully anticipated this, of course. Friday—every other Friday—was Henry Locke's day off. He had been setting unoccupied houses alight once a fortnight in order to make sure that Flanagan was usefully occupied for the evening. And I had deduced it.

One cannot defend an arsonist, yet I must admit to some sympathy for Henry Locke. It's a frightful shock to be caught *in flagrante* by anyone, let alone the Heir Apparent in a fireman's helmet poised atop a ladder.

I descended, stepped to the front door and knocked. Dymphna herself answered, having flung a garment over her head in the short time it took me to dismount from the ladder. She even managed a curtsey. Perhaps she hoped that I hadn't recognized her lover, for when I asked to speak to Engineer Locke she clapped her hand to her mouth. To his credit, Locke then stepped forward. There was a distinct whiff of paraffin coming from his clothes—more confirmation, if needed, that he was the arsonist.

It was not needed, for he confessed to the crimes. Manfully he refused to implicate Dymphna in the fire-raising, though I'm privately certain she was an accessory.

In November, 1870, Henry Locke pleaded guilty and was sentenced to penal servitude for life. You may think it a harsh sentence—as I do—for a *crime passionnel*, but that's the penalty for arson, and it *was* a dangerous way to court a lady.

Dymphna Flanagan parted from her husband soon after and took off to France with an onion-seller. Flanagan lost all his bounce and retired prematurely from the London Fire Brigade in 1873.

To end on a rising note, Captain Shaw kindly offered the unemployed servant Rudkin a job as a fireman third class, which he accepted. When I last enquired, he was performing ably. All things considered, I would recommend the fire service as a satisfying career for any man with a sense of public duty and a wife he can trust.

The Case of the
Easter Bonnet

Good Friday, 1995. In their usual box at the Theatre Royal, John and Olga Hitchman were enjoying the new production of *The Seagull* unaware that a thief had just forced his way into their mansion on Lyncombe Hill. There would be rich pickings. The Hitchman family had made millions out of Bath stone and expanded into mineral extraction world wide. John had succeeded his father as company chairman.

The thief was a high earner in his own line, a top professional, identified only by the name the press had given him: Macavity. '*For when they reach the scene of crime—Macavity's not there!*' runs the line in T. S. Eliot's poem. Burglar alarms and security lights didn't inhibit this cat burglar one bit. In the previous six months he had neutralised four expensive systems in the Bath area and profited by upwards of fifty thousand pounds. He picked his victims shrewdly, studied their routine and struck when they were not at home. He knew what he was after this time: Olga Hitchman was from a Russian emigré family. She owned a Fabergé egg her great-grandmother had been given by the Tsarina as an Easter gift in 1911. Gold, of course, intricately crafted, enamelled and inset with emeralds and rubies, it was insured for a six figure sum.

It was to be Macavity's present to his partner Jenny. Her Easter Egg.

Eventually he found the correct combination and removed the prize from the safe. The job had taken under two hours. He had left no prints and he took nothing else. He was out and into his black Alfa Romeo and away along the drive. Another coup for Macavity. Except that on his way downstairs he passed through a sensor he hadn't been aware of. It triggered an alarm at Manvers Street Police Station and a response vehicle passing down Wellsway was diverted to the house.

With screeching tyres the police car turned into the long drive leading up to the Hitchman residence. Macavity met them almost head on. His reaction was swift. He veered left onto the turf to bypass them. His powerful engine roared, he swung onto the road, and accelerated. The police had to turn to give chase, and he got away.

Bath's outsize detective, Superintendent Peter Diamond, ambled up the drive next morning and looked at the tracks the car had made. "Our mystery cat made a mess on your lawn, I see," he remarked light-heartedly to John Hitchman, who was unamused.

Those tracks were useful. The police were able to get a clear tread pattern and establish which tyres had been fitted to the car. Moreover, the driver of the patrol car was convinced that the thief had been driving an Alfa Romeo sports model. The Police National Computer carries records of all registered cars. The Alfa Romeos of that type in the Bath area can be counted on one hand.

Towards noon, Diamond drove over the cobbles in front of the Royal Crescent and found a space two cars away from a black Alfa Romeo. All other enquiries had proved negative.

This Easter weekend had turned out fine, but chilly, particularly on the exposed slope where the Crescent is sited. Diamond stood rubbing his arms by the sports car while the sergeant compared the tread pattern on the tyres. "No chance, I'm afraid," the sergeant said finally.

"You're certain?"

"These are another make altogether, sir. Mind you, they're new. They've still got some shreds of rubber where they were taken from the mould. It's worth asking when these were fitted."

A man in a blue sweatshirt and black jeans answered the door and before Diamond had opened his mouth said, "Piss off, will you? Out of it. Get some fresh air."

It was only when Diamond felt some pressure against his leg that he realized the remarks were meant for a cat, a large ginger tom that was trying to return indoors. The man put a foot against its rump and steered it away from the door. "You've got to be firm with them," he said. "I don't want it cluttering up the flat all day."

Diamond explained who he was.

The young man, whose name was Mark Bonney, invited him in. He introduced Diamond to his partner, a dark-haired woman in a denim suit. She offered to make coffee.

In the next twenty minutes, Bonney insisted that he had not been out at all the previous evening. He had watched a video with his partner and they had retired early. He had not used his Alfa Romeo since Thursday, two days before.

"I was looking at the tyres," said Diamond. "They're brand new. Changed them recently, did you?"

"Thursday afternoon," said Bonney. "Want to look at the receipt? It's right here."

It was from Tyrefast in Weston and the date was clearly written as 13/4/95. Thursday. The robbery had been on Friday evening.

"That seems to settle it," Diamond had to concede. "I've no further questions, Mr Bonney. Thanks for the coffee."

After the door was closed, Bonney and his partner watched discreetly from the window as the portly detective walked across to his colleague, shaking his head.

"You're brilliant," Jenny said. She had taken out the Fabergé egg and was holding it to her chest. "Brilliant! How did you manage it?"

"Manage what?"

"The receipt. You had the new tyres fitted only half an hour ago, for God's sake."

"No problem," said Bonney, putting an arm around her. "I changed the date myself, as soon as I was given the receipt. The lad wrote his 5 like a letter S. All it wanted was an extra stroke across the top. Now they're convinced I haven't used the car since Thursday."

They watched Diamond return to the police car, still shaking his head. Before getting in, he hesitated.

"What's he staring at?" said Jenny.

"My car," said Bonney. "Oh, Jesus! That bloody cat!"

The ginger tom was sitting forlornly on the Alfa Romeo, pressing itself against the still faintly warm bonnet.

Diamond strolled across and put his hand flat to the bonnet. Then he gestured to the sergeant and they approached the house and knocked again.

Macavity was about to be nicked.

Disposing of Mrs Cronk

"Foolproof."

Gary shook his head. "Too simple."

"The simple ideas are the best."

"What if he susses us?"

And now Jason shook his cropped head. He made you believe in his wild ideas, did Jason. Those pale blue eyes of his, as still as the stones in a mosaic, watching you. The mouth like a crack in the earth.

"What's my action, then?" asked Gary, weakening.

"Collect the readies."

"Five grand?"

"More if we like. We set the fee."

"Five is enough," said Gary with the measured calculation of a young man behind with his rent and trying to subsist on unemployment benefit of forty-two pounds a week. "And all I do is collect?"

"And look the part."

"How?"

"Suit. Tie. Shades."

"What do I say?"

"Not much. You just collect, I said."

"Alone?"

"I can't hold your bleeding hand, Gary. I'm doing all the heavy stuff, aren't I?"

There was a pause for thought.

"All right, Jay. You're on."

"How's it going, Mr Cronk?" Jason asked, grasping the crowbar he used to strip the casing from the frames of the wrecks that were brought in.

"Same as usual."

"Mrs Cronk still giving you grief?"

"Don't ask, Jason."

Jason hauled on the crowbar and exposed the burnt-out interior of a Vauxhall Cavalier. "Not much here worth keeping."

"Pity. Try the engine, son."

With two or three expert stabs at the front of the car, Jason forced up the bonnet. "Battery looks all right. I'll have that out."

His employer prepared to watch the swift dissection of the mangled vehicle. In other parts of the yard, other beefy youths were dismantling derelict pieces of machinery, fridges, cookers, lawn-mowers, for scrap metal. It was not a bad living in these grim times. There was money in scrap. Call it waste disposal, recycling, totting, what you like, it paid. Not many overheads. Low wages. These were young lads straight from the dole queue, glad of anything. With the basic tools, a breakdown lorry, a second vehicle to cart the good stuff down to the dealer and fly-tip the rest, you were set up. Cash for trash.

If only his domestic life worked as neatly as his business.

Jason leaned over the bonnet, peering at the way the hoses were fixed. Then he ripped them out with his large hands. He was the pick of the bunch, in spite of his aggressive looks, the nearest thing to a foreman on the site.

"I knew a bloke had grief from his old lady," Jason said, turning to pick up another tool. "Funny business. She couldn't get enough of it. Know what I mean, Mr Cronk? Big, healthy woman. Soon as he got into his pit, she was on him, regular, and when I say regular I mean three, four, five times a night and coming from all directions. Too many hormones, I reckon. No bloke could have stood it. Knackered, he was. His work suffered. His pecker was in permanent shock. He gave up going out with his mates. Got the shakes. Anyway, he faced facts in the end. It couldn't go on. So he went to the Fixer, paid the fee, and slept soundly ever after."

Mr Cronk reflected on the matter while Jason lifted out the battery.

"What do you mean by the Fixer?"

"I thought you'd know about the Fixer, Mr Cronk."

"I don't mix in your circles, Jason."

Jason applied himself to the heavy work, his biceps rippling.

"He takes care of problems. This geezer's problem was his old lady, so the Fixer fixed her."

"How?"

"Disposal." Jason ripped out the radiator and slung it onto a heap of rusted metal. Unlike the others, Jason never confused ferrous and non-ferrous.

"You mean he . . . ?"

"Yup. It wasn't crude, mind. The Fixer's a pro. No comeback. This bloke is free now. Free to marry again if he wants, but I don't think he will. Once bitten . . ." Jason gave a coarse laugh and picked up the bolt-cutter.

"What happened to the woman?"

"Accident, they said. She didn't know nothing about it, that's for sure. Drove her car off the road. The thing was, this road was next to a two-hundred foot drop. The coroner reckoned she fell asleep at the wheel."

"Accidental death?"

Jason grinned.

Mr Cronk gaped.

"The insurance paid up, easily covered the Fixer's fee."

He severed a bunch of cables and wrenched them out. There wasn't much left of that engine.

"What sort of fee does he charge?" Mr Cronk eventually asked.

"Ten grand."

"As much as that?"

"It sounds a lot, but it's like cars. You pay for a decent motor and you get value. Believe me, he's the Roller of his profession. He don't let people down."

Towards the end of the afternoon, Mr Cronk passed Jason again. The parts worth keeping had been stripped from the car, sorted and stacked neatly nearby. He was already sledgehammering another vehicle. He was a lad you could depend on.

"Er, Jason."

"Mr Cronk?" He rested the sledgehammer on his shoulder.

"You're feeling hot, I expect."

"What do you expect? I ain't picking daffodils."

"How would you like a cool swim? I've watched you working. You deserve it. Come home with me. I've got a thirty-foot pool."

"What, now?"

"Now's the right time."

"I'm covered in muck."

"You can take a shower at my place. We do have soap, you know."

Mr Cronk's house and garden were so palatial that Jason wished he had put the Fixer's price higher than ten grand. The pool had a glass roof that retracted at the push of a button like the sun-roof on a posh car. The bottom of the pool was lined with blue, green and gold tiles. There was money in recycling, more money than Jason had dreamed was possible.

He took a slow shower, soaping himself thoroughly in the shower-gel Mr Cronk had provided. He watched the grime go down the chromium plughole. Then he dried himself with the huge, pink, fluffy bath-towel and put on the boxer shorts Mr Cronk had lent him.

"So there you are, clean as a vicar," Mr Cronk shouted from across the water. "Come and meet my good lady."

Mrs Cronk.

She was reclining on one of those long, padded swing-seats suspended in a large frame. She must have been twenty years younger than Mr Cronk because she looked terrific in a black two-piece. Blonde, bronzed and superbly groomed, she was the biggest surprise yet.

Friendly, too. "Hi, Jason. Check those tattoos."

She didn't budge from the recliner, so he had to move in, crouch down and show her his biceps. She smelt expensive.

"Pure art. And on such an expansive canvas. Do you pump iron?"

"No, I break up cars for your old man."

She laughed. "So do I, but it doesn't give me muscle tone like that."

"You don't want it."

Mr Cronk said, more to himself than the others, "Many a true word." Then he turned to Jason. "Why don't you try the water?"

"Cheers. I will."

He wasted no time. He took a header, needing to get submerged fast, and not just because he was coming out in a sweat again. The water was deliciously cool. He was not a bad swimmer and he showed off a bit with his powerful crawl, doing a racing turn at the deep end.

After six lengths he stopped and stood up in the shallow end.

The swing-chair was no longer occupied.

"She's getting changed," her husband said. "She's got to get to her flamenco class." Mr Cronk had changed too, into a T-shirt, shorts and sandals.

"Is she learning flamenco?"

"She teaches it, four nights a week."

Jason swam another four lengths, lazily, on his back, thinking about Mrs Cronk dancing the flamenco. After a bit, he turned over and swam on his front.

When he got out, there was a fresh towel ready. Mr Cronk handed it to him. Jason sat on the edge of the pool with the towel draped around his shoulders, dangling his feet in the pool.

Mr Cronk handed him a can of lager, ice-cold. He said, "You look so cool, I think I'll join you, Jason." He stepped out of his sandals and sat beside Jason. The light on the water shimmered over the coloured tiles, distorting the shapes.

"That chap you mentioned today. The, em, Fixer."

"Yeah?"

"You said he was reliable."

"Hundred per cent."

"Ten thousand pounds, the man paid, for his services?"

"Ten grand, yes."

"Tell me, Jason. How does the money work?"

"Come again, Mr Cronk?"

"Well, is he paid by results? Does he get the money after performing the, em . . .?"

"I'm with you. No, there's got to be trust on both sides. Standard terms for that kind of job are half on agreement, half on completion. Five grand down, five at the death, so to speak."

After some reflection, Mr Cronk said, "It seems fair enough."

"Cash, of course. No point in cheques in a business like his."

"Or writing them, if you hire him," said Mr Cronk, churning the water with his feet, he was so amused by his own remark. "Do you know this fellow personally?"

"I've met him, yeah."

"Any chance I could meet him, just out of interest, so to speak?"

"No chance," said Jason.

"Oh."

"He doesn't meet no one on spec. Too risky."

"How did he ever meet the man you were telling me about?"

"It was set up by a third party. The bloke made it known he wanted to hire the Fixer. There was a meeting on neutral ground, the bloke and the Fixer. Five grand was handed over. Nothing spoken. When the job was done, the other five grand had to be left in a case in a left luggage box. The key was handed to the third party, who gave it to the Fixer."

"Neat."

"That's the way it's done the world over, Mr Cronk." Jason stood up. "I'd better get changed and toddle off. I'm sure you've got things to do."

"I'll drive you back. No problem," said Mr Cronk.

Towards the end of the drive back to the flat Jason shared with Gary, Mr Cronk said, "I suppose you couldn't act as third party."

"In what way?" Jason tried to sound puzzled.

"As a contact with the Fixer. You said you met him."

"Just the once, a while ago." He paused. "I suppose I could sniff around, see if he's about."

"I'd make it worth your while—later."

"Five hundred?" said Jason.

"All right. When it's all over."

They drove on for a while in silence.

"This'll be all right. Drop me here."

Mr Cronk stopped the car. "Don't think too badly of me, Jason. I'm a deeply wounded man. Mine is nothing like the case you mentioned. Almost the reverse."

"I don't judge no one, Mr Cronk."

"You'll let me know?"

"Get a grip, Gary. He's the one wearing brown trousers, right?"

"Right."

"You look great. Wear the shades, and your rings. Walk tall. And don't forget to check the money."

"Where will you be, Jay?"

"Where I said—down the tube with the cases and the tickets. Piccadilly Line to Heathrow, the night flight to Athens and six weeks bumming around the Greek Islands. Any problem with that?"

"No problem, Jay."

"There's nothing he can do. I lose my job, and you get the golden handshake, eh, Gary?"

"Yes, sure."

"Try and look the part, then."

Mr Cronk emerged from a taxi and entered the ticket hall of the tube station at precisely 4 p.m. He was carrying a sportsbag containing five thousand pounds in twenty-pound notes. As instructed, he waited to the left of the news kiosk. He was trembling uncontrollably.

At 4.03, a tall young man in dark glasses and a black suit and bootlace tie walked right up to Mr Cronk and said, "Is it all there?"

Mr Cronk fumbled and almost dropped the bag as he handed it over to the Fixer.

The young man unzipped the bag and made a quick assessment of the contents.

Mr Cronk said, "When will you . . .?"

"You'll get a phone call," the Fixer promised. He zipped the bag up again. Then he turned and walked quickly through the barrier and down the escalator.

Gary was all smiles on the platform. "Dead simple."

"Give us the bag," said Jason. He took it and looked inside. "Sorted."

The Heathrow train came in. They picked up the cases. On the journey, they opened one of the cases and stuffed the bag inside.

"It was a dream," said Gary, his confidence fully restored. "He was dead scared. You know what? If we played it right, we could roll him for the other five grand as well. Have a nice holiday, go back and screw him for the bloody lot. He wouldn't know it was a con till he got back and found his old lady still breathing."

Jason fixed him with those stone eyes and said, "You're a laugh a minute, Gary."

"Am I?"

"She's already dead."

"What?" Gary went white. "No! Jay, you never?"

"Couldn't let my old boss down, could I?" said Jason, enjoying this.

"For Christ's sake, mate, are you crazy?"

"Went for a swim with her this afternoon, didn't I? Pushed her face under the water and kept it there." He glanced at his watch. "He'll be finding her about now. He'll be saying, 'Jesus, that Fixer didn't waste time.' And when we get back to England, he'll pay up like a lamb."

Gary practically gibbered, "It was a scam, Jay, it was only meant to be a scam. We never agreed no violence."

Jason took pity. He'd had his fun, and other people in the train were starting to look at Gary. "I bet you still believe in the bloody tooth fairy and all. I never touched her."

Gary's breathing subsided. "Honest?"

"Honest. How could I? I was humping these cases to the station."

"Bastard."

"Get real, pal. We're on our way."

Their flight was due to take off at 23.10 from Terminal Four. They had plenty of time in hand. After checking in their cases and going through the passport control, they had a leisurely meal and a few drinks and started to get into the holiday mood.

"How long do you reckon it's going to take before old Cronk finds out he's been ripped off?" said Gary.

"Week. Longer," said Jason. "He might smell a rat when I don't come into work, but he'll think I'm ill, or something."

"And he can't do sweet f.a. about it. It's neat, Jay. Real neat."

"I'll drink to that."

Their flight was called. They walked to the departure lounge and showed their tickets and passports. One of the officials in suits said, "Would you come with me, gentlemen?"

"What for?" said Jason.

"This *is* your passport?"

"Yes."

"You are Jason Richardson and you, sir, are Gary Morton? You won't be boarding this flight. We're police officers with orders to arrest you."

After a scuffle, the pair were handcuffed and led away to the airport police office. They were cautioned and then questioned about their movements.

"You've got nothing on us," Jason said.

"We opened your luggage," the inspector said. "Almost five grand in twenties?"

"It's a long holiday," said Jason cleverly.

"Don't waste your breath, lad. We heard about you from Mr Cronk, getting yourself invited to his place and sussing it out for a robbery, knowing how scrap metal merchants have to handle large amounts of cash. That's naughty enough, but beating an innocent woman to death is evil."

Mrs Cronk dead?

Jason went cold. Suckered. He couldn't believe Mr Cronk had it in him.

Gary whimpered.

"Take their prints. See if they match up to the prints on the sledgehammer found at the scene. I'm confident they will. Armed robbery, murder and conspiracy to murder. Yes, it will be a long holiday, gentlemen."

The Mighty Hunter

George Blackitt sniffed the bottle suspiciously, poured some of the stuff on his finger-tips and sniffed again. This would be the first time in a life of seventy years that he had used aftershave.

He took another look at the label. *Surfaroma for Roughriders*. It certainly smelt rough, he thought, wondering how he had allowed himself to be conned into buying a product so overpriced. Embarrassment, really, he admitted. He wouldn't easily live down the giggles of the two young girls in the village shop when he'd given them his prepared speech. "I want it for my nephew in London actually. He's a bit of a ladies' man, wears the latest clothes and drives a sports car. Do you get the idea?"

Having sold him the bottle of Surfaroma, the pert little miss had caused a fresh eruption of mirth from her workmate by asking pointedly if his nephew required anything else from the shop. George had reddened deeply and fled.

In his day, it would have been unmanly to have used aftershave. Or the other things. He dabbed Surfaroma on his face and winced. It stung.

A large black tomcat stirred in his favourite armchair

across the room, opened his eyes and changed position. Catching a whiff of the aftershave, he raised his head just enough for a more informative sniff, then buried his nose under his tail.

"I don't blame you, Nimmy," George confided to his cat. "However, needs must, old friend. Can't expect a lady like Edith Plumley to entertain a gentleman smelling of soap, oh no. She's used to certain standards from her admirers. A sophisticated lady, Chairperson of the Darby and Joan Club, Queen of the formation dancing, Treasurer of the village fete committee. Quite a good catch, if she's willing to be caught, as I believe she is."

Nimrod had fallen asleep.

George gave up talking to the cat and talked to himself instead. He picked up his clip-on bow tie and stood in front of the mirror to adjust it. "You haven't seen action in a while, George Blackitt, but things are about to change." His reflection looked silently back, smart but strained, not totally impressed by this bravado. He turned away and reached for the jacket of his dark suit. "Well, you haven't worn this since Ivy's funeral." He sighed as he put it on. "Three years last month. Ivy, old girl, you wouldn't have wanted me to stay lonely for the rest of my life, would you?"

If a response had come from across the great divide, George wouldn't have heard it because he immediately started talking to the cat again. "Nimmy, old pal," he said, "it's time for another funeral. My own." He leaned over the chair and stroked the glossy, warm fur. "This is goodbye and R.I.P. to George Blackitt, the wretched widower. And welcome to George Blackitt, debonair, superbly groomed and shortly to cause a flutter in the heart of one Edith Plumley. Stand by for an announcement." He scratched Nimrod's head. "Come on, old fellow, I'd better get you fed. Who knows, it could be a long night. I'm not saying what time I'll be back. Come on, Nimmy. Nimrod."

Nimrod stood, arched his back and stretched. His name had been called in the proper tone, though the time was earlier than usual. At ten years old, the big, black tom had one companion he would never leave: the blue ceramic feed bowl just behind the door.

"Here we go, old chum," George said whilst filling the bowl with brawn. "This ought to keep you going till I get back." A fleck of meat jelly landed on one of his highly polished black brogues. The cat pounced on it in an instant. George looked down fondly. "I named you well, didn't I? '*Nimrod, the mighty hunter before the Lord.*'" No small mammal was safe within range of the cottage. In the summer Nimrod would be gone for hours, checking the hedgerows and the little wood across the meadow. Sometimes he went without processed catmeat for a week. He brought back what he couldn't consume and left it by the front door, birds, mice, voles and sometimes baby rabbits, hopeful always that when he went back and prodded one of the small corpses it would revive and test the reaction of his right forepaw.

George sang a line from an old song from years past. "Wish me luck as I go on my way."

Nimrod had his head in the feed bowl.

Two hours later, George was sitting uncomfortably in a rocking chair in Edith Plumley's cottage, regretting having agreed to a second helping of the steak and kidney pie. The meat had been tough and the pastry only semicooked. He sipped the tea she had given him and tried to wash away the after-taste.

"Biscuit, Mr Blackitt?"

"Well—"

"Do have one. I like a man who can eat."

George took a digestive. He bit with concentration lest the damned thing disintegrate into a pile of crumbs on his lap. "It was a meal to remember, Mrs Plumley."

"I'm so pleased you enjoyed it, Mr Blackitt." Mrs Plumley looked radiant and George noticed that she, too, had made an extra effort. She'd had her hair done and she was wearing a lace blouse. She had some kind of slip underneath, so it was perfectly decent.

He said, not untruthfully, "First class cooks are hard to find."

"I've had plenty of practice. You like steak and kidney?"

"You couldn't have made a better choice."

She smiled. "Most men seem to like it."

There was a pause in the conversation. The grandfather clock in the corner was ticking audibly.

"Nice weather for the time of year," said George.

A twinkle came to Edith Plumley's eye. "Next thing you'll be asking if I come here often. Please, just relax. I suggest it would help if we used first names."

He felt himself blush. "If you like." He still found her attractive, even if she couldn't cook. She was young in her manner. He guessed she was about sixty-three, but she could have passed for less.

"George."

"Yes . . . Edith?"

"I want to tell you something now, and I want to be sure I'm understood. I'm not in the habit of entertaining gentlemen in my home. In fact you are the first since . . . since I parted from Gregory. If I seem a little eager to be friends it's just that at our time of life I believe we have earned the right to dispense with—for want of a better word—the foreplay."

"Oh," said George, and accidentally set the chair rocking and slurped tea into his saucer.

Edith continued, "There isn't time for all that pussy-footing. Let's dispense with it, George. Let's admit that we're human beings with needs and impulses."

The digestive snapped. His crotch was covered in

crumbs. He moved his hand there to cover his incompetence. He managed to say, "I wouldn't argue with that, Edith."

"Good." She gave him a long, expectant look.

George swallowed hard. Why had she stopped talking? Why did her eyes beg his for a response? Why was a little drop of sweat rolling down his spine? Why hadn't he met her forty years ago?

"If you'd like to know," said George, "I really fancy you, Edith." He jerked his leg and set the chair going again. He was horrified. The statement sounded so crude. Where had it come from?

Edith laughed heartily. "You're a smooth talker, George, and an old rogue, too. I suspect you're making fun of me."

"No, Edith. Absolutely not. I didn't mean it. I mean I did mean it, in a way, but not in another way, if you know what I mean." He was no better than a tongue-tied schoolboy on his first date.

Like a lifebelt, Edith's command rescued George from his sea of embarrassment. "Come with me. You've been frank with me, and I don't mind admitting that you took me by surprise. And now it's my turn. After what you said, we should definitely hold nothing back. Put down your cup."

Without a word he got up and followed her ample form through the door beside the stone hearth. They entered her bedroom.

It was all so sudden. George felt a confusing mixture of guilt, elation and panic. Up to now he had always believed in the afterlife. As he stepped onto Edith Plumley's pink carpet and saw her double bed with its muslin canopy elegantly draped above the pillows, he told himself that atheism might, after all, be more appealing as a philosophy. He didn't want dear Ivy's immortal soul watching the witless ease of his seduction—on one glass of Australian sherry and a half-cooked pie.

And he wasn't entirely confident of satisfying Edith Plumley's expectations.

She turned and said, "This is the only way to get to it."

He said manfully, "I'm game for anything."

She crossed the room and opened another door. The *en suite* shower-room, he guessed. Fair enough. He, too, would be happier undressing in private.

She paused with her hand on the doorknob. "Come on, then."

He hesitated. "Both at once?"

She said, "There's room. Come on in." She giggled and disappeared inside.

George took a deep breath like a diver and followed her into the darkened room. It had a curious smell for a shower-room, a dry, musty aroma, vaguely familiar. George couldn't place it, but he didn't care much for it.

Edith felt for his hand and gripped it. Then she turned on the light. "Meet my little ones," she said. "Now everyone say hello to my friend George."

This wasn't a bathroom after all. It was a small dressing room, but instead of a wardrobe there were two shelves stacked with glass cages.

"You keep *mice?*" said George, too obviously in the circumstances. He knew the smell now. It was that of the local petshop where he bought Nimrod his supply of brawn.

"That's my secret," said Edith proudly. "Thirty-nine at the last count. All selectively bred over the last two years."

"Pedigree mice?"

"Well, of course! Look." She pointed to the back wall, a mosaic of rosettes and certificates. "One more win and I'll be a lifetime member of the National Fancy Mouse Society. That's my ambition, George."

George discreetly put a handkerchief to his nose and tried breathing through his mouth.

"I may have given you the wrong impression just now,"

said Edith, "bringing you through my bedroom, but that's the only way in, you see. I just loved the expression on your face."

"I wasn't expecting this," he admitted.

"You wondered what the invitation amounted to, didn't you, and I dare say you're heartily relieved," she said. "Heavens, we're too old to get up to things we shouldn't. I think I'd die if anyone saw me in bed."

"I can't think why," George gallantly said.

"Well, someone I hardly know."

"We could remedy that," said George.

"Given time, perhaps," said she.

"Not too much time," he said, feeling bolder now that the immediate challenge had been deferred.

"Any friend of mine would have to get used to the mice," said Edith. "And the smell. It all comes with me, I'm afraid. I keep them as clean as I can. Come and look at these." She indicated a cage set apart from the rest.

George peered politely at the two mice inside.

"Long-haired black and white hooded. The classic breeding pair," whispered Edith, her eyes rooted on the feeding mice. "The final show of the year is in Warminster in September. Only a short-haired silver-hood could possibly beat them. And there haven't been any shown at Warminster since 1985."

"You can see they're special," said George. He'd told white lies about the steak and kidney pie, so why not about these pesky mice?

Edith turned from the tank to look at George, her eyes shining. "You probably think I'm dotty, but these are my life. Would you really like to be part of it? Would you come with me to the Warminster show? I want someone to share my proudest moment with me. Then, who knows?"

"Edith, I can't think of anything I'd rather do," said George. Confident at last, he took her in his arms and kissed her. Their worlds collided gently amongst the sunflower seeds and sawdust.

He was home before eleven. Nimrod was out, enjoying his night life.

Ten days later, new neighbours moved into the empty cottage next door. George watched from his window in a fatalistic way as an immaculate Land Rover drew up. The place had changed hands several times in the past few years and he'd never got to know the people properly. They had been young couples from suburbia with unreal dreams of living in the country. One winter was usually enough; the familiar red and white 'For Sale' board would go up again and the garden would get overgrown until the new owners came in. Mind, the long grass made a happy hunting ground for Nimrod.

This time the young lady seemed friendly, knocking on George's door to introduce herself before the removal van arrived. In her middle twenties, with what used to be called a 'county' accent, but vivacious and attractive, she said she was Hannah from Dorking and her 'man' was Keith— which George took to mean that they were not married. He didn't object. The world had changed, and his own views on morality were changing too. He offered Hannah tea. They worked in television, he learned. She was a freelance researcher (whatever that meant) and Keith was a floor manager, which Hannah seemed to imply was something more exalted than keeping the floor clean, which was George's first assumption. Hannah said she had travelled on ahead of Keith who was with the removal gang to supervise the handling of some of the more precious items.

The van arrived and Hannah ran out to unlock for them. George settled down to watch the activity from the window. He was rather less obvious about it than Nimrod, who was sitting in the road gazing steadily into the back of the removal van. The Sutton boys from two doors up were out there as well, gaping. George had nothing but contempt for parents who allowed their children to be so blatantly nosy.

Keith, it appeared, was one of the four hefty fellows in T-shirt and jeans unloading the van. George had difficulty guessing which of them was the most likely to be the live-in lover of the elegant Hannah. She looked far too classy for any of them. But in mid-afternoon the van left, taking three in the cab and leaving one sitting on the drystone wall smoking a cigarette. He had cropped hair and a silver ear-ring.

George remarked to Nimrod, who had come in to be fed, "She's all right, but I'm not so happy about having him next door." He put on the kettle again, preparing do the neighbourly thing and take them both some fresh tea and biscuits.

"Into the fray, Nimmy, old friend," he said as he ventured out of the door, tray in hand.

Keith didn't even get off the wall. "For us? Nice timing, squire," he said without removing his cigarette. "Go right in, mate."

"George Blackitt, from next door," said George still holding the tray and therefore unable to offer his hand as he would have wished.

Keith shouted in a voice the whole village must have heard, "Han, are you there? Guy here with some Rosy Lea."

George stepped gingerly into the cluttered living room. Furniture and boxes stood in disorder everywhere.

"Mr Blackitt, what a marvellous thought!" said Hannah, appearing from the kitchen. "This is so generous."

"I'll leave it on the piano, shall I?" said George. "There's no hurry for the things. Tomorrow will do."

"Please don't rush off," she said. "Stay and have some with us. Don't worry, I've got a spare mug somewhere. That's one thing we have unpacked."

"Moving is a pain in the arse, ain't it, George?" Keith's voice said from the doorway. "Park yours on the chair, mate. Han and I don't mind squatting on the floor."

George took the mug Hannah handed him and sat like a throned king with slaves at his feet. Hannah offered some carrot cake that they'd brought with them. George politely declined.

"Don't blame you," said Keith. "Hippie food. We'll feed it to the mice."

"Mice?" said George.

Hannah laughed. "Don't worry. The cottage hasn't got mice, so far as I know. Keith has just bought this pair for breeding."

"Caged mice?"

"I'll show you." Keith was on his feet and searching among the packing cases. "Here we are." He brought out a glass tank and held it under George's nose. "Ollie and Freda, my latest investment. Still kipping from the journey."

George glanced into the tank with trepidation. The mice weren't visible. They were hiding under a shelter of sawdust and shredded newspaper in one corner. It moved in tiny spasms as Keith tapped the glass.

"Here, put the tank on your knees a sec," said Keith. Immediately he plunged his hand into the sawdust and hauled a mouse out by its tail. "It's either Ollie or Freda. Not easy to tell."

"Put it down, Keith," said Hannah.

"That's how you handle them," said Keith with nonchalance, but he then allowed the mouse to rest in his free hand. It crouched shivering. "I've never been without a pet, but fancy mice are something new."

"It looks a very fine specimen," said George, who was also beginning to know a little about mice.

"Short-haired silver-hood."

George felt his blood run cold. From all his conversations with Edith, short-haired silver-hoods were the only variety capable of outclassing her long-haired black and white hooded mice. And these people possessed a pair. "These . . . these are really rare, I believe."

"Yeah." Keith released the mouse into the tank. "They cost me a bomb. Well, if you're breeding, you don't want to use rubbish."

"Are you interested in mice, George?" asked Hannah.

"Well, em," George said guardedly. "A friend of mine keeps some and she and I . . . well, we take a passing interest."

"So you'll be going to the Fancy Mouse Show at Warminster, will you?" exclaimed Hannah, bringing her hands together in delight.

"Well, possibly. It's a long time off."

"Oh, do! It should be a hoot. We read about it in the local paper. Imagine, giving rosettes to mice." She giggled. "If Keith wins one, he says he's going to pin it up in the little room."

"Yeah," said Keith. "And if Ollie and Freda get on with it, we'll have a totally red silk bog this time next year."

"Cool," said Hannah.

"Yes, cool," said George dismally.

Two weekends later he was horrified to see Keith unloading ten glass cages from the Land Rover. They went straight into the shed at the bottom of their garden.

George slept fitfully that night. He hadn't slept so badly since the summer of 1940, only this time it wasn't the threat of German air-raids that kept him awake; it was the prospect of umpteen short-haired silver hooded mice in the garden shed next door. September was fast approaching and with it the culmination of Edith's breeding programme to secure her election to the National Fancy Mouse Society. He hadn't said a word to her about the newly-arrived competition. He knew it would break her heart.

"George, you look so downcast. I suspect that you aren't looking after yourself properly," she remarked in the men's outfitters when they were buying George a new linen jacket for the occasion. "Chin up, now. Is anything the matter?"

"Nothing, Edith," he lied.

"Come over on Saturday and I'll cook you a pie."

George had spent many hours watching the activity in the garden shed. Sacks of feed had gone in. And an electric cable, presumably to supply heating next winter. The shed was built on the far side of Keith and Hannah's garden, but if George weeded his verge by the dividing fence he could just see the darkened outlines of the mouse tanks inside. And often he saw Keith in there, handling his mice.

One August morning he called out, "How's it going, then?"

"What's that?" said Keith.

"The breeding."

Keith laughed. "They breed like mice, mate."

"Could I see them?"

"Love to show you, George, but I'm on location this week. Got to fly."

"You don't appear to have any lids on the tanks that I can see . . . Not that I've been prying, of course."

"George," said Keith smugly, "they're mice, not salamanders. They can't climb sheer glass walls, mate. Don't worry, none of the little beggars will get out. If they did, your old cat would have them, and who could blame him? But I keep the shed locked, so don't lose any sleep over it."

On the Thursday before the show, George had a stroke of luck. He had just been running Saturday's ghastly scenario through his head when Hannah called.

"Oh, Mr Blackitt," she said. "I hardly like to ask, but you

were so kind when we moved in. I wonder if you could do us a favour. Keith is doing a night shoot at the Tower of London on Friday. With it being open for visitors, that's the only time the cameras can get in there. I've never been and it's a wonderful chance. Would you mind keeping an eye on the cottage for us? It's just one night, but you never know."

A spark of hope glimmered in the ashes of George's sunken aspirations. "I'll be only too pleased. But what about the mice? Would you like me to feed them?"

"No, they'll be perfectly all right. Keith will feed them before we go and we'll be back first thing on Saturday."

"My dear, there's no need to rush back."

"Oh, but there is. We've entered for the Mouse Show, just for a laugh, as Keith says. We'll see you there, I hope."

Just as she turned to leave, Nimrod came in through the cat-flap. "Aren't you beautiful?" Hannah said, stooping to stroke him. "What's his name, Mr Blackitt?"

"Nimrod." Usually George explained the origin of the name. This time he chose not to.

Hannah tickled Nimrod under his chin. The cat, purred, arched his back luxuriously and boxed her hair with his paw. "You're quick and powerful, aren't you, Nimrod," she cooed softly, "but you'll promise to keep away from my Keith's shed, won't you?"

George slept better that night. By Friday evening he had worked out every detail of his masterplan.

Nimrod hadn't been fed since the morning and the cat-flap was wedged shut. He was prowling about the cottage like a caged lion.

George poured himself a large scotch. "You won't have much longer to wait, old friend," he said. "Fresh food for you tonight. Living food, none of that prepacked slop. How about mouse mousse for supper? Short-haired silver hooded mouse mousse. Patience, old friend, patience."

Nimrod's mewing was becoming positively feral in tone. He kept running to the table leg that he used as a scratching-post and clawing it agitatedly.

The plan was deliciously simple. At about nine o'clock, when it was dark, George would go out. Under one arm would be the football he kept for his grandchildren to play with when they visited the cottage. With the other, he would be carrying a travelling bag containing Nimrod, by now ravenous. George would let himself into next door's garden and go to the far side of the shed, the side nearest the Suttons' cottage. The Suttons had the three boys under twelve, the local tearaways. He would smash the window with the football and push it through. Then he would unzip the bag containing Nimrod and help him through the broken window. Nimrod would embark on an orgy of rodent-killing.

As soon as Keith returned to collect his prize specimens for the Fancy Mouse Show, Nimrod would make his dash for freedom, leaving the brash young punk to discover the mass murder and the football, and draw his conclusions. The next time George saw Keith and Hannah and heard the gruesome story, he would say that he thought he'd overheard some sounds in the garden about nine last night and guessed it was cats. He knew the shed was kept locked, so he hadn't gone out to check. Then he would apologize profusely for Nimrod's blood-letting spree and Hannah would say that you couldn't blame the cat—or George. And if Keith said that the Suttons disclaimed ownership of the football, George would give a shrug and say, "What else do you expect of modern kids?"

After two more scotches, George looked outside to check how dark it was and fetched the plastic travelling bag from his wardrobe. Nimrod actually came running to investigate, so it was simple to sweep him up and bundle him inside. He fought savagely to escape. "Save your energy, old fellow. You're going to need it presently," said George, zipping up the bag. "Okay, dinner should be ready."

He collected the football, picked up the bag, let himself out and moved stealthily past the unlit cottage next door and into Keith and Hannah's back garden. He rested the bag on the ground and took a precautionary look around him before pressing the football hard against the window. The glass shattered easily and he thrust the football through so hard that he heard it break another pane of glass in one of the tanks. He lifted the bag to the level of the window and unzipped it. Nimrod's head popped out, his fang-teeth bared. George helped his old friend safely through the hole and felt the strength in the struggling shoulders. The Mighty Hunter had got the whiff of the mice. The energy coming from the black fur was awesome.

George whispered, "*Bon appetit!*" Having released Nimrod, he picked up the bag and walked back to the house feeling twenty years younger.

The Fancy Mouse Show next day was a revelation. George wandered up and down the rows of tanks and cages in the municipal hall marvelling at the doting owners as much as the mice competing for the titles. They groomed and stroked their tiny charges in an attempt to catch the judge's eye. First there were the competitions to decide the best in each class. Later would come the accolade everyone coveted, for supreme champion.

Edith clutched George's arm. "See, George," she said. "See how exciting it all is? I'm not an eccentric old fool, am I?"

"I never said you were," George answered.

The judging of the long-haired black and white hooded class took place at noon. Edith's pair took first place. George and Edith embraced.

"I love you, Edith Plumley," George declared. "There isn't anything I wouldn't do for you."

"Just keep your fingers and toes crossed for me," she said tremulously. "They go forward to the supreme championship, on the stage at four o'clock. George, we're virtually certain to win. Only the late arrival of a truly rare breed would deprive my little beauties of the title."

"So what happens now?" said George.

"I just told you. We wait for the judging."

"No, what happens to us now, Edith. What about our future?"

A rough hand grabbed his shoulder.

"So here you are," said Keith.

George felt the hairs rise on the back of his neck. Fear gripped him. He was certain his neighbour was about to punch him.

But he did not. "George, old pal," he said, "I'd like to buy you a drink."

"That isn't necessary," said George, suspicious that this was only the prelude to violence.

"To celebrate, man," Keith said in the same friendly tone. "We just won first prize in our class. In fact, we're the only entry in our class. The silver-hoods. Extremely rare, the judge said. They created quite a stir. And they're going to win the supreme champion rosette. No problem."

George heard a whimper of distress from Edith. He'd almost forgotten her in his anxiety. "Edith, this is Keith, my neighbour," he said quickly.

He was about to add for Keith's benefit that Edith was a friend, but Edith said in a horrified voice, "Your *neighbour*?" Then she covered her face and fled. There was no point in going after her. He'd never explain it to her satisfaction.

"What's wrong with her?" said Keith. "Wasn't me, was it?"

George couldn't find words for some time. "I could do with that drink," he whispered finally.

After they had been standing at the bar some time while Keith held forth about the idiocy of Fancy Mouse Shows,

George managed to say, "Those prize-winning mice of yours—where do they come from?"

"What do you mean—where do they come from?" said Keith. "Other mice, of course." He laughed.

"No, where did you keep them? The shed?"

"Not the shed. They're valuable mice, mate. I wouldn't keep my silver-hoods in the shed. No, they live in luxury, on top of the piano. I just had time to get home and grab them and get them here for the judging."

"What about the mice in the shed?"

"They're nothing special. They're feeders."

"Feeders?" repeated George.

"Oh, Christ, Han didn't want me to tell you this. People living next door can get nervous, but there's no need. The mice are for Percy. You must have seen him on TV commercials. He pays for his keep. He stays coiled up in his tank at the bottom of our shed. It's got a glass top, mate, so Percy won't get out. He gets through hundreds of mice. Well, he would. In the wild, a fourteen-foot python would be swallowing live pigs and all sorts. They're terrific hunters. So quick. They have these dislocating jaws that . . . What's up, George? Hey, George, you look terrible."

Murder in Store

"Hey, miss."

"What is it now?"

"Something's up with Santa."

"That's quite enough from you, young lady," Pauline said sharply—unseasonably sharply for Christmas week in an Oxford Street department store. The Toy Fair was a bedlam of electric trains, robots, talking dolls and whining infants, but the counter staff— however hard-pressed— weren't expected to threaten the kids. The day had got off to a trying start when a boy with mischief in mind had pulled a panda off a shelf and started an avalanche of soft toys. Pauline had found herself knee-deep in teddies, rabbits and hippos. Now she was trying to reassemble the display, between attending to customers and coping with little nuisances like this one, dumped in the department while their parents shopped elsewhere in the store.

"Take a butcher's in the grotto, miss."

Pauline glared at the girl, a six-year-old by the size of her, with gaps between her teeth and a dark fringe like a helmet. A green anorak, white corduroy trousers and red wellies. She'd been a regular visitor ever since the school term ended. Her quick, sticky hands were a threat to every toy within reach. But she had shining brown eyes and a way with words that could be amusing at times less stressful than this.

"I think Santa's stiffed it, miss."

"For the last time . . ."

A man held out a green felt crocodile, and Pauline rolled her eyes upwards and exchanged a smile. She rang up the sale, locked her till and stepped around the counter to look for Mark Daventry, the head of the toy department. The child had a point. It was 10.05 and Santa's Grotto should have opened at 10.00. A queue had started to form. There was no sign of Zena, the "gnome" who sold the tickets.

It was shamefully unfair. Mark hadn't been near the department this morning. No doubt he was treating Zena to coffee in the staff canteen. When blonde Zena had first appeared three weeks ago in her pointed hat, short tunic and red tights, Mark had lingered around the grotto entrance like a six-foot kid lining up for his Christmas present. Soon he'd persuaded her to join him for coffee-breaks: the Mark Daventry routine familiar to Pauline and sundry other ex-girlfriends in the store. However, Zena wasn't merely the latest temp in the toy department. She wasn't merely an attractive blonde. She happened to be the wife of Santa Claus.

Big Ben, as he was known outside the grotto, was a ready-made Santa, a mountainous man who needed no padding under the crimson suit, and whose beard was his own, requiring only a dusting of talc. On Saturday nights, he could be seen in a pair of silver trunks, in the wrestling-ring at Streatham. This time, Mark was flirting dangerously.

"Coming, miss?"

Pauline felt her fingers clutched by a small, warm hand. She allowed herself to be led to the far end of the grotto, the curtain that covered the exit.

"Have you been sneaking round the back, you little menace?"

The child dived through the curtain and Pauline followed. Surprisingly, the interior was unlit. The winking lights hadn't been switched on and the mechanical figures of Santa's helpers were immobile. There was no sign of Ben and Zena. They generally came up by the service lift that was cunningly enclosed in the grotto, behind Santa's workshop. They used the workshop as a changing-room.

"See what I mean, miss?"

Pauline saw where the child was pointing, and caught her breath. In the gloom, the motionless figure of Santa Claus was slumped on the throne where he usually sat to receive the children. The head and shoulders hung ominously over one side.

It was difficult not to scream. Only the presence of the child kept Pauline from panicking.

"Stay here. Don't come any closer."

She knew what she had to do: check whether his pulse was beating. He might have suffered a heart attack. Ben was not much over thirty, but anyone so obviously overweight was at risk. She took a deep breath and stepped forward.

She discovered that he wasn't actually wearing the costume. It was draped over him. Somehow, she had to find the courage to look. She reached out for the furry trim of the hood, took it between finger and thumb and lifted it. She gave a start. She was looking into a pair of eyes without a flicker of life. But it wasn't Ben.

It was Mark Daventry. And there was something embedded in his chest—a bolt from a crossbow.

Pauline rushed the child out of the grotto and dashed to the phone.

She called Mr Beckington, the store manager, but got through to Sylvia, his secretary. Even suave Sylvia, supposed to be equal to every emergency, gave a cry of horror at the news. "Mark? Oh my God! Are you sure?"

"Is Mr Beckington there?"

"Mr Beckington? Yes."

"Ask him to come down at once. I'll make sure no one goes in."

When she came off the phone, Pauline looked around for the small girl. She'd wandered off, probably to spread the news. Soon the whole store would know that Santa was dead in his grotto. Pauline shook her head and went to stand guard.

She told the queue that Santa was going to be late, and someone made a joke about reindeer in the rush-hour. This is totally bizarre, Pauline thought, standing here under the glitter with these smiling people and their children, and "Jingle Bells" belting out from the public address, while a man lies murdered a few yards away. Her nerves were stretched to snapping-point.

Fully ten minutes went by before Mr Beckington appeared, smoking his usual cigar, giving a convincing impression of the unflappable executive in a crisis. He liked customers to be aware that he managed the store, so he always wore a rosebud on his pinstripe lapel. He nodded sociably to the queue and murmured to Pauline, "What's all this, Miss Fothergill?" as if she were the cause of it.

She took him into the grotto.

They stopped and stared.

The winking lights were on. The model figures were in motion, wielding their little hammers. Santa was alive and on his throne, dressed for work. Zena the gnome was powdering his beard.

"Ho-ho," Ben greeted them in his jocular voice, "and what do you want in your Christmas stockings?"

Mr Beckington turned to Pauline, his eyes blazing

behind his glasses. "If this is some kind of joke, it's in lamentably bad taste."

She reddened and repeated what she'd seen. Ben and Zena insisted that everything had been in its usual place when they'd arrived in the lift a few minutes late. They certainly hadn't seen a dead body. The Santa costume had been on its hanger in the workshop.

She gaped at them in disbelief.

Mr Beckington said, "We're all under stress at this time of the year, Miss Fothergill. The best construction I can put upon this incident is that you had some kind of hallucination brought on by overwork. You'd better go home and rest."

She said, trying to stay calm, "I'm perfectly well, thank you. I don't need to go home."

Ben said in the voice he used to his infant visitors when they burst into tears, "Now, now, be a sensible girl."

"If it's all my imagination, where's Mark Daventry?" Pauline demanded.

Mr Beckington told her, "He's down with 'flu. We had a message."

"Darling, I think some meany played a trick on you," Zena suggested. "That kid with the teeth missing is a right little scamp. Some practical joker must have put her up to it."

Pauline shook her head and frowned, unwilling to accept the explanation, but trying to fathom how it could have been done.

"If you're not going home, you'd better get back to your position," Mr Beckington told her. "And let's get this blasted grotto open."

She spent the rest of the morning in a stunned state, going through the motions of selling toys and answering enquiries while her mind tried to account for what had happened. If only the small girl had returned, she'd have got the truth from her by some means, but, just when the kid was wanted, she'd vanished.

About 12.30, there was a quiet period. Pauline asked Zena to keep an eye on her counter for five minutes. "I want to check the stock-lists in the sports department."

"Whatever for?"

"To see if a crossbow is missing."

"You still believe this happened?"

"I'm certain."

The sports department was located next to the toys on the same floor. Disappointingly, Pauline found that every crossbow was accounted for. She told herself that if the murderer was on the staff, he could easily have borrowed the weapon and replaced it later. But what about the bolt?

She examined the crossbow kits. Six bolts were supplied with each. She checked the boxes and found one with only five. She *hadn't* been hallucinating.

"What are you going to do about it?" Zena asked, when Pauline told her.

"I've got some more checking to do."

"Proper Miss Marple, aren't you? You're wasting your time, darling."

"Coming from you, that's good."

Zena said without a hint of embarrassment, "Jealous of my coffee-breaks, are you? That's all water under the bridge. Look, I still say this is someone playing silly games. It could even be Mark himself."

Pauline shook her head. "Zena, he's dead, and I'm going to find out why. Tell me, did you and Ben arrive together this morning?"

Zena smiled. "You bet we did."

"What's funny?"

"He guards me like a harem-girl since he found out Mark was chatting me up. We had a monumental row last week, and I told Ben straight out that he shouldn't take me for granted. Now he watches me all the time." She adjusted her pointed hat. "I find it rather a turn-on."

"But you definitely finished with Mark last week?"

"Absolutely. I wouldn't say he was heartbroken. You know how he is. Adaptable."

"That isn't the word I'd use," said Pauline, thinking of all the women Mark had "chatted up."

In her lunch-hour, she went downstairs and talked to the security man on the staff entrance, a solemn Scot who'd made himself unpopular with everyone but the management by noting daily who was in, and at what time. Pauline asked if by any chance Mr Mark Daventry was in.

"Yes, he's here. He arrived early this morning, just after 8.15."

She said, "Are you sure?"

"Positive."

"Someone told me he was down with 'flu."

To prove his point, the security man showed her Mark's overcoat in the staff locker-room. She knew Mark's camel-hair coat with the leather buttons and the shoulder-flaps. There was no question now that what she had seen was true.

She asked the security man about Ben and Zena. They'd arrived together at their usual time, 9.50—which was odd, not to say suspicious, considering how late the grotto had opened.

She decided to have it out with them. The grotto closed between 1.00 and 2.00, so she found them out of costume in the staff canteen. They'd finished lunch and Ben had his arm protectively around Zena's chair. They looked up like two choirboys on a Christmas card, innocence personified.

She warned them that she'd been checking downstairs. "I want a straight answer. Why weren't you ready to open the grotto at ten this morning?"

"There's no mystery, darling," answered Zena. "We had to wait ages for the lift."

A reasonable explanation. The lift was their only means of access to the grotto. Pauline had to accept it for the moment. She said, "I'm going to make a search of the grotto."

Ben said affably, "Fine. Let's all make a search."

They had twenty minutes. Pauline had hoped to find bloodstains on Santa's throne, but it was painted red. She went behind the scenery, where it was supported on wood and chicken-wire. "There's something under here."

It was a wooden packing-case. Ben dragged it out and pulled off the lid. There was a layer of the small white chips of polystyrene used in packing. Ben dug into them with his large hands.

Zena screamed as a tuft of dark hair was revealed. It didn't take much more digging to confirm that Mark's body had been crammed into the packing-case.

"I suppose all three of us are imagining this!" Pauline said pointedly.

"We'd better report it," said Ben in a shocked voice. Reassuringly, he and Zena gave every sign of being genuinely surprised at the discovery.

"Before we do," said Pauline, "would you mind looking in his pockets?"

"Why?" asked Zena, but Ben was already starting a search. In one of the inside pockets was the note that Pauline hoped to find. *Something* must have lured Mark to his death in the grotto early that morning.

It was a short, typed message: *See what Santa has for you, darling. Tuesday morning, 8.45.*

"I've seen that typestyle recently," said Ben.

"On our letter of appointment," said Zena.

"Sylvia?" said Ben, frowning. "Mr Beckington's secretary?"

Pauline and Zena exchanged a long, uncomprehending look.

They covered the body and took the lift to the management floor above. On the way up, Pauline said, "I've thought of something terribly important. Did you find out why you had to wait so long for the lift this morning?"

"Not for certain," Ben answered. "The usual cause is a storeman delivering goods."

Pauline said, "I believe it was the murderer, jamming the lift-door open at our floor so that no one would interrupt the killing. When it finally arrived, did you see a storeman?"

"No," said Zena, "it was empty." She hesitated. "But we smelt cigar smoke."

There wasn't time to reflect on that, because the lift-doors opened at the top floor and Mr Beckington was waiting there, a cigar jutting from his mouth. At the sight of the three of them together, his features twisted in alarm. He turned and made a dash for the emergency stairs.

"Ben!" shouted Zena.

Ben set off in chase.

The commotion brought people from their offices, among them Sylvia. Pauline grabbed her arm and drew her into the lift. Zena pressed the button for the ground floor and the three women started downwards.

"Mr Beckington," Zena blurted out. "He murdered Mark."

Sylvia's hand went to her mouth.

"But why?" said Pauline.

Sylvia said in a small, shocked voice, "He was jealous. Silly man. He was forever trying to start something with me, but I wasn't interested. I mean, he's married, with a daughter my age. Then last week Mark started taking an interest in me. I always thought him dishy, and . . . well, on

Friday evening we spent a little time together in the grotto."

"By arrangement?"

Sylvia nodded. "When everyone else was gone."

Pauline showed her the note they'd found in Mark's pocket.

"I didn't type this!" said Sylvia.

"Mr Beckington did," Pauline explained, "on your type-writer, to make sure Mark turned up this morning. He killed Mark in the grotto and he must have still been in there when the child sneaked in. He must have been hiding behind the scenery when I came in. I raised the alarm, and while I was standing outside like a lulu, he hid the body in a packing-case. I just hope Ben catches him."

"My man's strong," said Zena, "but fast he isn't."

The lift gave a shudder as they reached the ground floor. When the doors opened, a police sergeant was waiting. Two constables were nearby, standing at the foot of the stairs.

"All right, girls," said the sergeant. "Just stand over there, well out of the way."

In a moment, there was the clatter of footsteps on the stairs, then Mr Beckington ran straight into the arms of the waiting policemen. He offered no resistance.

Pauline felt a tug on her skirt and looked down at the small girl. "You?" she said. "You called the police?"

The child smiled smugly and nodded.

"And you believed her?" Pauline said to the sergeant.

"She's my daughter, miss. The way I see it, if my little girl tells me Santa's snuffed it, I've got to be very, very concerned."

Never a Cross Word

Poison, perhaps.

Quick-acting, if you choose the right sort. No mess. Simple to administer.

The problem with a poisoning is that science has progressed so far that you can't expect to get away with it any more. The police bring in people who make a whole career out of finding symptoms and traces.

Poison is not practical any more.

"I'm putting on the cocoa, blossom," Rose calls from the kitchen. "Did you switch on the blanket?"

"Twenty minutes ago, my love," answers Albert, easing his old body out of the armchair.

"And I thought you were day-dreaming. I ought to know better. My faithful Albert wouldn't forget after all these years. Is my kettle filled?"

He puts his head around the door. "Yes, dear."

"And the hottie—is it emptied from last night?"

"Emptied, yes, and waiting by the bed."

"You're a treasure, Albert."

"I do my best, sweetpea."

"I sometimes wonder how I ever got through the night before we bought the electric blanket. I've always felt the cold, you know. It isn't just old age."

"We had ways of keeping warm," says Albert.

"You've always had a marvellous circulation," says Rose for the millionth time. "You don't know how lucky you are."

Perhaps suffocation is the way. The pillow held firmly over the face. No traces of poison then. How do they know it isn't a heart attack? Mental note: visit the library tomorrow and find out more about suffocation.

"Nearly ready, honeybunch," says Rose, in the kitchen stirring the milk in the saucepan. "We're a comical pair, when you think about it: I make the cocoa to send us to sleep. You make the tea that wakes us up."

And wash up your sodding saucepan. And the spoon that you always leave by the gas-ring, coated in cocoa. And wipe the surface clean.

"I couldn't bear to get out of bed as early as you do," says Rose. "My dear old Mum used to say . . ."

Six hours sleep for a man, seven for a woman and eight for a fool.

" . . . six hours sleep for a man, seven for a woman and eight for a fool. I don't know how true it is. Sometimes I feel as if I could stay in bed for ever."

"It's coming to the boil, love."

"So it is, my pet. Where are the mugs?"

Albert fetches them from the cupboard and Rose spoons in some cocoa, pours in the steaming milk and stirs. She gives Albert a sweet smile. "And now it's up the stairs to Bedfordshire."

"I'll check everything first," he says.

"Lights?"

"Yes."

"Doors?"

"Of course, my darling."

"See you presently, then."

"Careful how you go with those mugs, then."

A fall downstairs? Probably fatal at this age. Maybe that's

the answer—the loose stair-rod near the top. Not entirely reliable, more's the pity.

In bed, sipping her cocoa, Rose says, "Nice and cosy. Pity it can't stay on all night."

"The electric blanket? Dangerous," says Albert. "They don't recommend it."

"Never mind. I've got my hottie and my kettle ready."

"That's right."

The hot-water bottle and the electric kettle are on Rose's bedside table ready for the moment, about two in the morning, when her feet get cold. She will then switch on the light above her head, flick the switch on the kettle and wait for it to heat up. Some nights Albert doesn't notice the light and the kettle being switched on, but he unfailingly hears the slow crescendo of the kettle coming to the boil. Then Rose will fill the hot-water bottle and say, "Have I disturbed you, dear? It's only me filling my hottie."

Depressed, Albert stares at the wrinkled skin on the surface of his cocoa. Separate bedrooms might have been the answer, but he's never suggested it. Rose regards the sharing of the bed as the proof of a successful marriage. "We've never spent a single night apart, except for the time I was in hospital. Not a single night. I look at other couples and I know, I just know, that they don't sleep in the same bed any more." So the guest bedroom is only ever used by guests—her sister from Somerset once a year when the Chelsea Flower Show is on and, once, his friend Harry from army days.

Rose says, "Did you notice the Barnetts this afternoon? Am I mistaken, or were they being just a bit crotchety with each other?"

A night in the guest room would be bliss. Uninterrupted sleep. Just to be spared the inevitable "Have I disturbed you, dear?" at two in the morning.

"Albert, dear."

"Mm?"

"I don't think you were listening. I was asking if you noticed anything about John and Marcia this afternoon."

"John and Marcia?"

"The Barnetts. At bridge."

"Something wrong with their game?"

"No. I'm talking about the way they behaved towards each other. It may have been just my imagination, but I thought Marcia was more prickly with him than usual—as if they'd had words before we arrived. Didn't you notice it?"

"Not that I can recall," says Albert.

"When he had to re-deal because of the card that turned face up?"

"Really?"

"And when he reached for the chocolate biscuit. She was really sharp with him then, lecturing him about his calories. He looked so silly with his hand stuck in the air over the plate of biscuits. You *must* remember that."

"The chocolate biscuit. I do."

"Unnecessary, I thought."

"True."

"Humiliating the poor man."

"Yes."

"I mean, it isn't as if John is grossly enormous. He's got a bit of a paunch, but he's over seventy, for pity's sake. You expect a man to have a paunch by then."

"Goes without saying," says Albert, who actually has no paunch at all.

Rose drains the last of her cocoa. "You know what would do those two a power of good?"

"What's that?"

"If they spent some time apart from each other. Since he's retired, she sees him all day long. They're not adjusted to it."

"What would he do on his own?"

"I don't know. What do men do with themselves? Golf, or bowls. Fishing."

"When I go fishing, you always come with me and sit on the riverbank talking."

"That's different, isn't it? We're inseparable. We don't need to get away from each other. We haven't the slightest desire to be alone."

There is an interval of silence.

Rose resumes. "They won't catch you and me saying unkind things to each other in public, will they?"

"Or in private," says Albert.

She turns and smiles. "You're right, my love. Never a cross word in forty-seven years."

"Forty-eight."

Rose frowns. "No dear, forty-seven. This is 1995. We were married in 1948. The difference is forty-seven."

"Yes, but we met in 1947."

"I wasn't counting that," Rose says.

"It's another year."

"Of course, looked at like that . . ."

"No arguments when we were courting. Lovers' tiffs, they would have been."

"But there weren't any. Ah, well." She puts her mug on the bedside table and switches out the light on her side. "It's far too late for mental arithmetic. Time to get my beauty sleep. Nighty-night, darling." She turns for the goodnight kiss. They've never gone to sleep without the goodnight kiss, in forty-seven years, or is it forty-eight?

Their lips meet briefly.

"Sweet dreams."

Albert gets rid of his mug and reaches for the light switch. He yawns, wriggles down and turns away from her, wondering what time the library opens.

He's in an aircraft about to take off for Australia. Off for a long holiday, time to adjust, to get over the grief, he has been telling everyone. The engines of the Jumbo are roaring, louder by the second, building to the immense power needed for take-off.

A voice says, "Have I disturbed you, dear?"

"What?"

"It's only me filling my hottie."

He emerges from the dream and looks at the clock. Five past two.

"I couldn't survive without my hottie," Rose says. "I don't know how you manage, really I don't."

"Marvellous circulation," Albert says silently, moving his lips unseen.

Rose says, "It must be your marvellous circulation. Well, there it is: a nice hot bottle for my poor cold feet. Now I'll be off to sleep again in two shakes of a lamb's tail."

Forty minutes later, Albert is still awake, thinking about ways of faking a suicide.

He is up as usual on the dot of six, groping for his slippers. He feels as if he could sleep three more hours, given the opportunity, but the habit of rising at six is too deeply rooted ever to change. He knows he'll feel better after the first cup of tea.

He edges around the bed to her side and unplugs the electric kettle.

Picking it up, he shuffles towards the bathroom.

Down in the kitchen, he cleans the saucepan and the spoon from the night before and wipes the surface clean. The kettle boils.

The tea is a life-saver.

In the library, while Rose is looking at the Romance section, Albert covertly inspects a volume entitled *Essentials of Forensic Medicine*. The chapter on Suffocation and Asphyxia runs to several pages. The list of post-mortem appearances, external and internal, is so daunting that he abandons the whole idea. But another chapter, Electrocution, catches his eye and captures his imagination.

"Do you want to borrow it?"

He snaps the book shut and looks to his right. Rose is at his side. He pushes it back into the first space he can see and says, "No, I was just browsing really."

"This is the medical section, isn't it?"

"Yes, I was only whiling away the time, checking up on my rheumatism. Have you picked yours, my love?"

"I'm going to borrow three, just in case I find I've read one of them before."

"Good thinking."

That afternoon, when Rose is deep in her romantic novel, Albert tries to slip away unnoticed to the bedroom.

"Where are you off to, honeybunch?"

"I think some air must have got into one of the radiators. I'd like to check."

Rose says admiringly, "My handyman."

"I shouldn't be more than twenty minutes."

"I think I *may* have read this. I'm not sure."

"If you have, you could always try one of the others."

He goes upstairs, straight to the bed and lifts up the undersheet on Rose's side. The electric blanket lies there, the single size, only on her side—because his marvellous circulation keeps him warm without artificial help. This blanket been doing its job for at least ten years and has lost most of its original colour. The fabric at the edges is getting frayed, and where her feet go, it has worn thin. He stares at it thoughtfully. He looks at the flex leading to the twin point where it is kept plugged in.

"Will it take long, dear?" Rose calls up. She must be standing at the foot of the stairs.

Hastily, Albert tugs the undersheet over the electric blanket again.

"Not long, my dear," he answers, adding in a whisper, "It should be very quick."

"Shall I put the kettle on? I wouldn't mind a cup."

"Good idea."

A few precious minutes. He folds the sheet back again, takes a penknife from his pocket, opens it, and begins scraping at the thin covering where her feet go. Cutting would be too obvious. It must look as if it has worn away naturally. He scrapes at several places and finally the threads begin to part and the copper element beneath is laid bare. He continues to work, exposing more of it, until he gets the call that the tea is ready downstairs. He scoops the loose threads into his hand, pockets the penknife and straightens the undersheet and tucks it in.

"Is that job done, my love?" Rose calls up.

"I hope so, my dear," answers Albert, planning the next part of the operation. It can wait until the evening.

"Have some tea, then. You deserve it."

About nine-thirty, after watching the news on television, he gets up as usual to take the kettle upstairs and switch on the electric blanket. Rose remains in her chair, knitting. Albert has done this so many times that he doesn't even have to tell her where he is going.

He collects the kettle, fills it with water in the kitchen, and carries it upstairs, placing it on Rose's bedside table. He switches on the electric blanket.

The hot water bottle is in the bathroom as usual, and has to be emptied. He unscrews it and stands it upside down in the wash basin to drain. Then he gets to work on the stopper. He pulls the rubber washer away from the base. This should ensure that the bottle leaks. To be quite certain, he makes a test, half-filling it, screwing in the stopper and holding it upside down. Sure enough, it drips steadily.

The preparations completed, he goes downstairs and joins Rose for the last hour before retiring.

When the milk is simmering in the saucepan, Rose asks, "Did you remember to switch on the blanket, Albert darling?"

"An hour ago, my love."

"So thoughtful."

"I think the milk—"

"Quick! The mugs."

Rose lifts the saucepan from the hob. Albert places the mugs beside the cocoa tin and Rose does the rest.

Everything is in place, as the politicians like to say. There is little else for Albert to do. At two in the morning, he will be wakened as usual while Rose fills the hot water bottle. She will push it down by her cold feet. In two shakes of a lamb's tail, as she will tell him, she will be asleep. For the next hour it will seep, seep over the undersheet, slowly saturating the electric blanket. While it remains warm, she won't notice. And when he judges the moment right, Albert will get out of bed, move around in the dark and switch on the blanket.

An unfortunate accident, they will decide at the inquest. Faulty equipment.

"Is it up the stairs to Bedfordshire?" says Rose.

"I think it is, dear."

"Will you lock the doors and turn out the lights?"

"Depend upon it," says Albert.

In bed, they drink their last cup of cocoa together, sitting up.

"People are so stupid," says Rose.

"What do you mean, dear?" says Albert.

"When you hear about so many marriages breaking up. So much unhappiness. If they'd only have a little more consideration for each other."

"True," says Albert.

You bloody old hypocrite, thinks Rose. Driving me to the brink of insanity with your sanctimonious smile and your "Yes, my darling," while you pursue your own selfish ways, waking me every blasted morning at six. Heaving yourself up with a groan and a yawn, to put on your slippers, regardless that it all causes a minor earthquake in the bed. Groping around the edge of the mattress to collect the damned kettle. Switching on the bathroom light. Flushing the toilet. Clumping downstairs and turning on the radio. Forty-seven years of it, I've endured. His farting, his fishing and his football on television.

And never a cross word between us. I wouldn't give you that satisfaction. I've held out all this time.

"Oh, dear."

"What's the matter, love?" says Albert.

"I've forgotten to go to the bathroom—and just when I was getting nice and cosy." She sighs. "I suppose I shall have to get out."

"That's one thing I can't do for you," says Albert.

"Snuggle down, dear. I shan't be long."

From the bathroom Rose collects a chair and takes it to the landing, stands on it and removes the bulb from the landing light. She returns the chair to the bathroom and collects the length of Albert's fishing twine she has earlier concealed under the mat. She takes it to the top of the stairs and attaches it firmly to a nail in the skirting board. Then she ties the other end to one of the banisters to form a tripwire over the top stair. In the dark at six in the morning he will never see it.

Rose returns to bed and gets in.

"Nighty-night, my darling."

"Sleep well, sweetpea."

They exchange the goodnight kiss and turn out their lights.

The Odstock Curse

"Finally, ladies and gentlemen, finally I want to come close to home, to your home, that is to say, to Odstock and the bizarre events that happened in your village almost two hundred years ago, events that I venture to suggest still have the capacity to chill your spines."

Dr Tom Staniforth peered over half-glasses at his awestruck audience. Truth to tell, he felt uneasy himself, not at his spine- chilling material so much as the fact that he had consented to give this talk to an open meeting in a village hall on—of all evenings—October 31st. The timing had not been his suggestion and neither had the title, *Horrors for Halloween*. He dreaded the possibility that some university colleague had seen the posters or otherwise got wind that a senior member of the Social Anthropology Department was sensation-mongering in the wilds of Wiltshire. He had come simply because Mother had insisted upon it. Pearl Staniforth had arranged the whole thing as a personal tribute to a former colleague of her late husband. And now, wearing one of her appalling red velvet hats, Mother was seated beside this old gentleman in the second row giving a sub-commentary and beaming maternally at regular intervals.

He was almost through, thank God.

"Forgive me if what I have to say about the Odstock curse is familiar to most of you, but I suggest it can still bear telling. I thought it would be instructive in the first place to relate the legend and afterwards to pick out the truth as far as one can verify it from reliable sources—by which I mean parish records, legal documents and, perhaps less reliable, the memoir of a contemporary witness, the village blacksmith. In the anthropological scale of things, it is all very recent." He paused, widening his eyes. Having abandoned his academic scruples, he might as well milk the subject for melodrama. Spacing his words, he went on, "In the churchyard is an old gravestone partially covered by a briar rose. The stone has an intriguing inscription: '*In memory of Joshua Scamp who died April 1st, 1801. May his brave deed be remembered here and hereafter.*'"

With strange timing came a distant rumble of thunder that cued an uneasy murmur in the audience. The storm had been threatening for hours.

"Thank you, Josh, we heard the commercial," Tom Staniforth adroitly remarked, giving the opportunity for everyone to laugh aloud and ease the tension. "The brave deed is a matter of record. The unfortunate Mr Scamp allowed himself to be hanged for a crime he did not commit. He was a gypsy accused of stealing a horse, which was a capital offence in those Draconian times. The real thief and villain of the piece was his feckless son-in-law, Noah Lee, who not only stole the horse but planted a coat belonging to Joshua at the scene of the crime. Joshua was arrested. He refused to plead and maintained a stoic silence throughout his interrogation and trial. He went to the gallows—a public execution in Salisbury—without naming the true culprit. You see, his daughter Mary was expecting a child and he could not bear to see her bereft of a husband, facing a life of misery and destitution.

"Joshua's heroic act might have gone unremarked were it not for the gypsy community, who protested his innocence. They recovered the corpse of the hanged man from the prison authorities, brought him home to Odstock and gave him a Christian burial. Hundreds attended. And later the same year the real horse-thief, Noah Lee, was arrested at Winchester for stealing a hunter. He was duly hanged, which you may think made a mockery of Scamp's noble sacrifice. But the truth emerged because Joshua's daughter Mary no longer felt constrained to remain silent. Great sympathy was extended to her and she was well cared for. And Joshua Scamp became a gypsy martyr. The briar rose was planted at the head of his grave and a yew sapling at the foot. Each year on the anniversary of his execution they would make a pilgrimage here, large numbers from all the surrounding counties.

"Now it seems that after some years the annual visit of the gypsies became a nuisance." Another clap of thunder tested Staniforth's powers of improvisation.

"Have it your way, Josh," he quipped, and earned more laughter, "but there must have been some justification for the rector of Odstock to have sworn in twenty-five special constables to keep the peace. Well, the blacksmith's memoir claims that the yew tree by the grave had become unsightly and the rector insisted that it was pulled up by the roots—a job that the sexton duly carried out. Unfortunately this measure deeply upset the gypsies and a mob of them descended on the church. There were scuffles as attempts were made to keep them off the sacred ground. The crowning insult was when Mother Lee, the Gypsy Queen, was evicted from the church, where she had come to pray, and the door locked behind her. The lady in question was venerated by the gypsies. She was the elderly mother of Noah Lee, the horse-thief, and she had earned enormous respect for disowning her son and praising the bravery of Joshua Scamp.

"Whatever the rights and wrongs of it—and I imagine there was cause for grievance on both sides—the gypsies were deeply angered. They took their revenge by breaking into the church and attacking everything inside. The pews, the windows, the communion plate, the vestments, the bell-ropes: nothing was spared. The constables were vastly outnumbered and powerless to prevent the desecration. This is all on record.

"Late in the evening, Mother Lee, having allegedly spent some hours in the Yew Tree Inn, returned to the church-yard where her people were still at work uprooting trees. Perched on the church gate, she called them to order and addressed a crowd that included most of the villagers as well as her own flock. Gypsies, as you know, have always claimed powers of divination. Speaking in a voice of doom Mother Lee pointed to the rector and told him that he would not be preaching in Odstock at that time next year. She told the church-warden who had engaged the special constables, a farmer by the name of Hodding, 'For two years bad luck shall tread upon thy heels. No son of thine shall ever farm thy land.' The sexton was informed that by next April he would be in his own grave. Two half-gypsy brothers unwise enough to have been employed as special constables were told, 'Bob and Jack Bachelor, you will die together, sudden and quick.' And finally she dealt with the door that had been slammed in her face: 'I put a curse on this church door. From this time whoever shall lock 'un shall die within a year.' And legend has it that all the curses came true."

Tom Staniforth let the drama of the story hold sway for a moment. He looked out at his audience and made brief eye contact with several. How gullible people are, he thought. They patently believe this codswallop.

"However, I promised to deal in facts, not legend," he resumed in a businesslike tone. "Let us see what survives of the Odstock curse when we test it against reliable sources.

The parish records are helpful. They tell us that the rector retired within a year, so that part is true, though we have no contemporaneous evidence for the throat cancer which was said to have robbed him of his power of speech. Nothing is known of bad luck afflicting Farmer Hodding except that his wife had a series of stillborn infants, which was not unusual in those days. I was unable to verify the story that his crops failed and his herd had to be slaughtered after contracting anthrax. The sexton, it is true, appears in the records of burials a few months after he was cursed. As for the Bachelor brothers, they are not mentioned in the register again, but superstition has it that a pair of skeletons found in 1929 in a shallow grave on Odstock Down belonged to them." Staniforth raised his hands to the audience. "So what? Even if they *were* the brothers, a supernatural explanation is unlikely. The possibility is high that the gypsies took revenge and disposed of the bodies. The so-called power of the gypsy's curse is undermined if they had to resort to murder to make it come true. To sum up, ladies and gentlemen, I have to say that I find the Odstock curse a beguiling story that, sadly for believers in the occult, falls well within the bounds of coincidence and manipulation."

He stepped from behind the table. "That concludes my talk. I hope you are reassured and will sleep peacefully tonight. I certainly intend to, and I have spent more time on these legends than most."

The reception he was given was gratifying. Pearl Staniforth, smiling this way and that as she clapped, prolonged it by at least ten seconds.

And there was a curious effect when the clapping died, because the storm outside had just broken over Odstock and the beating of rain on the roof appeared to sustain the applause. While the downpour continued no one was eager to leave, so the speaker invited questions.

A man at the back of the hall got up. He was one of the committee; earlier he had taken the money at the door. "What a wonderful talk, sir—a fitting subject for the occasion, and so eloquently delivered. I can't remember applause like that. Just one question, sir. I don't know if it was deliberate, only when you were discussing the evidence for the curse, you omitted to mention the gypsy's warning about the church door. What are your views on that?"

"I apologize," said Staniforth at once. "An oversight. I didn't mean to ignore it. The story goes that in the years since the curse was made, two people locked the door and suffered the promised fate within a year. But one is bound to ask how many hundreds, or thousands, must have turned the key and survived. You are up against statistical probability, you see." He smiled, a shade too complacently.

"No, sir," said the questioner in his broad south Wiltshire tones. "With respect, you're misinformed. The door has been locked twice since the curse, and only twice in almost two hundred years. The first time was in 1900, in defiance of the curse, when a carpenter was employed to make new gates. He was given the story, but he mocked it, turned the key and paid the price within the twelvemonth. They buried him under the path, between the gates he made and the door he locked. The second time was in the 1930s, when a locum was appointed while the rector was away. This locum dismissed the story as blasphemous and locked the door to uphold the power of the Lord, as he saw it. He was gathered shortly after. When the rector returned, he threw the key into the River Ebble just across the road and the church has never been locked since."

Deflated, Staniforth said, "I'm obliged to you. I stand corrected then, but I'd still like to see paper evidence of the two alleged deaths."

"If it didn't happen, why would the rector throw the key away?"

"Oh, the church rejects superstition as much as modern science does. No doubt he thought it the best way to put an end to such foolishness."

Happily for Staniforth the questioner was too polite to pursue the matter. The questions turned to the safer topic of witchcraft and after ten minutes a vote of thanks was proposed, coupled with the suggestion that as the rain had eased slightly it might be timely to call the evening to a halt.

For Tom Staniforth it had scarcely begun.

Old Walter Fremantle had invited the Staniforths back to his cottage for supper, not a prospect Tom relished, although he felt some obligation for the sake of his late father. Piers Staniforth and Walter Fremantle had gone through Cambridge together as history students and remained close friends even after their careers had diverged. Walter had become a museum curator and Piers a nationally known television archaeologist until his death abroad in the 1960s. From things Pearl had let slip occasionally it seemed that Walter had helped them financially after Piers died.

"Your father would have been so proud tonight," Pearl enthused while Tom cringed with embarrassment. "You had that audience in the palm of your hand—didn't he, Walter?"

"Oh, emphatically," said Walter, as he tried to pour brandy with a tremulous hand.

Tom offered to help. It was a case of all hands to the pump. Already his mother had supervised the microwave cooking and he had served the soup and the quiche. And it tasted good. Convenience food—but less of a risk than home cooking by a seventy-five-year-old bachelor.

They had not been settled long in deep armchairs in front of the fire when Walter launched into a confession. Frail as he appeared, he was still articulate and there could be no doubt that what he told Tom and his mother was profoundly important to him. "Your talk tonight has stirred me to raise a matter that has troubled me for many years. I didn't know you were an expert on the curse—didn't even realize you would mention it. Up to now I have hesitated to bring up the subject, mainly, I think, because I am a coward by nature."

"Far from it, Walter!" Pearl strove to reassure him.

Mother, will you shut up? thought Tom.

"It concerns Piers, your father. It was, I think, in 1962, towards the end of his life, that he came to see me for lunch one day. He was between expeditions, as I recall, just back from Nigeria and about to leave for South America in two or three weeks."

"Our life was like that," Pearl now chose to reminisce. "I scarcely saw him unless I went on the digs. I could have gone. The television people would have paid for me, but it was the travel, the packing and the unpacking. I was weary of it."

"Mother, Walter is trying to tell us something."

"Does that mean the rest of us have to be silent? It was never like that in the old days, was it, Walter?"

Walter gave a nod and a faint smile. "We were back from lunch and unpacking some of the objects Piers had generously brought back from Africa to present to the museum when I was phoned from downstairs and told that a woman had come into the museum and wished to donate an item to the local history collection. I'm afraid one gets all sorts of rubbish brought in and I was sceptical. This lady was apparently unwilling to return at some more convenient moment. However, Piers, ever the gentleman, insisted that I speak to her, so I invited her up to my office. The woman who presently came in was a gypsy, dressed like Carmen herself in a black skirt, white blouse and red shawl, which was most unsuitable because she was sixty at least, and large. I've nothing personal against such people, but she struck me immediately as someone I didn't care to deal with. My guess was that she wished to sell me something."

"They always do," said Pearl, "and if you don't buy they spit on your doorstep and give you the evil eye."

"Is that so? In fact, this person, who wouldn't give her name, incidentally, made herself a nuisance in another way, by relating the legend of the Odstock curse, at interminable length."

"How tedious," said Pearl, without much tact.

"I was familiar with the story," said Walter, "and I tried to tell her as much, but she would insist on giving us her version, which she claimed was gypsy lore. At another time I might have been more inclined to listen, because there is a lot of interest in preserving oral folklore, but my time with Piers was precious and she was invading it. Piers was extremely patient and good-mannered about the whole thing. I think it interested him."

"What was behind it?" Pearl asked.

"Mother, Walter is coming to that."

"Well, I've no need to keep you in suspense," said Walter. "She produced an iron key, heavily coated with rust, from under her shawl and placed it on my desk. Her son, she said, had found it on the river bank during the summer when the water level went down several feet. As a true Romany she knew it to be the cursed key of Odstock Church."

"Good Lord! And she expected you to buy it?"

"She was making a gift of it to the museum. She said she wouldn't offer it to the church in case someone tried to defy the curse. She said it would be safer in a display cabinet in a museum. I asked her if she seriously believed that the so-called curse was still potent. She gave me a look fit to shatter my skull and said that Joshua Scamp himself would deal with anyone so foolish as to lock the church door."

"The hanged man?"

"Yes. The curse is everlasting."

"Are you saying she actually believed that Scamp had some influence in the world of the living?"

"My dear boy, it's the gypsy version of the tale. I thought it poppycock myself."

"Exactly the point I was about to make," said Tom. "You were being asked to believe in a malevolent spirit, as well as the curse. There are limits."

Walter nodded. "That was my view when she presented me with the key. After she had finally been persuaded to leave, Piers asked me how much of the story I believed and I told him it was no doubt founded on a real incident that had been much embroidered over the years. Piers asked whether I proposed to display the key in the museum and I said certainly not. It seemed to me unlikely in the extreme that a key recovered from the river would be the very one that the rector had thrown in thirty years ago. Piers was more cautious in delivering a verdict."

"That's Piers all over," Pearl commented with a smile.

"My point was that we had nothing with which to authenticate the key except the gypsy woman's assertion. I said the only way to test it was to take the damned thing to the church and see if it fitted the lock. Piers advised me most adamantly not to take such a risk. He said the woman had impressed him and the power of the gypsies should never be under-estimated. We had an amiable dispute. I remember accusing him of superstition and he said he'd rather be superstitious and safe than sceptical and dead." Walter hesitated and stared into the fire. Some of the rain was penetrating the chimney and hissing as the droplets touched the embers.

Tom asked, "Did you ever try the key in the door?"

Walter turned and Tom noticed that his eyes were suddenly moist and red at the edges. "Yes, I did. It was from vanity, really. I wanted the satisfaction of telling my old friend that I had been right. I rose early the very next day, determined to prove my point. I was ninety per cent sure the key wouldn't fit, but if it did, I'd display it in my local collection with a note about the execution of Joshua Scamp and its aftermath. I remember it was a glorious morning and the rooks in the tall trees outside seemed to be chorusing me as I walked up the path to the door of St Mary's."

Pearl said impatiently, "Did it fit?"

"Oh, yes. It turned the mechanism inside. The bolt engaged. Only briefly, because I turned it back in the same movement. I was shaking at the discovery."

"Remarkable."

"And you lived to tell the tale," Tom said robustly to the old man. "Well done, Walter! You struck a blow for rational thought. What happened to the key? Did you put it on display?"

"It's in front of you, hanging on that nail over the fireplace."

Tom looked up at the notorious key, a rusty, corroded thing with a shank no longer than his smallest finger. It appeared innocuous enough. "May I handle it?"

"Please don't."

"It doesn't frighten me in the least."

"No. For God's sake hear me out."

"I thought you'd finished."

Walter shook his head. "Bear with me. This is painful. A month or so after trying the key in the door, I was afflicted with physical symptoms I couldn't account for. I became weary after no exertion at all and I lost weight steadily. My doctor put me through no end of tests. I had a full body scan. Everything. There was nothing they could diagnose, yet anyone could see I was wasting away. It was obvious to me that I wouldn't see the year out unless some miracle reversed the process. I kept remembering how I had defied the curse and locked the church door."

"It wouldn't have been that," said Tom. "Whatever was amiss with you, it wouldn't have been that."

"May I continue?" said Walter quietly. "One morning I was shopping in Salisbury and a woman approached me and asked if I would buy a sprig of heather for good luck. She was the gypsy who had presented me with the key. I said I needed all the good luck that was going and told her what I had done. She hadn't recognized me, I had lost so much weight. She was visibly shocked by what I told her. I'm afraid I was feeling so wretched that I begged for her help. I offered her any money if she would help me to lift the curse. She could name the sum. She would accept nothing, not even a silver coin for the heather. She said my only chance was to wait for All Soul's Night—Halloween— and then to invoke the spirit of Joshua Scamp by chanting his name three times. I was so desperate about my health that I was perfectly willing to try, but the rest of her advice was more difficult. I had to find a believer in the curse and speak that person's name aloud." His voice was faltering. "The curse would then be lifted from me and transferred."

Pearl's hand went to her throat. "Oh, my God!"

Tom felt his muscles tighten.

The old man said, "Yes, I thought of Piers. I remembered how he had almost pleaded with me not to try the key in the church door. He was a believer. In the few days left before Halloween, I wrestled with my conscience, telling myself it was all hocus-pocus anyway and Piers was an ocean away in South America. How could the shade of a dead gypsy who had never travelled out of England trouble a modern man in Peru? Yet I still hesitated. If I had not felt so wretchedly ill I would not have taken the risk. When you are reduced to shaking skin and bones, you will try anything. So on the night of Halloween, thirty years ago this night, I did as the gypsy advised. When I had three times invoked the spirit of Joshua Scamp, I spoke the name of my oldest friend." Walter bent forward and covered his eyes.

"What happened?"

His answer came in sobs. "Nothing. Nothing that night. For a week . . . no change. Then . . . the second week, my appetite returned . . . I felt stronger, actually recovering." He looked up, weeping uncontrollably. "In three months I was back to my old weight. The only thing I wanted was a postcard from my old friend in Peru." He paused in an effort to control his emotions and added, barely audibly, "It never came. I heard one evening on the television news about the mud-slip, the fatal accident to Piers. Devastating. What can I say to you both? Through my selfishness you lost a husband and a father."

Before Pearl could respond, Tom said gently but firmly, "Walter, it's typical of your generosity to tell us this, and I'm sure it seemed to make sense to you at the time, but really it's a misconstruction of events. It doesn't bear analysis. I'm sure I speak for Mother when I say you can sleep easy in the knowledge that you had nothing whatsoever to do with Dad's death. It was an accident."

"No."

"Your health improved because you threw off the effects of the virus, or whatever it was. We've all had mysterious illnesses that come and go. Yours was more severe than most."

"I know what happened, my son. Believe me, I was dying. I know why it went away. I don't deserve to be here. Your father should have been at that lecture tonight, not me."

Tom leaned closer to him and said earnestly, "The whole tenor of my talk was that superstitions are founded on coincidence and false reasoning and this is a classic example. You were too close to events to judge them analytically.

You accepted the supernatural explanation. Come on, Walter, you're an intelligent man of good education."

Pearl chimed in with, "I forgive you, Walter."

Tom swung around in his chair. He was incensed. "For God's sake, Mother—there's nothing to forgive! He had nothing to do with Father's death. This whole thing about the curse is mumbo-jumbo—and I'm about to prove it." He got up and snatched the key from its place over the hearth.

"Don't!" cried Walter.

Tom's mother shrieked his name, but he had already crossed the room, grabbed his coat off the hook and stepped outside.

Pearl screamed.

Tom strode along the road towards the church, regardless of the driving rain.

Odstock Church stands alone, a few hundred yards from the rest of the village. Distant lightning gave Tom Staniforth intermittent glimpses of the agitated trees along each side of the road. The castellated tower and steep tiled roof of St Mary's came into view, silvering dramatically each time a flash came. He refused to be intimidated.

Too far behind Tom to influence events, his mother and Walter Fremantle had started in pursuit. Neither was in any condition to move fast, yet they were trying to run.

Tom reached the church gates. Without pause, he stepped under the archway formed by two pollarded trees and up to the timber-framed porch. A lantern mounted on the highest beam lighted the path. The church doors were of faded oak fitted into a stone arch, with iron strap-hinges and a turning latch with a ring handle. A brighter flash of lightning turned the whole thing white. Tom found the rusted key-escutcheon, thrust in the key and turned it. The mechanism was a devil to shift. He was afraid that the key would snap under the strain. Finally it turned through a full arc and he heard the movement of the bolt sliding home.

Done.

He didn't withdraw the key. He wanted others to know that someone with a mind free of superstition had defied the gypsy's curse.

Hearing the footsteps of his mother and old Walter Fremantle, Tom stepped aside, away from the door. They would see the key in the lock. He was triumphant.

The glory was brief. Lightning struck the church roof. The thunder—an immense clap—was instantaneous. The ground itself vibrated. Scores of tiles loosened, slid down the pitched roof and fell. Two, at least, razor-sharp, cracked against Tom's skull and felled him like a pin in an alley.

Neither Walter nor Pearl saw the body when they first came through the gate. The porch-light had blown when the lightning struck. They groped at the door, feeling for the key in the lock.

Walter located it and gasped, "He did it. I tried to stop him. I tried!"

Pearl found her son lying insensible against a gravestone, with blood oozing from a head wound. Whimpering, she got to her knees and cradled his damaged head. He made no sound.

Pearl rocked her son.

"Is he . . . ?" Walter could not bring himself to speak the word.

Pearl ignored him anyway. The pride she had felt in the village hall when Tom was speaking with such authority had ended in blood and tears. She sobbed for the limp burden in her arms and the bigotry of rational thinking. She mourned her wise, never-to-be-forgotten husband and her rash, misguided son.

Gently, Pearl let Tom's bloodied head rest in her lap.

She brought her hands together in front of her, fingers tightly intertwined. Then in a clear voice she called the name of Joshua Scamp. She called it three times. She cried out passionately, "Take Walter Fremantle. He knows the power of the curse better than any man, having used it to kill my husband. He is a believer. Take him. For pity's sake, take him instead."

She remembered nothing else. She didn't see old Walter unlock the church door, remove the key and take it across the road to the river and throw it in. She didn't see him collapse as he tried to climb up the bank.

The next morning, in the intensive care ward at Odstock Hospital, Tom Staniforth's eyelids quivered and opened. His mother, in a hospital dressing-gown, watching through a glass screen, turned to the young policeman beside her, gripped his hand and squeezed it. "He's going to live!"

"I'm happy for you, Ma'am," said the constable. "Happy for myself, too. Maybe your son can tell me what happened last night. What with you having passed out as well, and old Mr Fremantle dead of a heart attack, I was afraid we'd have no witnesses. I'm supposed to write a report of the incident, you see. I know it was the lightning that struck the church, but it's difficult working out what happened, with all three of you going down like that."

"However did you find us?" Pearl asked.

"Wasn't me, Ma'am. Now I'd really like to trace the man who alerted us, but I'm not optimistic. No one seems to know him. Right strange chap, he was. Came bursting into a farm cottage soon after midnight, in fancy dress from one of they Halloween parties. Top hat and smock and a piece of rope around his neck. He nearly scared the family out of their wits, ranting on about a dead'un at the church door. Didn't leave his name. Just raced off into the storm. Drunk, I expect. But I reckon you owe him, you and your son."

*

Author's footnote: I should like to pay credit to three sources for the story of Joshua Scamp and the Curse of Odstock. *Wiltshire Folklore*, by Kathleen Wiltshire (Compton Russell, Salisbury, 1975) gives the version told by Canon Bouverie about 1904; *Wiltshire Folklore and Legends*, by Ralph Whitlock (Robert Hale, London, 1992) has Hiram Witt the blacksmith's memoir of 1870; and the fictional story of the lecture and its consequences was suggested by my son, Philip, who visited Odstock with me at Easter, 1993.

A Parrot Is Forever

That eye was extraordinary, dominated by the yellow iris and fringed by a ring of spiky black eyelashes. In the short time I had been watching, the pupil had contracted to little more than a microdot.

"It's magnificent, but it's a lot larger than I expected," I told the young woman who was its keeper.

She said, "Macaws are big birds."

At this safe distance from the perch, I said, "I was expecting something smaller. A parrot, I was told."

"Well, a macaw is a member of the parrot family."

This member of the parrot family raised itself higher and stared over my head, excluding me, letting me know that I was unworthy of friendship at this first meeting.

"No doubt we'll learn to get along with each other," I said. "I'm willing to try, if the bird is." I took a tentative step closer.

Too close for the macaw, because it thrust its head at me and gave a screech like a power drill striking steel.

I jerked back. "Wow!"

The keeper said, "It's a pity. Roger was just getting used to us. Now he has to start over again."

First lesson: you address parrots as you would humans.

The impersonal "it" was unacceptable. This was Roger, a personality.

Roger. About right for this rebarbative old bird. Roger is one of those names redolent of wickedness. Jolly Roger, the pirate flag; eighteenth century rakes rogering wenches; Roger the lodger, of so many dirty jokes. The glittering eye and that great, black beak curved over the mouth in a permanent grin would make you believe this Roger had been everywhere and tried everything.

"He's called 'Sir Roger,' according to his papers," said the young woman, wanting to say something in the parrot's favour. "We were taught a dance at school called Sir Roger de Coverley. I expect he's named after that."

Fat chance, I thought. My Uncle George, the parrot's former owner, was never a country dancer. He was a diamond robber. A long time ago, in May, 1954, Uncle George and two others held up a Hatton Garden merchant and stole twenty-seven uncut diamonds valued at half a million pounds. Half a million was a fortune in 1954. The advantage of uncut stones—if you steal them—is that they are difficult to identify, so it was also a clever heist. The only blemish on this brilliant crime was that the three robbers were rounded up within a week and given long prison sentences. But the diamonds were never recovered. Two of the robbers died inside. Uncle George served twenty-six years. After his release, he seemed mysteriously to come into money. He emigrated to Spain, the Costa del Sol. It was a wise move. He lived another fifteen years, without ostentation, but comfortably, in a villa, in the company of a *señorita* half his age.

In my ultra-respectable family, Uncle George was a taboo topic. My father rarely mentioned him, and never spoke of the robbery. I only learned of it after Dad died and I was going through his papers. There was a newspaper cutting about the release from jail of the old diamond robber.

Now my uncle was dead. He'd gone peacefully last Christmas, in his own bed, at the age of seventy-nine. It seemed he'd known his time was coming and he had made appropriate arrangements. This Blue and Yellow Macaw was bequeathed to me.

In January I had received a solicitor's letter advising me of my legacy. At first I thought it was a practical joke. I was told I must wait six months while the parrot served the six-month quarantine period that applies to all imported animals—as if I was impatient to meet this creature! I hadn't asked for the parrot. I knew nothing about parrots. I was an actor, for pity's sake. How would I fit a Blue and Yellow Macaw into my life? The solicitor informed me when I phoned him that he understood parrots make fine companions. As for my acting career, he'd heard that the late Sir Ralph Richardson had kept a parrot, and it hadn't held him back.

I was in a spot. Only a complete toe-rag would deny an old man's dying wish. My uncle must have been devoted to the parrot to make arrangements for it to be shipped to England. But oh, Uncle George, why to me?

True, I was the only surviving relative, but I have another theory. Uncle George may have seen me on cable television in the part of a wise-cracking villain in some corny crime series. It ran for some weeks. I think he identified with the part.

The crushing irony of all this was that the rest of the estate, consisting of the Spanish villa and all its contents and enough pesetas to provide many years of comfortable living, all went to the *señorita* Uncle George had shared the last years of his life with. The parrot came to me, I guessed because Isabella said she'd strangle it if Uncle George didn't get rid of it.

So here I was at Bird & Board, the aviary close to London Airport. Roger had completed his quarantine and now I had arrived to claim him.

"This is the box he travels in," the young woman informed me, opening the welded mesh grille that was the door of a sturdy plastic pet-container. It was the sort of box used for cats and dogs, the only concession to Roger's comfort being a wooden perch fitted some three inches off the floor and much chewed by his sharp beak. "He doesn't like it much. Would you like me to put him inside?"

"Please."

Roger had seen the box and was already getting agitated, swaying and ruffling his feathers. The moment the keeper started putting on a pair of leather gauntlets, there was a flexing of wings and a series of blood-curdling screams that started off all the other birds and created bedlam.

"They can be noisy," she said as if she were telling me something. "Hope you're on good terms with your neighbours." Skilfully avoiding the thrusting black beak, she grasped the big macaw by the neck and legs, lifted him off the perch and placed him in the box. "He'll calm down presently," she shouted.

And he did. She draped a cloth over the front and the darkness subdued him.

She asked me, "Have you kept a parrot before?"

"No."

"You've got treats in store, then. If Roger gets unbearable, you can always see if one of the tropical bird gardens will take him."

"Would you?" I asked hopefully.

"Couldn't possibly. We deal only with birds in quarantine."

"So I'm lumbered."

"Try not to think of it that way," she said compassionately, then added, "That will be a hundred and fifty pounds, please."

"What will?"

"Roger's account—for staying here. We can't do it for nothing, you know."

"Some legacy!" I said, getting out my chequebook.

"If you do sell him," she told me, "don't sell him cheap. They're worth a few hundred, you know."

"So I'm finding out," I told her as I wrote the cheque.

I carried the pet-container to the place where I'd left my car. Heaven knows, Roger had given me no grounds for friendship, but I muttered reassuring things though the ventilation slits. I continued to speak to him at intervals all the way along the motorway. At Heston I stopped at a garden centre and bought some heavy-duty leather gloves.

When I got home and opened the pet-container, it was some time before my new house-guest emerged. Having seen the size of his beak, and read a little about the damage one peck can inflict, I didn't reach inside for him. In fact, I was extremely nervous of him. After waiting some time, I left the room to get myself a coffee. When I returned, Roger had stepped out to inspect his new quarters.

If nothing else, he had brought some much-needed colour to my home. His back and wings were vivid sky-blue, his chest and the underside of the wings purest yellow, his crown and forehead dark green. Spectacular—but at what cost?

I'd gone to the trouble of making a perch out of beech wood and installing it in my living room. What I hadn't appreciated was that Roger wasn't capable of getting up there unaided. His wings were clipped. I wasn't ready yet to handle him, even with the leather gauntlets. But I didn't need to bother, because he made his own choice. After a cursory inspection of the room, he decided to occupy the sheet-feed of my printer, which projected at a convenient angle and left just enough room for his long blue tail feathers. He reached it by scaling the waste-paper basket and the top drawer of the desk, using his beak and claws.

Once on his new perch, he established his right of residence by hunching his shoulders, lifting his tail and depositing a green dropping on the script of my next TV part, which I'd left behind the printer. I felt the same way about the script, but I replaced it with an old newspaper.

There was sunflower seed and corn in the feeding bowl attached to the perch. I succumbed and moved the bowl close to the printer. The parrot appeared to have no interest in food. He watched me keenly from my office machinery, I suppose to see if I had plans to eject him. To foster confidence, I removed the pet-container altogether and put it in the spare room.

There is no doubt that parrots are exceptional in their ability to communicate their feelings to humans. They have eloquent eyes that dilate and contract at will. The skin around the face can blush pink. With the angle of the head, the posture of the shoulders and the action of the claws, they can express curiosity, boredom, sorrow, anger, approval, domination and submission. All that, before they let go with their voices. Mercifully, Roger hadn't yet screamed in my home.

That night, I left him perched on the sheet-feed. In the morning, although he still hadn't touched the food, he seemed interested to see me. Genuine trust was slow in developing on both sides, but he began to feed and the day came, about a week later, when he succeeded in manoeuvring his way across the furniture to the back of a chair I was seated in. Neither of us moved for some time. It was a distinct advance.

One morning the following week, perched on the printer as usual, Roger put his head at an angle, dilated his eyes and extended a claw to me. With some misgivings, I extended my arm. He gripped it at the wrist and transferred himself from the sheet-feed to me. Acting as a living perch, I walked slowly around the room. When I made to return him to the printer, he clawed his way higher up my arm until he was on my shoulder. He had decided I was not, after all, the enemy.

I suppose the discovery was mutual.

If all else fails, I thought, I can now audition for a part in *Treasure Island.*

In a couple of months, I learned to handle Roger, and he transferred to the purpose-built perch. He had a small silver ring around one of his legs and I could have chained him to the perch, but there was no need. He behaved reasonably well. True, he used his beak on things, but that is standard parrot behaviour. The worst damage he inflicted was to peck through my telephone cable. Sometimes it's an advantage to be incommunicado. At least a day passed before I realized I was cut off. I discovered the damage only when Roger fooled me with a perfect imitation of the phone's ringing tone. I picked up the receiver and the line was dead. This was the first inkling I had that he was capable of mimicry. In time, when he really settled in, he would greet visitors with "Hello, squire," or "Hello, darling," according to sex. He must have been taught by Uncle George. He had no other vocabulary and I didn't want to coach him. I think it undermines the dignity of animals to make them ape human behaviour.

As you must already have gleaned, Roger was winning me over. I found him amusing and appreciative of all the attention I could give him. There were moments when he would regard me intently, willing me to come forward and admire him, utterly still, yet beaming out such anticipation that I was compelled to stop whatever I was doing. The unblinking eyes would beguile me, seeming to penetrate to the depth of my being. As I went closer, he would make small movements on the perch, finally turning full circles and twitching his elegant tail. If I put my face against his plumage, the scent of the natural oils was exquisite.

One evening I returned late from a rehearsal and had a

horrible shock. Roger was missing. I dashed around the house calling his name before I noticed the broken window where the thief had got in. I was devastated. My poor parrot must have fought hard, because there were several of those spectacular blue tail feathers under his perch.

The police didn't give much comfort. "We've had parrots stolen before," said the constable who came. "It's just another form of crime, like nicking car radios. They know where to get rid of them. A parrot like yours will fetch a couple of hundred, easy. Did they take his cage as well?"

"He doesn't have a cage. He lives on that perch."

"How did you get him here in the first place?"

"In a pet-container. It's in the back room . . . I think." Even as I spoke, I knew it was gone. I'd been through the spare room and the box wasn't there. I should have noticed. Well, I had, in a way, but it hadn't registered in my brain until now. The bastards hadn't just taken Roger; they'd had the brass to take his box as well.

"We'll keep a look-out," said the constable in a tone that gave me no confidence. "Would you know your own bird? That's the problem. These Blue and Yellow Macaws all look the same."

I felt bereft. It was clear to me now how important that parrot had become to me. I was angry and guilty and impotent. I'm a peaceful man, or believed I was. I could have strangled the person who had taken Roger.

Each day, I called the police to see if there was news. They'd heard nothing. Almost a week went by. They advised me to get another bird. I didn't want another bird. I wanted Roger back.

I had to move the empty perch into the spare room because the sight of it was so upsetting. My work was suffering. I messed up an audition. I couldn't learn lines any more.

On the sixth day after Roger was stolen, a Sunday morning, my phone rang.

It was Roger.

Reader, don't give up. I haven't gone completely gaga over this parrot. Roger hadn't picked up the phone and dialled my number. Somebody else had. But I could hear Roger at the other end of the line. He was giving his imitation of the phone ringing.

The person who had dialled my number didn't speak. I said, "Who is this?" several times. Roger, in the background, was still mimicking the phone. It *could* have been a second phone, but I convinced myself it was not.

I guessed what it was about. The thief was checking whether I was home. He was thinking of breaking into my home again, perhaps to steal something else.

The line went dead after only a few seconds. Not a word had been spoken by the caller.

I was frustrated and enraged.

Fortunately, there is a way of tracing calls. I dialled the message system and obtained the caller's number. It's a computerised system and you aren't given the name or address.

I thought about going to the police and asking them to check the number, but I hadn't been impressed by the constable who had come to see me. He didn't regard a missing macaw as a high priority.

Instead, I waited an hour and then tried the number myself. It rang for some time before it was picked up and a woman's voice said, "Marwood Hotel."

Thinking rapidly, I said, "Is that the Marwood Hotel in Notting Hill Gate?"

She said, "I've never heard of one in Notting Hill Gate. We're the Marwood in Fulham. Gracechurch Road."

Fulham was just a ten-minute drive from where I lived. I told her I'd made a mistake. I put down the phone and went straight to the car.

Gracechurch Road was once a good address for the Edwardian middle classes. Now it stands under the shadow of the Hammersmith Fly-Over. The tall, brick villas have become seedy hotels and over-populated flats.

My approach wasn't subtle. I went in and asked the woman at the desk if the hotel welcomed pets.

She said in the voice I'd heard on the phone, "Provided they behave themselves."

"A parrot, for instance?"

"I don't know about parrots," she said dubiously.

"You have one here already, don't you?"

She said, "I wouldn't want another one like that. It makes a horrible sound when it's excited. Fit to burst your eardrums."

"Blue and yellow? Big?" I said, my heart racing.

She nodded.

I asked, "Does it belong to the hotel?"

"No, the foreign gentleman in number twelve. The top floor."

"When did he arrive?"

"About ten days ago."

"With the parrot?"

"No, he brought that in one day last weekend. In a box. He says it's only temporary."

"Is he up there now?"

She checked the board where the keys were hung. "He should be. If you want, I can ring up."

I said that on second thoughts I'd call back later. Simply going upstairs and knocking on the door would not be a wise course of action.

She didn't see me double around the side of the house to the back. These old buildings converted into hotels often have fire-escapes and this was no exception. It was the most basic sort, a vertical iron ladder fixed to the brickwork, with access to the large casement windows on each of the three upper floors. With luck, I wouldn't be visible to anyone inside.

This was a chance I had to take. I climbed about fifty rungs to the top floor. The window was a hinged one and it was open. Easy to open wider. There were extra rungs directly under it. All I needed to do was transfer sideways, put my leg over the sill and let myself in. First, I listened for sounds of movement from the room.

I could hear nothing.

I'm not much of an acrobat, but I succeeded in getting my legs through the window and scrambling into the room.

A voice I knew said, "Hello, squire."

Roger!

For me, that reunion was on a par with H. M. Stanley meeting Dr Livingstone.

Roger was perched on the footboard of a double bed. He recognized me. He lifted his claw—a signal that he wanted to transfer to my arm and so to my shoulder. Elated, I took a step towards him. There was a sound behind me. I was not conscious of anything else, except a crushing blow to the back of my head.

I don't know how long I was out.

When the world started up again for me, I was lying on the bed with my hands tied behind me. The foreign 'gentleman' had his thumb jammed into my eye, forcing it open. He spoke some words I didn't recognize.

My head ached. My vision was blurred, but clearing. He looked evil. His shoulders were huge.

I said, "I don't want trouble. I just want my parrot back."

He said with a strong Spanish inflexion, "You own this parrot?"

I told him who I was.

He spoke again. "This parrot Roger, he is stupid. He tell me nothing. Nothing."

I said, "He's just a parrot. What do you expect?"

"You ask what I expect. I expect you have talked to this parrot, yes? He tell you where diamonds are kept."

I said, "I don't know what the hell you're talking about."

He raised his arm and beat me across the face with the back of his hand. My lip split.

He shouted, "Your uncle had many diamonds, yes? Why he send you this parrot when he die?"

I said, "Just who are you?"

He grabbed my hair and forced my head back. "Now you are here, you will talk to Roger. Then he tell you some number, some number of box inside bank."

Box inside bank: I was beginning to understand. "A safe deposit number?"

"*Si.*"

"He doesn't speak numbers."

"Do it. Speak numbers now." Still grasping my hair, he hauled me off the pillow and towards the foot of the bed where Roger was still perched, looking uneasy, swaying slightly, just as he had when I'd first seen him at Bird & Board.

Feeling incredibly stupid and helpless, I started chanting numbers to my parrot. "One. Two. Three. Four."

Roger watched me in a stupefied silence.

"Five. Six. Seven."

"This no good," said the man. "Try three, four numbers together."

I said, "One two three. One two four." My lip had swollen. I could feel warm blood trickling down my chin.

Roger looked away.

"One two five."

I continued speaking sets of numbers, trying to think how this would end.

I said, "Roger is nervous. You've made him nervous. They don't speak when they're nervous."

This seemed to make some impression. Roger played his part by drawing his wings tight to his body and making a groaning sound deep in his chest.

The man produced a flick-knife and cut whatever it was that pinioned my wrists. I sat on the edge of the bed and wiped some blood away from my face. I needed to think. He was far too big to take on.

He said, "Now you try again."

I said, "I'd like to be clear what this is all about. You want a safe deposit number, and you think the parrot will speak it, right?"

He pondered how much to tell me. Then he said, "George, he had diamonds. Isabella, his woman, she search the villa. No diamonds."

"You were sent by Isabella?"

"*Sí*. She think maybe there is one deposit box in his bank in Màlaga. No name. Only number, *comprende*?"

"Yes."

"Isabella say George he was crafty old *gringo*. He teach the parrot this number and send it to you."

"I don't think so," I said. "I hardly knew him at all."

This didn't impress my captor. "Stupid old man, he do this to cheat Isabella."

"You're Isabella's friend?"

"Brother."

I doubted if that was true. I said, "I've had Roger for almost a year now. He's never spoken numbers to me. Basically, all he can say is 'Hello'."

Isabella's "brother" struck me across the face a second time.

Roger screamed and spread his wings.

He took a swipe at Roger and just avoided being pecked.

In extreme situations, the brain works faster. I said, "If you'll listen, I have a suggestion. You see the little silver ring attached to his leg? There's something written on it. Very small. I don't know if it's a number. We can look if you like."

"The ring! *Sí*!" His face lit up. He reached towards Roger, who dipped forward and tried to peck his hand.

There was no chance of Roger letting him examine that ring.

He said, "You hold him."

I said, "He's nervous."

He said, "You want me to kill you and the parrot?"

I spoke some encouraging words to Roger and held my wrist close to him. If ever I needed my parrot's co-operation it was now. After some understandable hesitation, he put out a claw and transferred to my wrist. Continuing to speak to Roger as calmly as I was able, I fingered the ring with my free hand.

I told the man, "I need more light. I can't read this."

He said, "You come to the window."

I stroked Roger's back and stood up. The man led me towards the light. He said, "No tricks. You show this number to me. You hold the parrot and show me."

Roger was amazingly compliant. He let me finger the ring again. In the better light, I gazed earnestly at the completely blank ring and started inventing numbers. "It looks to me like a three, a five, a nine. Is that a nine, would you say?"

The Spaniard moved to the only position convenient for viewing the ring. He didn't dare come within range of that vicious black beak. He had his back to the open casement window through which I'd climbed.

It was my opportunity. I was poised to give him an almighty push, but Roger forestalled me. He screeched, opened his wings and reared at the man—who rocked back, lost his balance and pitched backwards out of the window. It was a long drop, three floors to a concrete yard. I didn't look out to see the result.

I don't believe Roger understood the consequence of his action. My theory is that he thought he was being taken to the open window. In the year I had owned him—as I discovered later—his wing feathers had grown and he was perfectly capable of flying. He wanted to test those wings. For him, it was the best escape route. When the man blocked his exit, he acted.

I'm not proud of my actions after that, but I ought to set them on record. I grabbed my parrot and pushed him into his travelling-box, which was just inside the door. I carried the box downstairs and drove off without speaking to anyone.

The inquest on the Spanish guest at the Marwood Hotel resulted in an open verdict. Identification was impossible, because he was found to be using a false passport. It was assumed by most people that this was a sad case of suicide.

Within a week, I, too, changed my identity. I moved away from England, sacrificing my TV career for an early retirement to the tropics. For obvious reasons I am not disclosing the name of this island paradise. The climate is a lot better than I'm used to and it suits Roger well. I have a fine stone house, a large swimming pool, servants and a speedboat.

Maybe you are wondering where I got the funds. Roger discovered the seven large uncut diamonds. They were hidden in the hollow wooden perch fixed in the travelling-box he so disliked. He'd pecked through the wood before I got him home from the Marwood Hotel. So Isabella's "brother" had them in his possession for a short time, and never knew it. Sorry, Isabella—I'm certain they were meant for me. They were my legacy from Uncle George. Along with Roger, who is sitting on my shoulder as I write these words.

He's got life running as he wants it, I think.

Passion Killers

The doorbell chimed.

In the kitchen, Gloria looked at the clock. She had to be out of the house by half-past, or she'd certainly be late for choir practice. The tea was too hot, so she added some extra milk to cool it, took a sip and found it didn't taste like tea any more.

Her mother was letting a few seconds pass before going to the door. She wouldn't want it known that she'd been behind the net curtain in the front room for the past ten minutes.

Presently Gloria heard the caller being greeted in a refined accent her mother never used normally. "Is it actually raining outside? I must tell my daughter. She's about to go to choir practice. She's a soloist with the Surrey Orpheus, you know. Gloria, my dear," the message came, still impeccably spoken, like a headmistress in school assembly, "it appears to be raining."

"I know."

Tonight the choir were rehearsing the Cathedral Christmas Concert. "Sheep May Safely Graze" was open on the kitchen table. Nobody seemed to mind that the piece happened to be secular, from the Hunting Cantata; it was so often played in church. Gloria, who would be singing the part of Diana, supported the League Against Cruel Sports really and hoped people wouldn't say she was abandoning her principles just to get out of the chorus. She got up and tipped the tea down the sink, ran some water over the cup and saucer and reached automatically for the tea-cloth, but the tea-cloth didn't come to hand. Instead, of all things, she found that she was about to dry the cup on her mother's thermal knickers. They had been through the washing machine the day before and Mother must have hung them to dry on the towel rail, long-legged things in a hideous shade of pink described in the mail-order catalogue as peach-coloured. Even her mother laughingly called them her passion killers. Gloria clicked her tongue in annoyance and tossed them over the folding clothes-rack where they should have been.

The visitor was Mr Hibbert, the dapper man from number 31. For the last two Fridays he had called on Gloria's mother, Mrs Palmer, at precisely this time, just as Gloria was leaving for choir. The pretext for the visits wasn't mentioned, and Gloria hadn't asked. Her mother was only forty-one and divorced. She was entitled to invite a male friend to the house if she wished. It wasn't as if she was getting up to anything shameful. No doubt Mr Hibbert had a perfectly proper reason for calling. True, Mother had put on her slinky black dress and sprayed herself with Tabu, but it was just to make herself presentable. It couldn't mean anything else. Mr Hibbert had a wife and lived just four doors up the street.

At seventeen, Gloria viewed her mother's social life with detachment. Sometimes she felt the more mature of the two of them. Gloria worked in a small draper's shop in the High Street that had somehow survived the competition from department stores and mail order catalogues. It stocked a tasteful range of fabrics, haberdashery and wools. There were foundation garments discreetly folded away in wooden drawers under the glass counter. Nobody under forty ever went in there. Since leaving school Gloria hadn't kept up with her so-called friends, who had always seemed far too juvenile, obsessed with pop-singers and boyfriends. Even though she was the youngest in the choir by some years, the others talked of her with approval as old-fashioned. The way she plaited her fine, dark hair and pinned it into the shape of a lyre at the back of her head strengthened the perception.

In the hall, she put on her black fitted coat and checked her hair in the mirror. She called out, "I'm off, then. Bye."

From behind the closed door of the front room, her mother called, "Bye, darling." It was a pity she chose to add something else, a terrible pity as it turned out, but she did. First she called out, "Gloria."

"Yes?"

"If you're not in bed by midnight, you'd better come home."

The remark was meant to be funny and Mr Hibbert showed that he thought it was—or that he ought to react as if it was—by laughing out loud. Then her mother laughed too.

Gloria was deeply shocked. She gasped and shut her eyes. There was a swishing sound in her ears. The humiliation was unendurable. That her own mother should say such a thing in front of a man—a neighbour—was a betrayal.

And the way they had laughed together meant that Gloria must have been mistaken about them. Mr Hibbert's visit wasn't the innocent event she had taken it to be. It couldn't be. Decent people didn't laugh at smutty humour. By mocking her, they were affirming their own promiscuity—or at the very least their desire to be promiscuous.

She was disgusted.

To burst into the room and protest would only aggravate the injury. They'd tell her she had no sense of humour. They'd encourage each other to say worse things about her.

She turned towards the mirror again, as if the sight of the outrage on her own features would confirm the injustice of the offence. In the whole of her life she had never given her mother cause to doubt her moral conduct. She'd avoided drugs and smoking and she'd never allowed a boy to take the liberties most other girls yielded blithely. Keeping her standards high had not been easy. She was as prone to temptation as anyone else. She'd had to be strong-willed—and put up with a fair amount of derision from so-called friends who had been less resolute when temptation beckoned. Having to suffer taunts from her own mother was too much.

Mind, she knew that her mother had a streak of irresponsibility. Ninety-nine per cent of the time Mrs Tina Palmer behaved as a mother should. But Gloria could never depend on her. A certain look came over Mother at these times, as if she'd just tossed back a couple of gins (in fact, she didn't drink). Dimples would appear at the ends of her mouth, her eyes would twinkle, and then she was liable to do anything. Anything. Once, at a school speech day, seated in a privileged place in the front row because Gloria was getting a good conduct prize, Mrs Palmer had winked at Mr Shrubb, the PE teacher, who was up on the stage with all the staff. Most of the teachers had noticed and next day it was mentioned or hinted at in just about every lesson. Another time, bored in a supermarket queue, Mrs Palmer had started juggling with oranges and had swiftly drawn a large crowd. Gloria wasn't among them. Too embarrassed to watch the display, she'd slipped out through an empty checkout.

At this moment she wasn't prepared to accept what had been said as yet another example of Mother being skittish again. She was deeply humiliated and ablaze with anger. Her evening was ruined. She was in no frame of mind now to go to choir practice. How could anyone do justice to Bach feeling as she did? She opened the chest in the hall and dropped her music case into it.

She'd go out anyway. Anywhere. She couldn't bear to remain under the same roof while her feckless mother entertained her fancy-man in the front room.

Her hand was on the door in the act of opening it when she noticed Mr Hibbert's coat hanging on the antique hall-stand that was Mother's pride and joy. It was one of those elegant navy blue coats with black velvet facing on the collar. Gloria had once thought men who wore such coats were the acme of smartness. Now she was willing to believe that they were all playboys. She was tempted to spit on it, or pull off one of the buttons. Then a far more engaging idea crept into her mind, a wicked, horrid, but deliciously appropriate means of revenge.

She would give Mr Hibbert something to take home, an unexpected souvenir—the passion-killers, those unbecoming thermal knickers of her mother's. At some point Mr Hibbert would become conscious of something unfamiliar in his overcoat pocket and take it out. His immediate reaction on discovering such a revolting garment could only be guessed at, but he would surely think back and work out with distaste who the passion killers belonged to and try to interpret the message they were meant to convey, just as her mother would at first be mystified at mislaying her thermals and then mortified by the only possible conclusion—that her new friend Mr Hibbert was a secret collector of women's underwear.

Blushing or glowing, she was not sure which, Gloria tiptoed to the kitchen and lifted the thermals off the rack, this time actually grinning at their unspeakable shape and colour. She folded them neatly so as not to make too obvious a lump. Then she went back to the hall and slipped them into the left pocket of Mr Hibbert's beautiful coat: the left because the right already contained his leather gloves. She pushed them well down. In doing so, her fingertips came into contact with a set of keys. His car keys.

Now an even better idea dawned on Gloria.

How much more suggestive if the knickers were to turn up in Mr Hibbert's car, say in the glove compartment on the passenger side, where his wife would very likely discover them for herself. The prospect was delicious: Mrs Hibbert reaching in for a sweet, or something with which to dust the window, and pulling out another woman's drawers. Her wayward husband would really have some explaining to do.

It wouldn't be difficult. There were no garages in King George Avenue. The cars were parked in the street, and Mr Hibbert's was the only silver BMW.

Gloria fished out the thermals and the keys.

She held the thermals at arm's length. The passion killers. Would anyone believe they belonged to her mother? she wondered. Better leave them in no doubt. There was a way to do it.

One of the drawers in the antique hallstand was full of wrapping paper and padded bags people had sent that might be used again. Mother, being economical, kept everything that might be used a second time. When she needed to send a padded bag, she would carefully tear the stamps off one of her collection and cover the old labels with new sticky labels for readdressing. Gloria selected one of appropriate size, folded the pants and slipped them inside. She removed the stamps, but did nothing about the label, which still had her mother's name and address typed on the front. Just perfect. She didn't seal it, either.

As a precaution, just in case some nosy neighbour might see her in the street, she unpinned and unfastened her plaits. Nobody ever caught her with her hair loose. Like this, she suddenly felt a different person, not the high-minded young lady she liked to be known as usually, but a free agent.

She slammed the front door as she went out. The lovers could relax now, believing she was gone for at least two hours and a half. Sheep may safely graze.

The rain had stopped. Darkness had set in some time ago. The street-lamps in King George Avenue were more decorative than effective, but she spotted Mr Hibbert's BMW parked opposite number 31. There could be no question that it was his car because it was well known that he'd paid for a registration with his initials, HPH—a clear sign of vanity, in Gloria's opinion. Nobody seemed to be about, so she went straight across and tried the key on the passenger's side. It was a central locking system and she heard all the doors unlock. When she pulled open the door an interior light came on, so she got in quickly and shut the door and the light went out.

Simple.

The glove compartment opened at the press of a button. Inside were a couple of maps, a roll of peppermints, a half-eaten bar of chocolate and some petrol tokens. She stuffed the bulky envelope inside and closed it.

Now what? There was a sense of anticlimax. Gloria hadn't thought how she would spend the evening now that she wasn't going to choir practice. To go back to the house was out of the question. She'd be a prime suspect if she did. It was a chilly evening. She'd sit here a moment and think.

She'd never been into a pub unaccompanied and she wasn't going to start tonight. She wouldn't feel very safe walking the streets for long. And there was no one she could visit.

The best plan was to go to a film. She'd walk down to the Cannon and find out what was showing.

She was on the point of leaving the car when she heard footsteps close behind. She glanced into the mirror mounted on the side, but saw nobody on the pavement, so she turned her head.

A figure was walking slowly along the centre of the road between the rows of cars. She couldn't see too well, but she was fairly certain that it was a male wearing some sort of crested headgear, a fireman's helmet, perhaps, or a policeman's.

Panic-stricken, she ducked right down with her head over her knees hoping he'd walk past without looking in.

She could feel her heart thumping against her thigh.

Please, please go by.

The footsteps had the heavy tread of boots. They were agonizingly slow.

They stopped right next to the car.

She nearly died of shock when he opened the door on the driver's side and got in. The light came on in the car.

"Bloody hell!"

She remained quite still.

"Are you ill, or somefink?"

If he was really a policeman, he ought to have sounded more assertive, more in control, but she dared not check.

"You just give *me* a nasty turn, any road."

She was petrified. He took a grip on the hair at the back of her head and pulled her upright.

She had another shock when she turned to face him. The crested helmet was in reality a punk hair-style, a bright green Mohican tuft presently being squashed against the roof of the car. He was a youth of about sixteen. There were three silver rings through his left ear and a glittery stud through his nose.

He asked her, "This motor—is it yours?"

She shook her head.

"Your old man's? What you doing, then? Nicking stuff? You deaf, or somefink?"

She succeeded in saying, "Who are you?"

He said, "I asked you a question."

"You asked about five questions." She was beginning to feel safer with him. She was close enough to see that he was just a boy.

"I don't know you," he said, as if the fault were Gloria's. "I don't know you, do I?"

She said, "If you pulled the door properly shut, this light would go out." Immediately she'd said it, she realized that she might be misinterpreted. She was only anxious that nobody should see her sitting in Mr Hibbert's car, with or without a boy with green hair.

He closed the door and said, in the darkness, "Want a smoke?"

She said, "Look, this is someone else's car."

"He won't come out. He's watching telly in one of them houses, I bet. Long time since I tried a BMW." He put his hands on the wheel and it clicked. The steering column must have locked. "Bleedin' hell."

Gloria said, "Mind your language."

"Sod off."

At least she'd registered disapproval.

"If it ain't yours," he said, "how did you get in?"

"With the key. I, em, nicked it," she added, to forestall the next question.

"Jeez. Where?"

"From his pocket."

"Cool." He didn't ask about the circumstances. Instead, he said with admiration, "You're class."

She liked that. Nobody—certainly no boy—had ever referred to her in quite those terms before.

"What's your name?"

"Gloria."

"Gloria—blimey. I'm Mick. Want to go for a ride, Gloria?"

"What do you mean—in this?"

"What else? You just said you got the key."

"Can you drive?"

"I wouldn't be here, would I? Give us the key and I'll show you. I could start it easy, but the wheel's locked."

He was a joy-rider. He'd walked up King George Avenue trying the doors of all the cars to find one open and it had happened to be Mr Hibbert's.

The keys were in her lap. Mr Hibbert's keys. Mr Hibbert, who had laughed at the idea that she might spend the night in bed with someone. She handed them over. "Just a short ride."

He slotted the key in and turned it to free the steering wheel. The engine started first time.

"Nice motor," said Mick, switching on the headlights and revving the engine. He released the handbrake and they moved out of line and cruised quite quickly to the end of King George Avenue, where it met the High Street. Gloria felt an upsurge of excitement. She was joy-riding— and in Mr Hibbert's car.

"Open your window. Get some breeze through."

It worked electronically. She found the button and pressed. The wind was noisy. She glanced at the instruments and saw that the car was doing sixty in a built-up area.

"We can have a burn-up on the by-pass," said Mick apologetically. "These can do a ton, easy." He switched the radio on. A Mozart piano concerto was being played. "God 'elp us. See if you can get somefink with a beat."

She tried the controls, found some rock music and turned it up loud.

"Ace," said Mick.

They were flashing past parked cars at reckless speed.

Gloria was scared, but enjoying it in the way you can enjoy a roller coaster ride. She wasn't even using the seat-belt. That, to a full-blown punk like Mick, would surely have been chicken.

They succeeded in getting to the by-pass without being stopped by the police. On the triple carriageway, Mick moved out to the fast lane.

"Let's see what this heap can do."

Gloria's skin prickled. To think that this could have been choir practice.

The wind stung her face and stretched her hair in what felt like a comic-strip illustration of speed. Mick was steering one-handed, with his free hand resting on her thigh. She didn't mind.

They overtook everything. When anyone had the temerity to block the fast lane, Mick used the horn and headlights together. They weren't held up long.

Gloria looked at the speedometer and saw the needle hovering near 110. They passed the sign for a roundabout. She drew it to his attention in the most tactful way she could. "Let's go round and come back the other way."

"You go for this?" Mick shouted. "Does it turn you on?"

"It's magic."

The hand on her leg moved higher, exploring, but he had to use both hands to swing the car around the roundabout, the tyres screeching, and by that time Gloria had brought her legs up to her chest with her heels on the edge of the seat and her arms tucked around her shins. The one-handed driving was all very macho, but she felt it required Mick's undivided attention.

They raced back along the stretch they had just travelled. Someone in the fast lane refused to give way, so Mick overtook on the inside and made an obscene gesture as they passed. Gloria did the same. She had never felt so delinquent, or so alive.

"You know what?" shouted Mick.

"What?"

"You're neat."

"You're neat, too."

"I'll get you a present. What do you want—jewellery?"

She didn't know what to say.

"Somefink to wear? Leathers?" said Mick.

"There's no need," said Gloria. "You don't have to get me anything."

He reduced speed. They were coming to a slip-road that would take them off the by-pass.

"Have you got a telly? Portable?"

"Look, I don't want anything, Mick. If you want to get me a drink—"

"A drink? All right. You like fizz?"

"Fizz?"

"Champagne. You can have champagne if you want."

She laughed. "All right." If he wanted to be extravagant, she'd settle for a glass of champagne. Immediately she wondered if she'd made a wise choice. With some drink inside him, Mick might take even bigger risks with the car. Maybe she'd be wise to walk home.

They cruised at a mere seventy along the main road into town, ignoring several pubs. Gloria decided that Mick was driving them to his favourite haunt, some place where punks and rockers met, with wood floors and music and one-arm bandits.

In the High Street, he slowed and turned his head, as if looking for someone. He cruised quite slowly, past Woolworth's and Boot's and the Laundromat. Gloria didn't know of any pub along here. There was just the County Arms Hotel, with four stars in the RAC Guide, and that, surely, wasn't the sort of place Mick would frequent.

Like a mind-reader, he said, "We'll get it in the Wine Mart."

"Fine," said Gloria.

"Put your head down, right down, like you had it before."

"Why?"

"Why do you fink? We're going to ram-raid the place. These fings are built like bloody tanks."

She was horrified. "No, Mick!"

"Do what I say—if you want to keep your face." He spun the wheel sharply right.

She had a glimpse of the shop window of the Wine Mart straight ahead. She plunged her head between her knees. She felt the wheels mount the curb and then the terrific impact as the shop front was ripped apart. An alarm bell jangled.

Mick forced open his door and stepped through shattered glass into the shop's interior. Gloria sat up, twitching with fear and shock. The car's bonnet was covered in glass.

Mick was back, brandishing a bottle of champagne that he'd taken off a shelf at the rear of the shop. This was a nightmare.

Gloria said in a voice shrill with panic, "You're crazy!"

Mick shouted above the blare of the alarm, "Burst tyre. We got to run for it!" He opened the car door, grabbed Gloria's arm and tugged her out. "Come on! Let's get out of here."

They abandoned Mr Hibbert's car, still blocking the pavement with its front wheels inside the Wine Mart. Regardless of the people who must have heard and were certain to be watching from flats above the shops, Mick dashed up the High Street with Gloria following. At the first opportunity they turned left up a side-street.

Gloria leaned against a doorway to recover her breath.

Mick swung around. "You can't stop here. We got to go on."

If she'd had any breath left, she'd have shouted back at him, told him he must be a head-case to have done such a thing, made it clear that she would never have consented to it. That—far from impressing her—it proved that he was a pathological idiot.

A police siren frighteningly close interrupted her resentment. She forced herself to run again. They were coming into a paved area where cars couldn't normally pass, but she was sure the police car would pursue them if they were spotted. A couple of derelicts shouted at them from a shop doorway. They'd seen the bottle that Mick was still carrying and they were asking him to share it. Mick was too fast, but one of them stepped out to try and grab Gloria. He caught hold of her wrist with a filthy hand, and his face came close to hers, unshaven, bright pink and foul of breath. She screamed, pushed at his chest and managed to wriggle free. He stood in the middle of the walkway yelling obscenities as she dashed on.

Mick waited for her by the parish church beyond the shopping mall, a pathetic figure now with his stupid green hair in disarray like daffodil stalks after the flowers were picked. "Over the top, right?"

She nodded, too breathless to speak.

The wall around the churchyard was about four feet high. She put her hands on the coping and half-jumped, half-hauled herself off the ground. Mick shoved her backside unceremoniously higher and she scrambled onto the wall and jumped down. He followed, then stooped to pick up the champagne, which he must have tossed over first. Why he bothered with it, she couldn't imagine.

"Come on."

Stumbling between ancient headstones in the near-darkness they made their way as well as they could across the churchyard to the accompaniment of the police siren. At one point Gloria thought she could make out the sound of running footsteps quite close, but Mick was unconvinced. He'd stopped from sheer exhaustion, leaning against a tombstone. "They'd have searchlights and torches if they was trying to follow us."

Gloria said, "I can't run any more."

"Have some of this." He started fiddling with the foil wrapping on the champagne.

"I don't want any, you moron. I didn't want it in the first place."

He was loosening the wire around the cork. "You did. You said." He sounded like a six-year-old now.

"I didn't know you were going to break into a shop to get it and ruin Mr Hibbert's car."

The cork popped and Mick's hands were covered in froth. "Have a swig."

"I don't want any."

"I don't want any," he mimicked her. "Snotty-nosed bitch."

"I'm the one who stands to lose most," she pointed out. "I've never been in trouble with the police."

"Who says you're in trouble? We got away, didn't we?"

"Yes, but I took the keys from his overcoat pocket when he was visiting my Mum. It's going to be obvious."

"He was visiting your house?"

"Yes, he's probably still there."

"What's he doing with your Mum?"

"That's my business."

"Is he staying long?"

"I don't know—a couple of hours."

Mick fumbled in his pocket and produced the car-keys, dangling them in front of her face.

"You've still got them?"

"Now who's a moron? You can stick them back in his pocket and he won't never know."

"Give them to me."

He closed his fingers around them and hid them behind his back. "Who's a moron?"

"I'm sorry, Mick. I didn't mean that. Please."

"Come here."

"Mick, I said I was sorry."

He curled his finger, beckoning.

She felt her stomach clench. He wanted her. This was what it had all been leading up to, the joy-ride, the ram-raid, the champagne. Almost every day of her life since she had first learned about sex she had tried to imagine how it would happen to her the first time—the situation in which she would consent. Never, remotely, had she pictured it like this, among the gravestones in the bitter cold, with the police searching for her.

She said, "There isn't time." She could have added that it was dangerous and squalid and unromantic, but those were concepts that would make no impression on a punk. In his scale of values they might actually be incentives. And—in spite of everything that had governed her life until this moment—Gloria herself was being swayed. She was a different person now, a law-breaker.

Impulsively she stepped towards him and offered her lips.

He jammed his mouth against hers so hard that their teeth scraped. She could feel his hand fumbling low down at the front of her coat.

He said, "Take 'em, then."

It was a moment before she understood that he was trying to hand her the car keys. He pushed them into her hand.

Then he drew back and so did she, bewildered. Apparently all he'd wanted was the kiss.

"You'd better leg it now," he told her.

"Yes."

"See you." He turned and walked away.

She put her hand to her mouth as if the act of touching her slightly numb lips would somehow preserve the kiss. She didn't want him to leave her. She knew it was the sensible thing, the safe thing, but tonight she'd stopped being sensible and safe.

"Mick!"

He turned his head and said, "Leave it out, will you?"

Despairingly, she echoed the words he had used. "See you."

He walked on.

She bit back her distress. If she really wanted to be accepted by people like Mick she had to be tough with herself. She left the churchyard by a different route from Mick's and—to borrow his terminology—"legged it" through the streets towards home. So much had happened that she hardly expected to see the houses still lit—but they were—almost every one she passed. She couldn't believe that Mr Hibbert would still be in the house with his coat hanging in the hall, but in fact the entire adventure had lasted less than an hour and twenty minutes. It might still be possible to return the keys and pretend she had been at choir practice.

But when she turned the corner of King George Avenue she had a horrible shock. A police car was parked in the space where Mr Hibbert's car had been. The police? Already?

In two minds whether to run back and search the streets for Mick, she stopped at the corner and waited, going over in her mind what she could say if the police were with her mother now. She was in an appalling position. If she told the truth, she'd have to betray Mick. Then it occurred to her that the police might not yet have connected her with the theft of the car. It was possible that they were there for no other reason than to inform Mr Hibbert what had happened.

She was going to have to find the courage to walk into the house and act as if she knew nothing at all. It was no use waiting for them to leave, because Mr Hibbert was sure to leave as well. The only chance she had of returning the keys to his overcoat pocket was now.

With her heart pounding, she stepped up the street to the house. The light was on in the front room and she could hear the faint murmur of voices, but the curtains were too thick for her to see anything. Under the porch light she checked her clothes. Her shoes were muddy at the heels and her coat was dusty where she'd climbed over the church wall, so she did some rapid grooming with a paper tissue. She couldn't do anything about her hair; she'd just have to say that one of the plaits had come undone and she'd unfastened the other one. She took a deep breath, slotted her own key into the front door and let herself in.

The coat was still hanging on the hallstand, but there were others as well. And she didn't have time to do anything about the car-keys because the door of the front room opened and Mr Hibbert came out, followed by a police sergeant in uniform.

"You must be Gloria," said Mr Hibbert. "I've seen you several times, but we've never spoken. Your hair's different, isn't it?"

She murmured some bland response.

"Mrs Palmer's daughter," Mr Hibbert explained to the policeman. "Just back from choir practice, I believe." He sounded surprisingly chirpy for a man whose car had been stolen and wrecked.

Other people were coming out of the front room. Two women from up the street and old Mr and Mrs Chalk, from next door. Even the obnoxious Mrs Mackenzie from the house opposite, a woman her mother detested. So many witnesses?

And now her mother was there. "Gloria, help Mrs Mackenzie with her coat, there's a dear."

Nobody seemed unduly alarmed.

"I'll be off, then," announced the police sergeant, opening the front door. "Thanks for the coffee, Mrs Palmer."

Gloria reached for the fur coat that she recognized as Mrs Mackenzie's, just as Mr Hibbert was lifting his overcoat off the hook. He was saying something to her mother about coming again. In a swift movement, using Mrs Mackenzie's fur as a shield, Gloria succeeded in dropping the car keys into Mr Hibbert's coat pocket. Only just in time.

"Goodbye all." He'd put on the coat and was gone.

Some of the others were not so quick to leave. There was no sense of urgency. They were talking about what they would be doing for Christmas.

When Mrs Palmer finally closed the door on the last of them, she breathed a sigh of relief and said, "Let's have a fresh cup of tea, love. Have you had a nice evening? You're back early, aren't you? What have you done with your hair? I rather like it down. It suits you."

"Mum, whatever were all those people doing here—and the police?"

"Didn't I tell you? This is the third meeting we've had. We're setting up a Neighbourhood Watch. You know—keeping an eye on each other's property. It's becoming essential with all the crime round here. Sergeant Middleton was telling us how dreadful it is. He's the community liaison officer. It's his job to advise people like ourselves how to get organised."

"That's why they were here?"

"Well, yes."

"Mr Hibbert?"

"He *is* a neighbour, dear, and quite well off, I believe. He's got an interest in protecting his property. He's one of the moving forces. He's always the first to arrive."

"Yes, I noticed," said Gloria, wishing the earth would swallow her up.

The kettle had boiled. Mrs Palmer made the tea. "Of course, that Mrs Mackenzie from across the way came, and I'm convinced the only reason is that she wanted to see inside the house. She's so nosy, that woman. Do you know, when I made the coffee she insisted on coming out here to help me, as she put it. Of course, all she wanted was to get a look at my kitchen. Oh, and Gloria, darling, I'm *so* grateful to you for putting my thermal undies out of sight. Imagine if that woman had clapped eyes on them. I'd have died, I really would. I suddenly thought of them when she was opening the biscuits. The relief when I looked at the towel rail and they weren't there. I mean, they're not the most flattering things to have on display—my enormous bloomers."

Gloria tried to give the smile that her mother obviously expected.

Mrs Palmer added, "Tell me, where did you put them, dear?"

The doorbell chimed.

The Proof of the Pudding

Frank Morris strode into the kitchen and slammed a cold, white turkey on the kitchen table. "Seventeen pounds plucked. Satisfied?"

His wife Wendy was at the sink, washing the last few breakfast bowls. Her shoulders had tensed. "What's that, Frank?"

"You're not even bloody looking, woman."

She took that as a command and wheeled around, rubbing her wet hands on the apron. "A turkey! That's a fine bird. It really is."

"Fine?" Frank erupted. "It's nineteen forty-six, for Christ's sake! It's a bloody miracle. Most of them round here will be sitting down to joints of pork and mutton—if they're lucky. I bring a bloody great turkey in on Christmas morning, and all you can say is 'fine'?"

"I just wasn't prepared for it."

"You really get my goat, you do."

Wendy said tentatively, "Where did it come from, Frank?"

Her huge husband stepped towards her and for a moment she thought he would strike her. He lowered his face until it was inches from hers. Not even nine in the morning and she could smell sweet whisky on his breath. "I won it, didn't I?" he said, daring her to disbelieve. "A meat raffle in The Valiant Trooper last night."

Wendy nodded, pretending to be taken in. It didn't do to challenge Frank's statements. Black eyes and beatings had taught her well. She knew Frank's rule of fist had probably won him the turkey, too. Frank didn't lose at anything. If he could punch his way to another man's prize, then he considered it fair game.

"Just stuff the thing and stick it in the oven," he ordered. "Where's the boy?"

"I think he's upstairs," Wendy replied warily. Norman had fled at the sound of Frank's key in the front door.

"Upstairs?" Frank ranted. "On bloody Christmas Day?"

"I'll call him." Wendy was grateful for the excuse to move away from Frank to the darkened hallway. "Norman," she gently called. "Your father's home. Come and wish him a Happy Christmas."

A pale, solemn young boy came cautiously downstairs, pausing at the bottom to hug his mother. Unlike most children of his age—he was nine—Norman was sorry that the war had ended in 1945. He had pinned his faith in the enemy putting up a stiff fight and extending it indefinitely. He still remembered the VE Day street party, sitting at a long wooden bench surrounded by laughing neighbours. He and his mother had found little to celebrate in the news that "the boys will soon be home."

Wendy smoothed down his hair, whispered something and led him gently into the kitchen.

"Happy Christmas, Dad," he said, then added, unprompted, "Did you come home last night?"

Wendy said quickly, "Never you mind about that, Norman." She didn't want her son provoking Frank on this of all days.

Frank didn't appear to have heard. He was reaching up

to the top shelf of a cupboard, a place where he usually kept his old army belt. Wendy pushed her arm protectively in front of the boy.

But instead of the belt, Frank took down a brown paper parcel. "Here you are, son," he said, beckoning to Norman. "You'll be the envy of the street in this. I saved it for you, specially."

Norman stepped forward. He unwrapped his present, egged on by his grinning father.

He now owned an old steel helmet. "Thanks, Dad," he said politely, turning it in his hands.

"I got it off a dead Jerry," Frank said with gusto. "The bastard who shot your Uncle Ted. Sniper, he was. Holed up in a bombed-out building in Potsdam, outside Berlin. He got Ted with a freak shot. Twelve of us stormed the building and took him out."

"Outside?"

"Topped him, Norman. See the hole round the back. That's from a Lee Enfield .303. Mine." Frank levelled an imaginary rifle to Wendy's head and squeezed the trigger, miming both the recoil and report. "There wasn't a lot left of Fritz after we'd finished. But I brought back the helmet for you, son. Wear it with pride. It's what your Uncle Ted would have wanted." He took the helmet and rammed it on the boy's head.

Norman grimaced. He felt he was about to be sick.

"Frank dear, perhaps we should put it away until he's a bit older," Wendy tried her tact. "We wouldn't want such a special thing to get damaged, would we? You know what young boys are like."

Frank was unimpressed. "What are you talking about—'special thing?' It's a bloody helmet, not a thirty-piece tea service. Look at the lad. He's totally stunned. He loves it. Why don't you get on and stuff that ruddy great turkey, like I told you?"

"Yes, Frank."

Norman raised his hand, his small head an absurd sight in the large helmet. "May I go now?"

Frank beamed. "Of course, son. Want to show it off to all your friends, do you?"

Norman nodded, causing the helmet to slip over his eyes. He lifted it off his head. Smiling weakly at his father, he left the kitchen and dashed upstairs. The first thing he would do was wash his hair.

Wendy began to wash and prepare the bird, listening to Frank.

"I know just how the kid feels. I still remember my old Dad giving me a bayonet he brought back from Flanders. Said he ran six men through with it. I used to look for specks of blood, and he'd tell me how he stuck them like pigs. It was the best Christmas present I ever had."

"I've got you a little something for Christmas. It's behind the clock," said Wendy, indicating a small package wrapped in newspaper and string.

"A present?" Frank snatched it up and tore the wrapping away. "Socks?" he said in disgust. "Is that it? Our first Christmas together in three bloody years, and all you can give your husband is a miserable pair of socks."

"I don't have much money, Frank," Wendy reminded him, and instantly wished she had not.

Frank seized her by the shoulders, practically tipping the turkey off the kitchen table. "Are you saying that's my fault?"

"No, love."

"I'm not earning enough—is that what you're trying to tell me?"

Wendy tried to pacify him, at the same time bracing herself for the violent shaking that would surely follow. Frank tightened his grip, forced her away from the table and pushed her hard against the cupboard door, punctuating each word with a thump.

"That helmet cost me nothing," he ranted. "Don't you understand, woman? It's the thought that counts. You don't need money to show affection. You just need some savvy, some intelligence. Bloody socks—an insult!"

He shoved her savagely towards the table again. "Now get back to your work. This is Christmas Day. I'm a reasonable man. I'm prepared to overlook your stupidity. Stop snivelling, will you, and get that beautiful bird in the oven. Mum will be here at ten. I want the place smelling of turkey. I'm not having you ruining my Christmas."

He strode out, heavy boots clumping on the wooden floor of the hallway. "I'm going round Polly's," he shouted. "She knows how to treat a hero. Look at this dump. No decorations, no holly over the pictures. You haven't even bought any beer, that I've seen. Sort something out before I get back."

Wendy was still reeling from the shaking, but she knew she must speak before he left. If she didn't remind him now, there would be hell to pay later. "Polly said she would bring the Christmas pudding, Frank. Would you make sure she doesn't forget? Please, Frank."

He stood grim-faced in the doorway, silhouetted against the drab terraced houses opposite. "Don't tell me what to do, Wendy," he said threateningly. "You're the one due for a damned good reminding of what to do round here."

The door shook in its frame. Wendy stood at the foot of the stairs, her heart pounding. She knew what Frank meant by a damned good reminding. The belt wasn't used only on the boy.

"Is he gone, Mum?" Norman called from the top stair.

Wendy nodded, readjusting the pins in her thin, blonde hair, and drying her eyes. "Yes, love, You can come downstairs now."

At the foot of the stairs, he told her, "I don't want the helmet. It frightens me."

"I know, dear."

"I think there's blood on it. I don't want it. If it belonged to one of our soldiers, or one of the Yankees, I'd want it, but this is a dead man's helmet."

Wendy hugged her son. The base of her spine throbbed. A sob was building at the back of her throat.

"Where's he gone?" Norman asked from the folds of her apron.

"To collect your Aunt Polly. She's bringing a Christmas pudding, you know. We'd better make custard. I'm going to need your help."

"Was he there last night?" Norman asked innocently. "With Aunt Polly? Is it because she doesn't have Uncle Ted any more?"

"I don't know, Norman." In truth, she didn't want to know. Her widowed sister-in-law was welcome to Frank. Polly didn't know the relief Wendy felt to be rid of him sometimes. Any humiliation was quite secondary to the fact that Frank stopped out all night, bringing respite from the tension and the brutality. The local gossips had been quick to suspect the truth, but she could do nothing to stop them.

Norman, sensing the direction her thoughts had taken, said, "Billy Slater says Dad and Aunt Polly are doing it."

"That's enough, Norman."

"He says she's got no elastic in her drawers. What does he mean, Mum?"

"Billy Slater is a disgusting little boy. Now let's hear no more of this. We'll make the custard."

Norman spent the next hour helping his mother in the kitchen. The turkey barely fitted in the oven, and Norman became concerned that it wouldn't be ready in time. Wendy knew better. There was ample time for the cooking. They couldn't start until Frank and Polly rolled home from the Valiant Trooper. With last orders at a quarter to three, it gave the bird five hours to roast.

A gentle knock at the front door sent Norman hurrying to open it.

"Mum, it's Grandma Morris!" he called out excitedly as he led the plump old woman into the kitchen. Maud Morris had been a marvellous support through the war years. She knew exactly when help was wanted.

"I've brought you some veggies," Maud said to Wendy, dumping a bag of muddy cabbage and carrots onto the table and removing her coat and hat. "Where's that good-for-nothing son of mine? Need I ask?"

"He went to fetch Polly," Wendy calmly replied.

"Did he, indeed?"

Norman said, "About an hour ago. I expect they'll go to the pub."

The old lady went into the hall to hang up her things. When she returned, she said to Wendy, "You know what people are saying, don't you?"

Wendy ignored the question. "He brought in a seventeen-pound turkey this morning."

"Have you got a knife?" her mother-in-law asked.

"A knife?"

"For the cabbage." Maud turned to look at her grandson. "Have you had some good presents?"

Norman stared down at his shoe-laces.

Wendy said, "Grandma asked you a question, dear."

"Did you get everything you asked for?"

"I don't know."

"Did you write to Saint Nick?" Maud asked with a sideward glance at Wendy.

Norman rolled his eyes upwards. "I don't believe in that stuff any more."

"That's a shame."

"Dad gave me a dead German's helmet. He says it belonged to the one who shot Uncle Ted. I hate it."

Wendy gathered the carrots from the table and put them

in the sink. "I'm sure he was only doing what he thought was best, Norman."

"It's got a bullet hole."

"Didn't he give you anything else?" his grandmother asked.

Norman shook his head. "Mum gave me some chocolate and the Dandy Annual."

"But your Dad didn't give you a thing apart from the helmet?"

Wendy said, "Please don't say anything. You know what it's like."

Maud Morris nodded. It was pointless to admonish her son. He'd only take it out on Wendy. She knew from personal experience the dilemma of the battered wife. To protest was to invite more violence. The knowledge that her second son had turned out such a bully shamed and angered her. Ted, her dear firstborn Ted, would never have harmed a woman. Yet Ted had been taken from her. She took an apron from the back of the door and started shredding the cabbage. Norman was sent to lay the table in the front room.

Four hours later, when the King was speaking to the nation, they heard a key being tried at the front door. Wendy switched off the wireless. The door took at least three attempts to open before Frank and Polly stumbled into the hallway. Frank stood swaying, a bottle in his hand and a paper hat cocked ridiculously on the side of his head. His sister-in-law clung to his coat, convulsed in laughter, a pair of ankle-strap shoes dangling from her right hand.

"Happy Christmas!" he roared. "Peace on earth and goodwill to all men except the Jerries and the lot next door."

Polly doubled up in uncontrollable giggling.

"Let me take your coat, Polly," Wendy offered. "Did you remember the pudding? I want to get it on right away."

Polly turned to Frank. "The pudding. What did you do with the pudding, Frank?"

"What pudding?" said Frank.

Maud had come into the hall behind Wendy. "I know she's made one. Don't mess about, Frank. Where is it?"

Frank pointed vaguely over his shoulder.

Wendy said despairingly, "Back at Polly's house? Oh, no!"

"Stupid cow. What are you talking about?" said Frank. "It's on our own bloody doorstep. I had to put it down to open the door, didn't I?"

Wendy squeezed past them and retrieved the white basin covered with a grease-proof paper top. She carried it quickly through to the kitchen and lowered it into the waiting saucepan of simmering water. "It looks a nice big one."

This generous remark caused another gale of laughter from Polly. Finally, slurring her words, she announced, "You'll have to make allowances. Your old man's a very naughty boy. He's took me out and got me tiddly."

Maud said, "It beats me where he gets the money from."

"Beats Wendy, too, I expect," said Polly. She leaned closer to her sister-in-law, a lock of brown hair swaying across her face. "From what I've heard, you know a bit about beating, don't you, Wen?" The remark wasn't made in sympathy. It was triumphant.

Wendy felt the shame redden her face. Polly smirked and swung around, causing her black skirt to swirl as she left the room. The thick pencil lines she had drawn up the back of her legs to imitate stocking seams were badly smudged higher up. Wendy preferred not to think why.

She took the well-cooked bird from the oven, transferred it to a platter and carried it into the front room. Maud and Norman brought in the vegetables.

"Would you like to carve, Frank?"

"Hold your horses, woman. We haven't said the Grace."

Wendy started to say, "But we never . . ."

Frank had already intoned the words, "Dear Lord God Almighty."

Everyone dipped their heads.

"Thanks for what we are about to receive," Frank went on, "and for seeing to it that a skinny little half-pint won the meat raffle and decided to donate it to the Morris family."

Maud clicked her tongue in disapproval.

Polly began to giggle.

"I can't begin to understand the workings of your mysterious ways," Frank insisted on going on, "because if there really is someone up there he should have made damned sure my brother Ted was sitting at this table today."

Maud said, "That's enough, Frank! Sit down."

Frank said, "Amen. Where's the carving knife?"

Wendy handed it to him, and he attended to the task, cutting thick slices and heaping them on the plates held by his mother. "That's for Polly. She likes it steaming hot."

Polly giggled again.

The plates were distributed around the table.

Not to be outdone in convivial wit, Polly said, "You've gone over-board on the breast, Frankie dear. I thought you were a leg man."

Maud said tersely, "You should know."

"Careful, Mum," Frank cautioned, wagging the knife. "Goodwill to all men."

Polly said, "Only if they behave themselves."

A voice piped up, "Billy Slater says that—"

"Be quiet, Norman!" Wendy ordered.

They ate in heavy silence, save for Frank's animalistic chewing and swallowing. The first to finish, he quickly filled his glass with more beer.

"Dad?"

"Yes, son."

"Would we have won the war without the Americans?"

"The Yanks?" Frank scoffed. "Bunch of part-timers, son.

They only came into it after men like me and your Uncle Ted had done all the real fighting. Just like the other war, the one my old Dad won. They waited till 1917. Isn't that a fact, Mum? Americans? Where were they at Dunkirk? Where were they in Africa? I'll tell you where they were—sitting on their fat backsides a couple of thousand miles away."

"From what I remember, Frank," Maud interjected. "You were sitting on yours in the snug-bar of the Valiant Trooper."

"That was different!" Frank protested angrily. "Ted and I didn't get called up until 1943. And when we were, we did our share. We chased Jerry all the way across Europe, right back to the bunker. Ted and me, brothers in arms, fighting for King and country. Ready to make the ultimate sacrifice. If Dad could have heard what you said just then, Mum, he'd turn in his grave."

Maud said icily, "That would be difficult, seeing that he's in a pot on my mantelpiece."

Polly burst into helpless laughter and almost choked on a roast potato. It was injudicious of her.

"Belt up, will you?" Frank demanded. "We're talking about the sacred memory of your dead husband. My brother."

"Sorry, Frank." Polly covered her mouth with her hands. "I don't know what came over me. Honest."

"You've no idea, you women," Frank went on. "God knows what you got up to, while we were winning the war."

"Anyway," said Norman, "Americans have chewing gum. And jeeps."

Fortunately, at this moment Frank was being distracted.

Wendy whispered in Norman's ear and they both began clearing the table, but Maud put her hand over Wendy's. She said, "Why don't you sit down? You've done more than enough. I'll fetch the pudding and custard. I'd like to get up for a while. It's beginning to get a little warm in here."

Polly offered to help. "It is my pudding, after all." But she didn't mean to get up because, unseen by the others, she had her hand on Frank's thigh.

Maud said, "I'll manage."

Norman asked, "Is it a proper pudding?"

"I don't know what you mean by proper," said Polly. "It used up most of my rations when I made it. They have to mature, do puddings. This one is two years old. It should be delicious. There was only one drawback. In 1944, I didn't have a man at home to help me stir the ingredients." She gave Frank a coy smile.

Ignoring it, Wendy said, "When Norman asked if it was a proper pudding, I think he wanted to know if he might find a lucky sixpence inside."

With a simper, Polly said, "He might, if he's a good boy, like his Dad. Of *course* it's a proper pudding."

Frank quipped, "What about the other sort? Do you ever make an improper pudding?"

Before anyone could stop him, Norman said, "You should know, Dad." His reflexes were too quick for his drunken father's, and the swinging blow missed him completely.

"You'll pay for that remark, my son," Frank shouted. "You'll wash your mouth out with soap and water and then I'll beat your backside raw."

Wendy said quickly, "The boy doesn't know what he's saying, Frank. It's Christmas. Let's forgive and forget, shall we?"

He turned his anger on her. "And I know very well who puts these ideas in the boy's head. And spreads the filthy rumours all over town. You can have your Christmas Day, Wendy. Make the most of it, because tomorrow I'm going to teach you why they call it Boxing Day."

Maud entered the suddenly silent front room carrying the dark, upturned pudding decorated with a sprig of holly. "Be an angel and fetch the custard, Norman."

The boy was thankful to run out to the kitchen.

Frank glanced at the pudding and then at Polly and then grinned. "What a magnificent sight!" He was staring at her cleavage.

Polly beamed at him, fully herself again, her morale restored by the humiliation her sister-in-law had just suffered. "The proof of the pudding . . ." she murmured.

"We'll see if 1944 was a vintage year," said Frank.

Maud sliced and served the pudding, giving Norman an extra large helping. The pudding was a delicious one, as Polly had promised, and there were complimentary sounds all round the table.

Norman sifted the rich, fruity mass with his spoon, hoping for one of those coveted silver sixpenny pieces. But Frank was the first to find one.

"You can have a wish. Whatever you like, lucky man," said Polly in a husky, suggestive tone.

Frank's thoughts were in another direction. "I wish," he said sadly, holding the small coin between finger and thumb, "I wish God's peace to my brother Ted, rest his soul. And I wish a Happy Christmas to all the blokes who fought with us and survived. And God rot all our enemies. And the bloody Yanks, come to that."

"That's about four wishes," Polly said, " and it won't come true if you tell everyone."

Wendy felt the sharp edge of a sixpence in her mouth, and removed it unnoticed by the others. She wished him out of her life, with all her heart.

Norman finally found his piece of the pudding's buried treasure. He spat the coin onto his plate and then examined it closely. "Look at this!" he said in surprise. "It isn't a sixpence. It doesn't have the King's head."

"Give it here." Frank picked up the silver coin. "Jesus Christ! He's right. It's a dime. An American dime. How the hell did that get in the pudding?"

All eyes turned to Polly for an explanation. She stared wide-eyed at Frank. She was speechless.

Frank was not. He had reached his own conclusion. "I'll tell you exactly how it got in there," he said, thrusting it under Polly's nose. "You've been stirring it up with a Yank. There was a GI base down the road, wasn't there? When did you say you made the pudding? 1944?"

He rose from the table, spittle flying as he ranted. Norman slid from his chair and hid under the table, clinging in fear to his mother's legs. He saw his father's heavy boots turned towards Polly, whose legs braced. The hem of her dress was quivering.

Frank's voice boomed around the small room. "Ted and I were fighting like bloody heroes while you were having it off with Americans. Whore!"

Norman saw a flash of his father's hand as it reached into the fireplace and picked up a poker. He heard the women scream, then a sickening thump.

The poker fell to the floor. Polly's legs jerked once and then appeared to relax. One of her arms flopped down and remained quite still. A drop of blood fell from the table edge. Presently there was another. Then it became a trickle. A crimson pool formed on the wooden floor.

Norman ran out of the room. Out of the house. Out into the cold afternoon, leaving the screams behind. He ran across the street and beat on a neighbour's door with his fists. His frantic cries of "Help, murder!" filled the street. Within a short time an interested crowd in party hats had surrounded him. He pointed in horror to his own front door as his blood-stained father charged out and lurched towards him.

It took three men to hold Frank Morris down, and five policemen to take him away.

The last of the policemen didn't leave the house until long

after Norman should have gone to bed. His mother and his grandmother sat silent for some time in the kitchen, unable to stay in the front room, even though Polly's body had been taken away.

"He's not going to come back, is he, Mum?"

Wendy shook her head. She was only beginning to think about what happened next. There would be a trial, of course, and she would try to shield Norman from the publicity. He was so impressionable.

"Will they hang him?"

"I think it's time for your bed, young man," Maud said. "You've got to be strong. Your Mum will need your support more than ever now."

The boy asked, "How did the dime get in the pudding, Grandma Morris?"

Wendy snapped out of her thoughts of what was to come and stared at her mother-in-law.

Maud went to the door, and for a moment it appeared as if she was reaching to put on her coat prior to leaving, but she had already promised to stay the night. Actually she was taking something from one of the pockets.

It was a Christmas card, a little bent at the edges now. Maud handed it to Wendy. "It was marked 'private and confidential' but it had my name, you see. I opened it thinking it was for me. It came last week. The address was wrong. They made a mistake over the house number. The postman delivered it to the wrong Mrs Morris."

Wendy took the card and opened it.

"The saddest thing is," Maud continued to speak as Wendy read the message inside, "he is the only son I have left, but I really can't say I'm sorry it turned out this way. I know what he did to you, Wendy. His father did the same to me for nearly forty years. I had to break the cycle. I read the card, love. I had no idea. I couldn't let this chance pass by. For your sake, and the boy's."

A tear rolled down Wendy's cheek. Norman watched as the two women hugged. The card drifted from Wendy's lap and he pounced on it immediately. His eager eyes scanned every word.

My Darling Wendy,

Since returning home, my thoughts are filled with you, and the brief time we shared together. It's kind of strange to admit, but I sometimes catch myself wishing the Germans made you a widow. I can't stand to think of you with any other guy.

My heart aches for news of you. Not a day goes by when I don't dream of being back in your arms. My home, and my heart, will always be open for you.

Take care and keep safe,

Nick

Nick Saint (Ex-33rd US Reserve),
221C Plover Avenue,
Mountain Home,
Idaho

P.S. The dime is a tiny Christmas present for Norman to remember me by.

Norman looked up at his Grandmother and understood what she had done, and why. He didn't speak. He could keep a secret as well as a grown-up. He was the man of the house now, at least until they got to America.

The Pushover

During the singing of the Twenty-Third Psalm, the man next to me gave me a nudge and said, "What do you think of the wooden overcoat?"

Uncertain what he meant, I lifted an eyebrow.

"The coffin," he said.

I swayed to my left for a view along the aisle. I could see nothing worth interrupting the service for. Danny Fox's coffin stood on trestles in front of the altar looking no different from others I had seen. On the top was the wreath from his widow, Merle, in the shape of a large heart of red roses with Danny's name picked out in white. Not to my taste, but I wasn't so churlish as to mention this to anyone else.

"No handles," my informant explained.

So what? I thought. Who needs handles? Coffins are hardly ever carried by the handles. I gave a nod and continued singing.

"That isn't oak," the man persisted. "That's a veneer. Underneath, it's chipboard."

I pretended not to have heard, and joined in the singing of the third verse—the one beginning "Perverse and foolish oft I strayed"— with such commitment that I drew shocked glances from the people in front.

"She's going to bury Danny in the cheapest box she could buy."

This baboon was ruining the service. I sat for the sermon in a twisted position presenting most of my back to him.

But the damage had been done. My response to what was said was blighted. If John Wesley in his prime had been giving the Address I would still have found concentration difficult. Actually it was spoken by a callow curate with a nervous grin who revealed a lamentable ignorance about the Danny I had known. "A decent man" was a questionable epithet in Danny's case; "a loyal husband" extremely doubtful; "generous to a fault" a gross misrepresentation. I couldn't remember a time when the departed one had bought a round of drinks. If the curate felt obliged to say something positive, he might reasonably have told us that the man in the coffin had been funny and a charmer capable of selling sand to a sheik. I cared a lot about Danny, or I wouldn't be here, but just because he was dead we didn't have to award him a halo.

My contacts with the old rogue went back thirty years. Danny and I first met back in the sixties, the days of National Service, in the Air Force at a desolate camp on Salisbury Plain called Netheravon, and even so early in his career, still in his teens, Danny had got life running the way he wanted. He'd formed a poker school with a scale of duties as the stakes and, so far as I know, served his two years without ever polishing a floor, raking out a stove or doing a guard duty. No one ever caught him cheating, but his silky handling of the cards should have taught anyone not to play with him. He seduced (an old-fashioned word that gives a flavour of the time) the only WRAF officer on the roll and had the use of her pale blue Morris Minor on Saturdays to support his favourite football team, Bristol Rovers. Weekend passes were no problem. You had to smile at Danny.

I came across him again twelve years later, in 1973, on the sea front at Brighton dressed in a striped blazer, white flannels and a straw hat and doing a soft-shoe dance to an old Fred Astaire number on an ancient wind-up gramophone with a huge brass horn. I had no idea Danny was such a beautiful mover. So many people had stopped to watch that you couldn't get past without walking on the shingle. It was a deeply serious performance that refused to be serious at all. At a tempo so slow that any awkwardness would have been obvious, he shuffled and glided and turned about, tossing in casual gull-turns and toe-taps, dipping, swaying and twisting with the beat, his arms windmilling one second, seesawing the next, and never suggesting strain. After he'd passed the hat around, we went for a drink and talked about old times and former comrades. I paid, of course. After that we promised to stay in touch. We met a few times. I went to his second wedding in 1988—a big affair, because Merle had a sister and five brothers, all with families. They were a crazy bunch. The reception, on a river steamer, was a riot. I've never laughed so much.

Danny was fifty-seven when he died.

We sang another hymn and the curate said a prayer and led us out for the Committal. The pall-bearers hoisted the coffin and brought it along the aisle. I didn't need the nudge I got from my companion as they passed. I could see for myself that the wood was a cheap veneer. I wasn't judgmental. Quite possibly Danny had left Merle with nothing except his antique gramophone and some debts.

"She had him insured for a hundred and fifty K," Meanmouth insisted on telling me as we followed the coffin along a path between the graves. "She could have given him a decent send-off."

I told him curtly that I wasn't interested. God knows, I was trying not to be. At the graveside, I stepped away from him and took a position opposite. Let him bend someone else's ear with his malice.

Young sheep were bleating in the field beside the churchyard as the coffin was lowered. The clouds parted and we felt warmth on our skins. I remembered Danny dancing on the front that summer evening at Brighton. *Bon voyage*, old buccaneer, I thought. You robbed all of us of something, some time, but we came in numbers to see you off. You left us glittering memories, and that wasn't a bad exchange.

A few tears were shed around that grave.

As the Grace was spoken I became conscious of those joyless eyes sizing me up for another approach, so I gave him one back, raised my chin to the required level and stared like one of those stone figures on Easter Island. My twenty years of teaching fifteen-year-olds haven't been totally wasted. Then I turned away, said "Amen," and smiled benignly at the curate.

Mean-mouth walked directly through the lych-gate, got into his car and drove off. Why do people like that bother to come to funerals?

Most of us converged on the Red Lion across the street. A pub lunch. A corrective to nostalgia. It fitted my picture of Danny that his mourners should be forced to dip into their pockets to buy their own drinks. The only food on offer was microwaved meat pies with soggy crusts. Mean-mouth must have known. He would have told me that Merle was the skinflint, and on sober reflection it is difficult to believe otherwise. It seemed Danny had ended up with a tightwad wife. A nice irony.

And the family weren't partying at the house. They joined us, Merle leading them in while "Happy Days Are Here Again" came over the music system. Her choice of clothes left no one in any doubt that she was the principal lady in the party—a black cashmere coat and a matching

hat with a vast brim like a manta that flapped as she moved.
She was a good ten years younger than Danny, a tall, triumphantly slim, talkative woman who chain-smoked. I'd
heard that she knew a lot about antiques; at their wedding,
Danny had got in first with the obvious joke about his
antiquity, and frankly the way Merle had eyed him all
through the reception, you'd have thought he was a piece
of Wedgwood. Yet we all knew he was out of the reject
basket. Slightly chipped. Well, extensively, to be truthful.
He'd lived the kind of free-ranging life he'd wanted, busk-
ing, bar-tending, running a stall at a fairground, a bit of
chauffeuring, leading guided walks around the East End
and for a time acting as a croupier. Enjoyable, undemand-
ing jobs on the fringe of the entertainment industry, but
never likely to earn much of a bank balance. With his inno-
cent-looking eyes and deep-etched laughter lines, he had a
well-known attraction for women that must have played a
part in the romance, but Merle didn't look the sort to go
starry-eyed into marriage.

Someone bought her a cocktail in a tall glass and she
began the rounds of the funeral party, cigarette in one
hand, drink in the other, giving and receiving kisses. The
mood of forced bonhomie that gets people through funerals was well established. I overheard one formidably fat
woman telling Merle, "Never mind love, you're not bad-
looking. Keep your 'air nice and you'll be all right. Won't
'appen at once, mind. I 'ad to wait four years. But you'll be
all right."

Merle's hat quivered.

She moved towards me and I gave her the obligatory kiss
and muttered sympathetic words. She said, "Good of you to
come. We never really got to know each other, did we? You
and Danny go back a long way."

"To his Air Force days," I said.

"Oh, he used to tell wonderful tales of the RAF," she

said, calling it the 'raff' and clasping my hand so firmly that I could feel every one of her rings. "I don't know if half of them are true. The night exercises."

"Night exercises at Netheravon?" said I, not remembering any.

She took hold of my hand and squeezed it. "Come on, you know Danny. That was his name for that pilot officer whose car he used."

"Oh, her."

"Night exercises. Wicked man." She chuckled. "I couldn't be jealous when he put it like that. To Danny, she was just an easy lay. I envy you, knowing him when he was young. He must have been a right tearaway. Anyway, sweetie, I'd better not gossip. So many old mates to see." She moved on, leaving me in a cloud of cigarette smoke.

Another woman holding a gin and tonic sidled close and said, "What's she on, do you think? She's frisky for a widow."

"I've no idea."

"Danny's brother Ben must have given her some pills."

"Which one is Ben?"

"In the blue suit and black polo neck. Handy having a doctor for your brother-in-law."

"Yes." I glanced across at brother-in-law Ben, a taller, slimmer version of Danny. "He looks young."

"Fourteen years younger than Danny. They were stepbrothers, I think."

On an impulse I asked, "Was he Danny's doctor also?"

She nodded. "They never paid a bean for medicines."

Malice must be infectious. This wasn't Mean-mouth speaking. This was a short, chunky woman in a grey suit. She introduced herself as their neighbour. Not for much longer, it seemed. "Merle told me she'll be off to warmer climes now. She was always complaining about the winters here, was Merle."

"To live, you mean?"

She nodded. "Spain, I expect."

I remembered the life insurance payout. Merle's antique had, after all, turned out to be worth something if she was emigrating. Watching the newly-weds at their wedding reception, only four years ago, it hadn't crossed my mind to rate Danny as an insurance claim. Had it occurred to Merle?

What a sour thought to have at a funeral! I banished it. Instead I talked to the neighbour about the weather until she got bored and wandered off.

I did some circulating of my own and joined a crowd at a table in the main bar I recognized as more of Danny's close family. They all had large teeth and lop-sided grins like his. A man who looked like another younger brother was saying what a shock his death had been. "Fifty-seven. It's no age, is it? He was always so fit. I never knew Dan had a dicky heart."

"He didn't look after himself," a woman said.

"What do you mean—didn't look after himself?" the brother retorted. "He wasn't overweight."

"He didn't exercise. He avoided all forms of sport. Never learned to swim, hold a tennis racket, swing a golf club. He thought jogging was insane."

"He danced like a dream."

"Call that exercise? He never worked up a sweat. I tell you, he didn't look after himself."

"He had two wives," one of the men chipped in.

"Not at the same time," another woman said, giggling.

"What are you saying—that two wives strained his vital powers?"

There was some amusement at this. "No," said the man. "*You* said he didn't look after himself and I was pointing out that he had two women to do the job."

"That's what marriage is for, is it, Charlie?" the woman

came back at him. "So that the man's got someone to look after him?"

"Hello, hello. Have you turned into one of those feminists?" retorted Charlie.

"I'm sure being looked after wasn't in Danny's mind when he married Merle," said the giggly woman.

"We all know what was in Danny's mind when he married Merle," said the feminist.

Resisting the temptation to widen the debate by asking what had been in Merle's mind, I went back to the bar for a white wine. When I picked it up, my hand shook. A disturbing possibility had crept into *my* mind. The law allows a doctor considerable discretion in dealing with the death of a patient in his care. Provided that he has seen the patient in the two weeks prior to the death, and the cause of death is known to him and was not the result of an accident, or suspicious circumstances, he may sign the death certificate without reporting the matter to the coroner. Merle's brother-in-law Ben had treated Danny.

Across the bar, Ben was talking affably to some people who hadn't attended the funeral. This was his village, his local. Most of the family lived around here. He was at ease. Yet there was something more about his manner, a sense of relief; or perhaps it was triumph.

As for Merle, she was remarkably animated for a woman who had only just buried her husband. It must be an act, a brave attempt to get through the day without weeping, I tried telling myself. Watching her, I wasn't convinced. Her eyes shone like a bride's.

Another curious thing I noticed was that Merle spent time with everyone in that bar except her doctor brother-in-law, Ben. She kept away from him as if he were radio-active. Yet they were keenly aware of each other. Each time Merle moved, Ben would look across and check her position. Occasionally their eyes locked briefly. I was increasingly convinced that they had agreed not to be seen talking together. They weren't being hostile; they shared a secret.

When I left about six, the party was still going on. I didn't blame anyone for turning it into a wake. I was sure Danny would have approved. He would have been in the thick of the junketing, well pickled by this time, full of good humour, just as long as he didn't have to buy a round.

My unease about the circumstances of Danny's death dispersed within a week. I had more urgent things going on in my life that don't play any part in these events except that by February, six months after the funeral, I was tired and depressed. Then someone made things worse by breaking into my car and stealing my credit cards. The police were useless. The only positive thing they suggested was that I inform the people who issued the cards. When my shiny and pristine replacement cards arrived, I had an impulse to use them right away to give myself a boost. I walked into a travel agent's and booked two weeks in the sun. Immediately.

In Florida I spotted Merle Fox. By pure chance, or fate, I walked into the Guild Hall Gallery on Duval Street in Key West and there she was, looking at stained glass pictures of fish. She'd bleached her hair and cut it short and she was deeply tanned and wearing a skimpy top and white trousers that fitted like a second skin. Something new in widow's weeds, I thought unkindly—for I recognized her straight away. Of course she hadn't altered her features, but her stance was the giveaway, the suggestion of swagger in the shoulders. It was no different from the way she'd swanned around the bar of the Red Lion after Danny's funeral.

I didn't speak to Merle. In fact, I moved out of range,

hidden from her view by a rotating card-stand. But when she came out of the shop I followed, intrigued, you may say, if you don't call me nosy. I was pretty inconspicuous in T-shirt and shorts like most of the tourists strolling along the street.

Halfway along Duval Street she turned up a side road that was mainly residential and lined with two-storey Bahamian-style wood-frame buildings shaded by palms and wild purple orchid trees and fronted by white picket fences. She walked two blocks (with me in discreet attendance) and let herself into an elegant three-bay house with a porch and—more irony here—a widow's walk. Had I really seen Merle? The moment she'd stepped out of my view I became doubtful. It isn't the custom in Key West to have one's name on the mailbox, so it was difficult to make certain without speaking to the woman. I wasn't sure I wanted a face-to-face.

I crossed the street for a longer view of the house. The shutters were open, but the louvred windows effectively screened the interior.

You wouldn't believe that a leafy street bathed in sunlight could make you feel uneasy. After the crowds on Duval Street, this was eerie in its quietness.

A cat leaned against my shin and made a plaintive sound. I stooped to stroke it.

A voice startled me. "We call him Rocky, after the boxer. He has the most formidable front paws."

I looked behind me. This elderly woman had been sitting unnoticed in her porch swing in front of a small white house.

"He's a champion," I remarked, wondering if my luck was still running. "I was looking for a friend of mine who came to live in Key West. Mrs Fox. Do you know her?"

She paused some seconds before answering, "I can't say I do."

"She must have arrived some time in the last three months," I ventured. "She's a widow."

"The only lady who came to Southard Street since the summer is Mrs Finch in the house across the street and she's no widow," she informed me.

My confidence ebbed. "Mrs Finch, you said?"

"Mrs Merle Finch, from England. They're both from England."

"Ah. That wouldn't be the lady I know," I said, mentally turning a back-flip of triumph. "But thank you for your help, ma'am. Rocky is a cat in a million." I walked away, reflecting that Merle must have kept her hair extra nice to have charmed Mr Finch, whoever he was, into such a quick marriage. A little over six months since she had buried Danny she was re-married, settled in her new home. If her tan was any guide, she had already been in Florida some time.

The big insurance payout, the death certificate provided by her brother-in-law, the quick marriage and the escape to Florida. Had they all been planned? Was it any wonder I felt suspicious?

My holiday routine altered. Next morning I made sure of passing the house on my way to the shops. I lingered across the street for ten minutes or so. Wherever I went in Key West I was hawk-eyed for another sighting.

It came the next evening. Merle stepped out of Fausto's Food Palace on Fleming Street, crossed my path to a moped and put her bag on the pannier. My heart-rate stepped up. The hours of watching out for her, passing the house and so on, had made me feel furtive. Now I was ready to panic. Ridiculous.

I don't like being sneaky. That isn't my nature. I like to be straight with people. Confrontation is the honest way. So I steeled my nerves, stepped towards her and said, "Hi, Merle."

She stopped and stared.

"Remember me?" I said. "Danny's oppo from his Air Force days. Isn't this amazing? I must buy you a drink."

She couldn't deny her identity. Recovering her poise, she said in her very British accent that she would have been delighted, but she had to get back to the apartment. She had something cooking.

I almost laughed out loud at the phrase. Instead I insisted we must meet and suggested a nightcap later at one of the quieter open-air bars. She had a hunted look, but she agreed to see me there at ten.

"You got your wish, then," I said when we shared a table in a dark corner of the bar drinking margaritas.

"What do you mean?" She was tense.

"A warm place to live. I presume you live here."

"Yes, I do."

"And not alone. You're Mrs Finch now."

She frowned. "How did you know that?"

"I was told. Is he British, your husband?"

She gave a nod.

"Anyone I know?"

She said, "Why are you asking me these things?"

I said, "What's the matter? Don't you want to talk about them?"

She said, "I left all that behind. It's painful. I don't want to be reminded."

"I wasn't reminding you about the past, Merle. I was enquiring about the present. Your present husband. What's his name?"

She took a long sip of her drink. "Have you seen him?"

"No. But I'd love to meet him—if you let him out."

She pushed aside the drink. "I'll pay for these. I'm leaving."

I put a hand on her arm. "I'm sorry. That was insensitive. Don't take offence."

She brushed my hand away and got up. I didn't follow. I knew it would be no use. I *had* been insensitive. But she had fuelled my suspicions. She had behaved like a guilty woman. Meeting me had been an unpleasant shock. The geography of the Florida Keys—the long drive south from Miami over bridges that span the sea—fosters a feeling of escape, of reaching a haven in Key West bathed in sun and good will. You don't expect sharp questions about your conduct.

I believed Merle and her brother-in-law Ben had conspired to murder Danny. A lethal injection seemed the most likely means. Ben had written something innocuous on the death certificate and Merle had claimed the insurance, paid Ben for his services and escaped to Florida to marry her lover, the fascinating Mr Finch.

I believed this, yes. But it was only belief so far. The evidence I had was circumstantial. A cheap funeral, an alleged insurance payout, some sly glances and a quick marriage. None of this was sufficient to justify fingering Merle for murder.

Unable to sleep that night, I asked myself why I wanted to pursue the matter, for it was taking over my holiday. Was it anything as highminded as a concern for justice? Or was it morbid curiosity?

No.

It was more personal. Danny had been important in my life. The link between us was stronger than I'd admit to anyone. I was angry, deeply angry, at what I believed had happened. Our lives had touched only intermittently since 1961, and I regretted that. Face it, I thought. His murder killed a part of you.

Yet I knew if I pursued this, I was putting myself at risk. If I threatened Merle with exposure I would give her a reason for killing me. Or having me killed.

These were the thoughts I grappled with next day. They

made me sick with self-disgust because I had discovered I was a coward. I was scared to do any more about my suspicions. I despised myself.

So I became a tourist again, instead of a snoop. I lounged by the hotel pool in the morning and later took a trip to the coral reef in a glass-bottomed boat. I spent an hour in the cemetery. Morbid, you may think, but the gravestones are on the tourist trail. I found the famous epitaph "*I told you I was sick.*" It didn't seem funny when I saw it.

Late in the afternoon, I had a quiet drink in one of the smaller bars on Duval Street watching the movement of people towards Mallory Square. There's a tradition in Key West that people converge on the dock to celebrate the sunset. When I'd finished my drink, I joined them.

I didn't expect to meet Merle there. As a resident, she'd regard the sunset spectacle as a sideshow for tourists. Even so, as I sidled through the good-natured crowd I caught myself looking more than once at women who resembled her and the men they were with. I still wanted keenly to catch a glimpse of Mr Finch, the new husband.

The sky became pastel blue and the sun dipped towards the sea, becoming ever more red. The heads of some of the crowd were in silhouette. At one end a tightrope was slung between tripod posts and the performer was teasing his audience, keeping *them* in suspense with patter and juggling. I ambled on, past a guitarist and a dog-trainer. Ahead, someone else had drawn a fair crowd. A fire-eater, I guessed. There's something hypnotic about the sight of a flame, particularly in the fading light. But I decided the aerialist would be better value and I turned back. I was actually retracing my steps when I heard a scratchy sound that froze my blood, an old 78 record of a band playing some song from way back. It was coming from behind the crowd at the end.

I returned, fast.

I couldn't see for the tightly packed people. I circled the crowd in frustration while that infernal tune blared out. Unable to contain my feelings I scythed through the crowd saying, "I'm sorry, I have to get through"—until I had a view.

Danny was wowing them in his straw hat, blazer and flannels, hoofing it just as smoothly as he had in the old days. Far from dead, he had a better colour than most of his audience. The old gramophone was behind him on the ledge, grinding out "Let's Face the Music."

He saw me and winked.

I stared back, stunned. Maybe I should have rejoiced, but I'd grieved for this fraudster. I was more angry than relieved. It was a kind of betrayal.

Coward that I am, afterwards, when the sun had set and the crowds had dispersed I sat tamely with Danny on a ledge of the sea wall at the south end of the dock, our backs to the sea. He had a six-pack of Coors that he systematically emptied. Dancing, he explained, was thirsty work. He offered me some, and I declined.

"Merle told me she met you," he admitted. "She didn't want me to come out tonight, but I'm a performer, damnit. The show goes on. She doesn't understand that you and I go back a long way. You wouldn't blow the whistle on your old RAF buddy."

I didn't rise to that. "You've played some cool poker hands in your time, Danny, but this beats everything. I don't know how you managed it."

He grinned. "No problem. My stepbrother Ben is my doctor. He signed the death certificate. Merle picked up the life insurance and here we are—Mr and Mrs Finch. The fake passports cost us a packet, but we could afford them. Isn't this a great place to retire?"

"But there was a funeral."

"That didn't cost much."

"Too true."

"A lot of them were in on this," he confessed. "My cousin Jerry runs an undertaking business in the next village. He supplied the coffin."

"And a corpse?" I said, appalled.

"A couple of sandbags."

"You're a prize bastard, Danny Fox."

He chuckled at that. "Aren't I just? And the prize is in the bank."

"What you did is sick."

"Oh, come on," he said. "Who loses out? Only the insurance company. I had to pay huge premiums."

"There were people in that church who genuinely grieved for you."

"Horseshit."

That hurt. "I grieved."

"Jesus—what for?" His eyebrows jutted in genuine puzzlement.

I started to say, "If you don't remember—"

Danny cut me off with, "All that was thirty years ago. And then it was only—"

"Night exercises," I completed the statement for him.

"What?"

"Night exercises. That's what you thought of me, didn't you?" I stood up and faced him. "Admit it. Say it to my face, you skunk."

There was a pause. The night had virtually closed in. Danny up-ended his last can of beer. "All right, if that's what you heard from Merle, it must be true." He laughed. "Let's face it, Susan—that's what you were. P.O. didn't stand for Pilot Officer in your case, it stood for pushover."

I said, "That's unbelievably cruel."

Unmoved, Danny told me, "If you really want to know, I couldn't even remember your name that day we met in Brighton. I remembered your car, though."

That was one injury too many—even for a coward like me. The precious flame I'd guarded for thirty years was out. Our relationship had been the one experience in my life that I thought I could call truly romantic. Nothing since had compared to it. Danny had made me feel beautiful, desired, a woman fulfilled.

He knew the pain he had just inflicted. He *must* have known.

"Danny."

"Yes?" He looked up.

By that time Mallory Dock was deserted except for us. The water there is deep enough to moor a cruise liner.

The body of the middle-aged male washed up on Key West Bight a week or so later was identified as that of the man who sometimes danced on the dock at sunset. Nobody knew his name and nobody claimed the body for burial.

Quiet Please—
We're Rolling

A naked man on a tropical beach was chasing a small white dog that had just run off with his swimming trunks. The scene was shot from the rear. Once in a while, a bare bum is acceptable for early evening viewing.

Albert Challis, in his bedsit in Reading, reached for another can of lager, his eyes never leaving the screen of the small portable TV.

"Jesus! I don't know how they get away with this. It's bloody obvious most of it is faked."

His wife Karen continued mending the jumper on her lap, oblivious to Albert's ranting. She didn't enjoy the programme, and she had a long evening in prospect, repairing clothes. There was no escape from the TV when you lived in a bedsit.

Albert continued, after a belch, "When this show first went out, I reckon most of the clips were genuine. Then they started offering a few hundred quid for new material. Stands to reason people are going to fake the incidents. They set up someone making a fool of himself, roll the camera and cash in."

He watched in cynical expectation as a grey man in a

grey room began painting a door frame. A second later the door opened and the hapless decorator was dowsed in red.

"Well, knock me down with a feather," said Albert with heavy sarcasm. "I never saw that one coming. It's like I say, Karen. The whole thing's a set-up."

Karen folded the jumper and placed it on her 'done' pile, then turned her attention to a black woollen sock. It was one of Albert's, the survivor of a pair he had worn so proudly on their wedding day, eighteen years ago. Now it contained as much darning wool as original thread, but Albert insisted it wasn't ready for the rag-box yet.

On the screen a well-dressed woman in a stable yard started walking beside the half-doors where the horses were kept.

"Ay up!" said Albert. "Watch what happens to her big straw hat. There it goes!"

Sure enough, a horse's head appeared suddenly from one of the stables and got the woman's hat between its teeth and whipped it off her head and out of reach.

"I bet they rehearsed it three times."

Karen had looked up and watched the clip, prompted by Albert's "Ay up!" "If they did," she said, "they must have got through more than one hat. It's very destructive. I've never had a hat as nice as that."

Albert said, "It seems to me all you have to do is buy one of these bloody camcorders and the money's yours. They'll take anything, slipping on some ice, falling into a pond, being hit on the head by a football, any bloody thing. You could make one a week, I reckon. Shoot it on Saturday, send it to the television people on the Monday, and, bingo, the cheque arrives on Wednesday. We could live like kings on that sort of money, Karen."

Karen looked down at her darning again. "Well why not, if it's so simple? Why not get one of those cameras and try it?"

Albert had no immediate answer. He placed his can on the aged carpet and folded both arms across his ample beer-belly. The best he could manage in response was a smile that was meant to be superior.

Karen said, "You're all mouth and trousers, Albert Challis. You say it's all a con, but you don't have the bottle to prove it."

Albert found his voice. "I'm not sure I heard you correctly, my sweet," he said. "You did just suggest buying one of those camcorders, didn't you? When was the last time you looked in the bloody shop window? Have you any idea of the price of those things?"

Karen shook her head. They didn't have the sort of money most other people seemed to have. Nothing in their household had been bought new. They got it all secondhand. Whatever broke, burst or wore out had to be repaired.

"They cost a bloody fortune, woman," Albert ranted. "Hundreds of pounds. Can you imagine that, a little piece of black plastic costing five hundred quid?"

Karen shook her head, returning to the rhythmical comfort of needle and thread.

Albert finished his lager, watching a fat woman being chased across a field by a goat while the studio audience guffawed. "The point is," he said in support of his apparent caution, "I'm not prepared to splash out five hundred on a camcorder when we only stand to make two hundred and fifty back."

"But you just said you could make one a week and we could live like royalty," Karen reminded him. "Soon as I call your bluff, you back off."

Albert shot her a filthy look. "Don't you provoke me."

"It's not as if we haven't got the money," Karen persisted. "We must have more than five hundred in the bank."

"Never you mind what we have or haven't got in the bank, Karen."

"I do mind," she said. "It's mine as much as yours. I work to keep us going, same as you. The cooking, the cleaning, the mending. I think we ought to have a joint account and then I'd know how much we're worth."

"You'd spend it in a week," said Albert. "Look, if anything happened to me, God forbid, that money goes to you, right? All my worldly goods. Satisfied?"

The programme was coming to an end. The grinning host was saying, ". . . be sure to keep your home-movie clips coming in, because you could be the winner of our clip of the series prize, and that's worth a cool ten thousand pounds."

"Ten grand!" said Albert, deeply impressed. "Now that might be worth lashing out for. The clip of the series. We'd have to think of something really brilliant. Get me a pen and paper, quick. I'm taking down the address."

In bed, Karen was trying her best to sleep, drawing the thin blankets tightly around her, thinking of continental quilts, double glazing and central heating. She wondered how much they really had in that bank account.

Albert's voice broke into her fantasies. "It would have to be a really great caper. Something completely fantastic. They wouldn't give the money for one more silly kid messing about with a hosepipe."

Karen said, "Are you still on about that programme?"

"I'm on about ten grand."

There was an interval of silence before Karen spoke again.

"It would have to be believable."

"What do you mean?"

She raised herself onto her elbows, any hope of sleep impossible as long as Albert was preoccupied with the big prize. "Well," she said, "when you see most of those clips, the situation is just unreal. You couldn't believe in it."

The bed creaked and Albert rolled towards her. "Go on. I'm listening."

"Tonight, for instance," Karen said. "The chap who ended covered in paint. You yourself said it was probably all set up for the programme. I mean, who would want to film a door being painted?"

Albert clutched her arm. "You've hit the nail on the head. It's hardly a prime home-movie subject."

Karen explained, "That's why the ones they show at weddings work so well. You know, when they can't get the knife into the cake and they knock it off the stand. Or a breeze gets under the bride's gown and lifts it up to her waist. Stuff like that. People accept them as genuine accidents because a wedding is the place where you take your video camera."

"But you can't mess up someone's wedding just to get a laugh on video," Albert said, misreading the plot.

"That's just an example," said Karen. "All I'm telling you is that to win the big prize you'd have to find a situation when it would be perfectly normal to be filming. Then it looks genuine, and it's funnier, too."

Albert pondered the matter further. "Weddings, kiddies' parties, barbecues, village fetes. Where else do people take these little cameras?"

"Holidays," Karen dreamily replied. She yawned. "Night, night." She turned over, trying to find a comfortable spot between the thinly-covered mattress springs.

Albert's eyes were gleaming in the dark. He reached out and fondled Karen's rump. "You're brilliant."

"Shove off," she said, pushing his hand away.

"What I have, I hold," said Albert, replacing it. "You and I are going to take a holiday, my sweet. A caravan holiday."

"A *caravan*, did you say?"

"And I know where to get one. That bloke across the street who keeps it on his drive."

"Mr Tinker? He wouldn't let us borrow his caravan."

"I bet he will. He doesn't use it himself. Since the divorce, it's been stuck on that drive for two years. He'll be glad to be rid of it."

"Rid of it?" said Karen, failing to understand.

"We'll be doing him a favour," said Albert. "What does he want with a caravan? He'll make a few quid on the insurance. I'll speak to him tomorrow."

When Albert returned from his chat with Joe Tinker, he was practically turning cartwheels of joy. "He couldn't be more helpful," he told Karen. "Like I said, he's got no more use for the caravan. We're welcome to do just whatever we like with it."

"Take it on holiday?"

"We're doing him a favour," said Albert. "He won't have to park his car on the street any more. But that isn't all. I told him what this is about."

"You told him?" said Karen, horrified.

"Everything. To get his co-operation," said Albert. "He's seen the programme and he thinks the same as us. He says this is one hell of a stunt and he reckons we can't fail to win the big money. I've told him I'll give him a couple of hundred if we do. Fair enough, eh?"

"I suppose so," said Karen, "but can we trust him to stay quiet about it?"

"That's why he gets a cut. He's part of the conspiracy, then," said Albert. "But I haven't told you the best part. Joe Tinker also owns a camcorder. Yes, I'm not kidding. He's going to lend it to us for nothing. For nothing, Karen! What's more, he'll show you how to use it."

"Me?" said Karen.

"Unless you want to be making an idiot of yourself on television, you've got to be holding the camera, pointing it at me. And it's got to be done properly. Good focusing. No shaking. You only get one take, remember. It's got to be right first time, and it's got to be up to professional standard to win the ten grand."

She said nervously, "I don't think I can do it, Albert."

"Course you can! They're simple, these camcorders, dead simple. I told Joe you'll be over for some instruction this afternoon. He's a good bloke, and he fancies you anyway. He'll give you all the confidence in the world."

"What is this stunt, anyway?" said Karen.

"We take a holiday, like I said, towing Joe's caravan."

"Where to?"

"Some remote part of Wales. I'm going to study the map this afternoon while you're learning to be an ace camerawoman. If you get your certificate of competence we can drive down there next Saturday for the shoot."

"The shoot?"

"Of the film," Albert explained. "Get with it, love. We're shooting a film, remember? Like I say, we hook the caravan to my old Cortina. Joe's lending me his towbar as well. He's great."

"Is it strong enough?"

"The towbar?"

"Your car. Those caravans are big things to tow."

"No problem," said Albert. "We can take it gently, just tootling along. We'll be stopping every few miles filming bits and pieces of our journey."

"What for?"

Albert sighed. Everything always had to be explained to Karen. "Because it has to look like we're on a proper holiday. We need about twenty minutes of boring holiday stuff to divert suspicion from our real intentions. Can't you see how phony it will look if the only thing on the tape is the caravan going over the cliff?"

Karen gasped in horror. "Over the cliff? Mr Tinker's caravan?"

Albert smiled. "With only the seagulls as witnesses—apart from the camera and fifteen million viewers."

"It's insane!"

"That's why it's going to win ten grand. What a spectacle! I'm going to look at the Ordnance Survey and find a bit of the coast with a gentle slope leading to the cliff edge, and a good long drop to the rocks below. We park the caravan thirty yards up the slope. That way I have time to get out."

"Get out?"

"Before it rolls over. It's going to be sensational. You'll be outside filming the scenery from the cliff top. You pan around to me at the window of the caravan. I'll hold up a bit of metal and say, 'What's this, love?' The caravan will start to move. I'll shout something the TV people will have to bleep out—the audience always loves that—then I leap from the door holding the broken hand-brake of the caravan, to watch the thing roll over the edge." He laughed out loud and raised his arms like a boxer who has just heard his opponent counted out.

"It's so dangerous," said Karen. "I mean, it's a tremendous idea, but . . ."

Albert brushed the objection aside. "No risk at all," he said. "If you're nervous, we'll give the van fifty yards to roll, instead of thirty."

In the week that followed, Albert planned the "shoot," as he called it, with military precision. Having selected several possible clifftop sites, he drove down to Wales to make a decision on the most suitable. He found one on the Pembrokeshire Coast that was wonderfully remote, with a grassy slope leading straight to a two-hundred foot drop. In his spare moments he worked diligently on the script that he and Karen would have to follow, complete with stage directions.

"We only get one shot at this," he told her when he returned from scouting the locations. "It has to go like clockwork, while appearing totally unplanned. How are the lessons going?"

"All right," Karen said.

"You've been clocking in with Joe, have you, while I was away?"

She nodded.

"Mastered it yet?"

"I hope so."

"Hope isn't good enough," said Albert. "You've got to be certain. Are you going over to see him again?"

"This afternoon."

"Excellent. He's a good bloke, isn't he?"

"He's very good," said Karen, and she meant it.

"While you're in there, I'm going to do a bit of work on the old caravan. It could do with a clean. The smarter it looks, the better the effect."

So whilst Albert sponged and polished, preparing the caravan for its TV debut, Karen had more tuition from Joe. Really, as Joe explained, the camcorder was a simple machine that almost anyone could use, but if the attractive Mrs Challis wanted more practice with the thing, he was only too pleased to show her how to hold it. No woman had been inside his house since his wife had divorced him two years ago.

For her part, Karen was not displeased to feel Joe's arm around her shoulders steadying the camera from time to time. He was a most considerate man, and not bad looking, either. And he had double-glazing and central heating. "It seems a real shame that you're going to lose your caravan through this," she said.

"Not at all," said Joe cheerfully. "It's had its day. I've no more use for it. Besides, it's not in very good condition any more. The door has warped in the damp. You have to give it quite a tug to open it. Better mention that to Albert. A little grease around the sides will ease it."

Extremely early Saturday morning, when it was still dark and nobody was about, Albert went over to Joe's to attach the towbar. He'd arranged to collect Karen at the last minute. She sat in their front room with the lights off, mentally revising the instructions for the video camera. She had collected the camera from Joe after one last session of instruction the previous afternoon. Joe had been a tower of strength.

After what seemed like a couple of hours, Albert drew the caravan from its mooring and swung the car across the street. Karen climbed in, camcorder in hand.

"You'll do no filming in this light," Albert said tensely. "I don't know what you're holding it for. Chuck it on the back seat."

"It doesn't belong to us," said Karen.

Instead of "tootling along" as he'd promised, Albert drove fast for the first two hours. Two or three times Karen said she was nervous about the car, but he didn't slow down. Near the Welsh border, as dawn came up, she suggested a stop for filming. Albert said there would be opportunities later.

She reminded him of the reason for having some footage of other places as well as the clifftop, and he relented and let her film some sheep sheltering at the side of the road.

Albert looked at his watch. "I want to get on," he told her. "The light isn't so good in the middle of the day. It gets too bright."

"Joe said it doesn't matter what time of day you film with one of these."

"Will you shut up about Joe?"

As they neared their destination, Albert made a couple

of short stops to consult the map. The area was very remote.

About ten in the morning, the cliff came up on their left. Albert steered the car off the road and towed the caravan across the turf to the position he'd selected. He secured the brake on the caravan, uncoupled the car and drove back to a point near the road. They had a good view for miles around and no one was in sight.

"Smell it, love?" said Albert.

"The sea air?" said Karen.

"Money, stupid. Ten bloody grand."

"It's a good thing there's no wind," Karen pointed out as they walked towards the caravan. "This should be good for sound."

"You talk like you work for the BBC."

Albert walked towards the cliff edge and peered over. "Perfect," he enthused. "The tide's in. There's a thumping great drop, and it's going to get smashed to little bits and washed away and turn to driftwood." He came back to where Karen was standing with the camcorder. "Want to run over your lines?"

"It's all right," she said nervously. "Let's get on with it."

"Make sure it's working first."

She switched on and checked the battery level for the umpteenth time. She took some footage of Albert standing with his back to the cliff edge and they played it back through the eyepiece to check. The clarity was wonderful.

Albert seemed to be getting his confidence back. "Isn't it just like I promised? The gentle grassy slope, the impressive visual panorama, the sheer bloody suspense of the thing? And just look at that caravan!"

"Like ten thousand grand," she said, admiring the polished chrome and freshly-cleaned surface.

Albert walked her to her position. "Now you do know what to do?"

She nodded.

"And what to say?"

"Mm."

"Let's get on with it, then."

She watched him walk to the caravan. He had some difficulty opening the door, but he managed it at the second attempt, climbed inside, slammed the door and took his place by the window, opening it wide.

"Can you hear me all right?"

"Perfectly, Albert."

"Are we ready to roll, then?"

"Yes."

"Remember what I said. Establish the shot with a view of that cliff to your left, showing just how big the drop is, then pan around slowly along the cliff edge and across the grass to me. Right?"

"Right."

"Start the camcorder now. Action."

Heart thumping, Karen pressed the red *record* button, swinging slowly around to encompass the impressive-looking cliff. She didn't care any more that her hands were shaking. She watched the grass in the lens, then the white gleam of the caravan, then Albert at the window.

True to his "script," he held up a piece of metal. The caravan lurched on its mooring feet and for a second, Karen feared that it wasn't going to move.

Albert spoke his words: "Do you know what this is, love?"

The caravan began to roll.

"It's the brake, Albert! What is it doing in your hand? Get out—the van's moving!"

"Bloody hell!"

She saw Albert move fast towards the door and waited for the panic to set in for real.

Thirty yards to the edge.

She screamed his name as loudly as possible, mainly

to obscure his shouting. She had stopped filming, of course.

The caravan moved sedately on its way.

He was desperately trying to open the jammed caravan door. How many times had Joe stressed to her that she should tell Albert to grease the edges? Not once had she considered passing on the information. She wanted Albert to die.

Twenty yards to go, and it was picking up a little speed.

The worst thing would be finding a phone in this God-forsaken place. The closest must be miles away. Everything else would be simple. A few tears for the police. Then hand over the tape. "It must be all on here, officer. It's been the most awful accident."

Karen continued to scream, thinking of her future with Joe Tinker with his double-glazing and his central heating and his modern fully-sprung bed with the continental quilt.

Ten yards.

Five.

A moment before the caravan disappeared from view, the caravan door burst open, Albert flung himself out and hit the turf a yard from the edge. He had survived.

Karen was devastated. She flung down the camcorder and stamped her foot.

Fortunately, Albert was too shaken to notice. He still lay face down, panting.

Eventually she drew herself together and went to him. She could probably have pushed him over, he was so near, but she couldn't bring herself to do it. That would be too direct, a hands-on murder.

Albert said, "That was a bloody near thing."

"What went wrong?" said Karen as innocently as she was able.

"Couldn't get the bloody door open. I knew it was difficult. Found that out when I was cleaning the thing. Put some grease on it yesterday, but it wasn't enough, obviously. Ended up kicking my way out." He got to his feet. "Look at me. I'm shaking like a leaf."

Karen said, "Let's get you to the car."

"Where's the camera?"

"Oh, I dropped it over there," she said. "I'm not sure how much I got. God, I was frightened!"

"Doesn't matter, love," said Albert with unusual tenderness. "We can't use the video anyway."

"Why not?"

"Evidence. If they ever find anything at the bottom of that cliff and come knocking on our door, the last thing we want is a bloody video of the event."

She frowned. "They could only find the caravan."

Albert was shaking his head. "There's something else. With luck, the sea will take care of it."

"What on earth are you talking about?"

"Bloody Joe Tinker. When I went in to see him this morning, he said he wanted a half-share of the profits. *Five grand!* You know me, love. Mean as hell. I lashed out. Hit the bleeder against the kitchen stove and cracked his skull. Killed him outright. What could I do but shove him into his own bloody caravan and bring him down here for disposal?"

"Oh, God, no!" wailed Karen.

"Don't shed tears over him," said Albert. "Didn't you ever notice he fancied you something rotten, the jerk? Like I told you the other night, what I have, I hold."

Wayzgoose

A slight, worried woman in a leather jacket walked into Bath police station.

The desk sergeant eyed her through the protective glass. "Yes, ma'am?"

"Can I speak to someone?"

"You're speaking to me, ma'am."

"Someone senior."

The sergeant had been dealing with the public across this desk for twelve years. "I'm the best on offer."

Unamused, the woman waited. Her hair was dark and short, shaped to her head. She wore no make-up.

The sergeant coaxed her, "Why don't you give me some idea what it's about?"

"I just killed my husband."

The sergeant bent closer to the glass. "You what?"

"I came in to confess."

"Hang about, ma'am. Where did this happen?"

"At home. 32, Collinson Road."

"He's there now?"

"His body is."

"Collinson Road. I ought to know it."

"Twerton."

The sergeant gestured to a woman police officer behind him and told her to get a response car out to Twerton. Then he asked the woman, "What's your name, ma'am?"

"Trish Noble."

"Trish for Patricia?"

"Yes"

"And your husband's name?"

"Glenn."

"What happened, Mrs Noble?"

"He was in a drunken stupor at four in the afternoon when I came in from work, so I was that mad that I threw a teapot at him. Cracked him on the head. It killed him. Is that murder? Will I go to prison?"

"A china teapot?"

"Half full of tea. I've always had this wicked temper."

"Are you sure he's dead? Maybe you only stunned him."

She shook her head. "He's gone all right. I'm a ward sister, and I know."

"A *nurse?*"

"Shocking, isn't it?"

"You'd better come in and sit down," said the sergeant. "Go to the door on your right. Someone will see you right away."

The someone was Superintendent Peter Diamond, the senior detective on duty that afternoon. Diamond was head of the murder squad and this looked like a domestic incident, but as homicide had apparently occurred, he was in duty bound to take an interest. He made quite a courtesy of pulling forward a low, upholstered chair for the woman, then spoilt the effect by seating himself in another with a bump as his knees refused his buttocks a dignified descent. He had a low centre of gravity. A rugby forward in years past, he was better built now for anchorman in a tug-of-war team. "You're a nurse, I understand, Mrs Noble?"

"Sister on one of the orthopaedic wards."

"Locally?"

"The Royal United."

"So . . . ?"

"I came off duty and when I got home Glenn—that's my husband—was the worse for liquor."

"You mean drunk?"

"Whatever you want to call it." She closed her eyes, as if that might shut out the memory.

Mild as milk, Diamond said, "You came in from work and saw him where?"

"In the kitchen."

"Did you have words?"

"He wasn't capable of words. I saw red. That's the way I am. I picked up the teapot—"

"You'd made tea?"

"No. I'd only just come in."

"So he'd made tea?"

"No, it was still on the table from breakfast, half-full, really heavy. It's a family sized pot. I picked it up and swung it at him. Hit him smack on the forehead. The pot smashed. There was tea all over his face and chest. He collapsed. First, I thought it was the drink. I couldn't believe I'd hit him that hard. He'd stopped breathing. I could get nothing from his pulse. I lay him out on the floor and tried mouth-to-mouth, but it was no good."

She conveyed a vivid picture, the more spectacular considering what a scrap she was. She spoke calmly, her pale blue eyes scarcely blinking. I wouldn't mind mouth-to-mouth from you, sister, Diamond incorrectly thought.

The door behind him opened and someone looked in, a sergeant. "A word in your ear, sir."

Diamond wasn't getting out of that chair. He put a thumb and forefinger to the lobe of his right ear.

The sergeant bent over and muttered, "Report just in from the house, sir. Body in the kitchen confirmed."

Diamond nodded and asked Mrs Noble, "You said this happened at four in the afternoon?"

"Yes."

"It's twenty to six now."

"Is it?"

"Quite a long time since it happened."

"I've been walking the streets, getting a grip on myself."

"You're doing OK," Diamond told her, and meant it. She was a nurse and used to containing her feelings, but this was a stern test. He admired her self-control and he was inclined to believe her story, even if it had strange features. "You didn't think of phoning us?"

"I'm here, aren't I?"

"Earlier, I mean. When it happened."

"No point. He was beyond help."

He offered her a hot drink for the shock—and just stopped short of mentioning tea.

She declined.

"You said you saw red at finding him drunk," he recapped.

Her face tensed. "I disapprove of drink."

"Was he in work?"

She shook her head. "He was one of those printers laid off from Regency Press a year ago."

"Was he still unemployed?"

"Yes."

"Depressed?"

"Certainly not."

"It must have been difficult managing after he lost his job," Diamond said, giving her the chance to say *something* in favour of her dead husband.

"Not at all. He got good redundancy terms. And I'm earning as well."

"I meant perhaps he was drowning his sorrows?"

"What sorrows?"

"This afternoon bout was exceptional?"

"Very."

"Which was what upset you?"

She gave a nod. "It's against my religion."

Diamond treated the statement as if she were one of those earnest people in suits who knock on doors and ask whether you agree that God's message has relevance in today's world. He ignored it. "You're a nurse, Mrs Noble, and I imagine you're trained to spot the symptoms of heavy drinking, so I don't want you to be insulted by this question. What made you decide that your husband was drunk?"

"The state of him. He was slumped in a chair, his eyes were glazed, he couldn't put two words together. And the brandy bottle was on the table in front of him. The brandy he was given as a leaving present. He promised me he'd got rid of it."

"Didn't he like brandy?"

"It's of the devil."

"Had he drunk from the bottle?"

"Isn't that obvious?"

"Had he ever used drugs in any form?"

She frowned. "Alcohol is a drug."

"You know what I mean, Mrs Noble."

"And I've seen plenty of drug-users," she riposted. "I know what to look for."

"No question of drugs?"

"No question."

"Did he look for another position after the printing came to a stop?"

"There wasn't much point. All the local firms were laying people off."

"So how did he spend the days?"

"Don't ask me. Walks in the park. Television. Have you ever been out of work?"

He nodded. "And my wife couldn't find a job either."

"Then you ought to know."

"Unemployment hits people in different ways. I'm trying to understand how it affected your husband."

"You're not," she said bluntly. "You're trying to find out if I murdered him. That's your job."

Diamond didn't deny it.

"It wasn't deliberate." She raised her chin defiantly. "I wouldn't dream of killing him. Glenn and I were married eleven years. We had fights. Of course we had fights, with my temper. That's my personal demon—my temper. I threw things. Mostly I missed. He could duck when he was sober." Her lips twitched into a sad smile. "We always made up. Some of the best times we had were making up after a fight."

Trish Noble's candour was touching. Diamond sympathised with her. There was little more he could achieve. "We'll need a statement, Mrs Noble, a written one, I mean. Then you can go. Do you have someone you can stay with? Family, a friend?"

"Can't I go home?"

"Our people are going to be in the house for some time. You'd be better off somewhere else."

She told him she had a sister in Trowbridge. Diamond offered to make the call, but Trish Noble said she'd rather break the news herself.

2

To most of the staff at Manvers Street Police Station this room on the top floor was known as the eagle's nest. John Farr-Jones, the Chief Constable, greeted Diamond, who had arrived for a meeting of the high fliers. "You're looking fit, Peter."

"I used the lift."

"What's it like to be back in harness?"

The big detective gave him a pained look and said, "I gave up wearing harness when I was two years old." He took his place in a leather armchair and nodded to a chief inspector he scarcely knew. The wholesale changes of personnel in the couple of years he had been away had to be symptomatic of something.

"Mr Diamond's problem is that we haven't had a juicy murder since he was reinstated," Farr-Jones told the rest of the room. Since it was thanks to Farr-Jones's recommendation that Diamond had got his job back, he may have felt entitled to rib the man a little. But really the recommendation had been little more than a rubber stamp. In October 1994, a dire emergency had poleaxed Avon and Somerset Constabulary. The daughter of the Assistant Chief Constable had been taken hostage and her captor had insisted on dealing only with Diamond. The old rogue elephant, boisterous as ever, was now back among the herd.

"What about this teapot killing?" Farr-Jones persisted. "Can't you get anything out of that?"

There were smiles all round.

John Wigfull unwisely joked, "A teabag?" There was a history of bad feeling between Wigfull and Diamond. Many a time Diamond had seriously contemplated grabbing the two ends of Wigfull's ridiculously overgrown moustache and seeing if he could knot them under his chin. Now that Diamond was back, Wigfull had been ousted as head of the murder squad and handed a less glamorous portfolio as head of CID operations. He would use every chance to point to Diamond's failings.

Tom Ray, the Chief Constable's staff officer, hadn't heard about the teapot killing, so Diamond, wholly against his inclination, was obliged to give a summary of the incident.

When he had finished, it was rather like being in a staff college seminar. Someone had to suggest how the law should deal with it.

"Manslaughter?" Ray ventured, more in politeness than anything else.

"No chance," growled Diamond.

Wigfull, who knew *Butterworth's Police Law* like some people know the Bible, seized the moment to shine. "Hold on. As I remember, there are four elements necessary to secure a manslaughter conviction. First, there must be an unlawful act. That's beyond doubt."

"Assault with a teapot," contributed Ray.

"Right. A half-full teapot. Second, the act has to be dangerous, in that any sober and reasonable person would recognize it could do harm."

"Clocking a fellow with a teapot is dangerous," Ray agreed, filling a role as chorus to Wigfull.

"Third, the act must be a cause of the death."

"Well, he didn't die of old age."

"And finally, it must be intentional. There's no question she meant to strike him."

"No question," Ray echoed him.

Diamond said flatly, "It was a sudden death."

"We can't argue with that, Peter," said Wigfull, and got a laugh.

"I'm reporting it to the coroner. It's going in as an occurrence report."

Wigfull said, "I think you should do a process report to the CPS."

"Bollocks."

"It would be up to them whether to prosecute," Wigfull pointed out.

Diamond's patience was short at the best of times and it was even shorter when he was on shaky ground. He stabbed a finger at Wigfull. "Don't you lecture me on the

CPS. I refuse to dump on this woman. She's a nurse, for pity's sake. She walked all the way here from Twerton and reported what she'd done. If the coroner wants to refer it, so be it. He won't have my support."

Ray asked, "Have you been out to Twerton yourself?"

"I haven't had a chance, have I?" said Diamond. "I'm attending a meeting, in case anyone hadn't noticed. Julie is out there."

"Inspector Hargreaves?" said Farr-Jones. "Is that wise? She isn't so experienced as some of your other people."

"She was my choice for this, sir." He didn't want to get into an argument over Julie's capability, or his right to delegate duties, but if necessary he would.

He was first out of the meeting, muttering sulphurous things about John Wigfull, Farr-Jones and the whole boiling lot of them. He stomped downstairs to his office to collect his raincoat and trilby. He'd had more than enough of the job for that day.

Someone got up as he entered the room, a stocky, middle-aged man with black-framed bifocals. Dr Jack Merlin, the forensic pathologist. "What's up?" Merlin said. "You're looking even more stroppy than usual."

"Don't ask."

"Have you got a few minutes?"

"I was about to leave," said Diamond.

"Before you do, old friend, I'd like a quiet word. Why don't you shut that door?"

The "old friend" alerted Diamond like nothing else. His dealings with Merlin—over upwards of a dozen corpses in various states of decomposition—were based on mutual respect. Jack was the best reader of human remains in Britain. But he rarely, if ever, expressed much in the way of sentiment. Diamond grabbed the door-handle and pulled it shut.

"This one at Collinson Road, Twerton," said Merlin.

"The man hit with a teapot."

"Yes?"

"You don't mind me asking, I hope. Did you visit the scene yourself?"

Diamond shrugged. "I was tied up here. I sent one of my younger inspectors out."

"Good," said Merlin. "I didn't think you had."

"Something wrong?"

"You interviewed the wife, I believe?"

"Yes."

"She claimed to have topped him with a teapot?"

He nodded. "She's a ward sister at the RUH. Bit uptight, got religion rather badly, I think, which makes it harder for her."

Merlin fingered the lobe of his left ear. "The thing is, matey, I thought I should have a quiet word with you at this stage. Shan't know the cause of death until I've done the PM, of course, but . . ."

"Give it to me, Jack."

". . . a first inspection suggests that the victim suffered a couple of deep stab wounds."

"*Stab* wounds?"

"In the back."

Diamond swore.

"Not a lot of blood about," the pathologist added, "and he was lying face up, so I wouldn't be too critical of that young inspector, but it does have the signs of a suspicious death."

3

Collinson Road, Twerton, backs on to Brunel's Great Western Railway a mile or so west of the centre of Bath. Diamond drove into a narrow street of Victorian terraced housing, the brickwork blackened by all those locomotives steaming by in years past. Several of the facades had since been cleaned up and gentrified with plastic guttering, picture windows and varnished oak front doors with brass fittings, but Number 32 was resolutely unaltered, sooty and unobtrusive behind an overgrown privet hedge and a small, neglected strip of garden. The door stood open. The Scenes of Crime Officers had received Diamond's urgent instruction to step up the scale of their work and were still inside. Most of them knew him from years back and as he went in he had to put up with some good-natured chaffing over his intentions. It was well known that he'd been moodily waiting for a murder to fall in his lap.

The team had finished its work downstairs, so he went through the hallway with the senior man, Derek Bignal, and looked inside the kitchen. Almost everything portable had been removed for inspection by the lab. Strips of adhesive tape marked the positions of the table and chairs and the outline of the body.

Diamond asked if the murder weapon had been found.

"Who knows?" said Bignal with a shrug, practically causing paranoia in Peter Diamond so soon after his conversation with Merlin, the laid-back pathologist. "We made a collection of kitchen knives. See the magnetic strip attached to the wall over the draining-board? They were all lined up there, ready to grab. Some of them had blades that could have done the business."

"No other knife in the sink, or lying on the floor?"

"With blood and prints all over it? You want it easy, Mr Diamond."

He tried visualising the scene, which was no simple task with the furniture missing. According to her story, Trish Noble had returned from the hospital at four in the afternoon. If she was speaking the truth she must have let herself in at the front door, stepped through the hallway and found her husband seated facing her at the small table against the wall to her left as she entered the kitchen. In a fit of anger, believing him to be drunk, rather than mortally injured, she would have taken a couple of steps towards the table, where the teapot was, snatched it up and hit him with it. He had fallen off to the right of the chair—her right—and lay on his back on the floor, where she had tried resuscitation. That, anyway, was her version. The taped outline of the body didn't conflict with what she had stated.

To Diamond's left was a fridge-freezer. The doors were decorated with postcards and photos. The shiny surfaces bore traces of powder, where they had been dusted for prints. Holiday snaps of Glenn Noble, deeply tanned, in shorts and sandals, his arms around the shoulders of his pretty, bikini-clad wife. More of Trish Noble in her nurse's uniform, giggling with friends. A sneaky shot of her taken in a bathroom, eyes wide in surprise, holding a towel against her breasts, evidently unaware that her right nipple wasn't covered. Surprising that a woman who claimed to be religious kept such a picture on her fridge door, Diamond mused, then decided that nurses must have a different perception of embarrassment. Another that took his attention was clearly taken on some seaside promenade. Glenn and an older, stocky man were giving piggyback rides to two women in swimsuits, one of them Trish—but it wasn't Glenn's back she was riding.

Diamond sighed. To study people's private snaps systematically like this was an invasion of privacy, an odious but necessary part of the job. He wasn't in the house to look for evidence. Others had already been through for that. He was getting a sense of how the couple had lived and what their relationship had been. Having thought what a liberty it was, he stripped every photo off the fridge door.

"What's a wayzgoose when it's at home?" he asked Bignal.

"Come again."

"A wayzgoose. This picture of the two couples horsing about on the seafront has a note on the back. Wayzgoose, 1993, Minehead."

"Is it a place?"

"Minehead is."

"Could it be the name of some game, do you think?"

"I doubt it."

He looked into the other rooms downstairs. One was clearly the living room, with two armchairs, a TV and video, a music centre and a low table stacked with newspapers. The Nobles read the *Daily Mirror* and possessed just about every recording Freddie Mercury had made. On the wall were a bullfight poster and an antique map of Somerset. He picked an expensive-looking art book from a shelf otherwise stacked with nursing magazines. "Who's Eugene Delacroix?"

"A French romantic painter," Bignal informed him.

Diamond flicked the pages over. "Doesn't seem to go with Freddie Mercury and the Mirror."

"There were also two coffee mugs on the table," Bignal told him. "By the look of them, they were left over from last night. They're going to the lab."

It was not vastly different from his own living room. He moved on. The front room was used as a workroom by the couple, for sewing, typing and storing household bills and bank statements. They had a joint account and seemed to be steadily in credit, which was better than the Diamonds managed.

In another ten minutes the team finished upstairs. No signs of violence there, they informed Diamond. The aggro seemed to have been confined to the kitchen.

He went to see for himself.

The Nobles favoured a rather lurid pink for their bedroom, slept in a standard size double bed and had a portable TV on the chest of drawers Glenn used for most of his clothes. Trish Noble had a wardrobe and a dressing table to herself. She was reading Catherine Cookson and the Bible and Glenn had been into one of the Flashman books. If the quantity and variety of condoms in Glenn's bedside cabinet was any guide, their sex life hadn't been subdued by Trish's religion.

The second bedroom contained a folding bed, an ironing board and various items the couple must have acquired and been unwilling to throw away, ranging from an old record-player to a dartboard with the wire half detached.

He glanced into the bathroom. Nothing caught his attention.

"What's in the back garden?" he asked Bignal.

"Plants, mostly."

"Don't push me, Derek. Have you been out there?"

"Personally, no."

"Has anyone thought of looking for a murder weapon, footprints, a means of escape?"

"Not systematically," Bignal admitted. "It was already dark when we got here."

"Not systematically," muttered Diamond with heavy sarcasm. "It backs onto the railway, doesn't it?"

"Yes."

"Tomorrow, early, I want a proper search made. In particular, I want to know if there are signs that anyone got in or out by way of the railway embankment."

Bignal's eyebrows peaked in surprise. "You think someone else is involved, as well as the wife?"

"That's the way they would have escaped."

"*They?*"

"He, she, they or nobody at all. Let's keep an open mind, shall we?"

4

Julie Hargreaves may have expected a roasting for having failed to notice the stab wounds, but she need not have troubled. Diamond was more interested in roasting Trish Noble. "She had the kid-glove treatment from me yesterday," he summed up as they drove out to Trowbridge. "Today she's got to be given a workover."

"Do you see her as the killer?"

"Do you?"

She paused for thought. "It would be unusual, a woman using a knife as a weapon. The teapot, I can believe—but why would she hit him with the teapot if she'd already stuck a knife in his back?"

"To finish him off."

"Ah."

"However, there could be a second person involved." Diamond casually tossed in some information he'd received that morning from the SOCOs combing the back garden at Twerton. "There's evidence that someone climbed over the fence to the railway embankment. Two slats are freshly splintered at the top."

"An intruder? Nothing was stolen."

"Yes, but if she had an admirer, for instance . . ."

Julie didn't buy the idea. "That's pretty unlikely, isn't it?"

"You mean with her religious convictions? I said 'admirer,' not 'lover'."

"No, I mean he wouldn't need to climb over the fence. She'd let him in. And they would have to be real thickos to stab the husband and then go down to the nick and report it."

He responded huffily, "I didn't say it was a conspiracy. Unrequited love, Julie. The admirer is obsessed with Trish. She's unattainable while her husband is alive, so this nutter breaks into the house and knifes him. Trish comes home and finds Glenn dying, but mistakenly thinks he's drunk."

"And bashes him with the teapot?"

"Exactly. I think she told the truth yesterday. By now she may have something else to tell us."

"I wonder," said Julie. "I find it difficult to believe in this crazy admirer."

Diamond said loftily, "You may understand better when you meet Trish Noble. She's on the side of the angels and bloody attractive. Dangerous combination."

"That would explain everything," murmured Julie in a bland tone. "Shall I organize house-to-house to find out if anyone was spotted on the railway embankment yesterday afternoon?"

"It's under way," he told her. "Two teams."

Trish Noble's sister lived in a semi-detached on a council estate north of Trowbridge. But it was the bloody attractive young widow herself who answered their knock. In jeans and a white tee-shirt, with the height and figure of a pre-teen schoolgirl, she looked too frail to use a knife on a chocolate cake, let alone a man. The hours since the killing had taken a toll. Her big eyes were red-lidded and they seemed to have sunk deeper into her skull. Julie must have wondered at Diamond's ideas of attractiveness.

He introduced her and said there were things he needed to ask. Trish calmly invited them in, explaining that she had the house to herself because her sister was at work. In a narrow sitting room, watched by two unwelcoming spaniels, Diamond took the best armchair and launched straight into the workover. "You didn't kill your husband with the teapot, Mrs Noble. He was stabbed in the back."

She frowned and stared.

Julie said, "Why don't you sit down?" She stood behind the second armchair until Trish Noble acted on the advice.

"Did you stab him?" Diamond asked.

Trish seemed to have difficulty taking in what she had just been told—or she was making a convincing show of being stunned by the news. She shook her head.

Diamond said, "If you'd like to explain how it happened, we're ready to listen."

She said, "Stabbed?"

"Twice, in the back."

"That's impossible. He was sitting in the kitchen."

"Your story."

"It's true! He was at the table when I got in. I've told you this."

"You didn't stab him yourself?"

"That's insulting."

"We'd like a clear answer, Mrs Noble."

She said vehemently, "No, I did not stab my own husband."

"That's clear, then." Diamond glanced across at Julie, who had found an upright chair by the sideboard. "Got that? She denies it."

Julie opened her notebook.

"If you didn't stab him yourself," Diamond plunged in again, "we've obviously got to look for someone who did. Was there anyone else in the house when you got home from the hospital?"

The tired eyes widened. "No one."

"You're sure? You can't be sure, can you? Let's take this in stages. Did you see anyone?"

"No. This is unbelievable."

"Or hear them?"

"No."

"Is there anyone else living in the house?"

"What do you mean—a lodger? No."

"Does anyone have a key?"

"What?"

"Some friend, perhaps?"

"We don't give keys to our friends."

"I'll tell you what I have in mind," Diamond offered. "If someone let himself into the house unknown to your husband, he could have taken him by surprise and stabbed him shortly before you came in."

"Who would do that?" she said, and there was a note of scorn in the voice. She was getting over the shock.

"Do you have a lover?"

She reddened, but that wasn't necessarily an admission. Almost anyone would have blushed at the question. She told him with a glare, "You should wash out your mouth."

"Would you like it rephrased?" Diamond said. "A boyfriend? A fancy man? A bit on the side? Come on, Mrs Noble, you work in a hospital. Life in the raw. I don't have to pick my words with you, do I?"

"I am a married woman—or was," she answered primly. "I took vows before the Lord."

"No need for a boyfriend?"

The look she gave him was her response and he was convinced by it. Moreover, he'd seen inside her husband's bedside drawer.

"In that case, we have to consider what used to be called unrequited love. To put it crudely, some nutter who fancies you. You see what I'm driving at, don't you? This man obsessed by you murders your husband to have you to himself."

She sighed like a scythe and said, "I can't listen to these serpent-words."

"No secret admirer you're aware of? Let's look at another possibility. Did your husband have any enemies?"

The change of tack brought a more measured response. "Glenn didn't have enemies."

"Then did he have friends? Encouraging him in bad habits, perhaps?"

She said, "I can do without your sarcasm."

"These are friends, presumably?" He took from his pocket the photo taken at Minehead, the piggyback picture. "Were these people in the printing trade?"

She snatched it possessively. "You were the one who stole them, then. My photos are personal."

"Who are the people?"

The resentment remained in her voice. "The Porterfields. Friends of ours. We had a day out with them."

"Is Mr Porterfield a printer?"

"No. Basil is a businessman. He sells car-parts."

"And the lady?"

"His wife Serena. She's an art teacher."

"That's Serena mounted on your husband's back?"

She gave him a cold stare. "That was for a silly photograph."

"At Minehead?"

"Yes."

"For a wayzgoose?"

She frowned. "I beg your pardon."

"Look on the back. My dictionary says that a wayzgoose is a works outing for those in a printing house. A silly photo at a wayzgoose makes sense to me."

She glanced at the words on the back of the photo and shrugged. "It doesn't make any to me. Basil and Serena had nothing to do with Glenn's job. Besides, he was already redundant when we went to Minehead. He'd been out of work for over a year."

"I noticed an art book in your living room. French painter."

"Delacroix?"

"Yes. Was that a gift from Mrs Porterfield?"

"No. Glenn bought it himself."

"So he was interested in art?"

"Only in Delacroix."

"Are the Porterfields local?"

"They live up by the golf course."

"What's the address?"

"I don't want them troubled. They've got nothing to do with this. They're decent people."

"In that case, they'll want to help me find your husband's killer."

She said openly, "I can't believe this is happening. I thought I killed him. I was sure of it."

If she is playing the innocent, Diamond thought, she's doing it with style. He tried to resist making up his mind. First impressions were so misleading. In his time he'd made more mistakes over women than King Henry the Eighth. And this one with her martyred eyes was taking the steam out of his workover.

"After you hit him with the teapot and he fell off the chair, what did you do? Tell me precisely."

"I went to him at once. I could tell from the way he fell that he was out cold when he hit the floor. I found he'd stopped breathing, so I tried to revive him. Tilted back his head and drew the chin upwards. I don't have to go through the drill, do I?"

"Mouth to mouth?"

"Of course."

"Think carefully. While you were doing it, did you hear any extraneous sounds?"

"What do you mean?"

"If anyone else was in the house, in that kitchen, even, they may have picked this moment to run out." It was a wily suggestion. He couldn't have handed her a better opportunity of shifting the suspicion to some mythical intruder.

She hesitated, then said, "I didn't notice a thing."

Innocent, or refusing to be drawn? He couldn't tell.

"After the resuscitation had no result, what did you do?"

She bit her lip. "It's difficult to remember. It's just a blur. I was deeply shocked."

"Did you stay in the kitchen?"

"For a bit, I think."

"You didn't go upstairs, or in the other rooms?"

"I don't think so. I was horrified by what I'd done. I got the shakes. I think I ran out of the front door and wandered up the street asking the Lord to forgive me. It took Him a long time to calm my troubled spirit. In the end I walked all the way to Bath to confess to you."

"Did you speak to anyone between leaving the house and coming to us?"

"No."

"See anyone you knew?"

"I wasn't noticing other people." She made it all sound plausible.

"If there was anyone," said Diamond, becoming reasonable in spite of his best efforts to be tough, "it would help us to account for your movements."

"I've told you my movements."

"And we only have your word for them."

"That was after he died. Why do you want to know what I was doing after he died?"

He declined to answer. "Is there anyone you can think of who ever threatened your husband?"

"No."

Julie looked up from her notes and said unexpectedly, "Was he seeing a woman?"

Trish Noble blinked twice and flicked nervously at her hair. "If he was . . ." she started to say, then stopped. "If he was, I'd be very surprised."

"The wife usually is," Diamond added, privately wishing he'd remembered to ask. Smart thinking on Julie's part. "Anyone you can think of who may have fancied him?"

"How would I know? Look, you're talking about the man I loved and married. He isn't in his grave yet. Do you have to be so cruel?"

Julie said, "You want us to find the person who stabbed him, don't you?"

She nodded.

"There is someone, isn't there?" said Julie.

"I don't know."

"But you had your suspicions?"

She looked down and fingered her wedding ring. Speaking in a low, scarcely audible voice, she said, "Sometimes he came home really late. I mean about two in the morning, or later. He was exhausted. Too tired for anything."

"Drunk?"

"No. I would have noticed."

"How long was this going on?"

"When it started, it was once every two months or so. Lately, it was about every ten days."

"Did you question him about it?"

"He snapped my head off when I did. Really told me to mind my own business. It made me think there might be someone, but I had no way of finding out. He didn't smell of scent, or anything."

Diamond told her to collect her coat.

She looked seriously worried. "Where are you taking me?"

"Home. Julie will take you home. I want you to look at the scene and tell Julie everything you remember."

"Aren't you going to be there?" A question that might have conveyed disappointment was actually spoken on a rising note of relief.

"I may come later." He turned to Julie. "On the way, you can drop me off at the hospital."

Trish's anxiety flooded in again. "The hospital? Do you mean the RUH? You don't have to talk to them. They can't tell you anything."

"It isn't about you," said Diamond. "It's another matter." And it wasn't about his weight problem either.

5

"Believe it or not, I didn't come here to admire your sewing," Diamond told Jack Merlin.

There was no reaction from the pathologist.

"May I see the other side?"

"Not *my* sewing. My assistant Rodney does the stitch-work." In the post-mortem room at the Royal United Hospital, Merlin had the advantage of familiar territory. No visitor was entirely comfortable in the mortuary. Attendance at autopsies is routinely expected of detectives on murder cases. Diamond ducked out whenever he could think up a plausible excuse. On this visit he arrived late. The gory stuff had already been got over. With only a sewn-up corpse to view, he was putting on a good show of self-composure, but it didn't run to treating these places like a second home.

The assistant Rodney stepped forward and helped Merlin turn the body of Glenn Noble. Two eye-shaped stab wounds were revealed.

Diamond's hands tightened behind his back. "Not much doubt about those."

Merlin watched him and said nothing.

"They don't look superficial, either."

Still nothing.

"I reckon they tell a story."

There was a long interval of silence before Diamond spoke again. "You're a helpful bugger, aren't you? You know I'm pig-ignorant, yet you're not going to help me out."

Merlin shot an amused look across the corpse and then relented. "This one to the right of the spine did the main damage. Penetrated the lung two inches above its basal margin."

Diamond bent closer to the body to examine the wounds. "Obviously you've cleaned him up."

"You don't get much external bleeding from stab wounds. There was a pint or so in the right pleural cavity."

"So was that what killed him?"

"It was a potentially fatal injury."

"The cause of death, in other words."

"The potential cause of death."

Diamond straightened up, frowning. "Am I missing something here?"

"I can't be specific as to the cause."

"With a couple of stab-wounds like this and massive internal bleeding? Come on, Jack. Give me a break."

Merlin said, "As I understand it, the wife admitted to you that she cracked him on the head with a teapot."

"I believe her. Somebody certainly smashed a teapot. His shirt-front was stained with tea, as I'm sure forensic will tell us in their own good time. Probably tell us if it was Brooke Bond or Tetley's and whether she warmed the pot."

"There's bruising here on the head, just above the hairline," Merlin confirmed.

"Look, what is this about the teapot? The man has two deep stab wounds."

"And a bruised cranium."

Diamond screwed his face into an anguished expression. "Are you telling me it's possible that the teapot actually finished him off?"

"It's an interesting question. I can't exclude the possibility of a fatal brain injury. Of course I'll examine the brain."

"Haven't you done that?"

"It has to be fixed and cut in sections for microscopic examination."

"How long will that take?"

"Three to four weeks."

"God help us." He complained because of his own

frustration. He knew Merlin would give him all the information he could as soon as it was available. He was the best.

"And even after I examine the brain, I may not have the answer."

"Oh, come on, Jack!"

"I mean it. I've examined people who died after blows to the head and I could find no perceptible damage to the brain. We don't know why it happens. Maybe the shock wave passing through the brain stem was sufficient to kill them."

"So even after four weeks, you may not have the answer?"

"I'm a pathologist, not an ace detective."

There was an interval of silence.

"Let me get one thing clear in my mind," said Diamond. "Is it possible that what Mrs Noble told me is true that he was still alive when she clobbered him?"

"Certainly."

"With stab wounds like this?"

"A victim of stabbing may survive for some time."

"How long?"

"How long is a piece of string?"

"Your middle name wouldn't be Prudence by any chance?"

Merlin smiled.

"A few seconds? A few minutes?"

"I couldn't possibly say."

"And how would he have appeared? Unsteady, like a drunk?"

"Your guess is as good as mine."

"A distressed drunk?"

"Distressed is probably right."

"Unable to speak?"

"That's possible. The knife cut through some of the

blood vessels and airways in the lung, so there was bleeding not only into the chest cavity but into the air passages. That would have affected his power of speech."

"You see what I'm getting at?" said Diamond.

Merlin grinned. "You're testing the woman's story. I was at the scene before you, remember," he rubbed it in. "I saw the brandy bottle on the table. But I'm not given to speculation, as you know."

"Jack, I could be making an arrest very soon. Someone entered that house and stabbed him. Not the wife. I'm convinced she's telling the truth."

"Do you have a suspect?"

"I'm getting close."

"I wouldn't get too close. If you nab them for murder at this stage, you could be torn to shreds by a good defence counsel. Mrs Noble admits that she clobbered her husband with the teapot. She may have killed him, stabbing or no stabbing."

6

It was a five minute drive, no more, from the hospital to the murder house in Collinson Road. Frustrated by his session with Jack Merlin, Diamond looked to Julie Hargreaves for some progress in the investigation. He had left her there with Trish Noble, ostensibly checking the contents to see if anything had been stolen. More importantly, she would have been working on drawing Trish out, putting her at her ease and gaining her confidence in the way that she did with women suspects almost without seeming to try. If there were secrets in the lives of the Nobles, Julie was best placed to unlock them.

When he looked in, the two women were waiting in that chintzy living room with the bullfight poster and the map of Somerset. The television was on and coffee and biscuits were on the table. There must be something wrong with my methods, Diamond thought. While I look at a dead body, my sidekick puts her feet up and watches the box.

"Am I interrupting?" he asked.

Julie looked up. "We were waiting for you."

"What are you watching—a kids' programme?"

"Actually we were looking out of the window at the SOCOs in the back garden." She reached for the remote control and switched off. "They look as if they're about to pack up. Would you like coffee?"

"Had a hospital one, thanks." In a paper cup from a machine and tasting of tomato soup, he might have added. He wouldn't want another drink for some time. He reached for the packet of chocolate digestives and helped himself. "What's the report, then? Anything missing?"

"Most of the furniture from my kitchen," Trish Noble said accusingly.

"That'll be the scenes of crime team," Diamond told her. "They must have left you a check-list somewhere. You'll get everything back eventually."

"They weren't the ones who pinched the photos from my fridge door."

He said smoothly, "You'll get them back." He reached for the art book he'd remarked on before and leafed through the pages. "Is anything of value missing? Money? Jewellery?"

Julie answered for her. "We checked. Everything seems to be there."

"Speaking of money," Diamond said to Trish as if she had brought up the subject herself, "we'll need to look at the bank account and your credit card statements. You do have a credit card? How are you placed financially? I'm not being nosy. We need to know." He knew, but he wanted to question her on the details.

"We're solvent," she answered without looking up.

He hadn't Julie's talent for easing out the information. "Your husband must have been given a lump sum when he was made redundant."

She only nodded, so he talked on.

"It seems generous at the time, but it soon goes, I dare say. Where do you keep the statements?"

"They should still be in the front room if your people haven't taken them away."

"Would you mind?" he asked her.

In the short interval when Trish was out of the room, Diamond asked Julie what she had learned of importance.

"Glenn was up to something that she didn't care for," said Julie. "I think we touched a raw nerve asking if he had been two-timing her with some other woman."

"You touched the nerve," he said. "That was your contribution."

Julie flushed slightly. She wasn't used to credit from Peter Diamond. "Anyway, she's suspicious, but she isn't sure."

"She wouldn't have stuck a knife in his back unless she was damned sure."

Trish returned and handed across the statements. He studied them. "High standard of living. Shopping at the best boutiques. Meals out at Clos du Roy and the Priory. A holiday in the south of France."

"That's the way we chose to spend our money."

"But it doesn't seem to have hit your bank balance."

"Glenn had his redundancy cheque."

"What's this restaurant in Exeter that you visited twice in August?"

"The Lemon Tree? We often eat there after visiting his brother. Alec's home is a working paper mill, a lovely old place in the country near Torquay, but he forgets that people need to eat."

"I can take a hint. We'll get you back to your sister's," said Diamond.

Seated in the front, whilst Julie drove, he tried drawing out Trish by talking about the pressures that nurses had to work under. "My own health is pretty good, thank God, but in this line of work you get to see the insides of hospitals all too often. The RUH is one of the better ones. I still wouldn't care to be a nurse."

She didn't comment. Perhaps she found it hard to imagine the big policeman nursing anyone.

"How long have you worked there, Mrs Noble?"

"Three years."

"And before that?"

"Frenchay."

Another local hospital, in Bristol.

"It's a vocation, isn't it?" Diamond rambled on. "Nursing isn't a job, it's a vocation. So is doctoring. Better paid, but still a vocation. I'm less sure about some of the others who work in hospitals. The administrators. It's out of proportion. All those managers."

She didn't take his pause as an invitation to join in.

"They tell me the Health Service managers are the only lot who are on the increase," he said. "Oh, and counsellors. Counselling is the biggest growth industry of all. We need it for everything these days. Child care, education, careers, marriage, divorce, unemployment, alcoholism, bereavement. I don't know how we managed before. If there's a major disaster—a train crash or a flood—the first thing they announce after the number of deaths is that counsellors are with the families. We even have counsellors for the police. Something ugly comes our way, like a serial murder case, or child abuse, and half the murder squad are reckoned to need counselling. Watch out for the counsellors, Mrs Noble. If they haven't found you yet, you may be sure they're about to make a case study of you."

She didn't respond. She was looking out of the window.

"Me, too, probably," said Diamond.

7

"Give me the dope on the Porterfields," Diamond asked as Julie steered the car out of the police station yard and headed for Widcombe Hill. On his instruction, she'd spent the last hour checking.

"They've lived in Bath for the last five years. Moved out of a terraced house in Bear Flat at the end of 1993 and into this mansion by the golf course. There must be good profits in car parts."

He grunted his assent. "You're talking to a man who just had to buy a set of new tyres."

"She drives a Porsche and he has a Mercedes."

"And people like me paid for them."

"Oh, and her name isn't really Serena. It's plain Ann."

"What's wrong with Ann?" he demanded. "I once had a girl-friend called Ann. The last word in sophistication. Stilettos and hot pants. Don't suppose you know what hot pants are."

"Were," murmured Julie.

"Well, we can't arrest her for changing her name." Diamond wrenched his thoughts back from his steamy past.

"Who's your money on, Julie? Do you still think Glenn Noble had a mistress?"

"Yes—and Trish believes it, too."

"So who's the killer—an angry husband?"

"Or boyfriend."

He didn't mention Jack Merlin's bombshell—that Trish might, after all, have struck the fatal blow. "Any idea who? Basil Porterfield?"

She said, "I'll have a better idea when I meet him."

"You can spot a skirt-chaser at fifty paces, can you?"

"If you don't mind me saying," Julie commented, "that's a rather outdated expression."

"Un-hip?"

"Yes."

"Well," he went on, unabashed, "I have to agree with you that it was some visitor to the house."

"But who?"

He spread his hands. "Could be anyone. Could be the Bishop of Bath and Wells for all we know."

"The Porterfields were friends, close friends," Julie pointed out. "How many of your women friends would you hoist on your back for a photo?"

"All at once?"

She said on a note of exasperation, "Mr Diamond, *sir*, I'm trying to make a serious point. We know that Glenn was often out until the small hours. If we could confirm that he was sleeping with Serena . . ."

"Hold on, Julie. That's a large assumption, isn't it? Trish Noble doesn't seem to think he needed to go elsewhere for sex."

"She had her suspicions, believe me. You have to understand a woman's thinking. She may have said the opposite, but he was getting home so late that something was obviously going on. She's too proud or too puritanical to admit it to you and me."

"He could have been up to something entirely different."

"Such as?"

"A poker school. He wouldn't tell her if he was playing cards into the small hours. God and gambling don't mix."

Julie wasn't impressed by that suggestion. "She said he was tired when he got in."

"Well, it *was* late."

"Too tired for anything."

After a pause, he said, "Was that what she meant? This God-fearing woman who keeps a Bible by her bed?"

"That doesn't mean she's under-sexed."

"Fair point," said Diamond after a moment's reflection. "There's more bonking in the Bible than there is in Jilly Cooper and Jackie Collins together. So she interprets his reduced libido as evidence of infidelity? It's speculation, Julie, whether it's her speculation or yours."

She was resolute. "Maybe it is, but if she's right, Serena Porterfield is in real danger—if she isn't already murdered. We can't ignore the possibility, speculation or not."

The Porterfields' mock-Tudor mansion was on the slopes of Bathampton Down, with all of the city as a gleaming backdrop of pale cream stone and blue slate roofs. The house stood among lawns as well trimmed as the greens of the Bath Golf Club nearby. A gardener was on a ladder pruning the Albertine rose that covered much of one side of the house. A white Mercedes was on the drive. The chances of anyone from here being involved in a stabbing in a small terraced house in Twerton seemed remote.

Basil Porterfield opened the front door before they knocked. There was no question that he was the man in the Minehead photo —a sturdy, smiling, sandy-haired embodiment of confidence, even after Diamond told him they were police officers.

"Perhaps you heard that Glenn Noble is dead, sir?"

"Saw it in the paper. Devastating." Porterfield didn't look devastated, but out of respect he shook his head. "It's a long time since I saw Glenn."

"But you were friends?"

"He was the sort you couldn't help liking. Look, why don't you come in?"

The welcome was unstinting. In a room big enough for

the golf club AGM, they were shown to leather armchairs and offered sherry.

Diamond glanced at the teak wall units laden with pottery and art books. "This is a far cry from Bear Flat."

"We worked hard to move up in the world," said Porterfield evenly.

"You're in the motor trade, I understand."

"Curiously enough, we prospered in the recession. I don't sell new cars, I sell parts, and people were doing up their old vehicles rather than replacing them. The business really took off. We have outlets in France and Spain now."

"You visit these countries?"

"Regularly."

"And your business is based in Bath?"

"You must have passed it often enough, down the hill on the Warminster Road."

"Glenn Noble—was he a business contact?"

"Purely social. Through my wife, actually. She took a school project to the printers he worked for. Serena teaches art, print-making, that sort of thing. You can see her influence all around you."

"Is Mrs Porterfield at home today?"

"No. She's, em, out of the country."

Julie's eyes sought Diamond's and held them for a moment.

He remarked to Porterfield, "She must be devastated, too."

"She doesn't know anything about it."

Diamond played a wild card. "You said you haven't seen the Nobles for a long time. Perhaps your wife saw them more recently."

Porterfield asked smoothly, "Why do you say that?"

Julie, equally smoothly, invented an answer. "Someone answering your wife's description was seen recently in the company of Glenn Noble."

"Is that so? Funny she didn't mention it." He was unfazed.

"Just for the record," said Diamond, "would you mind telling me where you were on Monday afternoon between three and five?"

"Monday between three and five." Porterfield frowned, as if he hadn't remotely considered that he might be asked. "I would have been at the office. I'm sure my staff will confirm that, if you care to ask them."

"And your wife?"

"She's in France, like I said, on a school trip." He smiled. "She left last week. Last Friday."

"Where did you say she teaches?"

8

Cavendish College was a girls' public school on Lyncombe Hill. The Head informed Diamond that Mrs Porterfield was indeed on a sixth form trip to the south of France. She frequently led school parties to places of artistic interest in Europe. She was a loyal, talented teacher, and an asset to the school.

Diamond used a mobile phone to get this information. He and Julie were parked in North Road, with a good view of the Porterfield residence.

"Are you relieved?" he asked Julie. "Serena survives, apparently."

"I still say he murdered Glenn Noble."

"And I say you're right."

Her eyes widened. "Am I?"

"But he had the decency to do it while his wife was away. We'll arrest her when she returns."

"Whatever for?"

"Hold on a little and I'll show you, if my theory is right.

Serena's talent may be an asset to the school, but it's a bigger asset to Basil Porterfield. What time is it?"

"Ten past six."

"After our visit he's not stopping here much longer."

Twenty minutes, as it turned out. The Mercedes glided into North Road and down the hill with Julie and Diamond in discreet pursuit. Porterfield turned right at the junction with the busy Warminster Road. Three-quarters of a mile on, he slowed and pulled in to the forecourt of a building with *Porterfield Car Spares* in large letters across the front.

"Drive past and park as near as you can."

Julie found a layby a short walk away.

When they approached on foot the only cover available was the side wall of Porterfield's building. From it they had a view of the empty Mercedes parked on the forecourt. "I should have called for some back-up, but we can handle this, can't we?" said Diamond.

Julie lifted one eyebrow and said nothing.

Diamond issued an order. "When he comes out, you go across and nick him."

She lifted the other eyebrow.

He told her, "I'm the back-up."

Five minutes passed. The traffic on the Warminster Road zoomed by steadily.

"He's coming."

Julie tensed.

Porterfield emerged from the building trundling a hand trolley stacked with white cartons. He set the trolley upright, took some keys from his pocket, opened the boot of the car and leaned in.

Diamond pressed a hand against the small of Julie's back. She started forward.

Sending in Julie first may have looked like cowardice, but it was not. While her sudden arrival on the scene caught Porterfield's attention, Diamond ducked around the other side of the Mercedes. Just in time, because Porterfield produced a knife from the car boot and swung it at Julie.

She swayed out of range and narrowly escaped another lunge. Then Diamond charged in and grabbed Porterfield from behind and thrust him sideways against the car, pinioning his arms. Julie prised the knife from his fist. Diamond produced a set of handcuffs and between them they forced him over the boot and manacled him.

"Want to see what's in the cartons?" Diamond suggested to Julie over the groaning prisoner. "Why don't you use the knife?"

She cut along the adhesive seal of the top carton and parted the flaps. Neatly stacked inside were wads of French one-hundred franc banknotes.

"*Money?*"

"Funny money," said Diamond. "We'll find the offset litho machine and the plates hidden deep inside the building. What with Serena's artwork, Glenn Noble's printing expertise and these premises to work in, making counterfeit notes was a profitable scam. But just like you said, Trish got suspicious of all the late nights. Glenn hadn't dared tell her what he was up to, even though it helped their bank balance no end. She was too high principled to be in on the secret."

"Why French money?" Julie asked.

"Easier to make. No metal strip. I don't know how good these forgeries are, but Glenn would have got his brother in Devon to make the paper with a passable watermark." He picked one up and held it to the light. "Not bad. A portrait of Glenn's favourite painter, Eugene Delacroix. This has a nice feel to it. They coat the printed notes with glycerine. He'll have handpressed the serial numbers."

"And why was he killed?"

"Because of Trish. Unwisely he told Porterfield that she was asking about the late nights. She would have seen it as her moral duty to shop them all, and Porterfield couldn't risk her wheedling the truth out of Glenn." He hauled Porterfield upright. "You thought you could get rid of Glenn and do the printing yourself, didn't you, ratbag? Last Monday afternoon you called unexpectedly at the house. Glenn let you in, offered you a drink, and when his back was turned you drove a knife into him. You escaped through the back garden just as Trish was coming in through the front. Right?"

"How the hell did you get on to me?" Porterfield asked.

"Through something Glenn Noble wrote on a photograph. Someone took a picture of your day out in Minehead in 1993. Glenn wrote 'wayzgoose' on the back."

"What's that?"

"A word for a printers' outing. When I looked at it first, I couldn't understand why he called it that, since he was the only printer in the picture. Then it dawned that you and possibly your wife were involved in some printing activity. When I saw how well you were doing, and how large his bank balance was, I reckoned you were printing money. Julie, would you call headquarters and ask them to send a car?"

Porterfield asked, "What was that word?"

"'Wayzgoose'," said Diamond. "Funny old word. Worth remembering. It'll get you a large score in Scrabble. Where you're going, you may get the odd chance to play. You'll certainly have the time."

MYSTERY NOVELS
AND SHORT STORIES
BY PETER LOVESEY: A CHECKLIST

I. Novels
(In the following list, the publisher of the first British edition is followed by the publisher of the first United States edition.)

Wobble to Death. Macmillan, 1970; Dodd, Mead, 1970. Sergeant Cribb series.

The Detective Wore Silk Drawers. Macmillan, 1971; Dodd, Mead, 1971. Sergeant Cribb series.

Abracadaver. Macmillan, 1972; Dodd, Mead, 1972. Sergeant Cribb series.

Mad Hatter's Holiday: A Novel of Mystery in Victorian Brighton. Macmillan, 1973; Dodd, Mead, 1973. Sergeant Cribb series.

Invitation to a Dynamite Party. Macmillan, 1974; as *The Tick of Death* Dodd, Mead, 1974. Sergeant Cribb series.

A Case of Spirits. Macmillan, 1975; Dodd, Mead, 1975. Sergeant Cribb series.

Swing, Swing Together. Macmillan, 1976; Dodd, Mead, 1976. Sergeant Cribb series.

Waxwork. Macmillan, 1978; Pantheon, 1978. Sergeant Cribb series.

The False Inspector Dew: A Murder Mystery Aboard the SS Mauretania. Macmillan, 1982; Pantheon, 1982.

Keystone. Macmillan, 1983; Pantheon, 1983.

Rough Cider. Bodley Head, 1986; Mysterious Press, 1987.

Bertie and the Tinman: From the Detective Memoirs of King Edward VII. Bodley Head, 1987; Mysterious Press, 1988. Bertie series.

On the Edge. Century Hutchinson, 1989; Mysterious Press, 1989.

Bertie and the Seven Bodies. Century Hutchinson, 1990; Mysterious Press, 1990. Bertie series.

The Last Detective. Scribners, 1991; Doubleday, 1991. Peter Diamond series.

Diamond Solitaire. Little, Brown, 1992; Mysterious Press, 1992. Peter Diamond series.

Bertie and the Crime of Passion. Little, Brown, 1993; Mysterious Press, 1993. Bertie series.

The Summons. Little, Brown, 1995; Mysterious Press, 1995. Peter Diamond series.

Bloodhounds. Little, Brown, 1996; Mysterious Press, 1996. Peter Diamond series.

Upon a Dark Night. Little, Brown, 1997; Mysterious Press, 1998. Peter Diamond series.

II. Novels under the pseudonym Peter Lear

Goldengirl. Cassell, 1977; Doubleday, 1978.

Spider Girl. Cassell, 1980; Viking, 1980.

The Secret of Spandau. Michael Joseph, 1986.

III. Short story collections

Butchers and Other Stories of Crime. Macmillan, 1985; Mysterious Press, 1987.

The Staring Man and Other Stories. Helsinki: Eurographica. 1989. A signed limited edition containing four stories from *Butchers and Other Stories of Crime.*

The Crime of Miss Oyster Brown and Other Stories. Little, Brown, 1994.

Do Not Exceed the Stated Dose. Little, Brown, 1998; Crippen & Landru, 1998.

IV. Collaborations

The Rigby File. Hodder & Stoughton, 1989.
The Perfect Murder. HarperCollins, 1991.

V. Short stories

"The Bathroom." *Winter's Crimes 5.* Macmillan, 1973; *Ellery Queen's Mystery Magazine*, August 21, 1981, as "A Bride in the Bath." Collected in *Butchers and Other Stories of Crime.*

"The Locked Room." *Winter's Crimes 10.* Macmillan, 1978; *Ellery Queen's Mystery Magazine*, March 1979, as "Behind the Locked Door." Collected in *Butchers and Other Stories of Crime.*

"A Slight Case of Scotch." Collaborative story. *The Bell House Book.* Hodder & Stoughton, 1979.

"How Mr Smith Chased His Ancestors." *Mystery Guild Anthology.* Book Club Associates, 1980; *Ellery Queen's Mystery Magazine*, November 3, 1980, as "A Man with a Fortune." Collected in *Butchers and Other Stories of Crime.*

"Butchers." *Winter's Crimes 14.* Macmillan, 1982; *Ellery Queen's Mystery Magazine*, Mid-July 1982, as "The Butchers." Collected in *Butchers and Other Stories of Crime* and in *The Staring Man and Other Stories.*

"Taking Possession." *Ellery Queen's Mystery Magazine*,

November 1982. Collected in *Butchers and Other Stories of Crime* and in *The Staring Man and Other Stories* as "Woman and Home."

"The Virgin and the Bull." *John Creasey's Mystery Crime Collection*. Gollancz, 1983; *Ellery Queen's Mystery Magazine*, July 1983, as "The Virgoan and the Taurean." Collected in *Butchers and Other Stories of Crime*.

"Fall-Out." *Company Magazine*, May 1983; *Ellery Queen's Mystery Magazine*, June 1984. Collected in *Butchers and Other Stories of Crime*.

"Belly Dance." *Winter's Crimes 15*. Macmillan, 1983; *Ellery Queen's Mystery Magazine*, March 1983, as "Keeping Fit." Collected in *Butchers and Other Stories of Crime*.

"Did You Tell Daddy?" *Ellery Queen's Mystery Magazine*, February 1984. Collected in *Butchers and Other Stories of Crime*.

"Arabella's Answer." *Ellery Queen's Mystery Magazine*, April 1984. Collected in *Butchers and Other Stories of Crime*.

"Vandals." *Woman's Own*, December 29, 1984; *Ellery Queen's Mystery Magazine*, December 1985. Collected in *Butchers and Other Stories of Crime*.

"The Secret Lover." *Winter's Crimes 17*, Macmillan, 1985; *Ellery Queen's Mystery Magazine*, March 1988. Collected in *Butchers and Other Stories of Crime*.

"The Corder Figure." *Butchers and Other Stories of Crime*. Macmillan, 1985; *Ellery Queen's Mystery Magazine*, January 1986. Collected in *Butchers and Other Stories of Crime* and in *The Staring Man and Other Stories*.

"Private Gorman's Luck." *Butchers and Other Stories of Crime*. Macmillan, 1985; *Ellery Queen's Mystery Magazine*, July 1985. Collected in *Butchers and Other Stories of Crime*.

"The Staring Man." *Butchers and Other Stories of Crime*. Macmillan, 1985; *Ellery Queen's Mystery Magazine*, October 1985. Collected in *Butchers and Other Stories of Crime* and in *The Staring Man and Other Stories*.

"Trace of Spice." *Butchers and Other Stories of Crime.* Macmillan, 1985. Collected in *Butchers and Other Stories of Crime.*

"Murder in Store." *Woman's Own,* December 21, 1985. Collected in *Do Not Exceed the Stated Dose.*

"Curl Up and Dye." *Ellery Queen's Mystery Magazine,* July 1986. Collected in *The Crime of Miss Oyster Brown and Other Stories.*

"Photographer Slain." Contest story. *The Observer,* November 30, 1986.

"Peer's Grisly Find." Contest story. *The Observer,* December 7, 1986.

"Brighton Line Murder." Contest story. *The Observer,* December 14, 1986.

"The Poisoned Mince Pie." Contest story. *The Observer,* December 21, 1986.

"The Royal Plot." Contest story. *The Observer,* December 28, 1986.

"The Curious Computer." *New Adventures of Sherlock Holmes.* Carroll & Graf, 1987. Collected in *The Crime of Miss Oyster Brown and Other Stories.*

"Friendly Yachtsman, 39." *Woman's Own,* July 18, 1987; *Ellery Queen's Mystery Magazine,* May 1988. Collected in *The Crime of Miss Oyster Brown and Other Stories.*

"The Pomeranian Poisoning." *Winter's Crimes 19.* Macmillan, 1987; *Ellery Queen's Mystery Magazine,* August 1988, as "The Zenobia Hatt Prize." Collected in *The Crime of Miss Oyster Brown and Other Stories.*

"Where is Thy Sting." *Winter's Crimes 20.* Macmillan, 1988; *Ellery Queen's Mystery Magazine,* November 1988, as "The Wasp." Collected in *The Crime of Miss Oyster Brown and Other Stories.*

"Oracle of the Dead." *Ellery Queen's Mystery Magazine,* Mid-December 1988; *Best,* March 3, 1989.

"A Case of Butterflies." *Winter's Crimes 21.* Macmillan, 1989;

Ellery Queen's Mystery Magazine, December 1989. Collected in *The Crime of Miss Oyster Brown and Other Stories.*

"Youdunnit." *New Crimes.* Robinson, 1989; *Ellery Queen's Mystery Magazine,* mid-December 1989. Collected in *The Crime of Miss Oyster Brown and Other Stories.*

"The Haunted Crescent." *Mistletoe Mysteries.* Mysterious Press, 1989. Collected in *The Crime of Miss Oyster Brown and Other Stories.*

"Shock Visit." *Winter's Crimes 22.* Macmillan, 1990; *Ellery Queen's Mystery Magazine.,* February 1990, as "The Valuation." Collected in *The Crime of Miss Oyster Brown and Other Stories.*

"The Lady in the Trunk." *A Classic English Crime.* Pavilion, 1990. Collected in *The Crime of Miss Oyster Brown and Other Stories.*

"Ginger's Waterloo." *Cat Crimes.* Donald L. Fine, 1991. Collected in *The Crime of Miss Oyster Brown and Other Stories.*

"Being of Sound Mind." *Winter's Crimes 23.* Macmillan, 1990; *Ellery Queen's Mystery Magazine,* July 1991. Collected in *The Crime of Miss Oyster Brown and Other Stories.*

"The Christmas Present." *Woman's Own,* December 24, 1990; *Ellery Queen's Mystery Magazine,* mid-December 1991, as "Supper with Miss Shivers." Collected in *The Crime of Miss Oyster Brown and Other Stories* as "Supper with Miss Shivers."

"The Crime of Miss Oyster Brown." *Midwinter Mysteries 1.* Scribners, 1991; *Ellery Queen's Mystery Magazine,* May 1991. Collected in *The Crime of Miss Oyster Brown and Other Stories.*

"The Man Who Ate People." *The Man Who . . .* Macmillan, 1992; *Ellery Queen's Mystery Magazine,* October 1992. Collected in *The Crime of Miss Oyster Brown and Other Stories.*

"You May See a Strangler." *Midwinter Mysteries 2.* Little, Brown, 1992. Collected in *The Crime of Miss Oyster Brown and Other Stories.*

"Murder By Christmas Tree." Contest story. *The Observer,* December 20, 1992. Printed as a separate pamphlet to accompany Crippen & Landru's limited edition of *Do Not Exceed the Stated Dose.*

"Pass the Parcel." *Midwinter Mysteries 3.* Little, Brown, 1993; *Ellery Queen's Mystery Magazine,* Mid-December 1994. Collected in *The Crime of Miss Oyster Brown and Other Stories.*

"Murder in the Library." Contest story. *Evening Chronicle,* Bath, October 6, 1993.

"The Model Con." *Woman's Realm Summer Special,* 1994; Collected in *The Crime of Miss Oyster Brown and Other Stories.*

"Bertie and the Fire Brigade." *Royal Crimes.* Signet, 1994. Collected in *Do Not Exceed the Stated Dose.*

"The Odstock Curse." *Murder for Halloween.* Mysterious Press, 1994. Collected in *Do Not Exceed the Stated Dose.*

"Passion Killers." *Ellery Queen's Mystery Magazine,* January 1994. Collected in *Do Not Exceed the Stated Dose.*

"The Case of the Easter Bonnet." *Bath Chronicle,* April 17, 1995; *Ellery Queen's Mystery Magazine,* April 1997. Collected in *Do Not Exceed the Stated Dose.*

"Never a Cross Word." *You, Mail on Sunday,* June 11, 1995; *Ellery Queen's Mystery Magazine,* February 1997. Collected in *Do Not Exceed the Stated Dose.*

"The Mighty Hunter." *Midwinter Mysteries 5.* Little, Brown, 1995; *Ellery Queen's Mystery Magazine,* January 1996. Collected in *Do Not Exceed the Stated Dose.*

"The Proof of the Pudding." *A Classic Christmas Crime.* Pavilion, 1995. Collected in *Do Not Exceed the Stated Dose.*

"The Pushover." *Ellery Queen's Mystery Magazine,* June 1995. Collected in *Do Not Exceed the Stated Dose.*

"Quiet Please—We're Rolling." *No Alibi.* Ringpull, 1995; *Ellery Queen's Mystery Magazine,* December 1996. Collected in *Do Not Exceed the Stated Dose.*

"Wayzgoose." *A Dead Giveaway.* Warner Futura, 1995; *Ellery Queen's Mystery Magazine,* May 1997. Collected in *Do Not Exceed the Stated Dose.*

"Disposing of Mrs Cronk." *Perfectly Criminal.* Severn House, 1996; *Ellery Queen's Mystery Magazine,* December 1997. Collected in *Do Not Exceed the Stated Dose.*

"A Parrot is Forever." *Malice Domestic 5.* Pocket Books, 1996. Collected in *Do Not Exceed the Stated Dose.*

"Bertie and the Boat Race." *Crime Through Time,* Berkley, 1996. Collected in *Do Not Exceed the Stated Dose.*

"The Corbett Correspondence" (with Keith Miles). *Malice Domestic 6.* 1997.

"Because It Was There." *Whydunit? Perfectly Criminal 2.* Severn House, 1997. Collected in *Do Not Exceed the Stated Dose.*